# The
# SILENT
# HOUSE

# The
# SILENT
# HOUSE

*A Chronicle of Aglirta*

———◆———

# ED GREENWOOD

**TOR®**
fantasy

A TOM DOHERTY ASSOCIATES BOOK
NEW YORK

This is a work of fiction. All the characters and events portrayed in this book are either products of the author's imagination or are used fictitiously.

THE SILENT HOUSE: A CHRONICLE OF AGLIRTA

Copyright © 2004 by Ed Greenwood

A Tor Book
Published by Tom Doherty Associates, LLC
175 Fifth Avenue
New York, NY 10010

www.tor.com

Tor® is a registered trademark of Tom Doherty Associates, LLC.

ISBN 0-765-34726-1
EAN 978-0765-34726-8

First edition: June 2004
First mass market edition: July 2005

Printed in the United States of America

0  9  8  7  6  5  4  3  2  1

To Elaine, fellow explorer and great lady

And to Brian, for rescues above and
beyond the call

Furor Scribendi

But what are ghosts but the shadows of those who have died
but will not stop dreaming?
On battlements I see them standing,
eyes that are no longer eyes
fixed thoughtfully upon me.
About to speak, to warn
but forever silent
Cloaks billowing, they stride down stairs that are no longer there
On urgencies that have long passed
Yet not so long ago that pride, alarm, despair, and rage
have faded
Bright their swords
Brighter their love and hate and hunger for vengeance
Hunger for life, the chance again to feast
At the table they were snatched away from too soon
Things left undone
Things are always left undone
Regrets like smaller shadows follow them in long marching hosts
Sadly they mutely stare
Warning by their very presence
Cold their regard
Patient now
When time passes no more.
How I envy them
Their platters of trouble and travail cast aside
Where mine grows more heaped each passing day.
Haunts, come you and take my troubles
And I'll walk your battlements for you
And slowly forget how to shiver under the moon

> from "In Shadows I'm Never Alone,"
> a lament by Landre Szunedreth, Minstrel of Sirlptar

# Prologue

*C*old. I am always cold.

    *I hate this cold, crumbling place, this sprawling realm of stone, and yet I love it; I cannot be parted from it. It is alive, and it holds the magic I need most. I can feel it.*

    *I can also feel the House itself watching all I do within its crumbling walls and passages. In heavy silences it challenges me. Coldly patient, crushing . . . eternal. I must uncover its secrets to live again.*

    *It will fight me, and it will win. Yet a dead man cannot die again, and I have all the passing time I need take to succeed, though kingdoms rise and fall and the names of those alive today fade into windblown dust.*

    *So green the hills, so bright the sparkling river I stare out over. Halfway across it, the bright battlements of the palace that's crowded with the living, my friends among them, rise upon the green isle. Boats come and go, horsemen ride by . . . alive, so alive, so full of haste and vigor. I can see the white flashes of their teeth as they laugh and smile.*

    *Here, on crumbling battlements I share with the wind, I watch. I'll learn what I must, to rise again.*

    *I shall set forth the lay of this proud House, building its tale as I uncover and learn—and so keep ordered what I have unearthed, and lay bare the secrets of Silvertree House for all.*

    *Hearken, then, to the long and endless tale of the Silent House.*

The tall, fair-haired youth looked around at the trees and tall grass uneasily, unease sharp in his usually twinkling green eyes, and checked the storm-lantern in his hand again. Twice. "I feel . . . naked out here, without . . ."

The short, bandy-legged old man hadn't stopped looking in all directions since they'd come within sight of the great stone bulk of the Silent House, and didn't do so now.

"The stones of Sirlptar around you, lad? Aye, everyone feels that way the first time. But did you *really* think you could hide in the city? You're safe there only so long as you don't come to the notice of anyone with real power—or an ambitious thief like yourself who just happens to be a little faster, a little smarter, or a little luckier. Wh—"

The young man waved a dismissive hand. "No one's luckier than I am. The Three smile on me daily."

"Which is why you were fool enough to try to snatch a coin-coffer right off Tlarron's counter, hey? And think you could just stroll out into a Sirl cellar somewhere to count it— or outrun his two-score guards and factors?"

Dlan wrinkled his face into a momentary rictus of disgust. "So *yes,* you were right about it being a bad idea—yet I'm here, still alive, no?"

"Thanks to *my* swift aid and a lot of hiresword armor I had stowed away for just such needs, not out of any doing of the Three, youngling!"

The thief threw up his hands, and snarled, "So you say. Right, then: *yes,* I'm grateful, and yes, I'll aid you in this foray—fool-headedness of your own, mind—but I say again: the Three love my smile, and like to see it, often!"

The old man spat thoughtfully into the dead leaves and didn't bother to point out to young Dlanazar that the skulls of dead men never stop smiling.

Yes, this young fool would do just fine.

# BOOK ONE

———◆———

## Ravengar Silvertree

Born 112 Sirl Reckoning, Died 156 SR
First Baron of Silvertree to Be Made Lord Overbaron of Aglirta
and How the Realm Turned Against Him

# 1

## The Rise of the Raven

he fight is swift and furious. Blades skirl and clang on all sides as the panting men, stumbling with pain and weariness in their splendid but battered armor, hack and slash, too crowded in the churned mud of the hollow to back clear and fence with any care for the fate of their blades. Now all chases are ended, all proud taunts hurled, and it is slay or be slain.

The black-haired, wild-bearded man with the handsome face, his cheekbones as high and his eyes as large and dark as many a beauteous lady of the realm, has led the charge into the hollow, under thick, thorny tangles that forced all the combatants to abandon their horses, to this last dancing-place of death. The dark, gloomy trees press in close around the lurching, gasping men, and more than one of them thinks fleetingly of what prowling beasts must be slinking closer, drawn by the clangor of battle, fully intending to soon feed. . . .

Fleetingly is all the time anyone dare give for any thought but the fray, or—

"Ravengar!" one of his knights gasps at the black-bearded man. A dying man's desperate, futile pleading, a last despairing sob as the blade that's taking his life bursts out dark and wet from between the curved plates of his spurred and fluted armor, spraying lifeblood before it.

Baron Ravengar Silvertree, beset in the thick of the fray by bull-necked, heavy-armored giants snarlingly seeking his life with ringing two-handed blows of their reaping swords, hears and whirls, leaping high to bring his own sweeping blade over the steel of a foe and into the man's face, its tip biting deep into hawk-nosed helm. He heeds this slaying not, his gaze bent upon the dying Sorvren, who's been a true knight and a good friend, and rage sets his eyes afire.

Sorvren's fading, dulling gaze fixes upon that fire and goes down into the Great Darkness, clinging to it, lips weakly struggling to form a smile—and Ravengar Silvertree glares into the grin of Sorvren's slayer, revealed behind the slumping knight, and springs to meet the man. As he leaps, he whirls both of his blades back behind himself to stave off the blows of the foes he's just burst out of, leaving his breast and face unprotected.

Sorvren's slayer can't resist this bait, and leans forward in a roundhouse slash of his own, trying to slice out Ravengar's throat before the baron can reach him. As overbalanced as the Lord of Silvertree he's trying to slay, the man has no hope of keeping his feet as Sorvren crumples back into his thighs and knees, sending him sprawling helplessly forward—so both of Ravengar's armored knees can crash down on his head and neck, with a dull *crack* that can be felt more than heard in this forge-din of bloodshed.

Baron Silvertree bounds to his feet with the force of his landing and whirls around again, blades slicing air defensively, in time to see Baron Auroun—the gasping, grunting boar of a man who's dared to proclaim himself "King of Aglirta" in the teeth of the rightful King Thamrain—lumber forward with a blood-dripping boar-spear in his hands.

The two jutting points of Auroun's jowl-beard glisten with sweat and spittle, dripping like two tusks as the enraged baron abandons the shielding blades of his sycophants at last, rushing forward to strike at the unprotected back of his foe.

And wavers, finding Ravengar Silvertree turned about and ready for him. Ravengar grows his own savage smile as Auroun slows and bellows to his knights for aid. Even before his shouts they're hastening to join him, shoulder-plates clanking, eager to hew down the man who scant breaths before had been trapped in their midst—but Ravengar doesn't wait for them.

He lurches to the left, drawing the point of Auroun's spear, and then twists and ducks away to his right, so abruptly that his right elbow slams against his knee. Snarling, he hurls the borrowed-from-the-dead blade in his left hand into the baron's face. In its whirling wake, as Auroun shouts in alarm and pulls his head back and away, bringing his spear up, Ravengar's emptied left hand slaps down on the spear-shaft, tightens, and pulls.

Off-balance and blinded in the spark-splashing buffeting of Ravengar's flung sword, the baron stumbles helplessly forward—and Ravengar drives the blade in his right hand up in a cross-throat slash that smashes aside Auroun's gorget, its straps flying, and bursts through the throat beneath in a spray of eagerly jetting gore.

Silvertree continues both arm-swings, pulling his dying foe across in front of him by the spear to block the charge of one of Auroun's knights, and slapping at Auroun's greaves to bring his sword back past them and up to meet the other foremost knight.

Who is a great burly, helmless grinning giant of a man, a sword-scarred veteran who loves blood and killing, and is roaring his glee as he brings his own long, heavy, much-notched sword up in a gutting thrust.

That black blade hisses off the armored point of Ravengar's knee as the Lord of Silvertree turns side-on to the man, and rises up wickedly in front of Ravengar's nose. As the dying Auroun stumbles on Sorvren's corpse and falls, entangling the running knight behind him so that both plunge helplessly forward and down amid the shivering splinters of the bouncing boar-spear, Ravengar finds his own sword and the arm holding it free to swing—but beyond the thrusting blade that's flashing past his face.

So he launches himself towards the sword-wielder, bringing his sword arm down on his foe's forearm even before his shoulder slams into the man's chest, driving forth the knight's wind with a tortured groan and a spray of foetid spittle.

The man doubles up, or tries to, sinking down even as Ravengar lands hard on that extended sword arm and breaks

it, rolling over atop its grinding ruin to drive his armored elbow into the helplessly shrieking knight's mouth.

Shards of teeth fly as the man shudders back and away—
and Ravengar continues his roll, after the knight, bringing
his sword up and forward in a thrust that slides into that open
and ravaged mouth with wet ease.

Looking along it, he stares straight into the golden eyes of
a huge, half-seen forest wolf watching the slaughter from
between two gnarled tree trunks not six strides away. Ravengar kicks out and finds his feet, shaking his sword loose so
as to menace the wolf—and the eyes are gone, winking out
so suddenly that they might never have been there.

The Lord of Silvertree turns, drawing breath in a sudden
silence, to find himself gazing across bloody, trampled ferns
strewn with armored bodies and at—the broad, armored
mountain of King Estlan Thamrain, with two rumpled,
bloodstained knights flanking him and a royal smile widen-
ing on that normally wintry face.

"By the Three, Raven, you've done it!" Thamrain shakes
his head, half in admiration and half in disbelief, as he gazes
around the hollow at all the sprawled dead. "Auroun and
Belwyvrar and Galorfeather—all! Just as you promised!"

Ravengar leans on his blade for a moment to catch his
breath, and then goes to one knee, unable to keep a smile of
his own entirely off his face. "Luck was with us this day,
Majesty," he growls, fighting for wind enough to make his
words measured and fair, "and the favor of the Three. Blood
of Elroumrae, you *are* the only the rightful King of Aglirta,
and the gods know this and have aided us this day!"

Thamrain shakes his head again as he strides forward,
stepping on the bodies of his foes with no care for dignity or
lack of besmirchment. "I saw no gods fighting in this hollow
now," he says thickly, eyes bright. "I saw my only loyal
baron, the best warrior in all the realm, Ravengar Silvertree,
carry the day with battle wits and fearless bladework.
Raven, this day is yours."

"My King," Ravengar replies, bowing his head, "I am and
will remain true. A victory for you is a victory for us all—

and I am proud and happy to have been of service to Aglirta."

"Three Above," Thamrain says, drawing him up into a fierce hug, "but I seem to see both a matchless warrior and a bright-tongued envoy, in the same man! Your knights shall be barons in place of these dead traitors, and you shall be my 'Lord Overbaron.'"

"If it pleases Your Majesty, 'tis a title I shall be proud to bear."

"It does," the king laughs, as they grin nose to nose. "It pleases me well!"


"The man soars like a hunting falcon," Raevrel murmured, his strong arms crossed as he stared out the high window.

The darkly handsome man at the table whose left hand was always a taloned claw turned his head and told Raevrel's tall, straight back coldly, "Even falcons may be brought down, brother. Neither we nor the dead barons' kin are the only Aglirtans angered by Silvertree's rise."

"He raids Flowfoam's coffers like a conquering outland lord," Raevrel murmured. "Spending *our* inheritance."

"He does a lot of things, our proud and victorious Lord Overbaron," Thansel Snowsar said bitterly, setting aside his maps and parchments, and rising. "And our fool kinsman Thamrain is ever more grateful to him."

"Little Toad Thamrain," Raevrel whispered, clenched fists trembling. "*I* should be King of Aglirta now, not him. He was the youngest and most stupid of us all—and only a shade away from being the laziest, too."

"Aye, but he was *normal,*" Thansel replied softly, raising his ever-present scaled claw in pointed reminder. "Free of the taint of Prince Koglaur."

"*Taint!*" Raevrel almost spat, eyes like two gold flames as he whirled away from the window in a swirl of dark robes and darker hair. "The taint they still hunt us for! What makes them so right and so superior? Their fear of powers that can only have come from the Three?"

"Their numbers." Thansel shifted his shape, growing taller, a long fall of silken dark hair sprouting as breasts swelled beneath them, and hips. That taloned hand trailed behind one curvaceous leg as the beauty that never failed to take Raevrel's breath away glided near, and added in a purr, "Our time will come, Rae. Oh, yes, our time will come."

"But when?" Raevrel growled as they embraced, bodies shifting subtly to almost meld together, skin to skin.

"Soon," Thansel whispered in his ear, growing a swift second mouth to do so while the first kissed him. "Very soon."


"Silvertree's castle is becoming a great expense," Irsrar Matchet remarked, turning from the map of Aglirta on the sloping desk to look out the window over the bustling harbor of Sirlptar. This house stood on the seaward side of the ridge, many tall mansions and many-spired houses hiding any view of Aglirta itself from him. "How're they going to pay for it all?"

Feltorn chuckled and flicked a finger out from under his short, reddish beard as he always did, to wave it like a lecturing wand. "Ah, the eternal puzzlement of merchants in this city as they ponder any coffer but their own." He joined Matchet by the window.

"Baron Ravengar Silvertree has become Lord Overbaron Silvertree, remember, and 'tis fitting that his palace—begun, as he's essentially still but a wily lion of a warrior and back-forest hunter, as a defensible castle stronghold—be both large and luxurious. Large by our standards here in crowded Sirl-town, aye . . . but not what *we* would call true luxury. Banish all thoughts of great shimmer-tapestries and hanging Sardastan glow-paintings from your mind. Think of large, cold, dim stone rooms with a few heavy wooden chairs and tables. Large shaggy dogs wandering freely to warm Silvertree's feet with their snoring on chill nights, and armor hung up to rust everywhere because backcountry Aglirtans can think of no other adornment. Pay for it all? Matchet, have you yet seen any end to the forests of Aglirta? Or our

Sirl hunger for wood to build things with? Do you not eat—
and does not the daily simple fare of all this proud city
around us come from the farms of downriver Aglirta?"

Matchet sighed in exasperation. "You goldsmiths look
down your long noses at everyone, and see all as some sort
of tapestry spread out before you, with folk of Darsar but
ants scurrying about it. 'Tis all flows of coins and the doings
of countries to you. *I* see a small, struggling realm ruled
more by the great beasts of the forests than any of the armored barons who clank about Silverflow Vale shaking their
swords at each other! A few riverbank farms here and a few
there, endless war over who should rule, and the so-called
'royal' line spending half its time trying to slaughter its own
kin who have the Beast-Taint . . . I ask again: How are they
going to pay for it all?"

"Pay *whom,* dear Matchet? They needn't pay profuse coin
for Sirl crafters or the luxuries of all distant Darsar. The
sweat of building is their own, and the stone, food, and timber are theirs—theirs for the taking. Have you not seen by
now that we need them, but they don't need us? How do you
think Sirlptar grew so wealthy, hey? What river do we sit at
the mouth of? What comes down it, and why else would
trade come here rather than to older, larger Carraglas, Ragalar, Urngallond, or Arlund?"

"Yes, yes, I know they feed us and have more good ship-
timber left than anywhere else," Matchet replied testily,
waving a dismissive hand as he strode back to the map
again. "But you make your tapestry-gazing mistake again,
Feltorn: they're *not* a single-minded, trade-cunning legion
of merchants juggling debts, investments, and opportunities
like the moneylenders of Urngallond! They're a bunch of
brawling backwoods louts more interested in hunting each
other than bringing down stags! They neither care nor consider where their timber and turnips go, so long as they can
simply barge them downriver to us and receive handfuls of
gold in return! How would they even know our ways, and
how power is fought for in Sirlptar, and what's what in the
wider world?"

"Ah, good clock-merchant," Feltorn replied softly, "you forget what the Beast-Taint *is*. They can walk among us, and we'll never know. They could take your face, or mine, at will. One could be standing here beside you right now, and you'd not know it. And as for not knowing about the rest of Darsar . . . have you forgotten that this same brawling back-woods Silvertree has somehow taken to wife a sorceress of far Sarinda? A real beauty, too, with twice the wits of many wealthy and well-regarded merchants of Sirlptar; she could have wed almost anywhere, but chose your beast-roamed lout-pen of Aglirta. Have you forgotten that no less than *six* rich heiresses of Sirlptar took Aglirtan husbands this past decade? And left our crowded streets, every last one of them, to go live in backward, dangerous, baron-plagued Aglirta?"

Feltorn shook his head as he stepped softly closer to the clock-merchant. "You shouldn't forget things, Matchet. Bad things happen to merchants who forget things."

Irsrar Matchet stared at his colleague . . . and found himself shuddering at Feltorn's quiet but suddenly sinister tone. Suddenly he recalled his unfinished drink—and just how much he needed it. A fine cordial, too, silken on the tongue . . .

He reached for it as Feltorn smilingly raised his own glass—and so never noticed that his sleeve had brushed the decanter in turning, causing it to spin and start to topple . . . or how grotesquely long the fingers of the goldsmith's other hand momentarily grew to catch it and set it deftly back in place.

Matchet sipped thankfully at his warming, soothing cordial and then shook his head. "Shape-shifters here, in Sirlptar? With all our wizards and their head-singing wards? Bah. That could never happen."

Feltorn smiled faintly, and lowered his glass. "Indeed."


"Our descent from Queen Elroumrae is as clear and as strong as that of Thamrain, because it's the very same descent. If Prince Koglaur had survived that baronial ambush, he would have ruled as king—his shape-shifting then was deemed a curse laid on him by evil mages, not the 'taint' men talk of now. That word came to us from barons who desired to set aside House Snowsar and take the throne for themselves."

"But those barons are all dead," Samraethe whispered, her eyes large and dark. "Silvertree killed them."

"He killed the sons of the sons of those who first spread the tales of 'taint' and the Curse of the Three, and unfitness to rule. They used *us* as an excuse to challenge for the throne, and shed so much blood, and let the woods grow back and the monsters prowl unchecked. Ravengar Silvertree did us all that much service, in ending their bloodlines. There are no claimants for the throne now to rival Thamrain who can claim royal descent—save us. That won't stop Ravengar or his knights who now hold those baronies from considering themselves better fitted for the River Throne than 'tainted shape-shifters,' should something happen to Thamrain."

"Things often seem to 'happen' to men who rule realms or cities," Samraethe murmured.

"Ah, you have been paying attention to Eldreth's histories. Good. *That* is why our way, what the more restless of you younglings have begun to foolishly deride as 'the skulking way,' is the best way. Let others hate and fear kings and Lord Overbarons, while we Faceless stand near but never on thrones, steering the fools as we please."

"Raevrel and Thansel talk of doing murder in the Court, and stepping into the shapes of the senior courtiers and the king himself, and making war on Silvertree."

The large, tentacle-faced head turned to regard Samraethe for a moment, and then slowly looked back into the gloom, features hidden from her again. "Raevrel and Thansel grow restless, too, and talk of more than they should. They tend to regard our dead kin as just names, but I remember faces, laughter, their dreams. . . . Samraethe, along with the power to reshape ourselves, the Three have given us long years. Never forget that, or how deeply folk who lack our blood-powers hate and fear us, and how quickly and eagerly they have also helped to hunt us, when our 'normal' kin wanted us *all* dead. Hide, keep quiet, govern yourself with patience, and you can outlive the hunters. Stand forth in fury, as too many of us do and urge the rest of us to do, and you'll be marked, and watched, and intended for extinction."

"Uncle Belmur, how did it all begin?"

The tentacled head turned again. "You've begun to forget things, little one? So soon?"

"No, I've heard it often enough," Samraethe told him softly. "But I'd like to hear it from you."

"No one knows how Prince Koglaur gained his powers, but 'twas he who could first shape-shift. Alterations of his face, the length and shape of his fingers, and the size and consistency of his feet."

"Consistency?"

"Aye: sticky to walk up walls, hard to stride through fires . . . and of course he could alter their size. I saw him walk across a stream once, making his feet like lily pads, only larger than shields. The coming of his powers surprised him, but to me they seemed inborn, erupting from him rather than visited on him by someone's spell. The whim of the gods, the flowering of an older dalliance in the royal line none of us can do more than guess at . . . no matter. He had it, men knew about it, and all Aglirta started to watch us, to see if they could catch us at more of it."

The tentacled head emitted a soft sigh, and added, "They meant our deaths, all of us. Those Snowsars who lacked the powers had to denounce us as 'other,' or be swept away from the throne in a slaughter of every last one of us, that would have taken Aglirta down into endless war. Brigandage. Savagery.

"They called us 'the fey,' and themselves 'the Clean,' or 'normal.' They hunted us—their brothers and sisters—almost to extinction . . . and still do, when they can. Even if 'they' have now dwindled to just Thamrain, Ostel, Farlmeir, and their families."

"While we have grown strong," Samraethe murmured.

"More than a score of us, many of us strong in our powers—and some of us have mastered sorceries, too."

Belmuragath growled, "Aye, and grown bolder than those minor magics give us any right to be. 'Prudence' is but an amusing word to Thansel, Ammurak, Slaundshel, and those who study spells with them."

Samraethe opened her mouth to reply, but then closed it again without a word, and kept silence.

The tentacled head turned. "You rethink and leave words unsaid too loudly for me not to notice, little one. Speak truth, as things have always been between us."

Samraethe sat still and silent for what seemed quite a long time, and then said very quietly, "Uncle Belmur, I learn and practice spells with Ammurak. And have learned boldness from him, too."

Silence fell again, and stretched for a very long time before Belmuragath replied, not turning his head, "I see."

"Nay, my King," Ravengar said urgently, "they'll not come that way, riding right into our bows. They'll take the old bridge, here, and come round by way of Athalstance, up behind Hawkroost Hill. From its height they can do bow-work on *us*, and charge down at us if we struggle up to meet them."

Thamrain studied the map just in front of his Lord Overbaron's fingers, sighed, and sat back. "You've the right of it, aye," he said wearily, "but I'm too weary to remember, or think straight—or talk straight either. Let's meet again come morn, and go over it again."

Silvertree rose smoothly. "Of course. Shall I send in your page?"

The royal mouth yawned. "Nay, Raven. I'll just step out of my boots and into the arms of Alyss . . . and let her take off whatever she desires."

Silvertree gave him a tired smile. "In the morn, then."

"In the morn," the king echoed, rising with a muffled

groan from his chair. He still wasn't sure if his Lord Over-baron disapproved of his bedchamber-lass; that weathered smile hid everything. Raven's eyes weren't cold or afire, at least, and he'd never said a word about finding a queen and fathering heirs, something his Lord Steward and his Seneschal managed to mention to him, oh so politely, every single Lady-curséd *day.*

He waved at Silvertree, one warrior to another, as the man went out. Then Thamrain lurched into his bedchamber and groaned into the familiar low, warm lamplight, "Alyss?"

"Here, my King," her husky voice replied from the bed, its purr eager. Thamrain had a glimpse of bare flank and thigh as he turned his back to her to sit down heavily on the edge of the bed.

"This night, lovechild mine," he managed around a sudden urgent procession of yawns, "your raging lord wants nothing more than . . . than to snore, as soon as the Three grant. Could you . . . help me with my boots?"

"Of course," Alyss murmured from just behind him, her voice just a trifle strange. Deeper . . . she must be angry, aye, that would be it. Well, by the Three, she'd just have to . . .

"My King," she purred, gentle fingers stroking his chin, trailing down his neck.

Thamrain started to shake his head, and then shrugged and chuckled. Well, if she wanted to do it her way, well enough. . . .

Like gliding snakes her fingertips found his ears, his nostrils, his mouth, sliding in so caressingly. . . .

"Snore, my Thamrain," Alyss purred, her voice much deeper now, as the King of Aglirta roused into alarm: *How* many fingers did she—

"Snore and *DIE, LITTLE TOAD!"*

And the finger in his mouth bulged up in an instant into a thick, choking worm, stifling all breath and any cry he might make, in the brief moments before the tentacles in his ears and nose swelled, too, and the rich red blankets of his own bed were being whipped up around his head by still more tentacles. . . .

Thamrain's head burst like a rotten melon, spattering blood so profusely that the blankets were soaked in an instant, and the hissing shape-shifter was forced to pluck up the sheets beneath to contain the gore. The last semblance of Alyss melted away as its tentacles writhed and swirled, and a mouth that was sliding into something quite different hissed soft curse after disgusted curse.

"Rae," came a level voice from the doorway, "you're making near as much noise as if you were fighting him fists to fists. Let me take care of that, and shift yourself into Thamrain's likeness. There *are* guards just outside."

The tentacled thing on the bed snarled something angry and wordless, breathing heavily. Tentacles writhed briefly and then sank back into melting, shifting flesh that flowed and thrust and shuddered, until—

"That's it," Thansel said critically. "That's . . . aye, *just* like that. Stay like that."

Raevrel bared his teeth in a silent snarl, and got up from the bed, human-seeming arms coiling and flailing in distaste. Without a word the other Koglaur flung tentacles across the room and took hold of the slumping, blanket-shrouded body.

"Wait here for me," he muttered, sprouting so many tentacles that snake-like coils almost covered the dead king in a coccoon.

"What if someone sees you?"

A dozen gesture-echoing tentacles made Thansel's shrug impressive indeed. "'Twill be the last thing they ever see," he said briefly, as he bundled his burden out.

Raevrel looked back at the stripped bed thoughtfully, recalling the brief fun he'd had on it with the real Alyss before he'd broken her neck. She'd been . . .

He put those memories aside with a flare of anger and sent a pair of tentacles snaking into the next room in search of replacement boots. He'd forgotten to snatch them off before Thansel went out, and—

"Here," Thansel's familiar voice said flatly. "I figured you'd be wanting the boots." The words were coming from what looked to be a sleepy, irritated Lord Steward Narthar, in his night robe.

"Now we go together to Silvertree?" Raevrel asked, stamping his feet into the splendid-looking boots and looking around for a sword.

"We get your door guards to take us. That way we're brought to him without a lot of turning the palace upside down searching, and through whatever guards he might get here, with the smallest flasks of fuss and delay we can empty. Now look angry about something secret and urgent."

"What?"

"Invent something," Thansel said flatly, every inch the haggard, tousled steward of advanced years and bright loyalty as he hastened into the forechamber. "Real kings do it all the time."


Torches guttered low in wall-brackets in many a passage of the royal palace in the chill hours before dawn, but a surprising plenty of courtiers were still up and awake, backs to the walls in watchful pairs or threesomes in those stretches of hall farthest from the light, muttering together in low, careful voices. Many of those urgent, angry near-whispers included the words "Ravengar's rise," as if it were a calamity of the weather.

Their murmured discussions were hushed by the approach of hard-eyed guards with drawn swords in their hands, and Lord Steward Narthar and the King himself—bareheaded, sleepy, and grim, but striding with angry purpose. The courtiers' mutterings arose with fresh vigor in their wake, and a few of the most daring whisperers drifted along in the direction the royal procession had taken. The rest merely speculated on its destination.

Most of them were correct in their suppositions. In Flowfoam, these latter nights, all endeavors sooner or later regarded and carefully avoided, or passed through the presence and scrutiny of, Lord Overbaron Ravengar Silvertree.

Who'd discarded his sweat-damp shirt and unbuckled his

belt with a weary groan, lying down on his bed with boots still on and hand clasped over the hilt of his still-scabbarded sword, to leave all cares behind for however long the Three granted *this* time, before—

He came awake in an instant, sword half-out and sitting up alertly in the darkness. The sound came again, louder this time: someone pulling hard on the barred door to his room, causing the heavy wooden bar to thud against the wall and then fall back against its brackets.

Silvertree buckled his belt and rose from the bed in one smooth movement, darting a glance at the archway into the next room and the motionless tapestry that filled it. The window of the room beyond the tapestry could be unshuttered with two sweeps of his hand, pivoting swivel-catches aside, to offer an escape.

Of sorts. A long, hard fall onto a wooded hillside that plunged steeply to the river, with only a narrow guardwalk at the base of the palace wall—an unlit dirt track on this stretch of its run—between him and the cold rushing waters of the Silverflow.

Drawing his sword, the Lord Overbaron of Aglirta walked as quietly as he could to the barred door and stopped to one side of it, not uttering a word.

"I *must* speak with him!" Thamrain's voice snarled from somewhere beyond it. "Get it open—now!"

"My King," the tremulous tones of the Lord Steward said disapprovingly from even farther away. "Surely we need not *destroy* the palace! Lord Silvertree is doubtless exhausted and deep asleep—a condition brought on by his diligent and loyal service. Perhaps if this man hails him, in your name?"

Ravengar grinned in the darkness. Narthar loved him not, but liked doing things the right way more than anything else. But what urgent matter could the Lord Steward and the King together not deal with, that a newly anointed Lord Overbaron must be roused from his bed to deal with?

"Open," a guard's voice snapped. "Open, in the name of the King!"

Silvertree kept silent—and then, struck by a sudden

thought, turned soundlessly on his heel, went to the tapestry, and thrust it aside with his sword. Utter darkness lay beyond, and no sound or movement.

"Open, I say!" the guard called more loudly, and slammed what was probably both fists or his shoulder against the door, so the wood thudded as loudly as stout stone and older, more massive wood framing allowed it. "Open for King Thamrain!"

Silvertree kept silent. No man willingly opens the door to what could quite likely be his own death.

"Silvertree?" Thamrain barked, his voice as deep and as loud as if he'd been fresh and bright, rather than the tottering, yawning man Ravengar had left not long ago. "Open up, man! I must talk with you!"

The King waited, and then called more loudly and sharply, "Raven?"

"Enough of this," the steward said angrily. "Depart, all of you. Leave us. Go on, we'll be perfectly safe. Return to your posts. If we can't rouse him, we'll call you back, never fear. Go on!"

There was much shuffling of booted feet, men tramping away, swords and armored elbows scraping briefly against stone walls, and then silence.

"Lord Silvertree?" the steward called, his voice faint. He must have turned away from the door to speak down the passage, for the benefit of the departing guards. Stranger and stranger, this.

Silvertree slowly drew in a deep, carefully soundless breath, raised his sword behind his shoulder so as to be ready to chop down, and waited. A little light from the nearest wall-torch in the passage was leaking in around the door; it was all he had to see by as he stared at that stout barrier—and waited.

Abruptly, there was a flicker of movement in the gloom around the door. *Around* the door, aye, in the crack where it met its frame. Something—there! Something small and dark and wiggling, like a questing worm . . .

Like a snake. Silvertree took a swift step away and back,

to best position himself for a swing, and peered at the dark, undulating finger of . . . of whatever it was. It reached farther into the room, wriggling now and shifting its shape, bulges occurring within it and gliding together to meet at its tip, grow larger in their merging, and slowly stand forth from the ribbon-like body . . . whereupon an eyelid flickered in one bulge. Eyes! Eyes blinking in the darkness, seeking him—

In sudden fear he slashed out, spraying gore across the inside of the door and slicing those orbs away from the snakelike bulk that had grown them.

It convulsed and thrashed the air wildly, trailing blood, as something on the far side of the door hissed and then sobbed in furious pain.

Moving as quietly as he dared, Ravengar Silvertree returned to his stance, sword at the ready despite the slow drip, drip of unseen blood running down to his knuckles to seek the floor.

What this had to do with the King, he wasn't sure. Did Thamrain—or more likely old Narthar—have some sort of pet snake-beast, that could spy on—?

But nay, it mattered not, did it? Snake or not-snake or spell, this could mean nothing good for Ravengar Silvertree.

Perhaps Thamrain was alarmed by the success of his Lord Overbaron, and had invited him here to the palace expressly to slay him, and blame the killing on Ravengar's own treachery against the Crown. With the other barons gone, Thamrain's throne was secure—and he might well judge it safer with the man whose sword had confirmed him there dead, rather than keep Silvertree as a loyal and capable guardian.

A loyalty that had been heartfelt and unstinting until that—that *thing* had come wriggling through the door right in front of his face, a moment ago . . .

*Yes,* there 'twas again! More things, a dozen of them this time, or more, reaching through the door-seam like so many evil fingers . . .

He sliced and hacked in a brief fury, and heard a hoarse scream on the other side of the door this time—before something whipped around his ankle.

He hacked down with savage swiftness, not daring to bend to put his full weight behind those blows as other tentacles came questing up under the door to join the first. His blade clanged sparks from the floor with one blow, but thank the Three, he cut the tentacle around his ankle.

Without tarrying another instant, Silvertree raced away, ducking through the archway heedless of the tapestry, and plunging across the chamber beyond to thrust open the shutters in fumbling, do-this-*quietly*-damn-all-gods haste.

The dim, pale gray foredawn showed him no bowmen or guards below, and no tentacles swooping out of nearby windows, either.

Setting his teeth, Ravengar Silvertree scrambled up onto the sill as he heard his door-bar tumble to the floor in the darkness behind him. He swung his sword up and out into the air to gain some force for his leap, and followed the thrust of his blade into the empty night, plunging down, down—

To a bone-bouncing, breath-snatching crash through branches and then a thambar-bush to strike the ground hard amid much snapping wood, and spring stumbling to his feet in a frantic rush down into the uneven, vine- and stump-choked wooded gloom beyond.

Light blossomed above and behind him, flaring back sudden reflection from boughs and tree trunks ahead, and the Lord Overbaron of Aglirta ducked to one side and raced on in his bruising, tumbling flight down through half-seen trees, roots, and thorny tangles, panting for breath and sparing no time for a look back. He did *not*, he told himself fiercely, as he caught his sword on a branch with a blow that numbed his fingers and almost wrenched the weapon from his hand, need to see more tentacles, just now. Or ever.

And then, quite suddenly, the thickly standing tree trunks gave way to a pale gray light, and—he was in the water.

Its cold jolted him, clawing at his bare torso so fiercely that he shuddered for breath, almost lost his blade again, and then found the shock sliding away into numbness.

Too long in the river would slay him as surely as any strangling tentacle or guardsman's blade. . . .

He struck out for the unseen shore, letting the current take him along the Flowfoam bank, swimming with it rather than trying to struggle against it, hoping no seeking arrows would come his way. . . .

He did risk one look back—and wished he hadn't. Long, pale streamers of many-winged, palely glowing *things* were arcing down through the trees from his windows, which now blazed with the light of many torches. Helmed heads were crowded along the sills, watching as the two monstrous things pursued him, growing long needle-snouts and sleek flippers moments before they struck the water.

Ravengar Silvertree hurled a bitter curse at whatever gods might be listening in these chill moments before dawn, and started swimming for his life.

Or whatever short stretch of it might be left to him. The swift river flow was carrying him away from Flowfoam far faster than his splashing attempts to reach the south bank, but the chill waters would be carrying a cold corpse if he didn't get clear of them soon . . . or the blood and a few torn limbs of one, if those shape-shifting things caught up to him.

There were sleek, purposeful ripplings behind him, and splashings. Too close and drawing swiftly closer . . .

*Damn* the Three, and Aglirta with them! He was going to die here, torn or bitten or stabbed horribly in mere moments, alone without his Yuesembra!

"Sembra!" he gasped aloud, fighting his way towards the unseen riverbank. "My lady love, flee from this land before they take you, too! Oh, Yuesembra, may the Three spare you as they've spurned me, and—"

Something in the water slapped against his foot then, and as he twisted desperately away from it, the night around him burst into a brightness as blue and pale as soft moonlight, and he saw two bulks rising menacingly in the swirling water just behind him—and beyond them, racing across the river like little flames, the advancing edge of the blue radiance.

It was coming from the riverbank—where a lone, dark form stood, long unbound hair writhing and whipping about bare spread limbs as if in a gusty gale—and eyes two points of blue fire.

*"Sembra!"* Ravengar gasped, and clawed at the water in a fresh frenzy, trying desperately to reach his wife.

Her hands were weaving a spell, clawing the air in intricate gestures that trailed brief glows and swirls of sparks. Words tumbled from her lips in a swift, precise flow as she started to dance—not alluringly, but in a sequence of odd, briefly frozen poses in which arcs of fire sometimes briefly formed around her . . . and her murmured incantation never stopped.

Something that had more teeth than seemed possible raked along Silvertree's ribs and thigh, plunging him into burning agony. He thrashed, convulsed, swallowed water, and tried to scream.

Somehow he got his face up out of the water again and struck out blindly with his sword, even as tentacles, some of them growing eyes and eager fanged mouths with fearsome speed, thrust into his view, curving over and around him. . . .

The night caught sudden ruby fire, a blaze almost bright enough to hide the blood boiling into ragged red smoke as tentacles burst into tatters and melted away in midair, swept away in a struggling instant, waters hurled back in a great bowl of warm death that left Ravengar Silvertree suddenly on his knees on the stones of the exposed riverbed—and then, as the waters rushed back, snatched him ashore in a drenched and gasping heap, shivering around the slender ankles of his wife.

"Yuesembra," he managed to sob through his agonies, as silvery fish flopped and arched in the wet wrack around him.

Long-fingered hands dragged him to his feet with more sheer strength than he'd known she possessed, and familiar dark eyes looked into his from less than a finger-length away.

"Raven, my Raven," she whispered, and kissed him fiercely. Warm healing arose in his mouth and seemed to bubble through him, like a flood of caressing fire. As he arched and bucked helplessly in her arms, the woman folk of Aglirta called the Witch of Sarinda said into his bleeding ears, "Do you really think I'd let you sleep in yon palace, surrounded by dagger-wielding courtiers—and wantonly ambitious maidservants, too—without watching over you?"

Ravengar blinked at her, dazedly trying to form a smile. She shook her head, giving him a wry half-smile in return, and gave him a tug that cost him his hold on his sword at last and nearly sent him sprawling.

"Now *come*," she ordered, dragging the Lord Overbaron of Aglirta away up the riverbank in a tottering stumble before he could sag against her, "let's be away from here!"


# 2

## The Witch of Sarinda


"*B*ut—but—who are all of these people? This is not right! We must—"

"Learn to hold our tongues and do as we are told, old man," a guard said coldly, as one of his arms slid forward to an impossible length to take the courtier's throat in a crushing grip and then, with an easy shift of his fingertips, break the trapped neck. "Though I'll admit it's a bit too late for you. *Such* a tragedy."

Someone laughed shortly, and someone else joined in; the mirth sounded neither kind nor pleasant. The tallest of the small group standing in the darkened throne room lifted his head sharply and said to the guard, "Bar that door."

"Done," was the prompt reply, even before the heavy bar dropped into place.

"Good. Now, we mus—"

"Not *quite* so fast, if you please, Slaundshel. Raevrel gave orders—"

"To take the throne room and the shapes of the courtiers we knew to be important who came to it, until his return. And Thansel said 'You all have wits enough to do what is needful.' *My* wits tell me that by staying here, in the seat of what little power is left in Aglirta, we can't help but end up ruling, if we tread carefully in the days ahead. Thamrain is dead, and Raevrel wears his shape, as Thansel wears the semblance of that old fool the Lord Steward. Our war is begun and won almost in a single night: if we in turn take the shapes of the right folk, *we* are Aglirta henceforth—as is only right. We are its Blood Royal, and its proper rulers. Some of us, I know, have walked softly and hid in shadows so long as to now be comfortable walking no other way, but know this: *I'll* not yield up this chance without a fight—and I'll fight any of you, kin or not, if you try to ruin this victory." Slaundshel glared around the gathering of Koglaur like a lion ready to strike, defying anyone to speak against him.

The oldest and largest of the shape-shifters stirred and spoke. "I was as bold as you once, Slaundshel. As you seem to have adopted the blunt heraldry of issuing warnings, I'll give you one: Be always aware, as I was not at your age, that your admirable boldness is just that—and neither wisdom nor any sort of armor."

Slaundshel snorted. "Belmuragath, you'd have us all smell flowers and watch them wither with the passing seasons, doing nothing as the world changes around us."

"Yet the warning is well taken," Ammurak said firmly. "I have my spells as you have yours, Slaund, but overboldness has felled both wizards and our kin before this. I'm already uneasy about Thansel and Raevrel. They went to see Lord Overbaron Silvertree, I believe, and should have been awaiting us here."

"Now *there's* a dangerous man," Samraethe said quietly, speaking for the first time. Dauraunt and Vaesen, the most worldly of all the Blood of Koglaur, nodded in grim agreement.

"Can we not live with Ravengar Silvertree?" Belmuragath asked. "There aren't enough of us to replace all the courtiers as it is, and we could harness that fire of loyalty and battle-wits. If he never knows the King was slain . . ."

"Thansel and Raevrel didn't go to chat about nightbirds with him," Slaundshel said sharply. "They went to kill him."

"And if he lives yet, and knows not of our—"

"No," Ammurak said coldly. "That Witch of Sarinda sees all. She knows our secret, and if he yet lives, now so will he. They must both die."

*The Taint. I had it, too, though no hint of the Blood of Koglaur ran in my veins. I suppose royal vanity made the Faceless of Aglirta think themselves special. Exalted.*

*As if no one else in all wide Darsar could share their might. Or their doom.*

"How could they all have turned against me?" the embattled Lord Overbaron of Aglirta asked the sighing wind bitterly, as he stood on the battlements of Silvertree House watching yet another armed force cautiously advancing to encircle the walls. "What madness—?"

Words failed him, and he dismissed the empty air with waves of both exasperated hands and turned on his heel to glare down into the courtyard of his still unfinished home. Loyal but weary Silvertree warriors below were hastening this way and that, drawing water from the wells and shifting beams and heaped cobbles to brace the gates one more time.

"Men obey orders, Lord, no matter how foolish," one of his lancecaptains replied grimly. " 'Tis the King who gives them. The King is your problem." His gaze strayed to the tall, dark-haired figure of Lady Silvertree, and then swiftly turned elsewhere. A rumor had been spreading that King Thamrain did not hate and fear the Witch of Sarinda, as so many had thought for so long, but rather lusted after her—and now did war on his best baron just to lay hands upon her, darksome magics and all.

Ravengar clapped an agreeing, comforting arm around

the warrior's shoulders, and then stood back as the lancecaptain gave him a tight smile and started east along the battlements, to better see the mercenaries massing beyond the walls on that side of Silvertree House. At least the ramparts were finished, strong-standing under the fury of so many unexpected tests.

"Mahandor speaks truth," he murmured, "yet even when the King and I stood shoulder to shoulder, speaking with one voice and pointing out clear gain to barons, they were slower than this to muster their blades and ride to war for us."

"Those men are dead. The Koglaur wear their faces now, and press for our slaughter," Yuesembra told him firmly, taking one of his hands in both of her own. "You because you're the most capable battle leader in the realm, and so the greatest threat to them. I have spells most of them fear—and know who they truly are, and can tell all Aglirta so, until my tongue is stilled. These attacks will not end until we are gone."

Ravengar shook his head. "A dozen, now, not counting yon gathering rabble. Our food dwindles, and no fresh swords can spring up from the ground to replace our fallen."

"That's not quite truth," his wife replied softly.

Lord Silvertree's head snapped around. "*No,* Yuse. No. Absolutely not. I'll *not* have those who yet live, and fight loyally for me, see their dead comrades rise from the dirt to shamble into battle, rotting and plodding before their eyes to remind them with every step what their fate will soon be!"

"The risen dead are more frightening than the Faceless?"

"The Faceless are our foes, and fearsome only as they shift shapes. Walking corpses and shuffling bones would be blades of fear in the backs of our people—a peril caused by one of their own. They name you 'witch' and mistrust you already. The women fear and hate you for the way their men look at you. I . . . I fear for your fate at their hands, Yuse, if I fall and they know it."

"Don't," Yuesembra said softly, her eyes very blue. "If you fall, I shall embrace death as swiftly as I can find it—but I'll not find it alone. One hated and lusted-after witch of

Sarinda could well be worth three-score Aglirtans, or more; we shall see."

Ravengar swallowed, and then reached out to put his arm around her. Yuesembra settled against his armored chest as if it were a warm and inviting pillow, and said no more. In silence they watched their foes—mercenaries from across half Darsar this time, brought by barge from Sirlptar—make ready swords and bows under the flapping banners of Aglirta. Streams of messengers were trotting up to the well-armored men standing under those banners, and then hurrying off again, downslope and behind trees to the unseen hollows nigh the river, where the cart-road ran. The barons and court lords of Aglirta must be down there, out of sight of Silvertree bowmen and Yuesembra's sorceries alike.

"Every baron now a Faceless?" Ravengar murmured, after some time. "I'd not thought there were that many of them."

"If they were as few as courtiers would have you believe," his wife asked in reply, "how could Thamrain and those who wore the crown before him have failed to exterminate them?" She shook her head and drew him a little back, well behind the large merlon that guarded a stair-head—as the first catapulted kill-lances hissed through the air, amid shouted warnings, to clatter and shiver here and there around the battlements.

"If Prince Koglaur hadn't used the easy shiftings of his face to seem to be so many other men, and seduced fewer wives," Yuesembra added sharply, "the Faceless would now be but a fireside scare-tale, not an open royal secret. Even in Sarinda we knew the fey branch of the Aglirtan royal family outnumbered those of 'rightful blood' . . . and believe me, my lord, we knew little enough about green-forested Aglirta other than it had a great river winding down its heart, and stags and farms in plenty."

"And men who loved to make war," her husband added ruefully, pointing. "They're bringing up a ram for the first rush at our gates."

Yuesembra looked along Ravengar's arm at the purposefully moving helms below. Then she thrust him sharply away, raked a long-nailed fingertip along the line of his jaw, and snatched something from a pouch at her belt.

Biting back an oath, Ravengar slapped a hand to the gash she'd given him—but not before her longer, more nimble fingers had wiped a generous welling of his blood away, and brought it to her other hand in a slap that trapped whatever she'd snatched between her palms. She chanted something swift and strange over her laced fingers, and then threw what they held fiercely down at the stones before her, whirling to thrust an arm up in front of Ravengar's eyes in the same motion.

Her magic caused the nail—for that was what it was; he'd time to glimpse that much—and the glowing whirl of sorcery around it to burst apart with a roar that rocked the stones beneath their boots and sent stone chips cracking off the crenellations around them in fierce profusion.

An instant later, the great metal-shod wooden ram being slammed thunderously against the gates of Silvertree House burst apart, too, hurling the heads and arms of its wielders in all directions.

"Three bear witness!" Ravengar gasped, staring at the blood-drenched, screaming carnage. And then he snarled a cruder oath, and charged at Yuesembra, bruisingly driving her inside the stair-head—a scant breath before the battlements where they'd stood were raked by a hissing rain of kill-lances.

They'd not been the only ones looking at foes, it seemed.

"*Off* me, Raven!" the Lord Overbaron's wife hissed urgently, dusky skin sliding distractingly past the Aglirtan warrior's nose as she clawed her way back to her feet and darted forward.

"Yuse, *no!* Yon lances—"

"Were all fired in a volley, and by the time they've reloaded, working those winches like madmen, I'll have cast my next spell," the Lady Silvertree snapped. "*If* you belt up and let me incant, that is!"

Silently Ravengar gave his wife a warrior's salute, and she

smiled, stepped forward daringly into an embrasure, and sketched a swift and intricate gesture with both hands.

The Lord Overbaron of Aglirta looked around wildly, found the ready-shields littering a corner rather than the rack they were supposed to adorn, snatched one up, and rushed to protect his wife from stray arrows. Lance catapults might indeed take time to winch tight—he could hear the clattering, whirring chorus of many of them being rewound right now—but a bow took only an instant to bend, and a single lucky shot . . .

Yuesembra smiled tightly, struck a pose that might have been alluring in another time and place, and ducked down against his shoulder to share his shield—as a few arrows thrummed past overhead, far from their target.

"Walking dead you forbade, Lord," the dusky-skinned sorceress of Sarinda murmured nigh his ear, "but you said nothing about setting a few disembodied arms and heads to flying about striking at the living—*outside* the walls, and using only those who raise blades against us, upon their own fellows."

Howls of horror and disgust followed hard on the heels of her words, and Ravengar stared at her in awe and admiration—and then just *had* to see this handiwork, and clambered up with shield held before him, to peer and gape and peer again. A lone arrow splintered on a merlon close by, and he half fell back down into the stair-head beside his lady. "Claws of the Dark One!" he swore delightedly. "Some of them are running already! Hurtling heads thumping into faces, dancing arms slashing with swords at anyone near . . . *gods!* How long can you keep it up?"

"Not long," Yuesembra told him. "It eats at my strength already."

Ravengar stared at her in alarm, jaw dropping open, but his wife laid a comforting hand on his arm and murmured, "All powerful spells do. That's why wizards don't rule all Darsar already."

"But . . . but . . . ," the Lord Overbaron said in bewilderment. "Why have I never known this?"

Yuesembra sighed. "In sorcery, knowledge is power. Would you surrender all your blades to a foe, and face his steel bare-handed? Well, in like manner, we who work spells keep silent about our weaknesses, rather than trumpeting them to every passing battersword armaragor. Or even to Lord Overbarons, vital matter of strategy or not."

"Do you mean to tell me," Ravengar Silvertree asked quietly, reaching out to grip her arms in the gloom, "that every battle-spell you cast wounds you?"

Yuesembra gave him the smile that still stirred his ardor, and nodded.

"And if we face battle after battle, you'll waste away and dwindle and *die,* even if no war-spell or weapon touches you?"

"Quite possibly," the Witch of Sarinda confirmed. "Yet I've no intention of dying, Raven—and I have some secrets left to me yet. Some powerful secrets."

The Lord of Silvertree shook his head, took a deep breath, and asked levelly, "And is it the custom of wives in Sarinda to keep any number of powerful secrets from their husbands?"

Yuesembra smiled like a languid cat once more, lifted one shapely eyebrow in challenge, and said simply, "Of course."

*Ah, the maedra. As cold as I, yet alive. Sliding through stone. Eyeless snakes, yet with human arms, muscles mightier than those of any tall smith, taloned hands that can mold stone their spittle has softened.*

*I could take some beast-shapes, but never that one. I feared them when I first saw them.*

*And I fear them still.*

Ravengar hissed in pain, jerking under her fingers, but his wife merely rode his back to the next pose he settled into, and continued her gentle wiping. Spell-healing had served his worst wound, a deep stab into his guts where an armor-plate had failed; for the rest, he'd receive the same rough care any armaragor would give a comrade—save that the Lord Overbaron had refused the chew-herbs that dulled pain. He dared not be dream-walking if they broke through the walls somehow and came running to slay, with shouts and bloody swords raised. . . .

Yuesembra had already gone over the worst of his cuts with water, tracing their ragged ruin with a finger cloaked in linen. The vinegar she was using now, on her second tour of sliced and battered flesh, stung like the proverbial claws of the Dark One.

All day he'd hacked and stabbed and kicked at ladders and shouted orders and encouragement along the walls. All day and well into the night.

It was late now, the night of the ninth day since the mercenaries had first showed up at the walls of Silvertree House. Bargeload after bargeload of motley hireswords swelled the ranks under the royal banners—fast enough to more than replace those slain by the warriors of Silvertree.

The battered walls of his fortress home still stood, but the defenders on them were largely toothless now, all arrows long since spent. Someone under the flapping banners had been wise enough to order the volleys of arrows and catapulted kill-lances stopped, so the increasingly weary defenders could salvage no replacement shafts to fire back. Now all the catapults hurled were the stinking dead, to spatter, bounce, and spread horror and sickness. The horses hated it—but to make food stretch farther, Ravengar had already ordered the weakest beasts butchered and roasted.

Yet all the meat that hungry loyal armaragors could eat didn't make their sword arms less weary, or snatch reinforcements out of nowhere to bolster their steadily thinning ranks. Every day and night mercenaries scaled the walls on scores of precarious ladders, to be sworded or shoved screaming back down to their deaths below, and all day long they trudged forward to slam rams numbingly against the walls, avoiding the gates where the disembodied horrors kept flying beyond death by the Witch of Sarinda still reigned, and every fresh ram grimly advanced burst with fresh carnage just as the first one had.

The defenders had every advantage—save those of rest, relief, and numbers. Scores of hireswords died, and hundreds took their places, until every Silvertree man and wench who could lift a blade at all reeled with weariness—and sagged into snoring slumber in every idle instant. Slower and ruled by bone ache were their numbed sword arms, and as each loyal Silvertree defender died the dwindling ranks of those who remained saw their own deaths drawing closer.

This night the cooks had offered to defend the walls, and a gray-faced, stumbling Ravengar had lacked the fire to deny them. Everyone might go hungry on the morrow—but if his armaragors didn't get some rest, there wouldn't *be* a morrow. Only the outer fortress walls of the mansion were still theirs, the half-ruined and unfinished inner chambers long since abandoned to the catapulted dead, vultures, and increasingly bold rats. The chill dark rooms in and under the stout walls were home now, increasingly darker and colder as the Silvertree folk and their store of torches and lamp oil alike grew fewer.

Yuesembra was working by the light of a single lamp, and it was starting to die into dimness. Still in his breeches and boots, Ravengar was too stiff and pain-wracked to rise and refill it, and he'd learned in their early days together that she'd worked some childhood magic on herself—as did all in Sarinda who chose the path of sorcery—that let her see in the dark far more keenly than any cat. With her dusky skin, she looked like a hunting cat right now, in her supple, skintight dark leather breeches, high soft boots, and thieves' jerkin, throat-laced and sleeved to the wrists.

His own leather jack, stiff with sweat and blood, lay in a heap on the floor, marked where his armor had been driven hard into it—and where Yuesembra was sleek and dark, he was heavy-muscled and hairy.

Ravengar's naked sword lay ready under his hand as she

worked on him—and he looked up sharply, hand closing on it, when another glimmering light approached.

"Lord and Lady?" Eirendra's soft voice floated along the passage before her. Though bloodstains that had not been there earlier marked the hip and thigh of her plain gown, Yuesembra's maidservant seemed as serene as ever as she slipped through the archway into their bedchamber. She bore a covered platter in her hand, and over her shoulder hung a wineskin. Beyond the oil lamp she bore, a thick blanket was doubled over her other shoulder.

Steam was rising from her domed burden, and a sharp tang of cooked spices wafted with it. Ravengar smiled. Ah, trust Eirendra. . . .

She met his grin with one of her own—tighter and wearier than her usual sunny smile, of course, but that was only to be expected.

"I brought you the last dish Aunra was tending, before she went up to the walls," Yuesembra's maid murmured, as she bent over them both. "She said to feed it to someone or it'd burn, and I thought 'twas only right that the two of you see something more than cheese gnawed in haste, for once. So—" She lifted the dome from the platter.

And flung the glowing hearth-coals it held full in Yuesembra's face. The dome smashed sizzlingly into Ravengar's cheek a moment later, and he ducked his head as he launched himself up at her—in time to have the platter itself slammed hard into his nose.

Blinded, he roared in pain and fury, and slashed out at where Eirendra must be with his blade, slicing only empty air as he heard Yuesembra's gasp turn into a strangled, choking gurgle.

An instant later a tentacle slapped around his throat, another looped about the wrist of his sword arm, and he was struggling to breathe, staggering sideways through a stool to fetch up against the wall. The Three-cursed shape-shifters had slunk right into his bedchamber!

He couldn't get air, couldn't . . .

A red mist stole brightly up into the darkness before his eyes as Ravengar Silvertree sawed desperately with his blade at the strong, ever-thicker snakespan of flesh right in front of his chin, trying to . . . trying vainly to . . .

There was a flash of light—emerald radiance, flooding past his eyes in a rush that took him to his knees—and the crushing pressure around his throat and sword arm was suddenly gone. He sprawled on cold stone, gagging and groaning.

Three above, his throat hurt. When he could think about enough more than that to realize he'd been kicking the floor and writhing helplessly, Ravengar discovered the wheezing whistle of frantic breathing in his ears was his own, and that blood was running freely from his ears. At about that time, the light roiling somewhere behind him changed from green to an intense blue.

"Y . . . Yuse?" he croaked through the surging pain. "Lady, are you—?"

A rising roar was the only reply he received—a crackling like a kindling fire, wrapped around a thunder muted like a buried waterfall, great rushing power that could be felt more than heard. It was very close by, to his right, where the bed must be. The very air was throbbing and trembling . . . or was it just his own hurts making it seem so?

Ravengar struggled to master his spasms, and grunted his way up off the rough stone floor. He must find his blade and get to his wife, whatever had befallen her. She must need him, she . . . he took two unsteady strides, tripped in the discarded blanket, and crashed back down onto his knees, fresh pain making him howl and curse.

Hunched over against its fire, he groaned and kicked out angrily, trying to wobble to his feet again—and his sword rang on stone as he nudged it with his toe. The Lord Over-baron of Aglirta slapped a determined hand onto the floor, turned on it to fumble grimly around for his sword—and when he had hold of it again, dared to turn his head for the first time and try to see Yuesembra.

Tears were still streaming like storm-driven rain across his gaze, winking back echoes of light left behind by the

searing blow of the platter, but blearily he could see a
greater light through them: that bright, almost white-blue
fire, blazing up towards the ceiling in a torch-bracket that
should not have been there.

"Yuse?" he asked hoarsely, crawling forward on his
knuckles. "Yuesembra?"

A sound that was something more than a sob answered
him, and the torch-bracket moved. Hastily he sought his feet,
using his sword as a crutch, and trying to blink away tears.

Abruptly flame flared up from the floor behind him—the
lamp, by some whim of the gods unbroken, had ignited that
blanket the Koglaur had brought—and by its light he could
make out the bed, and Yuesembra hunched over on its edge
amid a tangle of scorched and shriveled tentacles, clutching
her face in her hands. That blue-white fire was raging out between her spread fingers, healing as it burned. The coals!
But . . . fire to heal burns made by . . . fire?

"Yuesembra?" he asked, and took a stride forward.

She flinched away from him, and Ravengar stopped uncertainly, sword raised. Had the—?

No. His gaze followed the tentacles down to the charred
thing on the floor, one long feminine leg bent out of the tatters that had been Eirendra's gown, the bloody fingers of a
rib cage arcing up out of blackened ruin, and beyond that: a
head that had only smooth flesh where a face should be—
smooth flesh split by a mouth frozen open in a grimace of
pain. He put his sword tip into that mouth, but the Faceless
did not move. Well and truly dead, then, burned by Yuesembra's magic.

The flames behind him were swiftly dying into threads of
drifting smoke—like everything else in these rooms within the
wall, the blanket had been damp—and Ravengar Silvertree
stepped rather dazedly across the room to pluck up the oil
lamp lying in its charred folds before full darkness came down.

"Raven," his wife asked from behind him, her voice a low,
insistent whisper, "do you trust me?"

Lord Silvertree whirled around, the lamp in his hand.
"Why, *yes*—"

Yuesembra's dusky smile was wry. "Just not enough to turn your back on me."

Ravengar lowered his blade, set down the lamp on a bedside table, and hastened to her. "Yuse, are you—whole? Well?"

"Yes. Do you trust me?"

The Lord Overbaron of Aglirta stood very still for a long moment, eyes fixed on hers, and then he said firmly, "Yes. Yes, I do. With my life."

"Then hear me and believe: no matter how strange—or sordid—my deeds may seem to you in the time that is left to us, all that I do is for you. To keep you and our children safe for as long as I have the power to do so. And to keep your name—and your vengeance—alive for even longer."

Yuesembra's eyes were very large and dark, her face within easy reach of his. Ravengar trembled in the air, wanting to kiss her, thinking she'd never seemed so beautiful as she did now . . . or so dangerous. Something in those eyes made him very afraid, something he'd never seen there before. Something that made him not dare come any closer.

"There's something you should know," she added, waving at the burned, tentacled corpse on the floor. "This isn't the first Koglaur I've slain. Or the tenth, since we've been shut in here. It's the twelfth."

"The—?" Ravengar stared at her.

"Repeatedly the Faceless have slipped inside our walls—somehow—and taken the places of your most trusted warriors and servants. They usually come to slay when you sleep, but twice now they've tried to get up onto the battlements to take you from behind while you're fighting."

"But—but how do they get in? And how many of them *are* there?"

Yuesembra shook her head. "I know not. I need all my strength to cast spells just to keep us alive; I've nothing left for prying or warding . . . or farspeaking. I don't need foresight, however, to know that there'll be more. So, husband mine: trust no one. Not even me, unless you're sure you're seeing *me,* and not a Koglaur in my shape. Be ready for an attack whenever a friend draws near. Weapon ready, space to use it, distance enough to avoid someone stabbing or just pouncing on you." She waved a hand at the blackened coils around her. "These tentacles . . ."

Ravengar nodded ruefully, still feeling the bruised tenderness at his throat—that rose into something much worse whenever he tried to swallow.

"Do those who remain loyal to us know about the—?" He waved at the dead Faceless.

"A few of them. Most learned the hard way, and now lie feeding the rats wherever the Koglaur left their bodies."

"I must tell Taranth; he can't command the walls properly when I sleep if he doesn't know that every man beside him could be a shape-shifter, just waiting for the right moment to betray him. More than that: he can hide this carrion, so your lady servants see it not, and spend their time to come doing something more useful than screaming in panic."

Yuesembra nodded. "If we send someone for him, from the ready-room, we can stay together. Raven, I don't want you out of my sight this night."

Lord Silvertree nodded, and held out his hand to her. Familiar long, strong fingers linked with his, and he tried not to flinch at the thought that they might twist into something bestial, tentacles seeking his life once more, with reaching fangs and . . . he shook his head to set such dark fancies aside as they hastened down the passage together.

Old Shamra was fat and shuffling, but she could move when she saw the need, and Taranth wasn't Ravengar's most trusted lancecaptain for nothing. He came down from the walls in haste, gleaming with sweat and someone else's blood, to stride along the passage with war ax in hand and risen fire in his eyes.

"Lord? You need me?"

"Taranth! I've something you must see," Ravengar greeted him with some relief, stepping back out of the passage to let the lancecaptain stride into the bedchamber. "It seems not all of our foes—"

Taranth took one step towards the bed, where Yuesembra

sat facing him with the burned, gaping Faceless sprawled in front of her, froze—and then flung his war ax into Ravengar's face and plunged forward, his body erupting into a reaching forest of streaking tentacles.

Ravengar got his sword up barely in time; the ax clanged deafeningly against it as its heavy blade laid open his right ear and then bit numbingly into the shoulder beneath as it fell. With a snarl he launched himself forward through a sudden wall of racing sparks.

Many of this second Koglaur's tentacles were shuddering in front of him, curling and convulsing back from the spark-spilling magic Yuesembra was lashing it with—but the rest were writhing like the shoulders of many men hauling of a net . . . and the net they were tugging at was Yuesembra's throat. She was hissing something through set teeth, nigh invisible in a halo of sparks and flailing tentacles—

And then Ravengar reached the shape-shifter, and drove his blade deep into its head. He wasted no time trying to see what damage he'd done, but left the sword where it had lodged—against bone, by the feel, though that might not mean much, against such a monster—but snatched out his belt dagger and stabbed like a madman, plunging the steel in and then hauling it forth and thrusting it in again, as fast as his weary arm could drive it.

Blood and not-blood drenched him, and a wet, keening wail arose and bubbled in his ears, but as a dozen tentacles or more left off strangling Yuesembra to dart back at him, the Lord Overbaron of Aglirta sprang away from the Faceless in a desperate, twisting leap that brought him down heavily atop two errant tentacles and the floor—with his hand on the shaft of the war ax.

He snatched, rolled, found his feet, whirled, and started hacking, dropping his dagger to use both hands as he advanced, heading through the shifting, sliding bulk and angry maelstrom of tentacles towards the hilt of his sword. Perhaps the Faceless would pluck it out and grow a hand to wield the blade against him, or perhaps he'd get back to it first . . . but it seemed as good a goal as any, when trying to wound something whose vitals could be anywhere.

The sword tore itself free when he was still the full reach of his tiring arm away, and circled, dripping, in the air. This was it, then . . .

Ravengar set his teeth against the pain that would come when it swept down—and then saw through the chaos of blood, tentacles, and sweat that no tentacle was touching the sword. It was whirling through their writhing weave on its own, as if a ghost held it!

Down it plunged. Not into the breast of the sweating, straining Lord Silvertree, but deep into the Koglaur's flowing torso, which shrank and split apart at its approach. The steel spun, flashing, to hack at the sliding flesh receding from it, and more blood spurted. Then Yuesembra gasped, somewhere beyond a wall of flailing tentacles, and the sword faltered.

But by then Ravengar Silvertree was only a long stride away from the writhing torso of the Faceless, where he'd wanted to be. He swung the ax so hard that both his feet left the ground to follow its whistling swing.

It bit deep, and the Koglaur shuddered like a tree hewn to the core. Ravengar kicked at that soft, slumping torso, managed to drag the ax free—and buried it again, viciously. Tentacles toppled, bouncing and writhing on the floor, and he struck again through the suddenly open space, afraid that if he let up for an instant, the thing would glide mockingly away, rise up again in some fearsome shape of talons and huge fanged jaws, and lunge at him as furiously as if it had never felt the ax at all.

His sword flashed past him, to transfix a desperately arching tentacle that had been reaching for his throat from behind, and Yuesembra gave him a grim smile as the Lord of Silvertree House shook his ax free of the shuddering, collapsing welter of gore and slithering wetness—and struck again, severing it in two this time and ringing one point of the ax head off the flagstone floor.

Tentacles coiled weakly, and then slid down to a slithering collapse. He grinned back at Yuesembra as she tore the last of the Koglaur from her neck and throat—tentacles that had sprouted a grotesque profusion of clutching human fingers—and came wearily towards him, arms outstretched for an embrace.

For a few swift, wary moments he peered about the room, trying to make sure this was Yuesembra and not a shape taken by the Faceless, while she lay lifeless beyond the bed. Her smile broadened and she nodded approvingly.

Then the din of battle-horns sounding from the battlements echoed down the passage. Neither Taranth nor Lord Ravengar were there to snap orders and swing swords, but it seemed at least one cook knew how to blow the warning of yet another attack.

The Lord and Lady Silvertree looked at each other wearily, still a blood-wading stride apart.

"I should be—" Ravengar began, looking around in the gore for his sword. There was a clatter of armor on stone in the passage behind him, and the thunder of running booted feet.

As he wheeled around, two of his senior armaragors rushed in, bearing his shield between them, his armor heaped upon it. "Lord," one of them snapped, snatching up the Lord Overbaron's helm from the pile in his free hand, "you must hurry!"

"Aye," the other agreed—and as the first one hurled the helm right at Ravengar's face and tentacles boiled out of his armor after it, shedding plates and gauntlets and greaves in all directions, the second drew his blade and hurled it across the chamber at the Witch of Sarinda.

Who was just finishing a swiftly snapped spell, blue fire bursting into life around her crossed, entwined wrists. As Ravengar staggered back, lifting the war ax to defend her, that blue fire leaped past him like an arrow shot from a bow. It split into two expanding whorls of spitting lightnings that broke over the two Faceless like waves striking rocks on the beach . . . and then ebbed and faded, leaving nothing but two slumping pillars of drifting smoke behind.

As the sword that sought her life rang off the wall behind her, bounced, and clattered thunderously to the floor, Yuesembra groaned and reeled, staggering back. Ravengar put out a hand to steady her, but she was falling away from him, stumbling against the nearest wall. She clung to it, sagging and shuddering, her face almost as gray as the dark stone, and murmured a word Ravengar had never heard before.

That word echoed strangely through the stone all around them, repeating as if the stones themselves were whispering it repeatedly to each other, a hissing chorus that died away and then swelled again menacingly.

Ravengar waved his ax and looked nervously about, expecting the stones themselves to erupt at him—but they stood as dark and as solid as always.

*As uncaring as always,* he thought savagely, as Yuesembra Silvertree gave a little moan and fell to the floor, ending up on her breast and knees, still moaning softly . . . almost senseless. When he held her and murmured her name, she seemed not to hear him, her eyes gone dark and dull, her mouth slack.

*"Yuse!"* he hissed, shaking her. *"Yuse!"*

From somewhere very far away, her murmur came, just the corner of her mouth moving: "I'm . . . not . . . dead yet, love."

And then there was a rush of booted feet in the passage again, and Ravengar set her gently back down on the wet and sticky floor and caught up the ax with a snarl.

Six hard-eyed armaragors burst through the archway, some of them sprouting tentacles as they came—and the others already sporting extra arms that menaced the Lord of Silvertree House with spears and axes and blades in sharp, steely profusion.

Ravengar gave them a defiant growl and waved his ax before him, swinging it back and forth, daring them to come within reach . . . but even as he sought to entice a few of these—these *things*—to die before the rest of them inevitably overwhelmed him, the walls around him seemed to stir.

The Lord of Silvertree backed hastily away, lifting his ax desperately. How had they got past him? How could they seem to be part of the very Three-be-damned *walls,* Dark One take them?

And as he raged in disbelief and despair, the great stones of the wall bulged like a tent thrust outwards by bodies moving beneath, rock bending and bowing as readily as soft fabric. The stones around Ravengar surged forward, ripples rushing past him towards the Koglaur, ripples that bulged forth into . . . dark, wet, smooth hulks that slid free of the walls, disgorged like birthed foals. Two, three, five of them.

They resembled upright snakes or eels with massively muscled, cruel-taloned arms, and were as large as war-horses, though they glided forward as softly and smoothly as a breeze through tall grass.

Ravengar stared at their backs in disbelief as these new monsters *flowed* forward to attack the Koglaur.

Then, as tentacles slapped and horrible wet shrieks and slobberings arose, he looked behind him wildly. These eel-things must be born of Yuesembra's magic! Was she—? Had she given her life casting a spell to try to save him?

The Witch of Sarinda was not where he'd left her. She'd crawled to the farthest, darkest corner of the bedchamber, and was clawing her slow and trembling way up the stones of the wall there, as weak and determined as an old woman Ravengar had once seen stubbornly fighting her way home in a gale. And one of her long-fingered hands had just done something to one of those blocks that made it sink inwards.

A door then opened in the wall beside Yuesembra, a way into darkness not on Ravengar's plans, and utterly unfamiliar to him.

"Y-Yuse?" the Lord of Silvertree House stammered, staring at his wife and at the door beside her, too dumbfounded to find words. "H-huh-wuh?"

Yuesembra Silvertree gained her feet, her skin more pale than he'd ever seen it. As he stared at her, she reeled, clawed at the wall to keep from falling, and gave her lord a wry smile. Her eyes were very large and dark. "Welcome to another of my secrets."

And with those words she pulled herself into the doorway—and collapsed forward into the unfamiliar darkness.

*"Yuesembra!"* Heedless of the noisy slaughter behind him, a wild-eyed Ravengar Silvertree whirled back to snatch up the flickering oil lamp the first Faceless had brought. Hefting the ax in his other hand, he bit back a prayer to the Three—for who else could have dealt him this much hurt in one night?—set his teeth, and ran after her.

# 3

## Maedra Rising

"*Y*use? Yuse! What is this place?"

"Raven, *trust me*. Later I'll tell all you deem needful. *Later*."

The walls around them shook, and small stones pattered down on Ravengar Silvertree's head. "What was *that?*" he snarled, as his lamp showed him whirling dust, a rain of stones—and then darkness, as it was smothered by a stream of rubble.

A long-fingered hand patted his arm as he peered blindly about, and soft lips kissed his cheek. "Let go the lamp," his wife murmured in his ear, "and use that hand to hold me . . . and we'll walk together."

Ravengar tossed the lamp behind him to keep its oil off them both, and reached out with his freed hand. Yuesembra's shoulder was against his chest, and he reached around until he was cupping her familiar curves, clasping her against him. "Huh," he told the back of her neck, "this is better than hacking tentacles that have slaughtered all my folk and friends, and taken their faces. *Much* better."

"I should hope so. Step carefully, now. I'm going to walk forward, and we'll have to move together, leg to leg, or stumble all over each other."

The Lord Overbaron of Aglirta did as he was bid, and after a few unintended kicks and missteps, fell into a rhythm with his wife's slow, deliberate strides. There was a lilt to her step, he noticed, that he must admire properly at some later and more appropriate time.

If such a time ever offered itself in what was left of their lives.

"What if the Faceless win the battle, back behind, and follow us? Or find that door later, and come after us?"

"They won't. There's no door there now."

"Ther—" Ravengar tightened his hold on his wife and dragged her to a halt. "Sembra mine, *will* you tell me what's going on here? I ordered a stout but simple palace be built, a ring-fortress of linked keep-towers, really, and . . ."

"And I," the sorceress of Sarinda replied calmly, "saw the Koglaur quietly breaking a neck here and slicing a throat there, as they stole their ways into the royal household. They feared you, Raven. They still do. The most loyal and capable man in the realm, the true power propping up Thamrain's throne. They knew what I was, too—and that doomed you. You could not be their dupe, so you must die."

"Aye, aye, I believe that, though it still seems more bards' fancy than the Aglirta I know . . . thought I knew. But all this! This tunnel! We must be clear away under the next tower by now, or even beyond the walls!"

"We are. Beyond the walls, that is—or rather, the ones you've been defending. There are some new ones, raised rather suddenly this night, close against the first. I'd hoped to crush and grind a few-score Sirl hireswords between new and newer, but I'm afraid I only trapped most of them. Still, they should starve before the walls crumble enough for them to climb out."

Ravengar listened to his wife's calm, confident voice with deepening awe. He'd known he was wedding a powerful sorceress, but *this* . . .

Yuesembra bent against his grip with sudden strength and strode on, half dragging his greater weight and bulk along. After a few strides he moved with her again, resuming their—for him—blind progress along a passage of damp stone.

And where by all the Three were they going? Halfway to Sirlptar, along tunnels he'd never even known existed? Or perhaps she'd cast an idle spell or two this morn, and with a wave of her hand ushered miles of caverns and crawl-passages into being. If every proud lady of Sarinda did this, that land must be as riddled with underways as worm-drilled cheese, constantly collapsing here and there as undermined keeps and hills and busy towns crumbled. . . .

His barony might do that, too, rich fields and forested hills and all falling into dusty pits of ruin without warning. . . .

Ravengar breathed heavily as he fought down any number of curses, and then said only, "I'd very much treasure, Lady, knowing what's going on. Knowing what your words just now *mean* would be a smaller prize, but one I'd still value. If 'tis not too much trouble."

His sarcasm won him the light music of her laughter, and the reply, "We're in a large chamber, now. Draw your dagger."

"I . . . Lady, I lost it in the fray."

The Witch of Sarinda clucked like a disapproving mother and then said in a voice that held a smile, "Then we'll have to make do with mine."

She slid free of him with a fluid ease that suggested she could have escaped his grasp at any time, leaving Ravengar to stand blind and helpless in the dark, his ax in his hand.

Something glowed faintly in the gloom before him. As he stared at it, the glow slowly grew brighter—a trifle stronger, not much—until he could see that its source was a tiny knife blade in Yuesembra's hand. His wife had evidently drawn it from that lower part of her large and ornamented belt buckle that dipped towards her crotch; the fingers of her other hand, still there, sketched a reassuring little wave at him.

"Here," she said, handing him the glowing fang, hilt-first. Her hand was not quite steady, and Ravengar wondered again how badly she was hurt.

"Yuse," he asked quietly, taking the tiny glow-lantern, "how are you? Truly?"

"Tired," she told him. "In fact, I'd very much like to sit down here with you, and just rest."

"While shape-shifters slaughter the last of m—our people? And start tearing apart this fortress trying to find us?"

The sorceress sighed. "There's nothing we can do about those loyal to you," she said in a small voice. "The few who are left. The Koglaur are too many, and my spells too few. I could barely save one man."

"Me." He thought about too many whirling things for a moment, while the rock suddenly boomed and shuddered again somewhere above their heads, and then asked, "The children?"

"As safe as my spells—and those of my sister Sameira— can keep them. Far from Aglirta, in hiding. Speak no more of them, lest the Koglaur remember their existence—and try to mind-pry their whereabouts out of me. Some of the shape-shifters can work spells."

Ravengar Silvertree went silent for a time, and then asked grimly, "What were those things you spell-spun? Those stone-eels?"

"Maedra. I didn't conjure them, or even summon them. You happened to build on stone they dwell in, and brought them food. My spells merely command maedra—steer them, as one wrestles a ship in a storm—for short periods."

Ravengar stared at Yuesembra. The darkness cloaked her, but her eyes shone back the dagger-glow like two winking stars. He shook his head, bewildered anew.

"I brought them *food?*"

His wife smiled. "Oh, yes. There's no flesh more to the liking of maedra than that of Koglaur."


Much later Ravengar stopped walking, the ax clutched very tightly in his white and trembling hand, and asked in a voice that trembled only a little, "Yuse? Is this stone moving past me one of these 'maedra'? It's touching my leg . . . *what do I do?*"

"Keep still, don't use that ax on anything, and calm yourself, my lord," the Witch of Sarinda told him firmly from the passage ahead, slipping back out of its gloom to stand facing him. "The maedra is . . . doing what a hound does, to be sure of just what man is standing near."

The Lord Overbaron of Aglirta drew in a deep breath, stared at the smooth stone ceiling above him—and how had it come to be so smooth? No pick or mattock had hewn that!—in the glow of the tiny knife his wife had given him, and fought down his fear. Then the quivering stone drew back from him, and passed by with the faint hiss of wind-blown sand.

The silence that followed was deep and very, very welcome.

"Suppose," he said pleasantly into it, when he trusted his voice again, "you tell me a little more about maedra. *After* you tell me where we are right now, that is."

"Where we always are in life, Raven: right here," Yuesembra said lightly.

He gave her a long, silent look, and she added quickly, "A little way west of Silvertree House, and about as deep underground as your walls rise above the soil. There's solid rock all around us; the damp is the water that always seeps through it."

"And the way we've come, behind us?"

"The maedra are changing it right now. When the Koglaur come seeking us, they'll find dead ends—and traps."

"And how will we ever get out?"

"The maedra open secret ways in the rock constantly, as they move. This is one of them; it soon doubles back east, and rises."

"And if the maedra turn against us?"

"We'll die."

"So much surprises me *not*," Ravengar snarled, fighting down fear, "but before I take a step more in this endless darkness, Yuse, I want to know just what these maedra are. Nurses scare children all over Aglirta—and younglings terrify each other far more, in their retellings to each other—with tales about the 'Snatchtalons' that live under the ground and pounce on wicked children . . . but I've never heard of anything else menacing that dwells underground, save corpse-worms. So: what's a maedra?"

"Creatures with wits to match you or me—eels as large as horses who can flow through earth and stone, digging with their talons. You've seen them."

"Arms like wrestlers, aye. But how do they 'flow' through solid rock?"

"Their spittle dissolves stone for a time, into something that can be shaped and smoothed, but then hardens again, in its changed shapes. I've seen their jaws gape wide enough to take in two men at once."

"A forest of fangs," Ravengar said with a shiver. "So they're making new tunnels behind us?"

"And rooms, thrusting up walls in our courtyard and outside, too. Any hiresword scared of sorcery will be trembling on the edge of headlong flight about now, as they see Silvertree House grow in front of their eyes like an awakening dragon."

The head of House Silvertree shook his head and said bitterly, "None of which lifts our doom. If Aglirta is overrun by clever shape-shifters and turned against me, my lands are lost—the realm is closed to me—and they'll close in and take my life, sooner or later. Probably much sooner."

Yuesembra put her hands on her slender hips, met his angry gaze, and nodded slowly.

Ravengar slammed the ax in his hand against the nearest wall, sideways so it rang like a bell rather than shedding shards of its blade. "Why then do you stay? Lady, you could snatch yourself away from this with your spells, could take me with you, too, and we could . . ."

The Witch of Sarinda shook her head. "You would not have agreed to leave," she said quietly, "and if I'd deceived you or forced you into departing with me, things would have been different between us, forever. Ruined."

The Lord Overbaron regarded her soberly for a long moment. "So much is true," he granted, "but you could still have saved yourself! Fled away from all this, back to Sarinda, to hide and guard our children!"

"I could have," Yuesembra Silvertree agreed in a whisper, "but that is not love, my Raven, and I'm not a defenseless bauble to burden you whenever 'tis the time of the sword. I stand with you."

She sighed, lifted one long-fingered hand, and added, "Now 'tis too late—the spells of the shape-shifters ring us around. They'll know every step you take, outside my wards, and be able to find and follow you behind every tree and under every stone in all Darsar. So why leave Aglirta? Let us bide here, and sell them our lives just as dearly as we know how."

Ravengar Silvertree regarded his wife in silence for some time, and then said roughly, "Lady, I love thee. The Three in their endless watching know that I reverence you, and think you the finest woman of all, above all others. Now I see you clearly, and say more: You're the greatest warrior I can think of, more fit to rule than any king . . . and I'm honored to fight at your side. From now on, for as long as is left to us, *I* follow *you*."

Dark eyes twinkled back at him. "Why, Raven, I do perceive you've learned to tongue-heave the ripest steaming dung as smoothly as any courtier." Yuesembra lifted her hand, lost her humor in an instant, and added warningly, "I ask you only to remember how you regard me right now, and when you come to feel very differently, remember what I said to you before: No matter how strange or treacherous my deeds may seem, all that I do is for you, and our children, and the memory of what Ravengar Silvertree has done for Aglirta. If men slay or dispute in your name, in centuries to come, I want them to be taking stands you'd be proud of, and agree with."

Ravengar nodded his head, hefted his ax, and growled, "Right. Enough talk. Let's start walking again."

Yuesembra touched the blade of the knife in her husband's hand, and its glow strengthened until it rivaled the brightest manycandle-lanterns. Briefly Ravengar saw branching passages stretching away lightlessly in several directions—before his wife turned to proceed along one of them, and he saw how thin she now looked, and how weary.

"Yuse," he asked quietly, not quite daring to demand again of her how she felt, "what if we took that passage? Or yonder way?"

Yuesembra shook her head. "Only if we must," she replied. "This one I know; the maedra may have left traps in the others, lest the Koglaur steal in."

Ravengar Silvertree shook his head, muttered something not quite audible, and waved at his wife to precede him along the correct passage. He seemed to have traded one set of herders over him for another. At least the new ones weren't seeking his own swift death.

He hoped.

"Behold the Great South Hall," Yuesembra announced with a flourish, indicating the vast chamber before them.

Much of its farther reaches were lost in unlit gloom and what seemed to be a grand forest of pillars, but both walls of the near end of the chamber, Ravengar noticed, were studded with protruding balconies at various levels—thrusting perches of stone that flowed out of the wall in curves sculpted to look like gigantic leaves, as if the walls were the side of some vast stone tree.

"Ah, yes," he observed in wry tones, "exactly as I'd planned it."

His wife threw him a look, and then stepped back to put a reassuring hand on his arm. "You'll always mistrust magic, won't you, Raven?"

"I . . . yes. Yes, I will. A spell that's like an arrow, even an arrow of flame, is one thing—born in front of me, hurled and then gone. Aye, that's . . . well enough, if I'm not the warrior being scorched by it. But creeping magics, both the spying sort and those that slowly change a man's face, or mind, or sap his strength . . ."

He flung out his hand at the darksome hall and said bitterly, "*I* planned my abode. A goodly keep, but nothing fancy. This is—"

He shook his head, groping for words, and then said grimly, "Grander, much larger . . . aye, awesome. Larger than Flowfoam itself, now. An empty city of stone I can get lost in. I'd never have spent coin and workers to build so large, when the same striving could have been better made use of elsewhere in the realm. Aye, I'm outcast and Aglirta is no longer under my hand, and aye, these maedra-beasts have done this, not my coin or the sweat of stonecutters of the Vale . . . but . . . but this seems a dream to me. A bad dream. I—I shouldn't be able to get lost in my own house!"

The Witch of Sarinda nodded. "You fear a home that surprises you."

"*Aye,* exactly! And not just the once, but over and over again! I feel as if I've been wandering here with you for days, and know not how the battle goes, or if the Faceless are lurking in all these dark halls all around us right now, or . . ."

"Raven," his wife told him gently, "you *have* been wandering here with me for days. I—the maedra are doing all of this, not at my bidding. These rooms and ways are . . . theirs."

Ravengar looked at her sharply, suddenly every inch the Lord Overbaron of Aglirta. "Can you not stop them?" he snapped, his voice as harsh as his glare.

Yuesembra shook her head. "I know how," she whispered, "but I no longer have the strength."

Something moved in the far reaches of the hall then. Something that slithered. Ravengar took two swift steps into the great room, to peer hard down the room, his ax raised . . . but could see nothing where the movement had been, or where its cause had gone. Not that he really needed to. What else could it have been but a maedra?

Then, far nearer, a floor tile as large as a great table suddenly bulged, rearing up into a stony, serpentine bulk that seemed to turn its head knowingly in Ravengar's direction as it arched forward—and plunged back down through the stone floor again, curving down into the solid stone with great power and slow grandeur.

The Lord of Silvertree House stared at the smooth, seemingly undisturbed tiles where the maedra had emerged and disappeared again, and asked quietly, "Your life is bleeding away all the time they work, isn't it? You're feeding them with your . . . your essence, aren't you?"

Yuesembra's mute nod was reluctant, but she met her husband's angry and fearful gaze steadily, even when he stalked back to stand glowering over her.

Ravengar looked down at her as if he'd never seen her before, and didn't quite know what sort of foe he was facing—only that it was a foe. And then he turned on his heel and strode a few paces away, whirling the ax around him in a sudden, steely flourish.

He turned again to face her before he stepped into the far wall, and asked flatly, "And is there any way to win your strength back from them?"

The Witch of Sarinda shook her head.

"Any other way to make you stronger?"

Yuesembra nodded this time.

*"Well?"*

She kept silent, and Ravengar stalked angrily up to her again. "Sembra," he said furiously, "don't treat me like some child, to be sent hither and thither and *not told anything*. Play me as your fool or errand-page if you must, but *tell* me what lies before us, what is likely and what might befall. How can we stand together, lord and lady, if you share not your secrets? *I* yield all to *you!*"

Yuesembra smiled. "You have no secrets."

"True enough," Ravengar replied shortly, starting to pace. "And that's no bad thing. A realm of plain-speaking warriors might be a brawling-ground, but there'd be precious little time and blood spent on lies and intrigue and hiding things; all Aglirtans would know just where they stood, and what the coming days would most likely hold. Forefather Look Down, Yuse, *tell me!*"

"I can gain strength," his wife replied in a small, tremulous voice, turning her head away to gaze down the Great South Hall, "by taking a little from you. You who need it, no matter how much I want it!"

Ravengar took a swift step and grasped her shoulder. "So work your spell, Lady mine! I'll *not* stand here and watch you die in front of me, the blood draining from you with every step until you shrivel and fall! Work your sorcery!"

Yuesembra smiled weakly up at him. "There is no spell."

"What d'you *mean*, woman? Speak plainly! I—"

Ravengar laid both hands on his wife's arms and shook her for the first time—and she sagged like an empty thing.

With a wordless sob of fear he plucked her from her feet, clasping her against his chest. Suddenly her lips were biting at his, and her fingers were clawing at the lacings of his breeches.

"T-this way," she gasped, and then kissed him hungrily again.

Lord Silvertree struggled for balance, let fall his ax with a wordless growl, and silently thanked the Three for one thing: in all of this bewilderment, he was at last not only doing something he enjoyed above all else, and had thought he'd never have time or safe opportunity to taste again—he was also doing something he knew full well how to do.

The glow of the knife faded entirely as Yuesembra took it from him, but not before it shone upon her happy, tearful smile.


"You didn't conjure up this fare, did you?" Ravengar growled, licking his fingers as he set down the last bones of the roast fowl and fixed his level gaze on his wife.

Yuesembra shook her head. "The maedra provided," she explained. "And yes, what you've not quite asked is true: food created by magic sustains for a little time, but robs life-essence of the caster to do so. You rob yourself to give yourself coin."

"Then I'll eat what the stone-snakes bring, and be happy," he said, drawing his war-gauntlets back on, "if only to have strength enough to . . ." He winked.

She shook her head. "Much as I love taking pleasure with you, Lord, our chances for that grow swiftly fewer. 'Twas no accident we came upon our old bedchamber this morn, so you could reclaim your armor. The maedra steered us there."

She sighed, waved at the passageways running away from where they stood in all directions, and added, "The Koglaur are hot at our backs now, roaming through Silvertree House. All our housefolk and loyal armaragors are long dead, and the realm told we two were slain as traitors. 'Twill not be long now."

*Until we die,* Ravengar thought, speaking in his mind the words she'd not said aloud. He shook his head, settling one hand back onto the war-helm slung at his hip, and the other onto the ready-scabbarded hilt of his heaviest broadsword. "And you know this—how?"

"The maedra," his sorceress wife explained, waving at the walls around. "Through the stone they speak to me. In mind-pictures. As you know from war trumpets, one can be quite eloquent by the pacing and combinations of simple, blunt signals."

"And if the Faceless close in," Lord Silvertree asked grimly, pointing down one of the six passages that met in the small chamber where they stood, the platter that had so incongruously held fresh roast fowl still gently steaming at their feet, "how shall I know if you're the real Yuse—or some shape-shifter?"

"I'd given some thought to that," the Witch of Sarinda replied, "but see no means more effective than a tether-rope linking our belts, yet mistrust its effects on our swiftness and your battle prowess. Perh—"

Figures suddenly reared up from all fours in the dim depths of five passages, to sprint towards the Lord and Lady Silvertree from all sides at once.

They swiftly acquired the faces of Ravengar's longtime friends and servants as they came. Though the deception, unfolding as it did before the Silvertrees' very eyes, was ludicrous, 'twas still jarring to see beloved, welcome faces coming to slay. Other, obvious distractions could be offered to slow a slaying Overbaronial hand, Ravengar realized, as some of the Faceless sprouted voluptuous female charms, swaying provocatively as they ran.

Lightning cracked blindingly across the chamber just before seemingly dozens of sprouting, already-sword-length claws could reach the armored Lord Silvertree. In its silver-white thrall several of the shape-shifters reeled, staggered back on their heels, or screamed.

One of them was seared twice, as Yuesembra's bolts rebounded in sizzling chaos from one Koglaur, who'd halted out of reach far down one passage to slide into the semblance of a tall, haughty man in robes, and was now advancing with slow, gloating caution.

One of the wizards among the Faceless, no doubt. Though this one waved drawn swords in both hands, other pairs of arms were busily weaving spells behind that menacing battle-array—and the handsome face above them all was favoring the Silvertrees with a sardonic smile.

"Yuse?" Lord Silvertree called sharply, as the wash of lightning that had left him numbed and trembling uncontrollably in his full metal armor receded enough to let him more than grunt. "This one?" He pointed with his broadsword at the Faceless wizard.

"Yes," she snapped, and ran past him to plunge into the passage first.

"Lady, wait!" he snarled, leaping after her. She wore but leather, and carried only daggers against two ready swords. He should be the one to confront the shape-shifter wizard, now that he wore armor that could keep strangling tentacles at bay for long enough, surely, to thrust home a good blade and—

Thin red lines of fire were racing through intricate patterns in the darkness down the narrow tunnel, following the fingers that had spawned them; the Koglaur was casting a swift spell.

Yuesembra, who seemed to be working no magic of her own, never slowed in her headlong charge.

Behind himself, Ravengar could hear painful hisses and groans, a few gasped, half-heard words in an unfamiliar tongue that sounded like curses, and then the slitherings of hurrying tentacles against the passage walls. The other four Faceless were giving chase.

Ahead, beyond Yuesembra's hurrying body, those red lines converged, brightened, the Koglaur laughed coldly—and all Darsar exploded.

The flash of light left Ravengar's eyes swimming, and the roar that rode with it smote his ears into sudden, eerie silence. He was tumbling back down the passage, hurled like a child's doll back into the other Faceless, and . . .

Something collapsed and crumpled wetly around his armor, and he had a momentary, blurred glimpse of a face with too many staring eyes and a two-fanged mouth agape in pain and fear . . . and then was past, crashing hard against a wall where two passages split apart in a juncture that was already adorned with the crumpled ruin of the platter he'd just dined from.

Something splattered against another juncture off to his right, where the next pair of passages departed the little chamber he'd been so forcibly returned to, and Lord Silvertree fought down the sudden urge to spew as a Koglaur that was half beauteous human woman, and half tentacles, staring eyes, and crablike pincers slid bloodily down to the floor, exposed organs tumbling and shapely human limbs sagging into something . . . else.

Ravengar was sliding floorwards, too, still deafened and struggling for breath. He didn't know how badly he was hurt, couldn't feel . . . much of anything yet.

Two Koglaur were lurching towards him, limbs spasming wildly and occasionally shifting into unintended forms that caused the host bodies to pitch over sharply, stagger, or even fall.

Ravengar found the floor, discovered that he still had hold of his sword, and started to roll to find his feet—a painful mistake that ended in agonized groaning when battered armor ground into broken ribs beneath.

As he winced, twisted away from that agony, and fought his way to his knees, the gasping and shuddering Lord of

Silvertree House risked a swift glance back down the passage he'd come from.

The passage now widened into a room that hadn't been there before, a brightly glowing space whose walls were writhing maedra bodies, and whose air seemed to be full of swirling sparks.

In their bright midst, Yuesembra and the Koglaur mage stood facing each other—or rather, floated upright in midair, their boots not standing on any floor Ravengar could see. Yuse seemed untouched by the blast, and must have had some sort of spell-shield ready against it. The face of the Koglaur, however, kept slumping into strangeness, and its left arm flailed limp and long as it fought to make the precise shapings of a spell-weaving. The Witch of Sarinda was casting a spell of her own, and—

A tentacle that was busily growing many snapping jaws thrust at Ravengar Silvertree's throat with an odd, bony rattle, and he was fighting for his life.

His blade was too heavy for bruised, numbed arms to wield swiftly, and twice Koglaur tentacles and swooping jaws got over it and gnawed at his armor, driving him helplessly back into a passage-mouth. The ax he'd discarded would have been even more useless, but he dared not drop steel and try to fight with his belt knives—some of these tentacles were as thick as his thigh, and none of them held anything vital that a tiny blade could reach. He needed to be able to sever them, to hack them aside, or . . .

The ceiling above him rippled and flowed, and a huge maw suddenly erupted from it, descending to bite through three flailing tentacles and most of the Koglaur body they were sprouting from.

The Faceless screamed and collapsed in a welter of blood, and the maedra descended farther into the room, tossing back its head like a fish hawk to swallow the struggling flesh it had already devoured.

Another maedra emerged from one of the walls, and Koglaur began screaming and trying to flee. Ravengar promptly pounced on the one closest to him as it turned, and slashed away a cluster of small eyes that had been watching him. When scales started to form under his gauntlets and its bulk surged, heaved, and thrust up a leonine head that curled in his direction, the Lord of Silvertree House fed the still-forming jaws the full length of his broadsword. Grunting and heaving, he fell onto the new neck to keep hold of his battle-steel—and drive it home to its hilt.

The gore that promptly fountained over him was hot and dark red, and held the bitter tang of iron. Ravengar shook it out of his eyes and tugged his sword free, kicking at a shuddering, convulsing tangle of half-formed talons to keep the Faceless at bay.

There was another flash of light, and a great rolling *boom*—it seemed he could hear again, though but faintly—from where Yuesembra was doing battle, and this time the Witch of Sarinda came hurtling down the passage, wrapped around the blood-drenched, riven length of what looked like one arm and most of the body of a maedra. Ravengar let fall his sword and reached out to try to catch and cradle his wife, but Koglaur tentacles sought the same prize, and he ended up wallowing in a swiftly growing net of flesh. "Sembra?" he gasped, seeing the swirl of her hair amid the chaos and reaching for it.

She was huddled into a ball, hands drawn in where he couldn't see them, and was black with beast-blood, so much that it might be hiding any mutilation of her own. "Yuse?" Ravengar gasped, trying to claw his way through the net of Koglaur-flesh to touch her.

For one horrible moment he feared this wasn't his Yuesembra at all, but a counterfeit shape taken by the Faceless wizard—and then she uncurled with a shout of triumph that unleashed a racing purple radiance that seemed to catch fire into flames of brilliant blue as she flung her limbs wide—a fire that slammed the Lord of Silvertree House back against a wall or ceiling in a crunch of protesting armor plate, and melted the web of Koglaur flesh in an instant.

A body that flowed and twisted through a bewilderment of shapes twisted past him, seeking to flee, but Ravengar half

fell onto it and wrestled it to a stop, his armored fingers sinking into bleeding softness as if he were handling something
rotten—and a shuddering maedra curled out of the nearest
wall to suck what was left of the Faceless from between
Lord Silvertree's hands, and left him holding nothing.

The maedra slid past him almost playfully and back into
another wall, leaving sudden silence behind it, and a dripping ruin of a room that held slumped and torn maedra bodies and a panting, disheveled husband and wife staring at
each other.

"My Lady," Ravengar asked, spitting blood, "are you—
well?"

"Better than you, my Raven," she replied with a smile,
plucking up his broadsword and handing it to him as if it
weighed nothing.

Ravengar looked at his wife in astonishment as he hefted
the heavy, familiar weight of his blade. He couldn't handle it
like that himself! How strong *was* she? And just what other
secrets did this beautiful sorceress keep, that he hadn't even
suspected yet?

Yuesembra gave him a wry smile, glided close to kiss
him—and send another surge of healing magic into him that
made his ribs itch as they shifted, and his pain ease—and
said, "That Faceless mage is dead, and 'twill be some time
yet before the only other powerful one comes here. Their
scrutiny is broken, which gives us both some time. You to go
fetch a lantern or candles and spark-steel down yon passage—'tis a long way, through four chambers, I fear—and
me to go do a thing that's needful. Try to come back to this
place, and then go on west, *that* way. If other Koglaur give
you chase, don't worry about where you go, but keep moving. If you stop, they can gather against you."

"I don't like this!" Ravengar hissed, trying to wrap an re-
straining arm around her—and failing, as she deftly ducked
and spun away from his armored reach. "Where are you—?"

Yuesembra stopped that question with another, deeper
kiss, broke it when he was trembling for quite another reason than battle-nerves, and whispered urgently, "Remember:

trust me." Then she bit Ravengar's ear gently, and as he turned to try to catch hold of her again—vanished.

"Bebolt!" He roared in frustration, staring at the empty air where she'd been and then around the blood-drenched chamber, which lacked all sign of Sarindan sorceresses. "Graul—*graul*—GRAUL!"

But all the curses he could roar did no more than awaken strange echoes in the distant dark, make the sting of his ear throb more painfully and his recovered ears ring again, and took up time that let the fading, falling sparks left behind by Yuesembra's spell-battle grow fewer and more dim.

The Lord of Silvertree Castle—and what a mockery *that* title was, in this labyrinth of unfamiliar rooms and halls not of his making, that were roamed by creatures far more deadly than he—realized abruptly that if he stood raging for much longer, the last light would fail and leave him in utter darkness, helpless against anything hungry that came creeping along.

He felt for the little blade Yuse had given him, drew it, and with its tiny, reassuring glow in his hand, set out down the passage she'd suggested. If the Witch of Sarinda said this was his best way and striving, then he'd do it.

After all, her guidance was about all he had left now.


It was a turbulent night outside the windows of Erard Bowdragon's high tower in Arlund. The storms were lashing other lands, far off, but the skies over Arlund-port were a deep, starshot blue clawed by darker fingers of racing clouds, like billows of smoke in a hurry to be elsewhere.

Erard loved to sit up in his great arch-backed chair and watch nights like this, sitting alone in darkness and letting his thoughts take him wherever they led.

And why not? No one dwelt with him, and no one in Arlund or elsewhere would dare tell a mage so mighty when he should seek his bed, or what he should do. Precious few wizards even had power enough to win past his gates and cross his garden to reach his tower—and wizards that strong were seldom foolish enough to try such boldnesses without a very good reason.

Wherefore Erard Bowdragon was expecting no visitors.

Yellowing skulls above three of his gates told the world the fate of his last few uninvited guests. Some of the others now shuffled Asmarand's wilds in shapes not their own, doing his bidding, though he was far from an evil man. The laws of kings and of fairness did not apply to wizards.

Erard rubbed his fingertips together and considered if crafting a great web of spells that could lay laws—or rather, enforced good behavior—on all wizards was possible, or even desirable. All other wizards but himself, of course. Such a—

There was a sudden burst of storm-blue radiance in the moonlit gloom off to the right of his chair, about four floor tiles away.

Erard stiffened in surprise, and hissed a word as he lifted his left hand. A wand whirled into it out of the darkness as two of the rings adorning his right hand glowed with sudden life.

The blue fire was spinning gently, and growing larger—taller, actually, reaching both up from its epicenter and down towards the floor.

Erard Bowdragon murmured a swift incantation and pointed at the floor with the wand. Tiny tongues of purple fire promptly rose into being in a ring around the tile beneath the uninvited blue flame—fires that scorched nothing, made no sound, and gave no heat.

The greatest mage in Arlund grounded the butt of his wand against the arm of his chair, which promptly reshaped itself into a hand to grasp and hold the wand upright. He then slapped the curved front of the chair arm, around which his fingers were wont to curl, and a brief winking of light heralded the appearance of a larger, thicker wand: a rod of dark, shiny wood floating horizontally in the air above his knuckles. Bowdragon reached up, took it into his hands, and stood, all in one motion, to pace closer to the growing intrusion.

Small cracklings of purple light were zigzagging like

lightnings up from his ring of flames, to form an intangible, largely unseen wall around the blue flame. This intrusion could be the arrival of a sent object, or a seeming, or an entity—but whatever it was, it could only be the work of a being of great magical power. Mighty sorcery was all that could pierce his wards, and persist in the face of the strengthening shields he was raising now.

Interest but no fear quickened Erard's steps, as he strode around the blue flame, peering at it narrowly, the magnificence of the storm-lashed night sky outside his windows forgotten.

Even if one of the fabled ancient Lords of Sorcery had somehow stepped out of legend and death-dust to menace him, the underside of that floor tile, like all of its fellows, was graven with a rune that could drink in castle-felling magics . . . and a quite-visible rune on the ceiling above could unleash a paralysis that had stopped the largest warsteed Erard had been able to find in midgallop, and held it there for over a month, until he grew tired of watching the dust accumulate on its wildly staring eyes.

The blue flame became a human-shaped form, about as tall as he was, and its feet touched the floor. Bowdragon smiled. Whoever it was was now in his power.

The flame faded from its lowest point upwards, as wardsearings always did, revealing . . . dark boots. Slender-ankled boots, on legs that seemed too shapely to be a man's. Well, well.

Leather breeches, and long-nailed, slender-fingered hands of dusky hue, laid straight down the sides of the legs they belonged to. Ringless, spread, and not moving to shape any spell. Sarindan? Feminine, definitely, even if the emerging bust had not been so lush and full in confirmation.

"Erard Bowdragon," a soft voice said, even before the flames fled from the face, "I apologize for my intrusion. I come here only in desperation."

The wizard aimed his blasting wand right at the shapely throat that moved with those words, and kept silent.

Only when the blue flame had entirely fled, and he found

himself gazing into the dark eyes of a slender, dark-haired woman in leathers who looked to have recently been in a battle, but who carried calm with her as easily as a casual cloak, did he speak.

"And who," he asked politely, over the wand that winked with warning power as it lifted to aim straight at his visitor's face, "are you?"

"My name is Yuesembra Silvertree, of Aglirta. You may have heard of me by another name: many men call me the Witch of Sarinda."

Well, now.

"I have another name, too," Erard observed. "The Unseen of Arlund. It was given me because I value my solitude. I do not welcome visitors, regardless of their contrition or beauty—and I destroy that which displeases me."

"You may destroy me," the sorceress replied, as serenely as if they'd been discussing the weather. "I'll not harm what you've built here by shattering your Hungry Rune below me, or your Rune of Stillness above. Nor have I any interest in hurling damaging magic around this room. If you prefer to slay me, I'd appreciate seeing your gardens briefly, before I die. I've heard much of their beauty."

She could see or sense a Hungry Rune through many-times-enspelled stone? "Yea, surprise pileth upon surprise, verily."

Like many men who dwell alone, Erard did not realize he'd said his thoughts aloud until Yuesembra smiled and said, "I find that, too, as my life unfolds. The Three must take delight in surprising us, I think."

Erard Bowdragon opened his mouth to say something sharp about dispensing with idle chatter—and then said instead, "You spoke of desperation. Tell me plainly why you've come here."

"To offer you a . . . bargain," the sorceress replied. "A binding blood-pact, if I can persuade you."

Erard Bowdragon lifted one eyebrow. "The Sarindan spells? My blood will take fatal fire within me if I break it?"

"Of course."

"And what would you have me do?"

"Bid farewell to loneliness, and raise my four children as your own—surrendering them to their proper name and station only when the time is right, and as it becomes needful."

Erard Bowdragon lifted his other eyebrow. "Your four children, Lady? What of the man who fathered them, who must be the Silvertree who's warlord in Aglirta? How soon can I expect him snarling at my walls with an army, if I do this?"

"He will soon be dead, and I with him. I would do this, if you'll agree to it, so that though my Ravengar must die in torment, Silvertrees descended from him will strike back at his slayers in time to come."

"And who might these slayers be?"

"The Blood of Koglaur, the shape-shifters who now rule Aglirta. There are wizards amongst them, and they see all Asmarand as their hunting ground."

Erard Bowdragon had run out of eyebrows, and contented himself with frowning. "Raise four children how? To be wizards?"

"As you see fit, sorcery or no sorcery at all. To be Bowdragons, and your own. Three sons, and a younger daughter. Present only the eldest son—and, only if he perishes, the second, and so on—to reclaim the lands and title of Silvertree."

"And buy myself a war with shape-shifters?"

"No. I need you to be a refuge only. You can profess total innocence of how we died and they came to you, if you desire."

"Some would call my end of this 'bargain' agreeing to a life of slavery, Lady. And what do I gain, in return for abandoning the life of study and spell-mastery I've chosen, to become a guardian nursemaid?"

"All of my wealth, hidden in Sarinda. All of my sorcerous knowledge, and whatever you like of what I know of folk and places and secrets. My mind, laid bare for you to plunder and to read the truth of my bargaining. My body, joined with you willingly in the making of pleasure."

The Archwizard of Arlund turned away abruptly and paced across his sanctum, but not before Yuesembra Silvertree had seen his eyes flicker. He paused before a table that bore a pair of exquisitely carved figurines, and stared down at them. The Witch of Sarinda watched the sudden trembling of his hand as he lifted one, and then the other, to gaze at it closely.

Death-images. They were remembrances. It had not occurred to her that Erard Bowdragon might once have had children of his own.

She did not now dare to ask what had become of them.

The Unseen of Arlund lifted his head, and said without turning, "Show me your children. Their seeming, mind: bring them not here."

The purple fires around her feet died away, and the air itself seemed to slump and relax with it.

Yuesembra drew in a deep breath, and then slowly and carefully cast a spell that would draw forth the likenesses of her children from her memories. To send a scrying to their real selves could alert someone spying on them to this tower room, and so to Bowdragon.

Silently, an image of four young folk standing laughing in a bright Sarindan garden unfolded in the air before her.

Bowdragon turned around, face somber. Yuesembra spread her hands, smiled a little unsteadily, and said, "Behold: Faerlun, Marask, Tesmer . . . and Belsaryl."

Erard Bowdragon took a step forward, and she saw that he was holding a tiny silver-bladed knife ready above his palm. "Lady," he said roughly, "Belsaryl looks as beautiful as you."

Yuesembra's heart leaped. "Have we," she whispered, her mouth suddenly dry, "a bargain?"

"We do."

Yuesembra reached for the lacings of her leathers, but Erard shook his head, held forth his hand—and brought his knife down.

"The blood-pact first," he told her. " 'Tis only right."

# 4

## A Feast of Swords

"*R*aven," the slender woman whispered in the darkness, reaching for him. "My Raven . . ."

Wild-eyed and weary, the man in armor stumbled back, slashing the air between them with his notched and bent broadsword. "Keep back!" he snarled. "Blood of Koglaur, keep away from me! I know not what you've done to her—or why you had to attack me at all, when we had a chance to make Aglirta great at last! If you'd given the land two seasons at peace, *two seasons* for the farmers to work unhindered, the realm could have been—"

"Yours, Lord Overbaron," the feminine form hissed, growing larger and leaning forward as fingers lengthened into tentacles. "*You* would have seized Thamrain's throne, if we'd let you!"

"Never!" Ravengar Silvertree snarled through sweat and tangled hair, as he hacked at the writhing forest of tentacles reaching for him. "I was loyal to Thamrain and to the realm! *I'm* not the one slaying by night and taking false shapes!"

"No, because you cannot," the Faceless hissed, drawing back from the still-sharp blade and shifting shape into something long and spidery, that could climb walls and thrust down on lone weary warriors from above. "Only because you cannot, Silvertree. You're a greedy hacksword brute, like all the rest!"

"*You* are twisted in mind as much as body, Koglaur," Ravengar replied wearily, stepping back through an archway into the next room and then immediately springing forward and up to slice through the first tentacle that came questing after him, "if you think that there's only *one* sort of greedy hacksword brute. We chase many aims, and follow even more widely differing codes. Now *get out of my house!*"

The shape-shifter howled as the severed tentacle fell to the floor, trailing a mist of strangely glinting blood. Silvertree sprang over its twisting splatterings and launched himself at the ceiling, his bent blade extended above his head like a thrusting spear.

It bit deep into yielding, flowing-away-not-fast-enough flesh, more blood sprayed, and a large and heavy shapelessness tumbled past his shoulder to splash wetly to the floor. Ravengar whirled and hacked at it before it could draw itself up, and kept on hacking as tentacles reached desperately through the archway, seeking to catch hold and drag the bleeding body out of the room and away.

"You . . . could . . . have . . . lurked . . . among us, and shared in a strong, prosperous Aglirta!" Ravengar panted, as he stabbed and hacked and stabbed again, struggling to hold his footing against increasingly feeble attempts to ensnare his ankles and tug him into a fall, where the thing could smother him. "You . . . could . . . have . . . gone on hiding in the . . . *uhh!* shapes of others . . . and we'd *never* . . . have known!"

"Tired of doing that," the shape-shifter gurgled faintly from several unseen mouths beneath him, in a strange droning, dying chorus. "So tired . . ."

The Lord of Silvertree House staggered away from its quivering, flattening bulk. "You're not the only one," he muttered, stepping carefully to avoid one last, feebly curling tentacle. He found a wall to put his back against, made thankful acquaintance with it, and leaned wearily on his sword, gasping for breath.

This was his sixth slain Faceless since Yuesembra had left him, and his second since his food had given out. There'd been no more steaming platters of food—the maedra liked his wife, it seemed, not him—and he hadn't seen any of the stone-eels for . . . days, 'twas now, he supposed.

He'd gone west, as she'd wanted, weighed down by lamps

and candles. The Koglaur, however, seemed to enjoy smashing lanterns and spilling oil, and Ravengar was now the lord of but a score of broken candles . . . and had lost all sense of where he was.

He tried never to go back *that* way—whatever "that way" was—and hoped he was about as far west as he could get in this new, unfamiliar, and seemingly endless labyrinth of dark, empty rooms, dark and Faceless-haunted passages, and short flights of steps that led up or down seemingly without reason. He'd learned to look up high often, to find the small, hidden-by-corners openings that led onto high ledges where he could sleep. Thus far, no Koglaur had found him as he snored . . . so perhaps the maedra were watching over him after all.

Thirst was no problem; water seeped through the walls to form little puddles here and there, and the icy, clear water tasted only of rock-tang. He supposed he was well underground, but cool air was blowing gently from somewhere down and through these underways. These miles of underways.

Ravengar shook his head in disbelief. The maedra, it seemed, were intent on carving out a kingdom of human-sized rooms and arches and passages. It seemed a rather vast palace just to entomb the bones of the Koglaur they devoured . . . and, soon enough, those of one Baron Silvertree.

There must be hundreds of maedra to fashion so much so swiftly—or had they been doing it for years, and he'd just happened to build atop them?—but he'd never seen more than four at once, and then only when there were Faceless to feed upon.

The Faceless. *Those* there must be dozens of. The maedra killed more of them than his paltry blade could down, and he'd slain . . . what, a dozen now? More.

It didn't matter. He slew and slew, and there were always more, creeping up behind him in the dark.

He just wished they'd stop taking the shape of Yuesembra, and cooing to him.

Something moved in the gloom beyond the archway, beyond the soft light of the little glowing knife he'd long ago thrust through his gorget-strap, so it shone from under his chin and let him see in this endless dark.

"Come out," he said wearily, "where I can slay you, and let's be about it!"

Several yellow eyes regarded him unblinkingly, but there was no reply. Ravengar hefted his battered broadsword and waited.

Those eyes belonged to several snakes—no, a single great serpent that glided along the floor with the faintest of whispers, its body about as thick as his thigh. Six necks rose from that bulk, and six fanged heads, each a little larger than Silvertree's fist, swayed at the ends of those necks.

"Well, Faceless, at least *you're* not pretending to be my wife," Ravengar told it as he advanced cautiously to meet it, swinging his sword tip back and forth, "and for that I thank you!"

Then he fed it his thanks with a sudden lunge and slash. Three of the heads struck at his steel with blinding speed, but his sword was just long enough to keep his hand away from their gaping fangs, and the serpent had only five heads when Ravengar danced away from its gliding advance and into a cross-passage, waved his sword warningly in case another Koglaur was creeping up behind him. These halls, however, seemed dark and empty . . . and a trifle colder than where he'd slain the last Faceless.

The snake slithered patiently after him, and Silvertree ducked to one side of the archway and hacked at the first head that showed itself. Two more heads promptly struck around the edge of the doorway, higher up, but Ravengar had expected that, and smashed them aside with his gauntleted hand, down to where his blade could slice them against the stone wall. Sparks flew as his blade took fresh abuse, but when he sprang away again, three heads hung limp, eyes dull, dangling in gore.

The two that were left reared back to hiss at Silvertree as the snake shuddered and turned to flee—whereupon something made it halt, tremble all over, sway, and then turn back to face him, for all the world as if an unseen hand was firmly guiding it.

"Three look down, but this . . . this is a real serpent!" Ravengar breathed, as he slashed those last two heads spinning from their necks and the serpent convulsed in a wild writhing of blood and pain. "And that was a spell sending it against me!"

He did not stay to see who the wizard was—a Koglaur, no doubt—but chose the most westward of the three passages, and ran.

Shape-shifters were bad enough, but against spells—without Yuesembra—he had no shield.

Not that he had a real shield, anymore, or a helm, for that matter. Both gone several battles back, in that room where the four stairs met, back by the—

"And so it ends at last, Lord Overbaron of Aglirta," a dry and sneering voice observed from the darkness ahead, "with one last service to your beloved kingdom: feeding hungry local corpse-worms. You've led us quite a chase, but—"

"Don't try to *talk* him to death, Slaundshel! *Kill him!*"

Ravengar didn't wait to find out what slaying Slaundshel might have in mind for him, or the voice that was upbraiding him, either. He flung himself sideways, fetched up against cold, hard stone, and spun around to race along it, his steel fingertips making the faintest of scraping noises as he reversed the broadsword in his other hand, so he could bring it to his chest and cover the glowing knife.

Sudden fire blossomed in the darkness behind him, and spun towards him with a hungry roar.

He spun around again, to see which way to dodge. A ball of whirling red flame was snarling towards him, heading to just where he'd been standing. When he took two steps farther away from it, it didn't veer to follow, but spun past, to burst against the wall with a flash and roar.

The coldly smiling wizard who'd hurled it was already hefting a second sphere in his hand, as it grew from a tiny dancing flame into another whirling conflagration with fearsome speed.

The wizard was standing in the center of a large chamber whose walls were studded with archways and balconies. Enough light for Ravengar to see this was emanating from the mage's shoulders, somehow, and growing steadily brighter. On the other side of the room stood another man—presumably the one who'd urged the wizard so sharply to slay the Baron of Silvertree—with a spear in his hands and angry eyes fixed on Ravengar.

Ravengar raced back the way he'd come, hoping there was some limit to how far that fire could be hurled. He swerved as he ran, twice—and then turned, sword raised wardingly, to see if either spear or hurled flames were seeking him.

The spear was already in the air, and Ravengar just had time to throw himself at the flagstone floor. Gorth's weapon thrummed past overhead, struck sparks well down the passage, and skittered along the stones into the distance.

"Gorth," the wizard remarked, "your aim grows not better. 'Tis a pity your brain's too feeble to master spells."

Gorth's reply was a wordless snarl of anger—as Slaundshel threw his second firesphere.

The Baron of Silvertree was up and running again, but as he'd feared, the flames bounced quite a distance after the hurled fire struck the floor and burst. The passage lit up in angry flame behind him, sharp pain flooded up his leg, Slaundshel barked unpleasant laughter—and Ravengar stumbled, danced helplessly off-balance, and crashed to the stones.

His slide was short, painful, and shrouded in sparks, ere he fetched up on his chin, staring at the spear an arm's reach ahead, with the stink of his own cooked flesh strong around him. *Gods,* it hurt!

"Didn't even have to shift shape," the Koglaur wizard observed cheerfully. "I don't know what sort of idiots Glasmur and Narthe were, to lose their lives to this dolt. Look at him: one throw and he's down to stay. Can't even drag himself to his knees to plead with us!"

"Oh?" Gorth replied, as Lord Silvertree rolled over and

up to his feet, almost fell as one scorched foot gave way, and caught himself with his broadsword, grounding it like a crutch. Groaning in pain, Ravengar swayed, caught his balance, and then fled down the passage, limping hard. "You do a lot of salting the spit before the stag's taken, Slaundshel?"

The wizard's snarl was just as loud as Gorth's had been.

Ravengar Silvertree was too busy to chuckle—and too despairing. He grunted his agony through set teeth as he hurried back east as best he could, seeking somewhere, anywhere, to hide.

He was going to die here. He had no defense against spells, and couldn't even stand properly to cross blades with the clumsiest of unshaven hireswords, now. He was . . .

"Doomed," Slaundshel observed with a wolflike smile, as he appeared right in front of the limping baron, the glow of the spell that had snatched him hither flickering around him. "Caught between us. And so, removed at last."

He strolled forward. "I'll take great pleasure in wearing your shape as I set about betraying all the folk you befriended, up and down the Vale. Oh, yes, Ravengar Silvertree will be remembered as quite a monster when I'm done with your face—he'll even be revealed as one of those deadly shape-shifters of legend! I find women swoon yet remember quite well, when abed with their husbands, and the face above them changes to something less than human!"

"You really enjoy this gloating and preening, don't you, Slaundshel?" Gorth said disgustedly from behind Ravengar, as he stalked up the passage with his reclaimed spear in his hands. Wearily, Lord Silvertree turned to meet him. "Just cook the rest of the man and let's be done here! *I* want to get back to Flowfoam before Ammurak does something stupid!"

"Then put your spear through him," the Koglaur wizard snapped. "I—watch*ware!*"

As Gorth broke into a run and swerved at the last instant to jab viciously at Ravengar's face, the Lord Overbaron stepped back, planting his good foot behind him. The spear tip reached for his throat, as he'd known it would—and his hand closed on it. Then he didn't need his blade for balance anymore, as Gorth tried to twist away, pulling Silvertree forward.

Ravengar threw himself in that direction, too, clawing his way along the spear shaft and swinging it hard to aid Gorth's twisting pull.

Like linked dancers they whirled around each other, and Ravengar planted his good foot again, bent, and—threw.

Still clutching his spear, Gorth crashed helplessly into Slaundshel. The two Koglaur stumbled back against the nearest wall, the wizard gasping for breath and starting to shift shape, and Gorth letting go his spear and cursing.

And then the wall swallowed Slaundshel, boiling forth in a wide maw that lunged at Gorth—who screamed and whirled wildly to flee.

Ravengar's broadsword took out Gorth's throat before he'd run a single stride, and the shape-shifter crashed to the floor and wriggled, fingers becoming tentacles that spasmed in pain and clawed at the flagstones as glinting gore spread wetly forth.

The maedra that had so suddenly eaten Slaundshel's upper half glided over to Gorth, spread its fangs—and struck.

It bore him into the floor and kept right on going, its long length sliding into the floor as if into wet mud, sucking the Koglaur with it and plunging its whole length into the stones. When it was done, the flagstones quivered slightly and then grew still. Only blood and two twitching ends of tentacles remained behind.

Shaking, Ravengar Silvertree looked at them and then back at the two half-shapeless legs that had been part of the Faceless wizard. It didn't take long to die in these dark halls. *I wonder if I'll stay alive long enough to get used to this pain.*

The Baron of Silvertree drew in a deep breath, leaned on his broadsword, and looked grimly in all directions, to see who'd try to slay him next.

The passage was dark and empty. He stood still and listened for a time, his ragged breathing loud in the silence, and then slowly limped back east, to where the three passages met. He'd take another way, this time, and . . .

* * *

He didn't know quite when he'd fallen, only that his cheek was against cold stone and there'd been a faint sound somewhere nearby, in the darkness that was all around him.

There it was again: a heavy weight descending on stone with infinite care, like the paw of a great cat stalking cautiously forward. . . .

It came again. Closer, and right—*there*. Did he still have hold of his sword?

No, but its pommel was cold against the side of his hand. If this was a Koglaur, it would reach out with tentacles rather than stepping within reach . . . unless 'twas an utter fool of a Koglaur. . . .

There came the faintest of liquid shiftings, very close by—and Ravengar snatched up his sword and flung himself to one side, rolling—

Two tentacles stabbed at his face, one of them slapping bruisingly across his throat, and he got his blade up just in time to strike it free of his neck before it could wrap chokingly around. . . .

Blue fire burst into being behind the Koglaur, outlining its nightmare shape. A handsome human face, grimacing at him in murderous glee as it slid down a rising black bulk that was as wet as any Sirlptar eel writhing in a basket—and erupting into black tentacles that couldn't help but choke and smother him, couldn't fail to—

The blue fire became maroon and then ruby red, its roaring rising into a howl. The black tentacles were flailing now in excitement or fear, but arching around towards the flames rather than reaching for Ravengar.

And then flames rolled over those tentacles hungrily, and the Koglaur screamed and clawed at the air with dozens of suddenly forming, desperate arms, seeking . . . seeking something it never found before slamming to the stones with a dying moan and starting to burn in earnest.

The red radiance died swiftly, but not before Silvertree saw several strange beast-shapes staggering back from it,

down various passages—a...
heart of it, dark hair swirlin...

Yuesembra!

Almost he cried her name a...
her—but no! This could well...
fighting with the rest to be the one...

"Keep back," he panted, lifting h...

And then a storm of tentacles, talon...
fang-snapping heads raced in at the Wi...
sides, and a hundred mouths roared Kog...

"Yuesembra!" Ravengar cried, launchi... desperately forward into that whirlwind of murde... us flesh.

His wife bent over, shouting an incantation with staccato
speed—and Darsar exploded.

*Sorcery. So thick does it cloak this place that waves of it wash
betimes through the miles of stone and dusty, darksome air, in
echoes that awaken phantoms, briefly kindle long-ago glows
once more into life . . . and give me power.*

*Aware and lively, to slowly fade until the next restless wave
comes. Biding here in this great tomb, cloaked in its chill.*

*Three deliver me from this eternal cold.*

The arms around him were warm and gentle—but they trembled. "Sembra," Ravengar breathed, knowing her smell.

"Y-yes," his wife said tearfully. "Oh, my Lord, I love you
so much. I'll never leave your side again, I swear!"

"That . . . that would be—good," the Lord of Silvertree
House managed to say, his throat suddenly tight. She was
real, she was here, she was soft . . . his hand had found her
breast, he realized, and he let go of it to reach up and take
hold of her chin, so as to draw her mouth down for kissing.

"Why are we—?" he asked, some time later.

"Unclad?" she supplied teasingly. "Well, I had to heal

, and—and *what* did you do with your
s . . . away?"

me dozen Koglaur," he growled, "used it as a
and . . ."

he was laughing soundlessly, and he dealt her a playful
cuff on the cheek. She captured that hand and kissed it—and
that was when he saw the tears in her eyes.

"Lady," he asked swiftly, "are you—well?"

She bent her head, swallowed, and then nodded. "As well
as anyone dying can hope to be," she told him, "because I'll
be dying with you."

Ravengar frowned, heaved himself up off his back, and
realized the pain of his burns was quite gone. "Dying? You
mean there are still Faceless left to slay us?"

"Oh, yes. And after healing us both, and summoning the
maedra to guard us and bring us food, I . . . I haven't enough
magic left to snatch either of us out of here. At least two of
the Blood of Koglaur who pursue us yet are wizards of
power—greater power, right now, than I have. They ring
these tunnels with wardings; we cannot escape."

The Lord Overbaron of Aglirta smiled mirthlessly. "I've
grown rather used to feeling that way. At least I'll not die
lonely." He cast his gaze around, and shook his head at the
state of his scraped and crumpled armor, lying in an unbuckled heap not far away.

They were lying together on a cloak he'd never seen before, in the heart of a little glow. All around them was another unfamiliar vast, dark, and empty chamber, this one
without balconies but sporting several thick, smooth pillars
rising from the floor in a seemingly random pattern. The
dark mouths of a few archways pierced the walls here and
there. He shook his head again.

"The Hall of Hlauntra," Yuesembra announced gently.
Ravengar gave her a look.

"Not my naming," she said with a smile. "The maedra.
Hlauntra is apparently an elder she among them, and fashioned this place."

"Well," Ravengar said, Lord of Silvertree House, names of at least a few chan to know how to find my way them."

"Follow the trail of dead Kogl voice, taking his hand, kissing it, her cheek. "I'm . . . I'm so sorry you

"So, Lady," Ravengar replied, look sword, "am I."

"So why," Lord Silvertree asked his lady, as he winced under her last bucklings and corners of his bent and twisted armor dug into him, "did you tell me always to go west?"

"To be farthest from where the Koglaur could easily enter these underways," Yuesembra replied, "and into the newest of the maedra delvings, where the passages would be fewest and you'd have the most hope of finding defensible bottlenecks where one alone can fight on a single front and not four or five flanks at once."

"Yet that's also farthest from food, and any chance at escape."

The Witch of Sarinda sighed. "With their warding-spells, there's no hope of escape," she told him, "and as for food—well, I didn't think either of us would be alive long enough for that to matter."

"I expect the Faceless thought that, too," Ravengar told her, looking along the ruin of his broadsword and deciding that trying to straighten it would probably snap it off short. "I wonder if we're close to outnumbering them yet?"

Yuesembra smiled thinly. "No, but much closer than we were that night you came swimming across from Flowfoam to me."

The Lord Overbaron of Aglirta sighed at that memory, his mouth tightening. That had been the night when his dreams for the Vale had all gone so wrong, and he'd been plunged

of what he'd thought were but chil-
re-tales.

a deep breath, patted at his sagging greaves—
were torn, and they had no way of repairing any-
—and then announced briskly, "Right. I'm ready to
start dying!"

"*Good,*" a dry whisper said right in his ear. Ravengar
whirled, sword flashing out—but there was no one there. He
cast a sharp look at Yuesembra, who grimaced.

"I can't waste magic on keeping their scrying away from
us," she explained, turning with hands on slender, leather-
clad hips to survey the gloom. Then she shrugged, took his
hand, and pointed to a nearby archway.

"Let's take that one, and—"

"*Head west,*" the Baron of Silvertree said in unison with
her. Yuesembra threw him a twinkling smile and strode
away, leaving him to hasten to catch up.

"Lady," he muttered, reaching her side again, "if 'tis all
the same to you, I'd rather hold hands, so I can be sure 'tis
you beside me, and not some confounded shape-shifter, if
you'd—"

The darkness erupted in blinding bursts of light, cold
laughter, and reaching, impossibly long limbs. Dazed,
Ravengar cursed, grabbed for Yuesembra's hand but found
nothing, and then abruptly spun away from her as tentacles
struck him in three places, and started hacking with all his
might at what he couldn't quite see.

Fresh bursts of radiance blossomed before his eyes, just
as he was starting to make out shapes again, and someone—
a woman? Yuesembra? 'twas high and shrill enough!—
screamed nearby. Then there was a wet, gurgling sound, like
a great beast wallowing in pain, and some snarls . . . and all
the while, the deep, wet thudding of his battered broadsword
biting into flesh.

"Sembra!" he snapped, hacking all the harder at what he
couldn't see, and keeping his blade up and circling to protect
his throat, "to me!"

That brought him a burst of shrill laughter, seemingly

down various passages—and a lone figure striding out of the heart of it, dark hair swirling.

Yuesembra!

Almost he cried her name aloud, and staggered to meet her—but no! This could well be just one more Faceless, fighting with the rest to be the one to slay him.

"Keep back," he panted, lifting his sword.

And then a storm of tentacles, taloned limbs, and reaching, fang-snapping heads raced in at the Witch of Sarinda from all sides, and a hundred mouths roared Koglaur blood lust.

"Yuesembra!" Ravengar cried, launching himself desperately forward into that whirlwind of murderous flesh.

His wife bent over, shouting an incantation with staccato speed—and Darsar exploded.

*Sorcery. So thick does it cloak this place that waves of it wash betimes through the miles of stone and dusty, darksome air, in echoes that awaken phantoms, briefly kindle long-ago glows once more into life . . . and give me power.*

*Aware and lively, to slowly fade until the next restless wave comes. Biding here in this great tomb, cloaked in its chill.*

*Three deliver me from this eternal cold.*

The arms around him were warm and gentle—but they trembled. "Sembra," Ravengar breathed, knowing her smell.

"Y-yes," his wife said tearfully. "Oh, my Lord, I love you so much. I'll never leave your side again, I swear!"

"That . . . that would be—good," the Lord of Silvertree House managed to say, his throat suddenly tight. She was real, she was here, she was soft . . . his hand had found her breast, he realized, and he let go of it to reach up and take hold of her chin, so as to draw her mouth down for kissing.

"Why are we—?" he asked, some time later.

"Unclad?" she supplied teasingly. "Well, I had to heal

you, and myself, too, and—and *what* did you do with your sword while I was . . . away?"

"Killed some dozen Koglaur," he growled, "used it as a crutch, and . . ."

She was laughing soundlessly, and he dealt her a playful cuff on the cheek. She captured that hand and kissed it—and that was when he saw the tears in her eyes.

"Lady," he asked swiftly, "are you—well?"

She bent her head, swallowed, and then nodded. "As well as anyone dying can hope to be," she told him, "because I'll be dying with you."

Ravengar frowned, heaved himself up off his back, and realized the pain of his burns was quite gone. "Dying? You mean there are still Faceless left to slay us?"

"Oh, yes. And after healing us both, and summoning the maedra to guard us and bring us food, I . . . I haven't enough magic left to snatch either of us out of here. At least two of the Blood of Koglaur who pursue us yet are wizards of power—greater power, right now, than I have. They ring these tunnels with wardings; we cannot escape."

The Lord Overbaron of Aglirta smiled mirthlessly. "I've grown rather used to feeling that way. At least I'll not die lonely." He cast his gaze around, and shook his head at the state of his scraped and crumpled armor, lying in an unbuckled heap not far away.

They were lying together on a cloak he'd never seen before, in the heart of a little glow. All around them was another unfamiliar vast, dark, and empty chamber, this one without balconies but sporting several thick, smooth pillars rising from the floor in a seemingly random pattern. The dark mouths of a few archways pierced the walls here and there. He shook his head again.

"The Hall of Hlauntra," Yuesembra announced gently. Ravengar gave her a look.

"Not my naming," she said with a smile. "The maedra. Hlauntra is apparently an elder she among them, and fashioned this place."

"Well," Ravengar said gravely, "that's good to know. As Lord of Silvertree House, I should be conversant with the names of at least a few chambers in it. It would be even nicer to know how to find my way twice to say, six or seven of them."

"Follow the trail of dead Koglaur," his wife said in a small voice, taking his hand, kissing it, and then holding it against her cheek. "I'm . . . I'm so sorry you had to fight them alone."

"So, Lady," Ravengar replied, looking around for his sword, "am I."

"So why," Lord Silvertree asked his lady, as he winced under her last bucklings and corners of his bent and twisted armor dug into him, "did you tell me always to go west?"

"To be farthest from where the Koglaur could easily enter these underways," Yuesembra replied, "and into the newest of the maedra delvings, where the passages would be fewest and you'd have the most hope of finding defensible bottlenecks where one alone can fight on a single front and not four or five flanks at once."

"Yet that's also farthest from food, and any chance at escape."

The Witch of Sarinda sighed. "With their warding-spells, there's no hope of escape," she told him, "and as for food—well, I didn't think either of us would be alive long enough for that to matter."

"I expect the Faceless thought that, too," Ravengar told her, looking along the ruin of his broadsword and deciding that trying to straighten it would probably snap it off short. "I wonder if we're close to outnumbering them yet?"

Yuesembra smiled thinly. "No, but much closer than we were that night you came swimming across from Flowfoam to me."

The Lord Overbaron of Aglirta sighed at that memory, his mouth tightening. That had been the night when his dreams for the Vale had all gone so wrong, and he'd been plunged

right into a nightmare of what he'd thought were but childrens' fireside scare-tales.

He drew in a deep breath, patted at his sagging greaves—
the straps were torn, and they had no way of repairing anything—and then announced briskly, "Right. I'm ready to
start dying!"

"*Good*," a dry whisper said right in his ear. Ravengar
whirled, sword flashing out—but there was no one there. He
cast a sharp look at Yuesembra, who grimaced.

"I can't waste magic on keeping their scrying away from
us," she explained, turning with hands on slender, leather-
clad hips to survey the gloom. Then she shrugged, took his
hand, and pointed to a nearby archway.

"Let's take that one, and—"

"*Head west,*" the Baron of Silvertree said in unison with
her. Yuesembra threw him a twinkling smile and strode
away, leaving him to hasten to catch up.

"Lady," he muttered, reaching her side again, "if 'tis all
the same to you, I'd rather hold hands, so I can be sure 'tis
you beside me, and not some confounded shape-shifter, if
you'd—"

The darkness erupted in blinding bursts of light, cold
laughter, and reaching, impossibly long limbs. Dazed,
Ravengar cursed, grabbed for Yuesembra's hand but found
nothing, and then abruptly spun away from her as tentacles
struck him in three places, and started hacking with all his
might at what he couldn't quite see.

Fresh bursts of radiance blossomed before his eyes, just
as he was starting to make out shapes again, and someone—
a woman? Yuesembra? 'twas high and shrill enough!—
screamed nearby. Then there was a wet, gurgling sound, like
a great beast wallowing in pain, and some snarls . . . and all
the while, the deep, wet thudding of his battered broadsword
biting into flesh.

"Sembra!" he snapped, hacking all the harder at what he
couldn't see, and keeping his blade up and circling to protect
his throat, "to me!"

That brought him a burst of shrill laughter, seemingly

from all sides. Bony talons jabbed at him in a dozen places, seeking spots where his armor had gaps. More than one plate fell and dangled, clanging against the rest, as straps parted . . . and through a sudden stagger of pain, Ravengar dimly saw bony talons draw back, dark with his own blood, and then lunge again—at his face.

He swung his bent blade at them desperately, spinning away as he did so to snatch himself away from anything curling around to smite at him from behind. He'd never in his life have thought he'd grow sick of fighting, but—

A tentacle slapped his head hard enough to make him cry out at the sharp pain in his neck, and something burst wetly as his sword sheared through it. A mouth somewhere down near his ankles promptly shrieked in pain, and he stabbed down, blearily seeing at least a dozen Koglaur in more or less human form crawling like swift spiders away from him, only long tentacles and snake heads rising from their backs to menace his blade and torso. Ravengar promptly leaped forward, feetfirst, and landed on one, stabbing down ruthlessly and then slashing out in both directions to strike aside the inevitable swarm of tentacles that sought to close over him.

There was a flash of ruby light and a loud *hiss*—and from somewhere above Lord Silvertree came a hot, smoking rain. He rolled away, wiping at his brow and cheek, and found his gauntlet trailing smoke from boiling Koglaur blood.

Then cooked, blackened tentacles were flopping onto the floor in a copious tangle, and a figure came reeling towards him, dusky face paler than he'd ever seen it before.

The Witch of Sarinda retched, staggered weakly, and reached for him.

"Lady? Yuse?" he snapped, frightened. He'd never seen such a sheen of sweat on her, or her eyes so bright.

"Can't . . . can't cast many more of those," she mumbled. "Takes . . . too much . . ."

Koglaur were slithering and scuttling everywhere now, through the drifting smoke of their dead brethren, and Ravengar curled an arm around his wife and rushed her away, across the chamber to—he knew not where, but just *away*.

Halfway there, tentacles snatched their feet from under them, slapped and lashed them rolling to the floor, snatched them apart, and—

More ruby flame, even as the Baron of Silvertree snarled and hewed aside whirling tentacles, and more Koglaur screams.

Spitting heartfelt curses, Ravengar Silvertree sliced aside the last reaching tentacles, stamped hard on a snake head that reached with its fangs at him, and ran to scoop up Yuesembra—only to skid to a helpless halt, staring.

Half a dozen Yuesembras were reaching beseechingly for his hand, on their knees, all of them pale, wide-eyed, and sweating.

"Help me, Raven!" one of them gasped, and the next sobbed, "Listen not to these Koglaur! I'm your wife!"

"No!" a third cried, "Lord, *I* am yours, and I alone!"

"In the name of our children, Raven, listen not to these—"

The Baron of Silvertree saw a tentacle glistening near the throat of one of the Yuesembras, and sprang into the midst of pleading sorceresses to hack it aside. A roar arose, and taloned tentacles flew at him in a dark storm of death, but he got his blade through the one he'd been seeking, and grateful eyes thanked him as the Witch of Sarinda gasped out a hasty incantation.

Or was it she? They were all doing it now, even as tentacles swarmed around Ravengar, stabbing at his face, tugging at his throat and his sword, seeking to drag him back and down. . . .

Something large and hungry plunged down from the ceiling overhead, and a score of tentacles were snatched stingingly away from Ravengar. The maedra thundered down beside him like a tree trunk of racing flesh and then was gone, rising smoothly to glide across the chamber as Koglaur screamed and fled in all directions. Other maedra, summoned by Yuesembra's frantic calling, were plunging and biting behind Ravengar, and tentacles were melting away as their owners fled for their lives, racing for archways

and dark shadows with maedra rising up terribly among them, biting and gliding and biting again. . . .

"Raven!" Yuesembra gasped, dodging wild-eyed through a tangle of severed, slumping tentacles to reach him. "Let's begone! I can't do many more such callings!"

She took hold of his hand—the one without the sword—and leaned in close for a hasty kiss.

Ravengar tightened his arm around her, lips reaching for hers . . . and at the last moment saw fangs gleaming in the triumphant crook of her smile.

He clawed at her, so as her neck thrust forward like a lunging snake for her jaws to savage him, and her arms became tentacles, he was turning her away—and thrusting his broadsword into the body that was sprouting dozens of fanged jaws and talons, and tearing anew at his battered armor.

Loosened armor plates clattered and clanged as a furious Lord Silvertree thrust home his blade again and again, twisting and pumping it in the same wound rather than withdrawing it and risking giving the Faceless time to really use the tentacles that were now slapping around his face and seeking to choke him or tear his head off.

Feminine mouths sobbed and spewed glinting blood as his steel slid in and out, in and out, and tentacles started to quiver and fall away. Ravengar kept moving, dragging the Koglaur around in a spin to try to thwart others that might be seeking to strike at him from behind.

And then a flash of light smote his half-covered eyes, a stink of flesh more fishlike than human arose around him amid crawling sizzlings, and the many-mouthed bulk of the shape-shifter fell away like a dead weight, tentacles dragging him down.

The Lord of Silvertree House struggled to sever them, slicing and sawing frantically to free himself before—

"My Lord, we must get away from here!" Yuesembra gasped, from close by his elbow.

Ravengar slashed out at that sound, snarling, "Keep away from me, shape-shifter!"

The reply was partly a gasp and partly a sob, and when Ravengar fought his way free of the dead Faceless and could stand and see properly, a dusky-skinned sorceress was huddled by his feet, clutching her breast and shoulder and moaning.

Silvertree took her by the hair and tilted her face back so he could see it properly, sword raised to her throat.

Dark eyes stared their pain into his. "R-Raven, please . . . ," she whispered, blood trickling from her lips. The Baron of Silvertree stared down at her in growing horror, seeking any sign of tentacles or snake mouths or . . .

There were none. Nothing but the lithe body of his wife, curled around his feet, blood dark upon her breast, leathers dripping.

"Oh, gods, Yuse," he whispered, as the last Koglaur shrieks ended and maedra began to glide into the walls around them. "Gods, I'm sorry."

"'Tis . . . 'tis all right," she hissed, voice fainter. And then she shivered. Ravengar cast a wild look all around and then sank down to his knees atop the carrion to cradle her.

"Sembra," he murmured, holding her against him. Three, but her skin was cold! Yuesembra closed her eyes, shuddered, and then whispered, "Just keep me as still as you can. I . . . I'll try. . . ."

Trembling hands lifted to sketch a single, simple gesture, then fell back like stones. Lips shaped a soundless incantation, and dusky skin began—very faintly—to glow. Helplessly Lord Silvertree stared at his wife's frowning face, his arm wrapped around cold shoulders . . . and saw the frown slowly fade, and the trickle of blood go dry.

Then she drew in a deep breath, and lifted one hand to cautiously explore the bloody ruin his blade had made of her breast. Probed gingerly, trailed about, and then ceased their work, not falling this time, as dark eyes opened and she gave Ravengar a weak smile.

He started to lift her, to stammer—but she murmured, "Keep still. Please." And her hand sought his face.

Her touch awakened a soft tingling, and Ravengar knew

magic was flowing into him once more, the healing she'd worked on him earlier come again.

"I—lass, save yourself," he protested. "Don't—"

"Together, Lord," she whispered fiercely. "We stand together, remember?"

Her face was pale again, and as the Lord of Silvertree House watched, sweat slid over it until there was enough to drip from her trembling chin.

"This is killing you," Ravengar growled, holding her close.

"Yes," she whispered. "Yes, 'tis. I can't work many more spells without dying. Help me up."

Lord Silvertree raised his wife to her feet as gently as if he were holding a thing of brittle feathers. The Witch of Sarinda clung to him, smiled wanly, and then leaned close to murmur, "My . . . words will go first, and then I'll lack the strength to stand—but unless a spell smites me, my mind will still be bright. Abandon me not, I beg of you."

"Lady, you need never beg me for anything," Ravengar growled. "I'll stand by you—*this I swear.*"

She smiled again, kissed him, and then stepped out of his arms to take a step unaided. And then another. Westwards she walked, towards an archway that was—suddenly full of grinning Koglaur!

Ravengar cursed and ran forward, as Yuesembra spun around to seek another way. "Flee!" she gasped, as she ducked under his arm, towards another arch. The Baron of Silvertree cast a quick glance at where she was going, half expecting to see more gloating Faceless blocking it, and backed to join her, waving his sword menacingly.

Koglaur chuckled or sneered, and followed, keeping together this time, advancing patiently.

So they'd learned to really fight at last. Aye, he and Yuse *were* doomed.

The wall of that southern passage bulged briefly as they retreated along it, and the Faceless faltered, going quiet . . . and staying that way until all trace of the maedra was gone. No hungry stone-eel erupted to bring down havoc, however, and after the shape-shifters had edged gingerly past where it had been, they grew bold again and hurried to catch up their pursuit.

By then the Lord and Lady Silvertree had crossed another chamber, found another westwards arch, and plunged into it. They ran along a dank, downsloping, noticeably cooler passage. Its long run was broken twice, for no discernible reason, by short descending flights of steps, and it came out at last in a large, low-ceilinged room that was studded with pillars—again, these supports were in no pattern, but scattered oddly. Ravengar peered about in vain for archways—but by the time he saw one, Koglaur were coming through it . . . and along the passage they'd taken here.

He glanced at Yuesembra, who murmured, "I can't run farther."

"Then I'll carry you," he snarled, reaching out his arm—but the Witch of Sarinda ducked away under it and came up shaking her head.

"No," she gasped, "you'll be swarmed and torn apart in a trice! Here we stand—here!—and here we'll fall. Together."

"Right here?" Ravengar barked, waving at the open flagstones all around them. They stood in the center of the chamber, with Koglaur—more than a score, now—flooding into it and starting to trot around to either side of them, keeping well back but moving to encircle the Silvertrees. "In the open, where they can come at us from all—?"

*"Trust me,"* she breathed, darting back in to kiss him. Her lips were sweet, and neither the Lord Overbaron nor his wife seemed to want this tenderness to end—but as the Koglaur stalked forward in bold unison, Ravengar broke away from his wife, hefted his sword, and growled warningly, "They're *coming* for us, lass!"

Yuesembra's reply was a whispered, "Don't jostle me!" and then she took a swift step away around behind him, to face the Koglaur on that side, drew herself up, and worked a swift spell.

The Faceless were slithering and padding and stalking forward, shifting their shapes into terrible, ever-changing nightmares of glaring eyes, gleaming fangs, tentacles, and hungry talons as they came.

Yuesembra dropped into a crouch, pointed at one of the largest—and there was a bright, eye-searing flash, a burst of oily smoke, and . . . the chamber held one less Koglaur.

There was a roar of anger and fear, and a great bellow among it of, "In at them! Don't let her—"

Yuesembra's next deathstroke ended that voice forever, and then she spun around on her haunches to fell a Faceless that was rearing up in front of Ravengar to menace him with six pairs of reaching arms. A dragon-headed Koglaur was the next to fall, reeling and toppling rather than vanishing, and Lord Silvertree cast a quick, anxious look over his shoulder at his wife.

She was hunched over in pain, on forearms and knees now, bleeding from her mouth, her face very pale and pale.

"Yuse!" Ravengar gasped, and ran back to stand over his wife. She reached up his legs with trembling hands and tried to drag herself to her feet—but fell back with a groan. Silvertree scooped her up in one arm, and she gasped in pain and clawed at his armor.

"Lass," he shouted, as hissing and snarling Koglaur closed in around them, "try not to—"

Yuesembra set her teeth in a snarl, tore free a dangling armor plate, and gasped, "To the floor! *Now!*"

Ravengar threw himself down, keeping his sword up and outstretched and himself under his wife. They bounced together on the flagstones, the Witch of Sarinda wincing, and then she was holding the scrap of metal aloft in one trembling hand and hissing something into Ravengar's chest, something that ended with the calm order: "Let there be a feast of swords."

And the armor vanished from between her fingers in a twinkling of sparks.

The chamber was suddenly full of swords—bright blades racing here and there like arrows fired in anger, dozens of them, whistling through the air to transfix Koglaur after grunting, reeling Koglaur.

Ravengar hugged his sobbing wife against his armored breast and watched death hiss past close overhead. Tentacles flailed vainly, Faceless shrieked and moaned, and still the web of racing steel went on.

It never slowed; as the Lord of Silvertree House watched, those lightning-swift blades simply . . . faded away.

Leaving behind silence.

When he dared to raise himself on one elbow, he found himself looking at a chamber that looked like a hog-slaughtering room. Shredded, slumped bodies were everywhere, tentacles and gaping serpent and beast heads strewn in great pools of glinting blood. A few shapes were still moving feebly, far away beyond the pillars.

"Sembra," the Baron of Silvertree said wonderingly, "you did it! You've slain them all!"

The Witch of Sarinda made a mewling sound. Ravengar shifted her with his encircling arm, edging her tenderly off his breast so he could sit up. She shook her head at him, denying his last words, and lifted a feeble hand to wave at the room all around. She was drooling.

"Yuse?" he whispered roughly. "Yuse?"

She shook her head again, eyes closing in resignation, and then opened them again to glare fiercely at Ravengar.

"You can't speak?"

She nodded, and Ravengar swallowed, set his teeth, and said slowly, "Well, my sword alone must see us through from now on, then."

"Don't worry," a coldly angry voice hailed him, across the carnage. "Your 'now on' won't last long."

Ravengar Silvertree scrambled to his feet, sword in his hand, and glared at the Faceless who'd spoken. Its great bulk was wet with glinting gore, but it rose tall among the pillars, and several smaller shape-shifters were moving to stand with it.

"For the death you've dealt us," the Koglaur added, taking man-shape to step over tangled tentacles and start its long, slow advance across the floor to Ravengar, "you must be slain. I shall take pride in being the one to fell you both. At last."

"And who might you be, Blood of Koglaur, behind your masks?" the Baron of Silvertree asked bitterly. "Thamrain a day ago, Lord Darse this morn, myself on the morrow?"

"I am called Ammurak. *Prince* Ammurak of Aglirta, to give you my proper title. King Ammurak, once I return to Flowfoam—for you seem to have harvested those of my kin who might best dispute my title. For that, I thank you."

"I have no need of your thanks," Ravengar growled, striding to meet the Koglaur.

"True enough, yapping man—for *you* have no more need of *anything*," Ammurak said smugly, raising his hand.

Small but hungry lightnings crackled forth from dark talons, bolts that stabbed at Ravengar as he launched himself into a desperate charge.

Desperate—and doomed. Lord Silvertree staggered, as sparks winked and raced all over his armor and his vainly reaching blade . . . and silently toppled, trailing plumes of smoke, into the waiting tentacles of the lesser Koglaur—who began to tear him apart.

Leaving Yuesembra weeping on her knees, alone in a slowly closing ring of shape-shifters.

"So heroic, your lord," Ammurak told her mockingly. "So manly—and so stupid. Without you, he'd have been nothing at all."

The Witch of Sarinda hid her face in her hands and sobbed something. The Koglaur prince chuckled, lifted his hand again, and gave her lightning.

It did not take long. Smokes arose from the huddled, dusky body of Yuesembra Silvertree, as she slumped slowly over onto her side.

Slowly, almost reluctantly, Ammurak of the Blood of Koglaur strode forward to stand over the body, cradling dying lightning in his palm. He stared down at it for a long, silent time, and the other Koglaur were wise enough not to disturb him.

They gave vent to an anxious chorus of cries when the chamber walls suddenly boiled forth with maedra—but the great gnawing worms turned away when Ammurak stalked towards them, and plunged back into the stone without devouring a single shape-shifter.

Koglaur cries became cheers as Prince Ammurak stepped around the rolling head of Ravengar Silvertree, wrenched from its body not long before, and strode out of the chamber without a backward glance.


The last, waiting spell had been coiling inside Yuesembra Silvertree for what seemed an agonizing eternity, since her feast of swords had died, and she'd been able to shape another spell in her mind.

Now all was done, all but the last whispered word—uttered now, through her hair and fingers, while Ammurak of the Koglaur gloated—that would bind her sentience to his.

Done.

Done and cannot be undone.

She'd have shouted her glee if the searing lightnings had let her, but contented herself with hurling herself up them, holding in her mind to the name of Ravengar, riding their spell-flows up into the Koglaur.

She burst into Ammurak's astonished mind like a stone hurled through glass, searing and savaging—*for Ravengar!*— and plunged deep into his memories, thrusting out questing thoughts like spears, flooding his depths with her light as she sank and slowed, sank and slowed . . . and then drew in his memories behind her like a cloak, to hide behind his eyes and wait for the right time.

Just to make sure of her control, she forced the Koglaur to walk over to her cooked body and look down at it. Ammurak tried to fight her then, his malice a slicing thing, but she won that war handily, and left him howling and fading, fleeing into a corner that she walled away until she could explore him at leisure.

Right now, it was time to go be crowned king.

Build for me, upon the southern bank of the Silverflow across from the royal isle of Flowfoam, a palace of stone. A defensible house; a fortress. Let it be encircled by a dry moat, with the trees cut back so no root may crack its outer walls. Build it deep, stone upon the bared stone of the earth, that no foe may slither like worm or serpent in by night and find a way through those walls, or ready chance to bring them crashing down in collapse.

Let those walls be everywhere as high as twelve men, with narrow bow-port windows only on the topmost floor of the outer face of dressed stone, and no windows on the ground floor of its inner face.

Let the walls be crowned by crenellated battlements, and at every hundred paces be raised a tower within the wall, that can be shut off by stout metal-shod and bar-braced doors from the rest, to be its own keep.

Let all those towers stand a hundred feet high, tall enough to overlook the trees down to the river, with bow-ports in their uppermost two floors. Let them be linked by a ring of tunnels beneath the earth, and a well sunk beneath each, and let every tower have a door into the inner yard but none in its outer face. Let the tunnel-ring lead to a single underway into the forest, to rise there in a defended and earth-covered chamber, and let as few men as possible know where this door among the trees lies.

And on the river side of the palace, facing Flowfoam, build me a great gate with portcullis and sally-ports and a "throat" of stone, flanked by two towers and leading into a foreyard with its own walls and lesser gate, which in turn shall give into the inner yard where shall be raised a stables.

Let all this be done speedily, for the greater glory of the King.

Ravengar Silvertree
Lord Overbaron of Silvertree

# BOOK TWO

———◆———

## *Sembril Silvertree*

530–568 ? SR
Lady Baron of Silvertree
And of the Strange Dread Doom That Befell Her

# 1

## Voice of a Dead Wizard

The servants had been barred from the Candletower. She'd locked all of its grand state doors behind the last of them, six successive thunders, and then the two secret doors. Yet as she turned away from that last locking, Sembril Silvertree could not shake off the uneasy feeling that she was being watched.

Her strongest revealment spell showed her . . . nothing. Long silent listenings, finest thread stretched across doorways, even positioning herself before mirrors and whirling around oft and suddenly had failed to show forth any intruder.

Instead, as she gazed at the reflections of her unsmiling face—emerald eyes watchful under dark brows, in a pale visage framed by long, dark red tresses—the feeling of everpresent, interested scrutiny had grown stronger, until it was almost a singing in the air. Something she could taste at the back of her throat, like the cold iron tang of blood.

She'd always felt . . . guilty, alive with excitement, with the thrill of doing something dangerous and disapproved of, if not exactly forbidden, when she shut herself up in the tower. From the first she'd made sure the servants "knew" it was to paint—the door-sized, ornately framed panels she splashed wildly with paints the moment the doors were shut, and left to drip and drink the settling dust for the rest of her solitudes. She'd even encouraged with carefully casual comments the unfolding rumor among the staff that she shut away the world with bars and locks because she liked to disrobe and dance as she "did her daubs."

Besides her sealing sorceries, those locks—great bargelocks she'd found in a House cellar, as large and heavy as severed heads—were all Sembril dared use.

All she'd dared since the day a spell she was trying some-how—she'd never found out just how—shattered her chains and sent them whirling around the chamber. Flailing death missed claiming Sembril Silvertree by a whisker, but had smashed her senseless to the ground and broken her leg. Not an arm, thank the Three, so she'd been able to heal herself by many slow, achingly draining spells.

She remembered the sickening agony of dragging herself across the floor to her books, and the long cold hours spent on the floor trying to muster the strength to cast another mending spell, and another . . . paltry little mendings never meant to knit bones in the first place. She'd never willingly lie down on a floor, ever again.

Another remembrance, this more exciting: blue sparks racing past her as if she were staring into the heart of a star, as her sorcery bonded great forged rings to the insides of one of her doors. The hasps forming under her hands so swiftly, she could scarcely believe it, the House changing to match *her* will.

And the dancing. Yes, the barefoot and betimes unclad whirling she'd done in these chambers, at first just to be sure her leg was whole, and then for the sheer pleasure of doing *anything* without the ever-present, mutely disapproving gazes of her servants . . . and then to exult in the sheer power of the magics she was calling up . . .

Sorcery *was* dangerous, and Sembril now knew enough about it to know just how perilous her paltry scraps of learn-ing—and much greater gulf of ignorance—of it was. 'Twas not for nothing wizards of power were rare and feared men, most of them mad or at least rashly rude and willful, yet tol-erated for their foibles because of what they wielded. Their ranks were always few. Not a season passed without some ambitious apprentice igniting himself like a torch, or trap-ping himself forever in beast-shape or the disfigurement of some lesser transformation, claws or fangs or worse, that could not be undone without the aid of another worker of magics . . . who would, of course, refuse to render it.

Two boots, trembling helplessly as the body above them

dissolved into greasy black smoke, with women screaming and everyone gazing in horrified fascination. She'd remember that horror to the end of her days, and knew she'd always wonder if that young wizard had been enticed into trying that spell at court purely to hand Sembril Silvertree a coldly pointed lesson.

Yet even with all of these waiting perils, sorcery was very nearly the only weapon Sembril could even dream of wielding, in an Aglirta that seemed to regard Silvertrees with . . . wary distrust, at best. King Amthrael seldom invited them to court, and no living Silvertree was styled "baron," though the arms and graces painted large upon the walls of the Lion Chamber, worked in metal on the Rivergate, and displayed on many banners throughout Silvertree House were as grand in their royal grantings as those of the baronial families. Her lineage was older and prouder than Adeln, Phelinndar, Tarlagar, and even Brostos . . . probably others, and possibly even all the rest, if she took the trouble to consult the full Rolls in Flowfoam. Yet Sembril could find no record of any great treason done by the Silvertrees in the past, or even a dispute. A Silvertree had even briefly been the first Lord Overbaron of Aglirta, before perishing with all his household in an unfortunate outbreak of disease that had swept through this house when it was new-built, and much smaller than it was now.

So she was quite used to being . . . thrilled, tense, and alert, even without the wonders of the unfolding spells, when she was alone in the Candletower. This heavy, watched feeling was different.

Different from the lurking that every dweller in Silvertree House learned to live with: the knowledge that the madworms in the walls could boil forth at any moment to devour you or change the very walls of the room you stood in, or simply ignore you and pass through the chamber out of one wall and into another, plunging through solid stone as if it were but cooks' oil. To them alone—for every wall was solid stone as they approached it and solid stone again in their wake, if they desired it so.

'Twas the madworms that drove her brothers to their goblets of calamanta and saal again and again, until they knew
no other release—goblets with bowls the size of Sembril's
head, though Relvaert, Taraunt, and Desmer spilled more
than they slaked, once they got to the singing and roistering.
Great hairy rutting beasts, all three, but their swift tempers
and even sharper swords at least kept the silk-tongued envoys of Maerlin and Phelinndar—whose heirs sought to wed
her purely to add the Silvertree lands to their own, Sembril
was sure—at bay.

There were times, many times, when Sembril heartily
wished she could be one of those empty-headed, high-
nosed elegant ladies who swept through much smaller
palaces than this—they could hardly do otherwise, for in all
Aglirta, only Flowfoam itself was larger than Silvertree
House—while men ruled, occupying themselves with nothing more strenuous than assembling ever-larger wardrobes
of the latest gowns, and working minor tyranny upon their
servants.

Nay, not in truth. She'd go mad of boredom if ever that
truly came to pass. A "walking gown" she'd never be. Yet
'twould be a grand day for all Silvertrees if her nature was
made moot by just one of her brothers standing forth to
show the realm he possessed one-tenth the spine and authority that had been the watchword of their father Throrn.

Throrn Silvertree had been something even rarer than a
mighty wizard: a gravely quiet, intelligent scholar who was
also a skilled warrior, and respected for both. Sembril's
brothers could remember him well, and hadn't shown more
than glimmers of their present brutish roistering while he'd
lived. Yet their mother, Suelyndra Tarlagar, was so long dead
that they'd never known her guidance—only the echoed
mothering of a variety of indulgent servant nurses and their
wasp-tongued sister Sembril.

Who was now damning herself in the eyes of the Three, if
the words of traveling priests could be believed, by seeking
out the powers of sorcery. "The Temptation of the Dark One,

offered to the weakest among us," the robed men called it, in their most fearsome tirades.

Well, *that* much was true. If ambitious Phelinndar or warlike Cardassa ever learned just how hollow the power of the Silvertrees truly was, they'd spend an afternoon riding or barge-floating their armaragors down the Vale—two dozen or so would suffice—and seize these verdant lands and great house for themselves, ending the name of Silvertree forever.

Now, if such conquerors were so foolish as to stop in the taverns on their way to victory—the Drinking Dragon down by the docks, or the Stand of Stags nigh Westbrook—and get into a brawl with Relvaert or Desmer, or try to conquer the Silvertree lands bedchamber by bedchamber, like Taraunt, they just might be vanquished. The handful of armaragors Silvertree could muster always rode, drank, wenched, and sported with the Three Scourges, leaving a handful of retired warriors who worked in the stables as the only men who could lift blade or bow to defend Silvertree House . . . and Sembril Silvertree.

So Sembril risked the weakness of being considered mad so as to shun visitors, and thereby conceal what even a halfbrained envoy could not help but see: Silvertree House, for all its sprawling size, housed a little more than a hundred servants, who clung to perhaps as many rooms, abandoning the miles upon miles of cellars and all the sprawling rest of the ever-changing chambers—from the great spire of Stonelion Tower clear west to Hawkheron Tower and the Southturrets—to the softly slithering madworms.

The mysterious madworms. The maedra, the great eellike beasts with chillingly human arms who lived inside stone and tunneled tirelessly. Her brothers had dared to challenge them with blades, or boasted they'd roast one for the feast-table . . . and come back sunk in fear and desperate for drink.

The rest of the realm had heard the tales about the madworms, but seemed to think it mere mad talk spun by the Silvertrees, who after all were old, proud, coin-thin . . . and crazed. The rest of Aglirta wasn't troubled by coach-sized worms that could pass through walls and stone like ghosts, now was it? Just as bards and saner men whispered around fires about the Faceless who lurked among us, shifting shape at will, yet no one ever saw such monsters in the bright sun of the markets and along the river road, now, did they?

That much was a good thing. Better to be thought mad or wastrels than to be feared as the keepers of monsters, and butchered by neighbors fearful of what the dangerous Silvertrees might do next. Sembril knew quite well how Aglirta saw her family: proud, old, poor, and of no account, headed by a sharp-witted, tall, and rather plain barren elder sister of three young, restless, lusty louts.

Perhaps she *should* fling wide the doors and dance naked in front of her paintings, some day. The servants deserved some entertainment, however paltry, in return for their loyalty. And their silence about the maedra.

"Or are they all spies and keepers, set here to watch over the Silvertrees, and keep us weak, unimportant, and ignorant?" Sembril asked the emptiness of her sanctum aloud. There came no answer that she could hear. The feeling of being watched, however, seemed to grow even heavier . . . and that was an answer of sorts.

Was one of the servants spying on her now, with magic? Or was it someone else?

She'd long thought some of the servants might be very much more than they appeared to be—might not even be human. She'd thought something more, too: that there was nothing, short of mastering sorcery, that she could even begin to do about it.

Not even be human. Yes. The Faceless *did* exist, and held no love at all for any who bore the name Silvertree. That much Sembril's books had already told her.

Her most precious treasures, these slender, crumbling old tomes of magic, kept hidden inside the urn that housed an aging starflower plant, beside the chair where some of the servants thought she indulged in private drainings of ithqual and dragondream, and others believed she summoned one of her brothers—or one of their own ranks, who'd cleverly kept his identity hidden for many a year, now—for trysts. The plant pot lifted neatly out of the round mouth of the urn to reveal her small stack of stored lore beneath. It was paltry enough, she knew. The meager results of *very* discreetly hiring daring adventurers to steal spellbooks from living mages, or retrieve them from wizards' tombs.

She only hoped she'd master enough of the magic they held, in time.

*Magic is never entirely spent when a spell is done. There are always scatterings. Magic is like . . . mold, spores scattered unseen here and there about the fringes of wherever it's been most boldly active, and then been scoured away. Lurking. Waiting.*

*Awaiting—for centuries, if need be—the touch of other magic, to awaken once more, usually to mere dim glows and half-remembered echoes.*

*For me, wrapped in my biting cold, so much is sufficient, for I am myself a half-remembered echo. Grass grows lush above my bones while I wander—a shadow, a drift of mist, an awareness unseen.*

*Many a hunted man might envy me . . . until their thoughts ran deeper.*

*Magic clings to nearly every stone of this vast palace, sometimes eight enchantments deep, and at my approach things stir, glows awaken. I can taste them all, if I take the trouble to delve into them directly.*

*Here, in this wall, I see a tall woman standing alone at a table strewn with open books, runes of magic winking and glowing on faded, stained pages as she walks restlessly back and forth, reading from them, frowning in thought. . . .*

*Making herself a sorceress . . .*

"If I had coin enough . . . and dared pursue this openly!" Sembril hissed in frustration, rapping her knuckles on the tabletop beside her latest acquisition. When she'd passed her hand over the lock of its metal clasp, a tiny green rune had arisen from the keyhole, floated there like a tantalizing emerald flame for as long as she kept her hand above it, and then vanished.

It betokened something magical about the lock, obviously—but what? If only she commanded more than mere scraps of knowledge!

Working magic was easy for her, almost as easy as walking . . . but she was like a child left alone with broken bits and pieces of unfamiliar tools. She didn't know the simple things about what went with what, why, what they were supposed to do . . . or how to make them do *any*thing. And she dared not ask anyone in Aglirta.

She'd found a few helpful lines about some spells in the court library at Flowfoam—but Sembril had been sure, later, that someone kept a watch over those books, and that her interest in magic had been noted. The only Aglirtan wizards she knew of were outlaws, or served one or other of the barons. None of whom would lift a finger to help a Silvertree unless they could take a grasping handful of gain as a result—but might stir their fists to reach out and seize the Silvertree lands if her asking just one question of their wizard led them to guess how weakly those lands were held.

Grasping gain. Sembril frowned down at the locked book. It seemed to stare back, mockingly. She couldn't afford to hire the wisdom of even a minor backstreet mage of Sirlptar, even if she'd dared to make the trip, or be seen seeking a wizard. She had the handful of spells in her few books— glowfire, the fetching-across-air, the shieldings too weak to be called proper wards that she cloaked the Candletower with whenever she studied magic, the spell that made magic announce itself, and the word that lit wood or paper—but nothing more.

And she needed *real* spells, magic to tame the maedra and win control of Silvertree House away from them, so that walls stayed where they'd been put, and Sembril's brothers could lay aside their fears and do something with their lives besides drinking.

Magic to find and hurl back the shape-shifters, to defend the Silvertree lands so well that even the proudest or most desperate baron wouldn't dare to send an army to her gates . . . or order their envoys to murmur increasingly-less-veiled threats and hints about her weak, unwed state whenever she attended court. As they did every time, now, almost lining up to oh-so-gently menace her.

And now this! The best pendant of her mother's jewelry this book had cost her, and it was guarded. That flame meant that forcing the lock would mean her death, or horrible maiming at best, or the book would be destroyed and its lore with it . . . or both.

Sembril clenched her fists so tightly that her nails cut into her palms, bit back a shriek of rage, and turned on her heel to pace and think.

The book lay on the table, challenging her. Its glow of magic had been so strong when the mercenary proffered it that she'd had to fight to keep the eagerness from her face. She'd failed, too, and saw as much in his face as he took the pendant almost reluctantly, as if on the point of demanding more.

She—*ohhhh!* Sembril whirled, skirts whirring about her ankles, and strode back to the table, to catch up her other precious tomes and put them carefully away in the urn. Returning the plant to its concealing perch atop them, she went back to the new book, took it up in her hands, and almost ran into the next room. If there was some sort of explosion or magical eruption, her other books should be far away.

Her feet took her to the Candle Stair, the great spiral of steps that linked her sanctum to the lower levels of the tower, but the watched feeling did not diminish.

Sembril stopped on the landing, set the book on the stone railing beside her, and traced its covers lovingly. Scaly hide of some unknown beast, dyed dark brown and made darker—almost black—by age. No word nor symbol worked into them anywhere, and a flap projecting from the back cover that curled around to overlap the front and guard the edges of all the pages, in a guardianship held close and secure by the clasps, two crossed bands of metal she did not know. Steel-shod corners, enspelled to keep off rust. Her new treasure, hers to hold but not to open.

Sembril glared at it. No, raging would do nothing. 'Twas time to either try to smash open the clasps and suffer whatever doom that would cause—or to think. Really think.

She laid her hand flat on the book and asked aloud, "Now if I was truly a powerful Silvertree wizard, how would I open you?"

And the book began to glow.

She almost sent it flying as she snatched her hand away, wild tinglings of power awakening under it. Tiny emerald lightnings were racing along the clasps, converging on the lock that had so frustrated her.

The lock which now obligingly opened, the crossed clasps folding back by themselves, to the echo of a faint but unmistakable male voice announcing calmly: "Silvertree."

So that had been the word of unbinding. *Why?*

Were the shape-shifting Faceless or some other unseen watchers toying with her? Had they sent her this tome as a trap, or a taunt?

The book lay still, and a suddenly fearful Sembril Silvertree hesitated a long time before daring to touch it.

When she did, no doom smote her timid fingertip. Nothing erupted into the stairwell. The book felt cold, and solid, and . . . ordinary. Aging parchment, not yet leaf-brittle, with the faint smells that almost always clung to old books. Its first page was blank, and the second held a badge Sembril thought she knew—or should know. She'd seen it once before, when . . . nay, she could not remember. Years back, when father was alive, just a glimpse from afar, when . . . at Flowfoam? No. She'd forgotten, if she'd ever truly known at all. This must be the mark of the one who'd created the book, or perhaps a wealthy patron who'd ordered it made for him . . . gingerly she passed her hand over the drawn device. Nothing.

She reached out to turn the page, and then impulsively touched the badge with her fingertip. Something stirred under her touch, like a spark too small to glimmer, and a voice announced calmly, "Erard Bowdragon, of Arlund." It was the same man's voice that had spoken before.

Sembril waited tensely, afire with excitement, but nothing more happened.

After a long, breath-tremulously-held wait, she touched the badge again. The announcement was repeated.

Erard Bowdragon. He'd been head of the Bowdragon family—strong in sorcery, all of them—years ago. He was dead, she was sure she'd once heard. Nothing more, which meant that nothing had been spectacular enough about his passing to gossip about, just that someone else was now head of House Bowdragon.

Sembril Silvertree turned the page.

It was covered with writing she could not read, script the like of which she'd never seen before, with little running lines of tiny characters beneath some of the boldly curved, swirling letters, and adorning two sides of others. When she touched one of those letters, a tiny emerald flame raced up her finger, the brief pain as sharp as if she'd been bitten by a kitten.

She felt an answering tingle beneath both of her ears, tightening and prickling, and then the voice said gravely, "Blood of Silvertree, Erard Bowdragon am I, and this you hold is the third volume of my more than dry account of my deeds and strivings yet unfinished. No spells will you find here. Yet every Silvertree should know the truth of my involvement with your kin."

Sembril kept her finger on the page, not daring to move it lest the voice should fall silent, and never speak again. Most spells unleashed but once. . . .

"I kept my pact," the voice of the dead wizard said calmly, "with Yuesembra Silvertree—and did as she bade me with

her three sons and daughter: Faerlun, Marask, Tesmer, and
Belsaryl. The younger two lived their lives as my own children, and whatever Bowdragons there be today in Arlund are
descended from them. The eldest I revealed as the Silvertree
heir in Flowfoam when I deemed him ready, as I'd blood-
promised his mother I'd do—and so delivered him to his
doom, as I'd known I would be. I think Faerlun knew it, too,
yet spoke no word of reproach to me, and for that I do him
honor."

Sembril Silvertree stood frozen, trembling. So to take Silvertrees to Flowfoam in Erard Bowdragon's day had been to
doom them?

"Yuesembra's second son, Marask, was of weaker stuff,
and I could tell the Koglaur were well pleased at that. From
the King on down, they smiled and offered me none of the
menace that had attended my first visit. Of more import to
you, they worked no harm on Marask . . . and so you came
to bear your name."

Sembril thought she saw a movement off to one side, by
the curving wall of the stairwell. She whirled around, keeping her finger firmly in place on the book.

There was no one there. She was alone.

Yet the feeling of being observed was stronger still; it
seemed as if a large and interested audience sat at her back.
She cast a swift glance in the other direction, but still found
herself alone, as Erard Bowdragon's voice rolled on.

"Marask was embraced and supported by the Koglaur not
out of any love or kind regard, but to gird and fortify the stability of Aglirta. The baronial families of Phelinndar, Tarlagar, Brostos, Cardassa, Brightpennant, Adeln, Glarond, and
Loushoond were growing in ambition almost as swiftly as in
coin, as their lands and power grew with them. In fractious-
ness they grew apace, too, with rival Koglaur behind every
baronial family, scheming and guiding—as is still the case
as I write this, and I daresay also whenever you hear this, if
there's a throne of Aglirta yet. The Faceless One who wore
the likeness of the King of Aglirta, and those eldest Koglaur
who posed as his most senior courtiers, wanted a noble fam-

ily they could wield as surely as a favored sword—and needed all Aglirta to see that laws and ranks and courtesy would and should prevail. Their acknowledgment and treatment of the long-lost Silvertree heir allowed them to demonstrate that. If they thought to deceive me or any other wizard of power—or plain man of level wits, for that matter—they were disappointed. Yet I fear Aglirta has as paltry a supply of plain, honest men of level wits who can see clearly, or choose to look at anything beyond their noses, as anywhere else in Darsar."

Erard's voice fell silent, and Sembril Silvertree lifted her hand uncertainly. The silence continued, and she looked up and down the stair and all around, seeking any trace of whoever was watching her so intently. Nothing.

Abruptly she took up the book, still open, and carried it back into the largely empty, nameless chamber between her sanctum and the Candle Stair. She set it on the old, scarred table just inside the archway that led into her sanctum, drew in a deep breath, and turned the page.

Nothing happened. More flowing, unreadable script, much the same as on the previous page. She set her finger down on it, magic surged unsettlingly up her hand—and Erard Bowdragon's voice spoke again. Sembril closed her eyes, threw back her head, and drew in a deep, shuddering breath of relief.

"I know not if Silvertree House yet stands," the dead wizard's voice said calmly, "or if you've ever seen it. I do know that as I say this, it is a place deemed haunted or cursed—a place where men say the walls themselves seem alive, and madworms roam through the very stones."

Sembril cast swift looks all around, seeing no one. As always. Yet she felt as if a multitude of folk were all around her, staring at her. As always.

"The walls do not live, but can be changed, sometimes with frightening speed—by the maedra. The same creatures men call madworms. Yuesembra spent her life-force in sorceries to command them. They delved, hollowed, shaped, and erected stone at her bidding, rather than at their own.

The result pleased them; they seem restless to expand Silvertree House, though they leave some chambers and passages to crumble into ruin. Even wizards cannot understand the minds of maedra."

Sembril sighed. So this tome wasn't going to be any path to mastering the madworms.

"They can flow through rock as an eel wriggles through the shallows, rock becoming as broth in their jaws. All but a few of the oldest keeps and ramparts of Silvertree House are their building—and since Yuesembra and her Ravengar fell to the Koglaur, the maedra have been uncontrolled. Silvertree House is their house, and they enlarge and change it almost daily."

Sembril glanced around, as if the nearest wall might vanish in an instant, revealing her to the birds and breezes . . . and the coldly amused scrutiny of a madworm as long as a coach-team, as a new wall grew like rising smoke in its hands. . . .

"I've watched Silvertrees wither as fear gripped them," Erard Bowdragon said gravely, "their own terror strangling life out of them—a fear of creatures that mean them no harm, and even take care not to discomfit them. Yet as their palace ceaselessly changes around them, fear grows in Silvertrees. Hear now the truth: The Koglaur slew Ravengar and Yuesembra to seize control of Silvertree House and exterminate all Silvertrees, but found themselves at war with the maedra. The stoneworms melted into stone to avoid most of their attacks—and when the Faceless Ones tried to use spells to mentally compel the maedra, they found *themselves* the mind-hunted."

. . . as so many halls and chambers and staircases had melted away, shifting into new shapes and linking to new places, Sembril thought, recalling the fear that lurked in her own belly, coiling and stirring, seeing Silvertree House changing around her as the days and months and years passed, the wizard's voice continuing half-heeded. . . .

"Hunted—and conquered. Broken-witted, the Koglaur swiftly descended into madness, wildly harming and soon killing themselves and each other . . . or being dispatched by other Koglaur of Aglirta, who came to fear them as Silvertrees fear Silvertree House. Yet perhaps you have found that one can smite and slay a man, but cannot slay a vast house, with all its towers above—and miles of cellars and tunnels below. I've watched Silvertree after Silvertree cling to a handful of rooms in desperation, unable to reshape their home—and forbidden by maedra strivings as frenzied as those of any fire-eyed priest to wall 'safe' rooms away from the rest. Few Aglirtans will set foot in Silvertree House—the Silent House, they call it now—to do more than repair doors and windows, or paint a wall. Word has spread that maedra always attack work gangs. Such words are true—and the truth beneath them is that they do this purely to strike at the Koglaur spies among the workers. There are always Koglaur spies among strangers entering Silvertree House."

Sembril nodded her head wearily. No workers came now, no matter how many coins hired Sirl trade-factors offered in that rich city, and she knew very well why. More than a dozen men dead, and the work of every gang smashed and ruined, their ladders and scaffolding and lives with it, time after time. Tongues wag, and tales grow in the telling, until the marching mountains themselves hear . . . and fail to forget.

Bowdragon's voice had fallen silent again. Sembril bowed her head over the page, suddenly shaking with weariness, the fire of excitement fled from her. She would listen to the rest of Erard Bowdragon's book—she had to hear every word—but it was not what she needed.

She needed something—a cloak of mighty spells, a scepter, one of the fabled Dwaer-stones, *anything*—that could win her control of her ever-changing home. *Even wizards cannot understand the minds of maedra.* If Erard Bowdragon was right, no such weapon of magic existed.

Which left her—not being a maedra—with nothing. No hope at all. So she must seize on the chance that Bowdragon was wrong, and that a more secretive, more powerful wizard just might have learned how to compel the maedra.

After all, Yuesembra Silvertree had.

Her ancestor, and a woman like herself, no war-baron with heaps of coins and hosts of cortahars and armaragors at his call. So she must hope to find—or have some daring hired adventurer find for her—an eloquent tome written by some wizard wiser and mightier than Erard Bowdragon, and read her rescue therein.

She closed Bowdragon's book carefully, and touched the clasps. As she'd expected, they moved by themselves, sliding smoothly together. Green flame encircled the lock for a moment as it clicked shut again.

Sembril regarded the tome in silence for as long as it took her to draw in a long, deep breath. Then she snarled at Erard's book, roaring wordless, frustrated fury until the echoes rang around her—whereupon she stopped abruptly, panting, picked the book up with gentle care, and headed back towards the starflower urn.

She'd read every word in all of the other tomes waiting there, but she'd just have to read them again, and hope she could see something she hadn't understood before. Or go as mad as a madworm trying.

If, of course, she wasn't that crazed already.

# 2

## Darkness Unleashed

"$\mathcal{E}$nd it," Thelmest Bowdragon said grimly, turning abruptly away. His face was white, and his brows slick with sweat.

His brother Presmur nodded and passed his hand over the spell-glows on the table—and the pale, gently drifting image of Sembril Silvertree, snarling her rage in a lofty room of Silvertree House, abruptly darkened and fell into writhing wisps of smoke. The four brothers staggered back from the table as if cords they'd struggled against had suddenly been cut, gasping in relief.

"Three Above, but that hurts the head!" Haljaster growled, shaking his curly tresses and wincing. "What's *in* those wards of hers?"

"Nothing," Presmur said coldly. "Our pain came from holding our own shields against the maedra. Something that would be easier, I might add, if you didn't flail about like a drunken warrior—or a youth afire with the flood of his first flagon inside him—when spell-linked to the rest of us."

"Now, Presmur," Farndorn said swiftly, "Hal *is* a drunken warrior—most of the time, anyway. And were he not, you'd never get a meal set in front of you, lost in all your fussing over spells and deep thoughts. Hal sees to the servants and food for all of us and guards at the gates so we can keep all this, remember?"

"I'd not forgotten," the thinnest and most studious brother said shortly. "Yet none of that excuses sloppy spell-work. It means doom as surely as an armaragor forgetting to strap on his blade before going to battle—a doom the rest of us might well share, some day, despite our own careful preparedness."

Haljaster strode across the room, plucked a decanter out of a tall, slender glassy forest, and told it, "Presmur, your life is consumed by scheming and worrying. I prefer to spend my time experiencing and *enjoying*. You might try it some time. A little experiencing and enjoying with, say, our feast-dancer Shalass should warm your frost for you!"

Presmur flushed, eyes narrowing, and Farndorn said sharply, "No, *don't* add that little remark to your ever-expanding grudge lists against the rest of us, Presmur. Hal's right: it's long past time you learned to *live* a little!"

"Enough," Thelmest said firmly, and his three brothers all seemed to relax and take another step apart. "As it happens, I agree with Dorn in this particular matter, but our time is better spent just now in discussing what we've just learned. Presmur, calm yourself and cast a thaenorn-ward."

"A full warding? But surely—"

Thelmest spun in a whirl of robes to stare down Presmur. "Is there *anything* more important to the conduct of the rest of our lives than coming to agreement as to what we've just learned, and what we do about it?"

A little silence fell, in which Presmur frowned and dropped his eyes—only to dart a swift glance at Farndorn and Haljaster, to see if they were smirking.

They were both nodding gravely at their elder brother, according Thelmest his right to command in family affairs. Behind solemn masks, their smirks would keep for another breath or two, until Presmur—prissy, predictable Presmur—turned his poisonous glare away.

"We'll all give power to your thaenorn," Thelmest ordered heavily, taking a half-step to one side to block Presmur's view of his not-quite-smirking kin. "Brothers, I want the strongest webwork of spells we've ever spun around us. Sooner or later, one of the servants is going to yield to the temptation to discover what we're up to whenever we order them all out of this tower—and lesser mages of Arlund, even if from nowhere else, pay close attention to House Bowdragon."

Presmur nodded, swallowed, spread his hands to wriggle his fingers with exaggerated care, and then cast the thaenorn.

It was the longest, most intricate spell any of them knew, its incantlets sung here and declaimed there, layer upon flourish-finished layer, and Presmur Bowdragon was a precise and careful caster. It took him a long time.

Each Bowdragon brother in turn glided forward with the glow of a risen spell bright about his hand, and proffered it at the right moment. Their magics melted into the unseen enchantment Presmur was building, until a shimmering, singing web of force was almost visible around his head and shoulders.

The quietest Bowdragon began to tremble in time with the pulsing surges of magic flooding through him, and then lifted his head, drew in a deep breath, and announced, "Done. We are alone, and shielded so that none can see or hear in. The Serpent itself could not break through our thaenorn—nor the Dragon in full fury, for that matter."

"Not that you've ever seen either, to be able to make such a judgment," Farndorn muttered, an observation that earned him a sharp look from Thelmest.

"Brothers," the eldest living Bowdragon said heavily, "I know not where that book has been or precisely how Sembril Silvertree came by it, but I see no reason to doubt its veracity. She was upset by what she heard; I judge her no actress, to feign a reaction for our benefit."

"Agreed," Haljaster said firmly. "If she expected us—or, more likely, the maedra—to be watching her, she'd take care to pretend ignorance of such things, or trusting in a ward-spell she could easily miscast for us. Instead, she looked about herself as if suspicious of watchers, more than once."

Farndorn nodded. "I, too, believe we saw her true reaction. Presmur?"

"I know less of women than the rest of you," the most studious Bowdragon said grimly, "as Haljaster never tires of reminding me. But yes, I saw nothing to make me think otherwise than we saw surprise, dismay, and frustration that she truly felt. I, too, believe we heard Erard Bowdragon's voice. If *he* was telling untruth, down the years, I have no way of knowing. Yet why not believe his words? It wounds him not at all to speak truth, and profits his bones nothing to work mischief among his descendants. I'd say we heard his great secret. We are all Silvertrees."

"No," Thelmest said firmly, "we are Bowdragons. Only we and Sembril Silvertree—a lady who won't live much longer, I'd judge, and has no one to tell our lineage to who'd care or believe her—know otherwise. The question is, do we make this *our* secret, and pass it down to our eventual offspring?"

"No," Haljaster said promptly. "I see no benefit in becoming encoiled with the troubles of swift-darkening Aglirta. The reach of the Serpent-lovers—and the Faceless, too, for that matter—is too long."

Farndorn nodded vigorously. "I agree. Win ourselves a maedra-infested ruin of a palace, at best, with a claim many

Aglirtans will never believe, just to take a seat at a table where a feast of war and murder is about to be served up? Not with my wits in hand!"

Presmur frowned. "Forgive me, brothers, but I know less about the situation in Aglirta than the rest of you. Studying spells profits me; listening to gossip about foreign lands does not."

"Well, it *should*," Haljaster growled, "seeing as how most of the food eaten in Arlund and every other city of this coast comes from Aglirta. Whenever no open war rages elsewhere, Silverflow Vale is the true battleground for all in Asmarand; to know what befalls there is to raise a seeing-glass to all we know of Darsar."

"Again, brother, I agree with you," Thelmest put in, "yet Presmur's mastery of magic far outstrips our own, with good reason. He bends his wits to spellcraft, more than any of the rest of us. Know then, Presmur, that Aglirta is both the granary of Asmarand and the seat of its greatest power—*not* wealth, but 'tis not the backwater folk of Arlund and Sirlptar and far Carraglas like to think it. The Dwaerindim were made there—and they've gone missing again."

"*That* I've heard of," Presmur agreed, "though nothing was said of Aglirta. Surely they could be anywhere?"

"Indeed," Farndorn agreed, "for someone's obviously hiding them, biding the right time to burst forth and use them—to conquer. But conquer what, and where? Proud cities, yes, but Aglirta—yes, that wet riverbank forest studded with little backland farms—is where the Koglaur live, and the maedra crawl, and the Serpent-priests hiss. Somewhere near Aglirta the Serpent himself sleeps, and if he awakes—"

"*When* he awakes," Haljaster interrupted.

"Aye, when he awakes," Farndorn continued, "the Dragon will arise in Aglirta to battle him . . . and 'tis Aglirta they'll fight over, not Arlund or Sirlptar or any of the proud cities of the coast."

"Aye, and that war is stirring even now!" Haljaster felt for the hilt of a warblade he wasn't wearing, and added, "Methinks we'll see the Serpent rise in our lifetimes."

Presmur shook his head. "You spout old nursery-fears, and wave them like war-banners. I—I can scarce believe I'm hearing this, from the three of you."

"Yet your ears fail you not," Thelmest said in a voice of quiet thunder, "and you *are* hearing it from the three of us. We're neither children in a nursery nor backfence fools, Presmur. *We* heed the winds, and face the coming weather."

Presmur shook his head again, and said wearily, "Well enough, I'm misinformed, and all eyes should look to Aglirta. Whereto it seems, if I've heard you all a-right, 'tis best if the Bowdragon clan has no known connection."

Three heads nodded soberly, and Presmur spread his hands and said, "So we stay Bowdragons, and forget we ever heard that Yuesembra Silvertree bore our forefathers. This meets with no dispute from me, and so it seems we're agreed. Yet has it not occurred to you, my brothers, that if Aglirta is such an important backwater, roamed by so many powerful folk, that Sembril Silvertree—the eldest of her family, mind, as Thelmest is here—may be slain by someone who first turns out her mind with spells to learn all her secrets? She has magic, after all, and possibly great treasure hidden in that vast ruin of a house, and . . . then we'd have a foe seeking our deaths or spell-thrall that we might not even know about! Should we not slay her first? *Now?*"

"Before she has any chance to share our secret?" Farndorn asked. "Brother, your ruthlessness surprises me."

"Your prudence is admirable," Haljaster said, "but there's no need. Making a foray into Aglirta, to risk being seen embroiling ourselves openly in Aglirtan affairs, would be a mistake."

"A mistake," Thelmest echoed, nodding.

Presmur frowned at his brothers, and shook his head. "So you grant that the risk is real, but consider moving to end it a mistake? And what is this 'no need'?"

"There's no need," Thelmest replied, "because Sembril Silvertree is going to die very soon now—and by the hand of no stranger."

Haljaster nodded. "Aye. She'll be gone before the season

is out . . . when the darkness now unleashed in her own house reaches her."


Sembril stiffened, her hand on the concealed latch of the outermost secret door. There had come a muted booming, a faint shuddering thunder amid the soft scrape of her own striding, and she realized it was the second one. At least the second one.

As if someone was breaking down the doors.

Madworms! But no, they could just slither through the stone *beside* a door, and pass on their way with nary a pause. So who—?

Should she cower and hide on this side of her secret—but no, everyone knew where it led. Even strangers could hardly fail to notice an entire *tower,* right on the river side of Silvertree House. This door might be hidden, but there were other ways into Candletower, if one dared to go deep into the cellars and work a long way south to the Ravenskull Stair. She'd best get through this door, and hope to hide her secrets a few days longer. She had a few spells, tingling deep inside her, and there was a sword hanging on the wall in the next room, by Quaycel's Tallglass. . . .

Sembril slipped through like a hurrying breeze, peering across the dimly lit hall. Its door was still closed. Good. Now in case the intruders had bows, she'd best get up onto the gallery, to where its stone front could shield her from arrows. That sword—

It was a sturdy, plain old warblade, set in a place of honor by the ornate mirror because some loyal retainer had wielded it to save a Silvertree life, in some past strife or other. *Yes, we've had a lot of past strifes—and a plentitude of present ones,* Sembril thought wryly, plucking it down. Heavy it was, but still strong, and well-balanced; it felt good in her hand. She caught sight of her soft, wavering reflection in the tallglass as she hefted it: an old skirt and open, unbelted robes worn over leather tunic, breeches and warriors' boots, long unbound hair the hue of old polished copper, severe green eyes in a pale, unsmiling face . . . tall, taller even than the old mirror made her look—

Hmmph. Not that any man of Aglirta was interested in her, beyond her name and the lands that went with it. Sembril whirled away up the stair, wondering who wanted to see or slay her so badly that they were willing to brave the blue ravening fires of her paltry shielding spells. Every door they'd burst through should wreath them in searing flames as it fell—not slaying fire, but enough to leave most men groaning on the flagstones for much of a day, their limbs weak and numbed.

Interestingly, the intense feeling of being watched was gone. Perhaps the watchers had seen enough, or heard Erard Bowdragon's words, and decided they could now just come in and kill her. Who they might be, exactly, w—

There was a sudden, sharp splintering crash of rending wood, followed by a rolling *boom* that could only be the door of the next room shuddering back off the wall—and then a louder slam that shook the floor and sent echoes racing across the chamber. That door must have torn off its hinges and toppled. Sembril winced at the thought of what must have happened to anyone caught underneath it.

And then she shrugged off her robes to free her arms for swordplay, wishing she'd practiced with steel more often, and the blade in her hands didn't feel so Three-cursed *heavy*. She'd been trained as thoroughly as her brothers, but even she hadn't expected to—

"This is the last one, lads!" someone shouted, just beyond the door.

It was Emeruld, Seneschal of the House. A man that until a breath ago she'd trusted absolutely—as her father had trusted him before her.

"Stand back!" Emeruld snapped, and then came closer to the door and called more gently, "Lady Sembril? Mistress?"

Sembril stood on the gallery, sword in hand, and held silence.

Waiting. She was good at that. *Decide for me, Emeruld.*

"Lady Sembril?" he called, more loudly.

*Let me not put a foot wrong.* If she said and did nothing, this door, too, would be struck down.

"Emeruld?" she called back, sharply, taking a swift step to one side. There were wands that could hurl slaying magic through keyholes, and if they were trying to learn just where she stood . . .

"Lady Sembril!" His voice sounded relieved—just a trifle relieved. "Grave news!"

Sembril started down the stair, trying to tread as softly as possible. "What news?"

"I—Lady, uh, your ears should hear this first, before . . ."

"Emeruld, I have no secrets. All of House Silvertree knows what I do, it seems, and I see no reason why all of you shouldn't know this, too. The men with you know it already, don't they? Or don't they?"

It was Emeruld's turn to hold silence, for the time it took her to descend the stair and start across the floor, keeping carefully to one side of the door.

"They do, Lady," the seneschal said finally. "We all do. Yet I'd prefer not to . . ."

"To shout it through a door? Which you'll break down to come in and get at me if I don't open it?"

"Nay, Lady. Not now I know you can hear. I'm . . . Sembril, lass, we're not coming in seeking to harm you, or drag you forth. Yet this is too urgent—"

"To wait until highcandles? *That* bad? Now I'm not sure I *want* to open the door."

"I daresay, Lady," Emeruld replied wearily. "I daresay."

Sembril banished her fires with the necessary gesture, did the second one that caused the lock to release and the bolts to slide back by themselves, and swung open the door.

A ring of grim, worried faces stared at her—men of the household, all of them girded for battle. Sembril waved her sword at Emeruld standing red-faced at their fore and said gently, "I'm here. Tell me."

"The Lord Desmer, Lady, rode to war against Maerlin some days ago," the seneschal said tersely. "His excuse: the wording of the last letter of entreaty sent you by young Lord Imdraeth Maerlin, which I fear he . . . saw . . ."

"One or other of my brothers intercepts and reads everything sent to me," Sembril said calmly. "I know this, Emeruld. I did *not* know of Desmer's . . . doing. He took hireswords to help him, I suppose? Or has he hazarded—and by your face, I'd say lost—cortahars and armaragors we can't afford to lose?"

"Hireswords and all, Lady," the seneschal said heavily, "and lost many. A rider's just reached us, with word that Lord Desmer lives, but that he and every sword who rode with him are defeated and scattered, fleeing here all by their own ways—with the armies of Maerlin hot behind them."

"And Maerlin, without hireswords or even a full mustering, can easily field twelve blades to our one," Sembril said softly, seeing doom finally closing its fingers around her. Well. Imdraeth Maerlin wouldn't have to bother wedding her, after all.

She drew in a deep breath, threw back her head, and said briskly, "Mount a light watch, and have everyone else bring all the food and drink—water especially—to the innermost habitable rooms of the House. Shieldcourt Hall, I think, and Flaertrumpet Hall. When they come, we can fall back, defend the Dragonfire Door and the Broken Stair . . . and let the maedra do some of our fighting for us."

"Ah, Lady . . . ," Emeruld said slowly, lips twisting as he searched for words to thrust through them. "That's just . . . ah, it. The mad—the maedra. They're . . . fleeing."

Sembril asked nothing, but merely lifted an eyebrow. The seneschal eyed her and struggled on. "Uh—up from . . . something below. They've been wriggling out of the walls past us all morning, and into the woods, as fast as they can slither. Dozens of them."

Sembril felt cold—and somehow, at the same time, numb. She knew the color must be draining from her face. Everyone in Silvertree House feared the maedra, and she couldn't even begin to imagine what would scare *them*. Or had some clever wizard finally crafted a spell to compel them, and was using it to aid Maerlin? Or to just empty Silvertree House, heedless of the clashes of hard-riding, warring Aglirtans, so he could come striding in to claim its treasure? Sembril knew of no rich hoard of gems or coins that could begin to echo what minstrels claimed Silvertree House held, but it was possible Silvertrees beyond her grandsires had hidden coins or gems enough to fill a lofty hall—a hall the maedra could well have since moved, or hidden—and gone to their graves not telling all their secrets to their kin. And no wonder. *Had my sons been like Relvaert, Taraunt, and Desmer, telling them about coins would be to watch them fall over their own boots in their haste to spend it all.*

"How many," Sembril asked, because it had been in her mind and it was something to say, "loyal men of the house were harmed getting here to me?"

"Seven, Lady."

"Eight," one of the oldest cortahars said firmly, his boldness betraying how upset he was.

"Bring them in here and lay them down, as gently as you know how," Sembril commanded, tossing her sword onto the room's only sturdy table. "There's a spell to ease pain. . . ."

"And then, Lady?"

"And then, Emeruld, gather everyone in the Ghostwynd Tower—with the food and the drink I mentioned earlier. We'll do our own defending there."

"While you, Lady, will—?" Emeruld asked gently, eyeing the white-faced Lady of the House.

Sembril sighed. "There's a spell I've never tried yet. I'd better look at it now."

"For blasting armies?" The seneschal sounded more bitter than hopeful.

"For meeting minds with beasts," Sembril Silvertree told him.

"Talking to horses and such? How's that going to keep us alive? If you turn aside the Maerlin mounts, they'll just get off and come at us afoot. They'll have to do that anyway, if we're in Ghostwynd Tower."

"I don't know how to find out what's scared the maedra

without talking to them, or at least seeing into their minds. Do you?"

Jusper Emeruld stared at her as if she'd suddenly turned into King Amthrael—a King Amthrael who had three heads, with crowns glittering on each of them. "L-lass—*Lady*—you'll be burned witless!"

"Then I won't mind being married to Imdraeth Maerlin, will I? You can put me into a pretty gown and march me out to him, save your lives, and get gone while his armaragors are taking turns enjoying me. After all, I won't know or care, will I?"

The men of Silvertree were all staring at her now, open-mouthed. One or two of them made the warding sign against either madness or the Curse of the Three, but at least two others stood tall and looked at her with—respect? Admiration? Dawning hope?

"And how," the old seneschal asked her heavily, "will knowing what the maedra fear help us?"

Sembril Silvertree gave Emeruld a level look, and picked up the sword again.

"This," she told him flatly, "I know how to use. Not as well as any of you, and not well enough to keep myself alive for more than a few breaths against a good bladesman—or any two foes. How many folk of the House can do more, beyond you men? Emeruld, we're going to *die*. They're going to hack us down like foresters clearing saplings, with about as much trouble. You know it—you all know it. I can see your faces as well as you can see mine."

She turned and put the warblade back on the table, slowly enough that they could all see how much her hands trembled. "So what weapon can we raise against them? Whatever scared the maedra is something powerful enough to be a *big* blade in our hands, if it's something we can wield."

Emeruld blinked. "And if it's not, Lady Sembril?"

Sembril Silvertree shrugged. "Then I'll at least die trying to do *some*thing. Something besides brooding and drinking and running off fetching trouble. Does anyone even know where Relvaert and Taraunt are?"

One of the older cortahars smiled thinly. "Three Above," he whispered, "but you sound like your father now—like your father when he was raging. I saw him that way only twice." Another man nodded.

Sembril looked back at them, throat tight, and whispered, "Bring in the men who got hurt. Please. Before I start to cry."

"Lady," Emeruld said smartly, bowing, and wheeled to give orders.

Behind him, Sembril Silvertree sagged against the door-frame and watched men scramble to do her bidding. Men who'd done no more than nod politely and turn away from her before.

"Desmer," she murmured under her breath, glancing at the sword on the table. "I wonder which Faceless One you handed an excuse for attacking us? There's one standing be-hind every baronial throne . . . and with the maedra gone, there's nothing to stop them from becoming you, or Emeruld, or the undercook. Aglirta may never know of our fall, but the Silvertrees are doomed."

She shook her head and turned away to gaze at the cold, dust-filled gloom of this lofty, nearly empty room—just one of so many like it, chambers upon chambers built by the maedra in an ever-growing labyrinth that made Silvertree House seem as large as some cities . . . yet as empty as most ruins. Her home, part of her, even if she'd never seen more than a tenth of its rooms and halls and dark lower levels. If she could melt into stone and dine on stone and drip-water, she could live here no matter how many Koglaur lorded it over Silvertree House.

As she could not, this dark, watchful, waiting place was far more likely to soon serve as her tomb.

Gasps, scrapings, and scrabblings behind her told her that the wounded men were being brought in. She turned to find Emeruld, to—

And then there were different sorts of gasps, and the ring-ing of blades being hastily drawn, and a sudden stillness.

Sembril saw men staring—everyone staring—off to her left. She looked there, too.

The largest maedra she'd ever seen was racing across the room towards her in a long, continuous, *looming* glide, arched up like a snake about to strike. It was as long as the high table in the Blue Chalice Chamber, its tail only now emerging from the blank, solid far wall—and it was headed straight for her, eyeless head lowered like a ram's.

Sembril froze, not knowing what to do. There was no point in fleeing if it wanted to catch her, and she was already busily—and thus far victoriously—fighting down the urge to scream and retreat. . . .

She stared at it. Huge, brawny shoulders rippled as mighty-thewed, humanlike arms spread wide as if to catch her. Its talons hadn't risen to menace her—yet. That sword was far out of reach, over on the table, and sword points on either side of her were wavering in trembling hands. . . .

No one lunged or slashed at the maedra as it slid up to her, laid the back of one cold, smooth-as-marble hand on her cheek for one long, long moment—and then slid past and was gone, the wall behind her swallowing most of it ere she could turn.

Turn she did, staggering as a yellow mist of confusion flooded blindly around her eyes, wanting to ask questions, wanting to cry out commiseration and—and—

It was gone, the wall swallowing the tip of its tail as blankly and as thoroughly as if it had never been in the room.

Sembril Silvertree fought for balance, nigh-overwhelmed with the rich and vivid force of what she'd been mind-shown, a racing flow of mind-pictures all red-purple around the edges in the wake of the yellow mist's dying. . . .

Glimpse after gliding glimpse of maedra racing river-wards through the House in fear, all fleeing from something dark and tentacled and terrible—an upright, ungainly glistening black column of tentacles that narrowed into a serpentine body as long as six maedra the size of the one that had just burst past Sembril.

"Arau," they called it, knowing it only from legends as a fell creature of the earthy deeps, a burrowing thing, insatiable. *The* Arau, the feeder on maedra, unintentionally un-

leashed by maedra tunneling far beneath Silvertree House—
rearing up triumphantly to shred and slay, doomed maedra
battling it in a frenzy, shredded and broken bodies tumbling
around it in a gory dark rain as those tentacles stabbed and
coiled, lashed and *struck*—

"Lady? Lady *Sembril!*"

She groaned, shaking her head as if to drive away the
nightmare visions of slaughter, but knowing she could not,
her gorge rising, fear making her shiver as every hair she
had thrust out rigid. . . .

"Lass!" It was Emeruld, cradling her arm and shoulder,
shouting into her ear as if over roaring surf. "Sembril, what
did it *do* to you?"

Sembril shook her head again, found him through swimming eyes, and announced grimly, "It is my belief, men of
Silvertree, that what the maedra are fleeing—the *thing* that's
killing them—is not a blade we can wield. Unless it scours
the House of us all and is yet hungry, when the armies of
Maerlin reach our gates; then it'll be *their* turn to cower."

"So what do we do now?" someone asked, his voice rising
in fear.

Sembril turned towards that man, with eyes like two dark
flames, and replied, "Die defending our home. The Three
deem it a rightful task, as I recall."

# 3

## Sembril's Greatest Spell

"Three curse you all! Have you *forgotten* how to draw a
bow?"

"We're out of arrows, Lord," Jusper Emeruld replied
grimly.

Relvaert Silvertree gave the seneschal a surprised look,
and then grinned his usual wide "what care I?" grin, spread

his war-gauntleted hands and shrugged, battered armor plates flashing. "Well," he announced, "I always wanted to die fighting!"

And snatching up a shield from a fallen Silvertree corta-har, he charged through the doorway into blood-drenched Foxheart Hall—tall, square-jawed and handsome, long black hair flying about his metal-clad shoulders.

That lofty, usually deserted chamber in the depths of Silvertree House was strewn with corpses. Silvertree corpses, reaped in the shouting, screaming time just past by humming storms of Maerlin arrows. Endless those shafts had seemed, and though they came only singly or in pairs now—a sure sign that quivers were nearly empty, and prudent orders had been uttered at last—they'd done more than enough damage to the meager Silvertree ranks. Less than a score of battle-tested warriors still stood, huddled behind their shields all around Seneschal Emeruld.

An arrow thudded into Relvaert's borrowed shield, promptly followed by another. A third hissed past to crack into shards against the wall beside the stout, broad-shouldered seneschal's head, but Emeruld never flinched.

He'd watch Relvaert's end—reckless, wench-hungry wastrel or not, the man who'd never conducted himself as the head of Silvertree House was owed that much.

Not that seeing it through would cost much time. Relvaert's splendid armor might stop a shaft or two, but any war-arrow from a decent bow that caught him squarely . . .

Two such shafts slammed into the shield together, and the scion of House Silvertree was snatched off his feet and hurled two paces back. He landed on his heels, staggered a step or two sideways, reeled . . . and ran on.

Relvaert was trying to reach the archway across the hall whence the bowmen were firing. Half the mailed might of Maerlin were waiting cautiously beyond that gap for those archers to clear the hall. They knew not much more than a handful of Silvertree swordsmen remained, but were wary of this dark, endless stone labyrinth of a palace, with its traps and sally-points and fabled lurking monsters. Moreover, they could afford to be slow and careful. No one would come riding hard to this sprawling tomb of a place to rescue Silvertree lives.

It would not be long now. A goodly way across the hall, a war-arrow had caught Relvaert Silvertree's shield squarely, piercing it with a *thud* like dull thunder, pinning it to his arm and spinning the scourge of Vale lasses half-around. He was smiling still, Emeruld saw, black hair drenched with sweat as he turned back to face his foes, wrestling the shield up to face the first rush of Maerlin cortahars edge-on, using its nether point like a prow to force them back and away—to where his long warblade could reach them, and their own shorter blades bite nothing.

It might have worked, had he faced only one or two, but the men of Maerlin knew well the importance of preventing this well-armored lion of a man from reaching the narrow arch, and making a stand there that could cost many Maerlin lives ere he was overmatched and driven down. They came at him in a swarm, stumble-booted in their haste, hacking with clumsy enthusiasm in a rain of steel that couldn't help but overwhelm Relvaert's strength and batter his arms down.

The eldest living Lord Silvertree spun away from that rush, managing to drive his blade around the guard of one warrior and deep into the man's ribs—where it lodged as the man squalled forth gore and life together. Still grinning fiercely, Relvaert used his blade like a handle to move the shield of reeling, dying flesh athwart other reaching Maerlin blades.

Jusper Emeruld plucked two daggers from the belts of sprawled and still Silvertree warriors who'd never know of their loss—or of anything else, ever again—and threw them at Maerlin faces. One blade glanced away after drawing but a thin line of blood, but the other took a man in the nose or mouth and sent him toppling in a flood of gore.

Relvaert Silvertree gave the seneschal a grin of thanks as he turned again, slashed open a Maerlin throat—and then vanished under a swarm of reaching, hacking blades, ar-

mored shoulders, and bobbing helms. One Silvertree armaragor stirred as if to charge forth into the Hall and hack at
all of those armored backs, but Emeruld caught the warrior's
eye and shook his head bleakly. One man was hurling his life
away before their eyes; two would simply be that much more
of a loss. Neither was weakness they could afford.

But then again, doomed men can afford anything.

The scream and clang of misused warsteel underscored
that grim truth for the long, loud stretch of a few good
breaths, and then . . .

Emeruld had been right. It had not taken long.

Relvaert bellowed, "For *Silvertree!*" in the sword-skirling
heart of that bitter fray, and then cried out again in ragged,
wordless pain and defiance, snarling out his last bubbling
breaths with three or more warblades buried in him—and his
own long sword clanging clumsily and heavily as his
strength failed.

The folk of Silvertree watched helplessly as Maerlin cortahars and armaragors hacked Relvaert Silvertree to death.
Then the invaders turned from their bloody work with gleeful yells and charged across Foxheart Hall.

"Stand and hold!" Jusper Emeruld snapped, fire in his
bristle-browed brown eyes as he settled the gorget dangling
from his plain, heavy war-helm into place. "Let no man of
Maerlin gain this threshold and keep his life!"

And then there was no more time for orders or words of
bold defiance. Warblades, shortswords, and daggers thrust
and rang and rained sparks down amid stamping, whirling
boots. Men crashed together, gasping and swearing, and did
vicious hacking and stabbing murder until too many men of
Maerlin had fallen—and the rest fell back.

No one cheered. The panting, bloodied Silvertree warriors among the arches knew the respite would be all too
short . . . and the next foray might well mean their deaths.

Jusper Emeruld leaned against the archway he'd fought so
hard to defend, not looking down at the blood streaming
from his smashed and ruined left gauntlet, and glared at the
cold stone around him bitterly.

Since Desmer had sprinted desperately through the gates with hard-riding Maerlin armaragors close behind him, Silvertree bows had twanged to pluck some from their saddles, and this attack had begun, not a single madworm had been seen in Silvertree House.

Not one, reaching so much as a lone talon forth from the solid stones to claw or clutch.

They'd have made all the difference against this Maerlin rabble, tearing the overbold invaders limb from li—

"Seneschal!"

The call was more of a gasp, and the young and frightened Silvertree warrior who'd made it was stumbling with pain and weariness as he emerged into the light. Nul . . . Nulthen, that was his name, one of Desmer's—

"Seneschal, Lord Desmer is dead—slain in the Long Hall by Maerlin cortahars. They're coming south now, slow and careful, by way of Galard's Hall and the Banner Gallery."

The seneschal lifted his helmed head as if he could see through the stone walls to the rooms named. "What of Lord Desmer's command?"

"Dead. All dead but a few who've fled deep into the House—a handcount, no more. I ran ahead . . . and . . ."

The cortahar gestured helplessly, and Emeruld gave him a grim smile. "Well done. With us will be a less lonely death than lurking alone in the back halls, waiting for a Maerlin sword—or something else—to take you."

He lifted his head and voice together, and snapped, "Lords Relvaert and Desmer are fallen, and in the absence of Lord Taraunt, *I* give orders for House Silvertree. Hear me: Fall back, everyone, to the East Forehall! Induth, you lead. Nessur and Beldred, to me; we'll stand rearguard. When I fall, heed the orders of Phaern."

Men stared back at him with doomed and weary eyes, and Emeruld raised his notched sword and snarled, "*Move,* Three lash you!"

They moved, slowly at first, like so many sheep. So did the Maerlin warriors, trotting forward across Foxheart Hall again with their longest warblades—and a glaive they'd managed to find somewhere in the halls—at the fore.

Beldred and Nessur were already shaking their cramped and numbed hands, spitting, and striding forward to take up stances in the archway.

Emeruld gave his retreating warriors a last glance and wave, and turned to join the two men he'd selected to die next. And him with them, unless the Three plunged into a whimsical mood for miracle-making in the next few breaths.

No maedra, young Lords Silvertree who were every bit as hotheadedly idiotic as lust- and drink-ridden . . . baron's sons, and—and Lady Sembril's spells might have helped a little in the defense of Silvertree House, too, if she'd deigned to emerge from the secret ways she'd walled herself into, so soon after that pretty little speech, and done at least a little fighting.

As the old Vale saying went: *There are three things a man dare not trust in: women, sorcery, and his luck.*

Jusper Emeruld smiled bitterly, hefted his blade, and stepped forward to be a fool the third time, by trusting in his luck. "*Thank* you for your timely aid, Lady Sembril," he murmured mockingly, as he chose the particular flagstone where he'd die.


Far away in the cold, stony gloom, Sembril Silvertree brought her fist down on a table in frustration and burst into tears. Emeruld's bitter face swam into a swirl of angry flesh in the depths of her crystal.

Relvaert and Desmer both gone, and so many Silvertree warriors and retainers, too—now arrow-festooned food for rats and flies in a nameless anteroom near the Red Chamber. All she had left now was Ruala, who'd become a friend as well as as the best maid any lady could hope for.

Like a silent shadow, Ruala came up behind her and put a comforting hand on her lady's shoulder. Sembril covered those gentle fingers with her own, but found no comfort. If this went on, she'd soon be alone in Silvertree House . . . with the Arau slithering on one side of her, and the murderous Maerlins on the other.

"No," she whispered. "No." She reached for the crystal as if her fingers could pluck Emeruld somehow to safety . . . and then let her hands fall.

She could do nothing.

Nothing but stare helplessly as three armored men—cortahars of House Maerlin—crashed into the burly seneschal, chopping at him with their blades. Emeruld snarled in their midst, ducking and swinging his own steel, and one of his attackers sagged backwards and fell. The seneschal drove his sword over that man's collapse, into the narrow eyeslit of another cortahar's helm—but the third armsman, with a vicious grin, thrust his blade in and along that reaching arm, into the seneschal's armpit and . . . deeper.

Jusper Emeruld reeled, spitting blood, and tried to turn towards his foe, but the man moved with him, twisting the blade as he shoved it farther in, hilt-deep against Emeruld's armor. The seneschal groaned, a long, bubbling growl of agony that sank in tone and volume as he slid off the blood-slick Maerlin blade towards the floor.

Emeruld bounced once, heavily and slowly, the blood pounding in Sembril's head as she stared wide-eyed through her tears. And then, as the blade wet and dark with his own blood swept down at his throat, he gasped, "Curse you, Sembril! I *know* you're watching, girl—why couldn't y—?"

Maerlin steel strangled his last words in a flood of gore, and the seneschal's eyes lost their fire and stared at the ceiling in frozen wonder.

And then real tears came, a blinding flood that left Sembril Silvertree head-down on the table, struggling for breath, sobbing so hard that she couldn't see, couldn't feel, couldn't think. . . .

Yet could remember, as Ruala swarmed over her, murmuring soothing words—empty, hopeless words that brought no shred of comfort.

Sembril tried to swallow, tried to breathe.

"He meant it not, milady! He was wild-minded, he was desperate—"

*Yes.* Desperate, these last days had been, as incant after incant fell into failure, weariness settled over her like a steadily heavier succession of smothering cloaks, and people died. Her people.

"Milady, be at ease! Three look down and soothe you, where I cannot!"

Sembril laughed bitterly at Ruala's words, or tried to. The attempt plunged her into a fit of choking and coughing.

Three indeed! She had a darker, closer guest. . . .

The Arau. That darkness stalking the depths of the palace had slain so many Silvertree folk that she'd been forced to ignore the Maerlin warriors and spend her spells trying to learn more about the foe within Silvertree House. Reaching out from behind their backs to softly quench life after life, it was the greater threat—perhaps to all Aglirta, or wider Asmarand beyond—and she couldn't hope to fight it until she knew more about its true nature.

Sembril slowly mastered her shudders and swallowed her weeping, shoving herself upright despite Ruala's clinging hands, and glaring down at Emeruld's dead face in the dimming crystal. Clenching her teeth, she turned away to stride across the gloomy chamber, pulling free of her faithful maid.

If Maerlin blades hacked bloody trails through the halls of her home, and dying Silvertree warriors cursed Sembril Silvertree for abandoning them to the Maerlin wolves, so be it. "A graver task faces Sembril," she whispered aloud.

"Milady?"

Sembril made no reply. *She* must find or spellforge a weapon to slay the Arau . . . or far more than the folk of Silvertree would soon be slain and cursed.

"But *how?*" she asked aloud, in a whisper that the darkest corners of the room had heard six-score times already, or perhaps a few times more.

As usual, the room declined to answer, and Ruala's reply was her usual bewildered echo of, "Milady?"

"Ruala," Sembril said warningly, her tone telling her maid to find silence, and spread her hands to gaze down at them.

So what, as she drew breath here and now, was the measure of Sembril Silvertree?

Her battle-magics were paltry things. A little fire-hurling that was most deadly against foes who'd obligingly doused themselves in pitch or flammable oils; a blood-boiling spell and a poisoning one that both required the caster to mingle blood with the victim and maintain that mingling throughout the incant—in an intimacy that would be rare indeed outside a lovers' bedchamber—and a mindsword to war with the wits of a single foe . . . again with overmuch intimacy.

She could mindspy from afar, a little—a *very* little, against nonhumans—and she could change her own body in limited ways and for brief times, though such transformations gave her no facility at wielding, say, the tentacles of the Arau, or even its snakelike body. Some wizards, if the tales could be believed, could blast down castle keeps with a single incant . . . but Sembril Silvertree was not one of them.

Well, then, perhaps she could mind-pry the Arau from afar and learn something of its nature, and its whereabouts, too.

And perhaps it could learn just as much about *her* and just where she was, through her prying.

Sembril shivered. The crystal was dark now, but she could still see Emeruld's angry eyes as clearly as if it shone like the sun and he stood bathed in its light glaring at her.

She was dead already, as dead as her faithful seneschal, as doomed as every other living thing in Silvertree House. So long as the Arau lived, unharmed and—and *hungry*—the great house around her was a death trap, and all Aglirta was threatened.

"Truly," she whispered bitterly, "the Three smile upon me. Relvaert and Desmer, all our armaragors and household, swept away. And now this . . ."

Silence fell, and she glared around at the cold stony gloom as if the room itself was to blame. As before, the chamber seemed unimpressed. Ruala quivered, not yet daring to speak, but leaning forward, ready to rush to her lady's aid if Sembril but said the right words.

Sembril said nothing. Drawing in a deep breath, she clenched her fists, scowled at her crystal—and got to work.

Trimming and lighting new candles, she set out her most precious spellbook with stones on the corners of the pages to hold it open at the right incant. Ruala started forward uncertainly, and Sembril waved her back with a furious sweep of her arm. Her maid returned to trembling immobility, her eyes large and dark with fear.

Gathering and arranging the few tokens the spell needed, Sembril windmilled her arms to stretch them, and closed her eyes.

Drawing in an even slower, deeper breath, she opened them again to find the room unchanged around her.

Sembril smiled and folded her arms with as much satisfaction as if she hadn't a care in the world. That confidence was vital.

Wearing it like a cloak, she stepped forward to the table in the same brisk manner as her father had once blessed harvest feasts, and carefully cast the mindspying spell.

All at once the room seemed darker, and tentacles coiled at the edges of her vision. Restless, malicious . . . and very much aware of her.

More than that: eager now to claim Sembril, as if their owner had been impatiently awaiting her. The Arau was very close—just inside the wall to her right—and it wanted sorcery.

Sembril shivered; it thought it could master magic by devouring sorcerers—humans actively wielding magic—and so it was delighted she'd finally cast a spell. One frightened human woman, alone in a door-barred room far from any aid . . .

Almost gloatingly it slithered through the stones and out into the candlelight, to take her.

Ruala screamed.

Sembril froze her into a wavering near-statue with a hissed incant, and turned calmly back to the book, as if what she did now was the usual and proper next step of her mind-spying magic.

Filling her mind with Ruala's terrified face and her own irritation at it, she began the casting of the mindsword. It was a short incant, but Sembril slowed it so it seemed . . . casual. The Arau was touching her mind just as she was peering into its thoughts, and it must suspect nothing until too late.

If the mindsword failed, she was doomed. If it did its harm but could not slay, she was also doomed. If she tried to flee, yet again she was—ah, behold: three fates spun by the Three—doomed.

Sembril finished the spell with a flourish, closed her spell-book, and told it in a wry murmur, "There's entirely too much doom to share around Silvertree House this day."

And then she turned, stepped boldly forward before fear could make her falter, and embraced the slithering darkness that was reaching for her.

*Three, what courage! It warms me, every time I behold it.*
*Warms me, and sickens me with the terror I know lies ahead.*
*And leaves me sad again, here in my cold.*
*The chill that changes not.*

"They say this place is haunted, don't they?" Dlan's voice was as firmly confident as ever—but Horl noticed that it was much quieter now than it had been outside, in the leaf-dappled sunlight.

He avoided smiling, and contented himself with the gruff reply. "They say a lot of things, but I've been in and out of it more than once, and I still live . . . in my old and aching fashion."

Dlanazar cast a thoughtful look back at the tiny rectangle of sunlight behind him, and then another, longer one at the old man. "Just so as to avoid any unpleasantness later," he said softly, setting down the glimmering lantern, "suppose we go over the terms once more, Lord Whitehair."

Old Horl lurched when he walked—one of his legs was

twisted and shorter than the other—and looked his years. His
shoulders were broad and his hands callused, but they trembled slightly, all the time. His face and arms were covered
with knotted, crisscrossing white scars, and he had a face that
looked like a piece of old barn-board. Except when Horl
showed open anger, amusement, or contempt, Dlan couldn't
read that weather-beaten face—and Dlanazar Duncastle hated
not being able to read faces.

Not that he had much to fear from this old man. Horl
lacked Dlan's strength and reach, and obviously needed him
for this little treasure-foray. Yet if the Silent House was a safe
place, it would've been picked clean centuries ago . . . and
word would have gotten around.

The old man leaned against a wall, his movements slow
and patient, and said, "While we're inside these walls, you
follow my orders—because there are traps here, and places
where things are not as they seem. I know many of these perils, and you do not, so obeying me is only good sense—even
if the Three *do* clasp you as safe as a lover."

That earned him a sharp look from the younger procurer.
The Three didn't chant in Dlan's head or bestow visions upon
him nightly, as the priests claimed to receive—things just always worked out right, every time. His hunches, the chances
he took . . . Life seemed simple enough, and his road to riches
and fame both easy and inevitable. Many struggled for years
and enjoyed nothing of the success that fell into his hands,
again and again—so yes, no matter how skeptical sour old
men were, the Three smiled upon Dlanazar Duncastle. Yet
hold the tongue, and let old Lord Whitehair have his say. Hu-
moring him was a small price to pay, if half the riches he'd
claimed they'd find fell into Duncastle hands ere nightfall.

"In return for such trifling obedience, and the aid you render me in undergoing it, you are welcome to everything we
find—that I don't warn you away from, mind—except a
handful of coins for me, and that copper hand I spoke of."

"Which you want because?"

"Because the magic in it can heal this hand of mine." Horl
held up his left hand, which looked normal enough, though

Dlan had noticed he never seemed to uncurl his fingers from where they hung, half-grasping empty air. "I can barely carry a blade or a crutch with this, lad—let alone use it."

"So you get the magic, and I—"

"Dlan, lad, there'll be *plenty* of magic. Enchanted blades, glowstones, and baubles galore, unless something's gone very wrong, and most of them with power to beggar the one little healing thing I want. Don't worry, lad, there'll be plenty to make you rich, when you sell them, and powerful, after you keep what you don't want to sell, and probably some things that can heal you or anyone much better than the hand . . . things I don't know quite how to use. However, if you find the right sage, and bribe him with one bauble, you could well walk away from him knowing how to use a dozen more, hey?"

Dlanazar nodded slowly. "Don't betray me, old man," he said softly. "I'll be watching."

Horl sighed, scratched at his grizzled red chin, and stretched, his leather armor rippling. It was old, very old, and had worn smooth, bright, and thin. "I'll be watching too, lad, so make me the same promise, hey?"

"By the harbor-horn," Dlan said shortly, and picked up the storm-lantern. "Right; let's be up and sharp, then!"

The old man nodded. "Indeed. I grow no younger." Thrusting himself away from the wall, he lurched off down the passage.

Dlan tensed when Horl drew his sword, a moment later— but then relaxed again in disgust, when the old man started to use it like a walking stick.


"Fall back!" Taraunt Silvertree shouted, and then added a wordless snarl of rage as he slashed a Maerlin cortahar across the face so hard that the man's severed jaw clanged against the crumpling cheekguard of his helm.

The blued metal of Taraunt's armor flashed as he raised his other slender arm in a wave and bellowed, "Back to the North Forehall, and rally to me!"

"Silvertree!" old white-haired Ulburt roared, taking up the order. "Silvertree! Rally to the Lord Taraunt in the North Forehall!"

Abruptly men were shouting and calling all over the crowded chamber, the Maerlins trying to drown out and confuse the dwindling Silvertree defenders, and the veteran armaragors of Silvertree House seeking to make this retreat seem a heartening thing to the wide-eyed and blood-drenched coachmen, gardeners, and chamber-knaves who were tremblingly fighting alongside them.

They might be led by the youngest, smallest, and most pretty-faced of the Lords Silvertree, but by the Three, he'd show them all he could fight!

Taraunt killed another enemy armaragor—at least his score-and-five slaying of the day, though in truth he'd lost count four chambers back—by kicking the twisting, gurgling body of the cortahar he'd just felled into the man's shins, and opening the Maerlin knight's throat as he toppled helplessly forwards. Thank the Three Above these Maerlins had no bowmen, so the fight could at least be steel to steel, and not whistling shafts and death, death, death to all in about as much time as it takes to draw breath for a scream.

The stout, intricately carved stone columns that marched down the spine of Gryphonpost Hall had served the Silvertrees admirably as shields for a long, slaughter-filled time, helping them reap a harvest of heaped and broken Maerlin bodies, but Silvertrees had fallen, too, and the survivors were now too few to hold every gap between pillars. It was time to fall back again, down narrower halls and passages, deeper into the labyrinthine gloom of Silvertree House.

Taraunt slapped the armaragor Narbuth on the shoulder and jerked his head in the direction of the distant Forehall. The tall knight nodded and led the way, Silvertrees plunging after him like scared rabbits as Ulburt brought Lammarth and a handful of the other veterans across like a closing curtain of brandished swords, to join Taraunt as a rearguard.

Four Maerlins fell with blades darting into them from

both sides before someone shouted an order and the invaders fell back.

"I know Desmer's fallen, and I heard Relvaert's command is broken and scattered, too," Taraunt growled to Ulburt as they met and began to back down the passage behind them, "but what of the Lady Sembril?"

"Naught, Lord. Not a word heard. There's some as say she fled, and others that she has a secret place deep in these halls, and went there to hide or work great slaying magic against these Maerlin wolves, but—"

Ulburt shrugged, as if to say that the truth was beyond him, and all a wise old armaragor should concern himself with at such a time was butchering Maerlins while not getting cut down himself, not wondering about women or magic that might or might not be bursting forth into the battle—and might or might not harm friends just as much as foes, if it did.

"Indeed," Taraunt agreed with a wry smile, lunging at a Maerlin who'd dared to charge after them, and setting the man back on his heels to stumble on a fallen blade and crash down. "There's bound to be some as says 'thus,' and some as says 'so,' and—"

"And some as just dies obligingly," Ulburt grunted, driving his blade through the throat of the fallen foe as Taraunt lunged forward again to menace the next two Maerlins, "an' makes the unfolding entertainment of the Three that much simpler. Bards may begin the tales—but blood always ends them. And my job, these days, is simple bloodletting."

Taraunt Silvertree laughed mirthlessly in reply as they retreated down the passage together.


"Milady! Milady, noooooo!"

Sembril could dimly feel cold, wet slime on her limbs and throat, tentacles sliding gently over her and into every gap and seam of her garments. It didn't seem to matter, even if jaws followed, and the tentacles twisted over to favor her

arched body with their swordlike edges, or reared back to
stab and impale. . . .

She had worse and more fascinating matters to consider.
Both in front of her eyes and in her mind behind them, she
was in the same place: floating in cold yet welcoming darkness, adrift in a mind old and fell and ever-hungry, eager for
sorcery and curious to learn what her own mind held.

She should have been screaming by now, as she felt her
clothes torn from her and tentacles slithering over her every
curve, worming wetly into every cleft and opening of her
body, sliding down her throat chokingly. . . .

It all seemed very far away, even when tentacles pulled
her limbs wide with a sudden surge of strength and other
tentacles thrust into her, coiling and wriggling, their bone-
spear tips somehow retracted so that all she felt was shockingly deep and insatiable softness.

Ruala's screams ended abruptly, in a sound that was both
wet and final.

The Lady Silvertree scarcely noticed. The awareness coiling around her was slithering and reaching and exploring,
breaching many doors in her mind that yielded up memories
in floods, remembrances bursting forth in torrents that
should have overwhelmed her . . . that would have torn her
asunder if Sembril hadn't clung sobbingly to the mindsword
and then . . . melted into it.

The Arau soon found a place in her mind that made her
limbs jerk and thrash in spasms not of her own bidding.
Then its tentacles fell away from her wrists and ankles because they were no longer needed: Sembril's body was tugging at invading tentacles eagerly, pulling them on deeper
into her despite the ever-rising pain of being torn apart inside. The Arau was moving her limbs for her now, making
her help in literally tearing open her body and turning it inside out. . . .

As she sank deeper into that coldly coiling mind, Sembril
began to see her heaving body from many angles at once,
views overlapping. She was . . . she was gazing through the

myriad eyes that studded the tentacles of the Arau, and from their many vantages saw her own torso arching as if in rapture amid the black, slimy serpentine forest that held and impaled it, as her belly split open in a sudden wet flood of gore, innards spilling out, one breast riding up incongrously as steaming red ribs parted around wriggling tentacles. . . .

Her pain was a surge of tingling excitement to the Arau, and to her, as well. Sembril rode it like a racing storm through tentacles and the webwork of darker nodes within the great serpent body, flashing everywhere, her awareness like a flame shedding streamers of anger, rage, frustration, grief, and fear in its wake, brightnesses seized on by the cold dark mind all around her, shimmering sparks that flashed, sparkled, and drifted on outwards through the mindgloom. . . .

Ancient it was, and lonely, so lonely. Its kind had always been few, and sorcery had slain some and enslaved others, causing the rest to flee. Sorcery it feared and hungered after, seeking it as true power, for in the deep places of the earth other creatures were no match for it and were consumed almost casually in its endless explorations. . . .

Node after node yielded up its thinking, her brightness both gorging it and cleaving it as readily as its tentacles had ravaged her body. Sembril found a place at last that resisted her, rising up dark and whispering to cloak itself in secrets even as it sought to shield them from her, crouching and turning away, trailing them like tatters. A murmuring thing of bone that faded into something akin to the delicate skeleton of a crumbling leaf before her light . . .

She flooded through that place in an instant of darting ease and found it surrendering to her, offering itself as she'd offered herself, her mindsword fading into mastery that became oneness. She *was* the Arau, now, and it was her, at once the proud and powerless sister of the Silvertree family of Aglirta, and an old, lonely, gnawing thing of tentacles and maedralike stoneslithering.

Almost affectionately it showed Sembril her own head

and shoulders. The rest of her body was entirely gone now, even the wide-spattered gore sucked out of the stone and subsumed again. The flesh of her shoulders melted under the assault of many small wormlike jaws sprouting from restlessly roving tentacles even as she watched.

The tendons of her neck were standing out like sword blades of flesh with the strain of taking in the tentacle she'd swallowed, now so deep and thick that it had unhinged her jaw. Her eyes were staring wildly yet somehow still alive and aware . . . and to think of them brought what they were seeing to the forefront of her great dark shared sea of a mind. She was still seeing out of them, and out of the tentacles sucking at them, too . . . and she, Sembril, could remember everything, and—she willed four tentacles to slash at a wall, and watched them do so with satisfaction—control this mind she now shared.

Her gamble—her sacrifice—had worked.

Fascinated by her sorcery and by conquering her body, the Arau had let her in, and she'd mastered its wits. So now—she watched her head vanish almost absently, pausing only to briefly shape a tentacle into a dark semblance of it while she still had a clear vision of it before her—the Arau with its powers, tentacled serpentine body, hungers, and nature was in the thrall of . . . the mind of Sembril Silvertree.

She laughed then, wildly, not stopping until the stones all around echoed back her shrieks of mirth.

They were still thrumming with the after-echoes of her exultation and doom-fear when Sembril plunged into them in a rolling flood of tentacles and raced through the cold, thick, somehow *choking* darkness.

Raced to a small, nameless chamber near the Hall of the Sunrise where old Ulburt had just growled his valiant last, taking two Maerlin blades that had been meant for Lord Taraunt Silvertree as he slid floorwards, his much-notched blade falling from stiffening hands.

Dark power rose snakelike within her, darkening her vision, awakening a hunger to slay . . . as Sembril lowered the head that was not hers, and growled. The icy black power to

shape stone rose up in her like a surging wave—and like a
wave she flung it out across the chamber, flagstones rippling
up in a tumbling torrent to fling warriors of Maerlin back
and away from her last surviving brother.

Taraunt was groaning from a deep wound in his shoulder,
too pain-wracked to gasp as she flung up encircling walls of
stone around him, the hurled swords of shouting Maerlin
cortahars ringing back futile sparks from their entombing
flanks . . . in the brief time before the stones beneath their
feet rose like the charging fin of a purposeful shark and
drove them to bone-shattering dooms against walls and pillars and archways.

She rained stones down upon them, whirled rocks around
them, and thrust up rocks like spears beneath them, crushing
them into bloody, shapeless smears and scraps of riven armor. And when nothing moved in that hallway, she surged
on, seeking the next Maerlins.

Futile arrows greeted her tentacled coming, and the Arau
choked back what was Sembril in its coldly eager rage to slay.
With all the power it could muster, it—Sembril—lashed out
with the stones of the House, slaughtering every last invader.

And then she went hunting more of them.

The third band, and the fourth, she crushed and slew, but
the fifth was nigh the entrance, and fled out into Aglirta in
shouting terror. Sembril sent tentacles after them and toppled some of the stones of the outer walls onto them, reaping
a bloody harvest and walling a dozen or so inside Silvertree
House. Their screams annoyed her, so she sent her tentacles
out of the stones on all sides of them and tore them apart as
swiftly as she could.

And then silence fell in Silvertree House, but for the
moans and awed curses of the score or so loyal Silvertree
men still alive. She left them be, sliding back through the
cold dark ways to where she'd entombed Taraunt.

Rats and men alike cowered aside as she slithered past.

* * *

Stones in front of him fell away suddenly, gloom flooding into the utter darkness around him like blinding sunlight. Taraunt Silvertree struggled to his feet, hope leaping up from despair within him. His sword was in his hand, and—

"Three Above!" he gasped, almost dropping it.

The slender column of glistening flesh towered over him from the other side of the wall its busy tentacles were dismantling. Scores of eyes blinked at him out of dozens of tentacles as thick as his thighs, many of their ends gaping open into many-fanged mouths. Such a thing could not be, outside nightmares, *should* not be—

*Taraunt.*

The mindvoice was gentle, almost a caress, as comforting as his sister's rare motherly embraces. . . .

With a sudden snarl of rage and fear, Lord Taraunt Silvertree sobbed his way out of awe—who could hope to escape such a beast alive?—and sprang over the steadily tumbling wall of stones, sword flashing as he swung it in both hands, as hard as he could.

Tentacles melted away in a suddenly urgent dance, and he stumbled forward as his mighty swing sliced only air, off-balance and helpless. He was doomed, he was—

*Dead without laying blade to it,* he recalled the old warriors' saying, about men felled like sheep before some mighty beast. It was going to twist his head off, tear him limb from—

Tentacles stabbed past his face like seeking arrows, plucking and coiling, and Taraunt felt his sword snatched away. He clutched for it, vainly, a tentacle like an iron bar before his throat and a finger-burning racing forest of them in front of his hand.

*Taraunt, have you learned nothing but killing? Is the bite of a warblade the only greeting you can give me?*

The voice was in his mind, not his ears, yet its tone was unmistakeable this time.

"S-Sembril?" He couldn't believe it.

This—this *thing,* black and slithery and many-tentacled,

as large as a wagon! *No!* Oh, no! She must be spell-thralling it from hiding, and mindspeaking him with another spell . . . before the Three, this beast *could not* be his sister.

*But I am. Relvaert and Desmer are dead, and I am become—this.*

"Gods, no! What *happened,* Ril?"

*I defeated the Arau, and it devoured me.* No longer mind-scolding him, his sister's voice sounded wry, wearily amused. *So now you are the last living Silvertree, the last of us all. Father's last hope.*

Taraunt sat down against what was left of a wall, collapsing as suddenly as if all the breath and fire had fled from him together. He felt empty . . . discarded. Forgotten. A name out of yesterday, like the snatches of names that clung to the overgrown stones of the long-fallen down-Vale castles. He was become a Maraunt, a Tornsar, a Varthallow. A word adrift in the wind . . .

"You're going to lay a doom on me," he murmured, barely caring. "Something I must do for the Silvertrees. Whether I care to, or not."

Something flashed in the gloom; his sword, returned to him as deftly as if it weighed no more than a feather, and the tentacles that proffered it was the hand of a master swordsman.

*You* could *fall on this,* Sembril's voice said, as gently as she'd ever soothed his childhood tears. *There are worse fates.*

Taraunt looked up at her, anger flaring, and then froze, gazing upon that serpentine bulk and the tall forest of tentacles. Anger died into ice inside him. Worse fates indeed.

"Oh, Ril," he said, almost weeping for her. "Ril!"

*Taraunt, stop this. Please. Take your sword now, and hasten. Sneak away like a thief—I'll lead you to a door far from those the Maerlin know—and get you to Sirlptar. There, hide and breed.*

"Breed?"

*Yes. Take a new name, lay aside fame and high airs, and work for a living. Wed, sire children, and forget high pride.*

*and Silvertree banners. Send your offspring back to claim their heritage only when they're ready, never more than one at a time. The Faceless hate us, and they rule the Vale now, wearing the faces of the king and the barons.*

Taraunt closed his eyes, face tight, and shook his head violently—as if to refuse her, and to deny the world away.

"I'll do it," he whispered slowly, "and hide the name of Silvertree." He shook his head again, regretfully, and then opened his eyes and said, "I was growing tired of Vale wenches anyway."

*After several thousand of them, I'm hardly surprised.*

Taraunt gave her a lopsided grin, ducked his head in the same gesture of embarrassment he'd made since he was six summers old, and murmured, "Sister . . . Sembril, you were always our lady, the only true lady we three louts ever knew." He looked up at her almost fearlessly and asked, "What will become of you?"

*I'll dwell here, slay Koglaur, and become the Curse of Silvertree House. I am what I am, now.*

"Oh, Lady save you, Ril," Taraunt whispered, gazing up at her. "Forefather protect you."

Tentacles stirred restlessly in the darkness. *So much I might have had.*

Her mindwhisper seared him with sudden bitterness. *So much, had you men—all of you men—not snatched my life away from me. Yet this is my home now. Here I'll rule and abide, and yearn for a handsome lord of my own no more. Go, Taraunt. Go, before the Arau's hunger makes me slay you, and never return here.*

Taraunt scrambled up, sword in hand, and backed away in the direction three long tentacles pointed.

*Go through that arch, and watch for my tail far away. Then follow it, until you see the way out. GO, Taraunt.*

Sembril's youngest brother hastened to do as she bid, but turned beyond the archway and looked back at her with the eyes that had melted a thousand hearts. "I . . ." He swallowed. "Ril, will I ever see you again?"

*See me? No. But listen, sometime when your dreams are
still, and I'll whisper to you. Just once or twice, before you die.*

The maedra are curious creatures whose true nature
no honest wizard or sage can say they with certainty
comprehend. Through stone they glide, as effortlessly
and as swiftly as a man strides through mists, and stone
serves them: they can shape it as a child in a river shallows shapes mud, and builds with it. Yet unlike mud
that slumps as soon as the child's hand leaves it,
maedra-shapings stand as solid as if the stone had always and ever been that way.

And the maedra have minds seemingly as sharp as
our own. They can fashion straight, smooth walls, level
floors, spiral stairs, and archways as intricately ornamented as any skilled mason can hope to carve. They
often seem whimsical to us, yet have been proven (by
Marethko and Dunstable recently, and by such long-
ago loremasters as Ingamaerus and Urun Thoul) to remember human promises, faces, and deeds, and to form
friendships and dislikes very much as humans do. They
can be silent, even when passing in and out of stone,
and their snakelike bodies and human-seeming arms
betimes have the strength to break tempered warsteel,
and their claws to rend flesh and sometimes splinter
bone. They seem plentiful in and beneath Silvertree
House and in that northern spur of the Talaglatlad that
men now call the Warfangs, less so elsewhere. Other
Houses of Aglirta claim to know of them only as creatures of fancy-myth, yet tales of them are told in very
backcountry village and woodcutters' glade in all the
Vale, even unto the stinking alleys of Sirlptar. The maedra seem powerful enough to rule humans if they chose
to, though sorcery might prove their scourge (their mastery of it and resistance to it is unknown), but they seem
creatures of the earthy deeps, who seldom stray far
from stone.

Many have observed them hunting humans and

beasts of like or greater size by reaching out of solid stone to rake or strangle, and such prey they devour. I know not if this is their only food, but it is my belief that their stone-shaping involves the saliva of their fanged jaws. It temporarily dissolves stone into something that can be shaped and smoothed, only to harden again in its new configuration.

I believe claims by some sages that maedra are but beasts are rooted in the folly and pride of our kind more than dispassionate and alert observation. Maedra seem our equals in wit and thought, though their aims and schemes are unknown to us, and I believe prudent defenses of Silvertree House must include a close watch over them, and researches on my part into magics that will allow us to see (and ultimately, if such a thing be possible, influence) their thoughts.

I can only speculate (and that fancifully and in truth baselessly) as to why the maedra alter and reshape the House around us all, and here set forth only the most important of the over seven thousand observed and noted changes they've wrought (which I estimate to be no more than a quarter part of their doings, in that part of the House that is above ground).

Saensummer: Built the Orntower and Wyvund's Wing, what we now call Ottro's Gate, and the Southserpent Wall. A great expansion south that included the provision of a well that can only be for our (human) use, given that the maedra can glean moisture from rock and freely tunnel to wherever waters flow, underground.

Draethsummer: Built Highdragon Hall and the domed Raethcra that links the Orntower with the Emmerhall. Extended Wyvund's Wing to a new westernmost tower shaped like a cone, which you dubbed the Netherfang that winter. These constructions increased the size of the House twofold; Wyvund's Wing alone could in comfort house the entire household twice over.

Draethwinter: Added the tower we now call the Naethneedle to the northern end of Highdragon Hall, and filled the Summer Yard with a new hall, larger even than Highdragon. We called it "Skeldaert" after your senior forester, Iruth Skeldaert, who died in the coldest days.

Tzoondsummer: Built the Swordarm Wing, east and south, and divers arch-pierced, low but crenellated walls to enclose five courtyards between it and Wyvund's Wing. These walls have no corner towers, and are laid out at odd angles for no discernible reason.

Tzoondwinter: Brought down Malandar's Hall in the oldest part of the House one night, causing the death of armaragors Rorin Yandarth and Ursandro Thaelen, and raised in that space the tower now called the Moonspire.

Brindynsummer: Opened the floor of Blackwyrm Hall to reveal a great pit reaching down seven dungeon levels, and caused stairs to be placed linking the ground level of the Hall with the three uppermost lower levels. Raised a small and apparently impenetrable tower adjacent to the Netherfang.

Lalaethsummer: Joined the fourth level of Baldimur's Tower and the fifth floor of the Ladytower with a flying bridge in the form of a covered hall with two floor hatches promptly dubbed "the Death-holes" (and almost as swiftly used by young Lord Relvaert to dispose of a hound that had bitten him).

Lalaethwinter: Built a new linking wing between Wyvund's Wing and the Darkhall, which I believe to be one of the first maedra additions to the fortress built by Lord Ravengar Silvertree. Caused the Netherfang to rise another two levels.

This summer, thus far: Raised a new tower beside the Zanderspire, and pierced the floor of the South Forehall to create a new well that yields water of such force and clarity that it can be piped as far as Starstairs Hall. The maedra have thrice removed our pipes and replaced them with smooth-carved channels in the stone of the floor.

Although the river impedes significant building to

the north of the House, all other directions remain available to the maedra, yet they demonstrate a liking or preference for crafting additions to the south and southwest. The Warfangs lie in that direction, across a great distance of wild uplands. I must stress that no conclusion as to maedra purposes can be reached that is not wholly invention; no man knows enough about the creatures to speak or write with authority.

Avulanxyus Havaddun
House Wizard to the Lord Throrn Silvertree

# BOOK THREE

———◆◆◆———

*Taerith Silvertree*

906–948 SR
Lord Baron of Blackgult
And of the Greatest Surprise of His Life

# 1

## A Capture in the Night

Horl paused in front of an empty archway, his hand still held up in the signal that told Dlan to keep the lantern shuttered. "Lost yet?"

"Why? What d'you mean?" the younger man asked sharply.

"Do you still know the way back outside, lad? In case something happens to me?"

"I . . . I think so. Yes."

Horl quelled a chuckle. Dlan was a good liar—but not good enough, in the present company he was keeping.

He made the gesture that told Dlan to unshutter the lantern and point its beam of light *thus*.

Its radiance stabbed out through the archway and roved about in accordance with Horl's always-half-clenched left hand. They surveyed the empty chamber beyond together. Still no beasts . . . just more rubble, dust, and emptiness.

Dlan stifled a sigh. He was beginning to think the fabled fortress had been plundered, long ago, and they'd find nothing.

"They call this Lord Taerith's Hall," Horl murmured, as if remembering something interesting and slightly amusing, long put out of mind. "Though he never set foot in it."

"Oh? How do you know that? And who was Lord Taerith?"

"Well, lad, let's rest a bit, here, and I'll tell a bit of his story. Come to think of it, he was a young Sirl thief living by his wits, too; called himself 'Taerith the Blade.' "

He smirked. "You look glaze-eyed enough to have been listening to old tales for hours, but heed me: there'll be treasure enough to please you before long."

"Three willing," Dlan muttered, but set the lantern down,

and then followed it to the floor, his drawn sword cradled across his thighs.

Horl smiled. Yes, this young fool would serve him just fine.


The storm had grown bored with hurling lances of lightning around the spires of Sirlptar and moved along the coast, leaving only occasional growls of distant thunder behind— along with the busy gurglings of downspouts and the harsher hissings of water dripping onto thousands of already-drenched flagstones. The sea mist hanging in the air was as wet as either, and as thick as smoke. It was just the sort of night Taerith the Blade liked best.

Storms made such a familiar din in Sirlptar that folk huddling inside their houses heard no little noises arising from where no sound should arise, and the clinging damp held smoke close around its cause, keeping lit lamps and fires to a minimum. Just the working conditions most desired by a handsome young thief and kidnapper-for-hire.

And Taerith the Blade was young, handsome, lithe, and alert. "Alert enough," as the Sirl saying went. In his case, that meant sufficiently wary that he'd not yet been caught.

Which was a good thing for Taerith, because being caught thieving or attempting a kidnapping in the house of a noble was usually a death sentence—rendered on the spot, without any need for all the fuss and delay of a public trial.

Taerith knew this very well, and was not quite young enough to think himself invincible or the personal pet favorite of all Three smiling gods . . . but he *was* good at what he did, and a shrewd judge of anyone who spoke with him. Thus far (a matter of some six seasons, which was four more than most of "the best" ever managed) he'd managed to make quite a good living as a thief and kidnapper-for-hire in the bustling city.

It was work he enjoyed, and Taerith was smiling now. That arch crook of a mouth that charmed ladies easily, the one that showed no flash of teeth, and sat so well on his fine-boned face, under dark brows and dancing blue eyes. Long and lean, tousled dark hair a-whirl above dark leathers, he stalked forward like a prowling cat. He hefted the ready capture-hood in his hand, almost purring in satisfaction as he crept through the darkened house of the noble lady he'd been half-paid to capture.

The as-yet-unwed Lady Kaedyth Mramsurr, of the Mramsurrs of Teln. Tall and gravely beautiful, and possessed of quick wits, an enchanting smile, and a midnight flood of long, dark hair. Her vices seemed to consist of nothing more than avidly reading books of all sorts, enjoying an occasional tall glass of something exotic, and dancing alone to her own soft singing. He'd been watching her for three days now, and had to admit that his client—fat, sweating, and greedy though the man might be, with pudgy over-beringed fingers and an oily, perfumed oh-so-pointed smallbeard— could not be faulted in this particular matter of taste, at least.

And Aunjoszmur Hamoraunth, dealer in gold finechains and jewels of distinction, had paid a handsome weight in gold to buy the attention and preparation time of Taerith the Blade. The delivery of the Lady Kaedyth's person would bring as much again, unless Hamoraunth was far more stupid than his reputation suggested, and dared practice deceit. Sirl law frowned upon thieves and kidnappers, but it positively scowled—a scowl involving whips, goads, salt laid in slicing wounds, and hot irons until the remains were ready for the grave—on swindlers and trade-cheats. A thief carries off the goods of today, but a dishonest trader harms the takings of all merchants on the morrow, and for many days thereafter.

Enough of Hamoraunth's greedy leerings; what should be in the mind of an accomplished procurer right now was the goods of today: the Lady Kaedyth.

Who at this moment should be just *there* in the gloom ahead of him, alone in her bedchamber at the far end of this wing. Guards were posted at its outside doors two floors below, and a pair of loyal serving-maids slept in rooms beneath those of his quarry, but all the rest of this end of her house should be deserted. Such were her orders, and she was accustomed to being obeyed.

Yes, she was the sort of wench Taerith liked, and that would make his work all the more enjoyable. There'd be a trap on her door, of course, and probably a second one involving a coffer of body-jewels "carelessly" left open on a moonlit table in her outer room . . . but there'd be nothing to bar her maids from reaching her up a private back stair, if she rang for anything. A maid's room would be his ready road to the prize.

He took a side-stair down to the darker hall below, and softly opened the door of the room belonging to Sharalta, the fatter of the two maids. A heart of tender love and eyes that missed no need or anticipation of the Lady Kaedyth, but their owner liked a little plate of skoavies and a thimble-glass of calamanta before retiring, and it had been the work of but an idle moment to drop a pinch of aumurt into the decanter her lady kindly provided for her.

Gentle snoring came from the large bed to his left, and the faintest of glows came from the hooded lantern on its stone-bowl table beside . . . the narrow, unadorned door he sought.

The stair beyond was inky-dark, and Taerith drew a disk of stone from his belt and held it against the lantern-hood until the light aroused its own eerie glow, and he could use it as the dimmest of hand-lamps, seeking trip-threads, unusual steps, and the like. He found none, and returned the stone to its pouch ere he reached the turn of the stair. With slow care he flexed his fingers inside the capture hood, making sure once more that it wasn't twisted or tangled, and drew the door open, just a crack.

Darkness beyond, and faint, regular breathing.

Taerith opened the door boldly, and then froze again, letting his eyes learn the gloom. Distant lightning flickered at the windows, and fresh rain began to pelt down on the roof. He waited.

Nothing.

He stepped into the room, and immediately to one side of the door, to a spot on the thick rugs he'd already surveyed narrowly. Twice.

No movement, nor light. The canopies of the great bed hung

unmoving, a handspan apart, just as they'd been at his first glimpse of them.

Taerith strolled almost casually—and soundlessly—across the room, around behind the head of the bed, keeping well away from the storm-flicker and that gap in the canopies. Those who sleep with their draperies parted usually do so to have a glimpse of the night outside and the light of the morning, and rarely turn their backs on the openings they've caused. And those who come to kidnap usually prefer to pounce with a capture hood from behind, ere a quarry can draw breath to scream or have time to get a hand up to claw at the hood—or deliver a knife from under a pillow into an even tenderer place.

The bed had a high back and foot, of ornately carved wood flanked by slender spiral decorative pillars. The draperies were gathered and tied to those pillars with tasseled cords by day, but by night hung free, and it was the work of but a moment to—bring the capture hood up as he leaned in, and then smoothly down over the serenely sleeping face. He whipped the long-tressed head up from the pillow to drag the hood down, putting a firm elbow into a noble gut to drive forth her air in a gasp that strangely did not come. . . .

Which was when two arms that felt as heavy and as strong as a great ship's mooring cables slapped around Taerith's throat from behind, clasping him so tightly that they seemed to have instantly turned to unyielding stone.

He could not even turn his head. His arms were pinned to his sides, the capture hood falling from straining fingers as he struggled to breathe, struggled to—

A darkly beautiful face leaned around from behind his shoulder to smile at him, so closely that her faintly spicy breath tickled his cheeks. The noblewoman's head seemed to float at the end of a grotesquely long, flexible neck.

"Oh, dear," the Lady Kaedyth Mramsurr observed lightly. "It seems the procurer has been . . . procured. Fair evening, Taerith the Blade."

"Uh . . . urkh . . . ," Taerith remarked brightly, terror choking him more than the unbreakable but not overly tight grip. "How——?"

Something that looked like an impossibly long worm, or snake, reached out of the darkness and lifted a nightcloak away from a glowstone on a side table, flooding the bed with soft light. Taerith gaped down at the hooded woman on the bed in front of him, her limbs sprawled sleepily in a silken gown. One of her legs ended in a shapely foot, but the other narrowed to an ankle that became a long, snakelike tendril of flesh curving down over the edge of the bed only to rise up again into—a tree of flesh, now moving another branch or tentacle slowly towards Taerith's face. Two others were the coils already entwined around his torso and neck, flanking the *second* body of Lady Kaedyth Mramsurr that was now gliding around in front of him, neck shortening smoothly as it did so, to join the face that was smiling at him.

"I'm not a noblewoman of Teln, as you can see," she said, her face changing subtly. Her eyes became larger and darker, and her cheekbones higher—still beautiful, but somehow older, and wiser, and knowingly formidable rather than serene. "I'm a Koglaur—oh, yes, we do exist—and I call myself Maretta."

"Does—does—?"

"Aunjoszmur Hamoraunth know what he sent you to bring back to him? Oh, yes." The third tentacle glided a little nearer to his nose, and he shrank back from it.

She shook her head. "Fear not my appendage, Taerith— unless you're foolish enough to scream, or try to work magic."

Taerith swallowed. "And if I did?" he whispered, trying not to let his teeth chatter.

"I'd give your mouth this to choke on, and buy silence that way," came the calm reply. Yet another tentacle reached out from behind Taerith to touch something else on the table by the glowstone. "I dislike noise and tumult."

Whatever it was flashed once, like an emerald star finding a gap in night-clouds, and the Koglaur purred, "Your patron should join us momentarily. No recriminations, please.

Near-silence is our customary goal, as it is yours. Let us all try to make shared calmness prevail."

"W-what do you want of me?" Taerith gasped. He was going to *die* here, torn apart or devoured by this fey monster! He should scream, bring someone . . . hah! By the Dark One, it'd be but the smaller, more slender maid, unless one of the doorguards heard. And either way, these tentacles would tear his head off long before . . .

"The right choice," the shape-shifting thing told him, its body shifting again. Below Maretta's face now was the most voluptuous female form he'd ever seen, thrusting ardently towards him, offering . . .

The effect was grotesque, not alluring. He swallowed, shuddered, and twisted his eyes shut, his gorge rising.

"Get—get—," he choked.

"Away? Very well." A tentacle took him around the hips, and another behind the knees, lifting him as easily as if he'd been a babe and putting him on the bed. There seemed to be no sleeping woman, counterfeit or otherwise, lying there any longer, but when Taerith opened his eyes, the smiling shape-changer was gone from his view. The tentacles around his hips and legs remained, however, just as firm and hard as those holding his neck and torso. She was behind him, holding him prisoner. And the tentacle with which she'd promised to choke him waited just to one side of his mouth, pointed at his teeth like a spike. Helplessly awaiting his doom, Taerith tried not to tremble.

He was sitting on the high bed where the sleeping "Lady Mramsurr" had lain. The draperies of its canopy were now drawn back to show him the nightdark chamber with its occasional flickers of distant lightning . . . and a particular flagstone, well beyond the bed, that was starting to glow.

The radiance was a faint amber at first, a thin line like firelight seen under a door that ran along one edge of the stone. It grew swiftly in brightness and size, outlining the entire flagstone—which was large enough for an embracing couple to stand together on, or a procurer clasping a hooded captive from behind—with a pulsing glow.

The light looked like a fire, if a fire could rage without fuel, heat, or smoke. On another night and in another place, Taerith might have been fascinated to see such a thing, but now he scarcely cared. It was a magic that had something to do with bringing the jewel-merchant Aunjoszmur Hamoraunth here . . . an arrival that could only hasten his own doom.

In silence the stone grew brighter, and then quite suddenly someone was standing on it, in the heart of that glow. A fat, all-too-familiar figure, shuffling forward towards the bed, rubbing those fat-fingered hands with a gleaming-eyed, leering smile.

Aunjoszmur Hamoraunth, of course. The moment the fat merchant's feet left the glowing flagstone, its light winked out—and there was an instant of deep gloom before one fat hand waved almost lazily towards the side table, and the glowstone flared into astonishing brightness that made the room brighter than the full sun of dayheight.

"He seems unharmed," Hamoraunth commented, in a voice deeper and clearer than Taerith had ever heard from him before.

"He's had a bad fright, of course," the Koglaur replied from behind Taerith, "but yes, I don't think I broke anything."

The dealer in gold finechains and jewelry nodded and suddenly straightened, a shimmer of spell-sparks heralding his own shape-change. He stood taller, now, with a high bare forehead and forbidding dark eyes, the oily beard gone white and sharp-curled, all the rings gone from long-fingered, almost womanly hands. He lifted one wintry eyebrow, and in that same deep, clear voice asked Taerith, "Do you know who I am, procurer?"

Taerith stared at him helplessly, and then shook his head.

"My name, Taerith," the man said almost sternly, "is Garlen Blackgult."

The procurer shivered. The greatest wizard in all Sirlptar. He opened his mouth to speak, and found his mouth so dry that he had to try shaping his first words twice before any sound came out. "Au—Aunjoszmur Hamoraunth's dead, isn't he?"

"No, he's merely growing steadily thinner than my false seeming of him, in a dungeon far below our feet," Blackgult said. "Neither Maretta nor I slay needlessly."

Taerith stared at him. "Is . . . is my death 'needful'?"

"I hope not," Blackgult said gravely. "It all depends on the choice you make."

"The right choice," Maretta added, "or another one."

Taerith shook his head in bewilderment. "And the Lady Mramsurr? The—ah, real one?"

The Koglaur smiled. "The more secrets a man knows," she said almost merrily, "the more daggers he holds against his own heart. Know less, and be safer."

The Sirl wizard smiled almost sadly. "You already know far more than enough to be dead, procurer. I'm sure you've realized that already."

"I am trying to find a way to stay alive," Taerith replied carefully. "Would you like your half-payment back?"

Blackgult smiled. "Not unless you make the wrong choice."

The procurer drew in a deep breath, tried to master his fear—these two were *playing* with him, dark laughter of the Three—swallowed, and said, "So you hired me to capture a noble lady whom you knew to be this . . . Maretta. You did this to lure me here, where the two of you will now force me to make a choice. May I be permitted to know clearly what my choices are, or is it 'guess wrong and die'?"

"Your choice will be as blunt and clear as we can make it," the wizard told him, "and we'll begin the clarifying now. Taerith, who were your parents?"

The procurer frowned, and then spread his hands in a shrug of helplessness. "Dead before I was old enough to remember. Locksmiths, I suppose, given that it was locksmiths who shared me as a fetch-and-runner, rather than folk of one family. Or perhaps they were folk who owed debts to more than one lock-maker."

Blackgult shook his head.

"What was your father's name?" Maretta asked quietly, her voice coming from just behind Taerith's left ear.

The procurer tried to shrug, but found that the tentacles binding him were as immobile as castle walls. "I know not," he replied. "I've never known."

"Any hint of your kin, a family name?"

"None," Taerith replied truthfully, trying to shake his head.

"Let me give it to you, then," Garlen Blackgult said in suddenly brisk tones, striding forward to stand close by the bed. "Silvertree."

Taerith frowned up at him. "Silvertree? *That* Silvertree? The haunted nobles of Aglirta?"

"*That* Silvertree," the wizard said firmly, a faint smile fading onto his face. "Treasure and huge haunted palace and all."

Taerith gaped at him, and then tried—really struggling against the tentacles for the first time since his first frantic reaction to them—to turn and stare at Maretta. Surprisingly, she let him swing around . . . to see her nodding in agreement. She was not smiling anymore.

"Tell us what you've heard of the Silvertrees," she suggested gently.

Taerith stared at her. "I . . . uh . . . ah . . . they used to be powerful in Aglirta, they have lands on the Silverflow shores south of the king's isle, and there's a huge ruined palace there that no one lives in, that folk say ghosts change and build upon constantly, so it grows and grows, and no man knows all its rooms and ways. Everyone says there's magic there, and rich treasure. Many adventurers have gone in seeking those riches, but few have come out again. Only a handful have found wealth, though they say a man called Rarauthin and a few companions, and someone else— Laercel? Laersor?—ended up *really* rich."

Taerith smiled weakly. It all sounded fabulous and fanciful as he said it. Blackgult gestured for him to continue, a slashing, commanding wave of a hand that did not welcome refusal.

Taerith eyed that hand for a moment, and added, "The Silvertrees did something bad or disloyal, or got themselves cursed somehow; everyone has different tales. The great wizard Harabrentar of Sirlptar, before he died, boasted that he put a curse on the Silent House that drives Silvertrees mad. The mage Gorstal of the Isles says a Silvertree is destined to take the crown of Aglirta amid blood and fire, and then renounce it."

He waved a hand. "There're dozens of tales more. As for the Silvertrees, they're all hidden, and most years one or two of them appear out of nowhere, and try to claim their title and lands. There's some royal decree or other that makes slaying or hiding them a crime, so the barons keep bringing them to the king of Aglirta. He sends them under guard into Silvertree House—where some get torn apart the first night. Others go mad and slowly waste away, and either wander into the far ways of their palace, or slay themselves in madness after fleeing it. Men say this is part of their curse, though no one seems to agree on just what this Curse is, or how they acquired it."

"You think you're telling us lies and rumors and exaggerations," Maretta said gently, "but truth underlies all your words. Those Silvertrees who die their first night in the palace are false claimants, but those who go mad *are* of the blood Silvertree. Both magic and riches can be found in Silvertree House, but as you say, only a handful of adventurers emerge from it; most vanish forever in its shadowed halls."

The wizard nodded. "Taerith Silvertree, it's not yet time for your choice. First, we'll tell you *why* both true and false Silvertrees keep emerging from shadows, and why the kings of Aglirta haven't simply seized their lands years ago, and hurled down Silvertree House into rubble."

Taerith sighed. "You're going to want me to go in there, aren't you?"

Blackgult held up his hand in a "cease" gesture, and then lifted it to Maretta, who said, "We'll speak of this in good time, Taerith. Yes, in good time. When we've told you all you need to know to make a clear choice."

Using his newfound freedom to turn his head, Taerith nodded.

She smiled faintly. "Men make war and dispute with one another, and so do—my kind. *Our* war is for rule over Aglirta."

"Faceless fight against other Faceless?" Taerith asked tentatively.

Blackgult nodded. "Various Koglaur desire to use Silvertrees as weapons against rival Koglaur in this covert struggle, which has been going on for . . . centuries."

The procurer shook his head in disbelief. "Centuries? Without armies? And no hint of it in rumor or Vale lore, or the warnings of priests?"

"My kind," Maretta said, with just a hint of a sharp, icy edge to her voice, "do not believe in damaging or destroying what they fight over."

"Taerith," Blackgult said firmly, "just—hear us. Believe or not later, but heed now, until you've heard it all." He waved a hand at the windows and added, "Some Koglaur who desire to control your kin have, ah, 'adopted' the Silvertrees of Sirlptar."

"You make it sound as if I belong to a strong and numerous family," Taerith murmured. "Are we all . . . in hiding, here in the city?"

"Numerous Sirl families are descended from Silvertree stock. Most, like you, know nothing of their heritage—until someone tells them. That 'someone' is always a Koglaur."

"Various of my kind," Maretta added, "have manipulated and aided Silvertree after Silvertree into trying to reclaim their lands and title. Some of the false Silvertrees have been tests arranged by Koglaur, and some have been humans hunting treasure. Yet the true Silvertrees all go mad and die once they try to inhabit Silvertree House, regardless of our aid—and we want to know why."

"Yes," Garlen Blackgult said, folding his arms across his chest and looking down at Taerith expressionlessly. "We want to know why . . . and so come at last to your choice."

Taerith looked up at him, but asked nothing.

Maretta smiled as if his silence pleased her, and remarked, "I see three roads before Taerith the Blade. One is death—for you know far too much, now, to walk Darsar freely. As I'd not want to waste a chance to . . . experiment on a Silvertree, your passing is likely to be slow and painful. I say this not as a threat, but merely to make your choice very clear."

"That's your choice of outright refusal," Blackgult added, "but there are two other choices. One is feigning agreement but fighting against us or seeking to flee us, which will result in your soon entering Silvertree House as a mind-thrall controlled by our spells, a 'Baron Silvertree' who's little more than a marching puppet. There, as we watch from afar, you'll presumably suffer the same fate as your kin who've gone before you."

"And my last choice?" Taerith asked, in a voice that was almost calm.

"Work with us willingly, and enter the palace under our spellwatch but with full freedom, as our partner. We'll suggest and advise and provide what aid we can as you explore—and hopefully uncover the secret of the so-called 'Curse.'"

"With such clear choices, I am compelled to accept this third and last," the procurer said without hesitation. "As you expected me to."

Both the wizard and the Koglaur smiled. "That's good," Maretta said. "I should add that we don't intend to tarry overmuch, once your decision is made."

Taerith Silvertree nodded and said almost wearily, "So cast your spell."

Blackgult's smile, as he raised both hands and the tingling radiances flooded out to engulf the procurer, revealed more than mere satisfaction.

It seemed almost . . . proud.


"So they led him by the nose through this place? Like you're doing to me?"

"Easy, lad, easy. There'll be chances enough for excite-

ment and the Three smiling on you and treasure glittering in
your hand soon enough. Trust me."

Dlan eyed him thoughtfully over the faint, hot glow of the
shuttered lantern. "So you keep saying . . ."

Old Horl spread his hands. "Now, then: Who got you out of
Sirlptar a few running paces ahead of men who'd have flayed
your hide right off you and then broken all your fingers—and
*then* slit your throat?"

"You did," the young procurer said grimly, and then lifted
his head. "Yet if you hadn't, I'd've won through somehow!
The Three—"

"Yes, *yes*," Horl said gruffly. "I thought that once, too. See
these scars? Turns out I was wrong a time or two, or there
were too many other young and overconfident fools for the
Three to be paying attention just at the moment I needed
them. Taerith Silvertree, now . . ."

Dlan sighed. "Yes?"


"Everything seems . . . green," Taerith muttered suspiciously, peering around.

*That's one of the spells I cast on you,* Blackgult's voice
murmured in his mind. *Without it, you'd be groping blindly
right now, in utter darkness.*

*(DON'T move about),* Maretta added sharply. *(There are
many traps. Silvertree House is never as empty and lifeless
as it looks.)*

"I find myself unsurprised," Taerith muttered wryly, and
was startled at a sudden dancing mind-caress that seemed to
be Maretta's mirthful reaction to his tone. It felt wonderful,
and he shuddered against the nearest wall for a moment or
two as her chuckle passed. Then he drew in a deep breath
and asked, "Where exactly in the House am I?"

*A north-south passage linking the Orbarlum with Mur-
crester's Hall,* the wizard mind-told him. *Beware the traps.
Step on no flagstone that has dagged edges.*

"Does that warning hold true throughout the House?"

*No. In a few places only—but everywhere the flagstones hold meaning. The maedra can shape stone, and so have no need to use fitted paving stones.*

"So which direction do you prefer I proceed?"

*The way you're facing, towards the Orbarlum.*

"Why?"

*(We can sense awakened magic, a little, through you.)* Maretta's mind-voice held excitement. *(The magic is strongest in that direction. Others have in the past reported the same thing.)*

Taerith drew his slender sword and hefted it as he glanced up at the ceiling, seeking nooses or drop-blocks or clinging beasts. All that met his eyes was smooth stone and deeper darkness. He stepped cautiously forward in the gloom, peering at each flagstone.

Around him, the vast stone House was empty and dark. It was cool but dry, and free of the dust and spiderwebs he'd expected. Though the passage he was in had a high, bare stone ceiling, his movements awakened no echoes.

It was a long, long hallway, pierced at irregular intervals with closed, unadorned stone doors not quite twice his own height. He could not see how they opened or what held them shut, and did not care to find out. Blackgult's magic had delivered him to the midst of this passage, leaving him no refuge to retreat to.

Abruptly, something slithered across the passage, far ahead. Something large and scaled and serpent-tailed, that had apparently failed to notice him. Taerith froze, peering and straining to hear any sign of its return, or doings.

"Was that one of those . . . what did you call them? Maedra?"

*Probably. Continue along the passage.*

Taerith thought of a rude and derisive reply as he moved forward, again, but something akin to tolerant amusement rippled through his mind: Blackgult's reaction. Maretta mind-sighed, and Taerith felt suddenly ashamed. He was going to die here, but there was no need to spend his last breaths cringing and cursing. He was the best procurer in all Sirlptar, he was. . . .

Springing back in scrambling haste as a large section of floor in front of him suddenly sank with a deep, floor-shaking rumbling, rising sharply on his right—and flipped over, falling back into place with a crash that snatched him off his feet and rattled his teeth as he came down.

Taerith fell heavily on the still-shuddering floor, convinced he'd caught a glimpse of a man's hand, just for a moment. Its owner must have been tumbling down into the grinding gulf revealed by the moving stone, and presumably crushed and slain in that great crash.

"Claws of the Dark One!" he gasped, his nose scraping still-thrumming flagstones. "Who—?"

"*You* did that!" an unfamiliar voice snarled. "You killed Flarult!"

Taerith rolled hastily to one side and up to his feet, making sure he still had hold of his sword.

A door ahead of him on the passage wall to his left was open, and three grim-looking men were peering out of it. They seemed to be able to see in the dark just as well as he could . . . and they were looking at him.

Two of them wore well-used armor and bore drawn swords in their hands, but one in the middle—the one who'd spoken—wore an ill-fitting jack of battle-leathers that left his arms bare . . . and those arms were swiftly sketching intricate gestures in the air.

The man was casting a doom-spell on Taerith.

# 2

## Men with Horns

*Stand your ground. Look unafraid. Ignore his casting.* Blackgult's mind-voice was calm and firm—but then, the wizard could afford to be. He was safe back in an opulent bedchamber in a grand house in Sirlptar, far from this monster-roamed ruin and three angry men.

Taerith swallowed and did as he was bid. After all, where could he run to? The passage was long and straight behind him, sporting only closed doors and many of the flagstones whose shape Blackgult had warned him meant that traps— like the one that had just swallowed and crushed a man, right in front of him—lay beneath them.

Taerith the Blade stood his ground and tried to look unafraid. Three Above, what a night! Everything changed, his life swept away, and—

The air around him exploded in ruby flame with a white-hot heart. Tongues of ravening fire reached for him with a roar.

In spite of Blackgult's reassurances, Taerith flinched—but the wizard's magic flooded over and past him, dwindling into a cloak of blue smoke and shadows in an instant . . . and was gone.

Leaving the three grim men blinking at him in astonishment, the leather-jacked wizard most of all. He gaped, ruddy face paling in its frame of sweat-soaked hair and beard, and gasped, "Who *are* you?"

*Tell him Taerith Silvertree.*

The procurer did that, and the three men stirred in wary amazement. "Are . . . are you a ghost?" one of the armsmen demanded.

*Say nothing.* Taerith gave the three men a wordless smile,

and whispered under his breath, "No, I'm a doomed puppet. *Much* better a fate."

A cold darkness that could only be Blackgult's anger touched his mind in answer, but the brief ecstasy of Maretta's mirth joined it.

The armsman was eyeing Taerith narrowly and fumbling at a belt-pouch. His companion-at-arms took a quick pace to one side, as warriors do when they want to outflank a foe and strike at him from two sides at once—but stopped and held his ground when the first warrior plucked something out of his pouch and tossed it to Taerith.

It was a silver coin, winking once in its flight. Rather than have it strike his chest, the procurer snatched it out of the air with his free hand.

It did not explode with magical fury, and he uncurled his fingers, regarded its unfamiliar minting—it was shaped like the blades of a double-sided ax—and raised his eyebrows.

"My rates are rather higher than this, I'm afraid," he told the man who'd thrown it. "But as you can see, I'm no ghost. I had nothing to do with—" He pointed at the floor with his sword. "—*that,* or the fate of your friend, either."

*Ask them why they're here.*

The wizard frowned at Taerith, and waved at the armsmen to spread apart and advance on Taerith from two sides. "So, do you dwell here?" he asked.

*Ask rather than answering. Tell him it's your turn to hear answers.*

So Taerith did that, and the three men exchanged swift glances. The older of the two warriors growled, "Fair dealing. We were . . . drawn here by the dreams."

"Dreams?"

"Sent by the Three, perhaps," the other warrior said, "Though which of the Blessed I couldn't say."

"Dreams that would not let us sleep until we were journeying here," the wizard put in. "To fight the horned men."

"Horned men?"

The three men frowned at Taerith, and the two warriors

took a step closer. "Have you not seen—?" the wizard asked softly.

*Sheathe your sword and raise both your hands.*

Taerith did as he was bid, and blue lines of lightning promptly crackled between his fingers, causing the three men to halt.

"I see enough," Taerith told them gently over the crackling bolts, hoping his calm speech would sound menacing. "Maedra. Others. But no horned men, as yet."

"The maedra dwell here," the wizard said, eyeing the lightnings with new respect, "in the walls. They battle the stag-headed sorcerers alongside us, but for the most part ignore us."

"Who are 'us'?" Taerith asked, before Blackgult could tell him to.

"Adventurers who came here to plunder—many, from all over Asmarand—and a few Aglirtan hedge-wizards who cast the wrong spells and got plucked here."

"Plucked by what?"

"The dream-spinner. Whatever it is that wants us here, fighting the horned men."

"And if you just look around for treasure, or try to leave? What then?"

"The whispers start," one of the warriors blurted. "In your mind. Warning, threatening . . . pleading. You mustn't listen, for she guides you false. Always you find yourself headed back—*there*." He jerked his head down the passage towards the Orblarum, in the direction Taerith had been heading.

" 'She'?"

"The voice that whispers in our minds seems female," the wizard said, frowning again at Taerith. "I'm surprised you don't hear it." He took a step forward, raising something that hung on a fine chain around his neck as if to ward Taerith away, and added, "And it's more than time for *you* to answer *us* again, stranger. You claim your name is Silvertree, so I ask once more: Do you dwell here?"

Blackgult gave him no guidance, so Taerith replied, "Not yet. I hope to, when—"

"You proclaim your lineage to the King of Aglirta and demand your lands and title," the wizard said almost wearily. "You'll be the seventh this season."

"Eighth," one of the armsmen corrected. "That fool who rode in the front gate three days back, remember?"

The wizard snorted. "And died braining himself on an archway because he was too crazed to dismount, so he fell from his saddle straight down the forecourt well. Leaving it undrinkable for the rest of us, Three take him!"

"Who are these horned men? Are they Silvertrees, or—?"

"Strangers," the wizard replied. "Sorcerers, invading from a far land—a warm land called Omnthur, they claim, that's not on any map of Darsar *I've* ever seen—through a gate opened by their magic. It lies in the room beyond the Orblarum, and as far as I can tell, they come to explore and plunder like any Sirl or upland adventurer."

*Did you see his eyes flicker? He's just decided he's told you too much, and you'll have to die. Get over to the wall on your left, right away.*

Taerith obeyed Blackgult's mind-voice with a casual air, stroking his chin and frowning as if seized by thought. The wizard snapped his fingers to attract the eyes of the two warriors and made a certain swift, circling finger-gesture. Rather reluctantly the armsmen started to move forward.

*Take a step back. Notice the wedge-shaped block in the wall? Put your fingers on it, and say "Silvertree."*

Taerith did as he was bid—and the wall suddenly swung away under his fingers, a narrow door opening inwards into darkness.

*Get through!*

He sprang to obey as both warriors shouted and charged, swords thrusting.

*Duck to the left, and run!*

As he shouldered through the narrow opening, magical radiance suddenly flared in front of him, illuminating two passages curving off into dim distance—but Taerith whirled around to the left, into darkness, and ran.

*Now halt, turn around to watch, and keep quiet.*

Again he obeyed, in time to see the armsmen burst through the door. They eyed the two passages and each other, cursing, and then chose one way and plunged along it. A few moments later, one of them screamed, and the other shouted in fear. There was a frantic clanging and ringing, as if a sword was hacking wildly at stone, and then the choked-off, gurgling beginnings of another scream. Then silence.

*Stay still.*

Taerith had been going to do that anyway. Breathing heavily, he watched the open door. The wizard peered cautiously in, looked this way and that without seeing Taerith, and then called two names.

The reply was silence, so he shouted them, which won him some echoes and then silence again. Cursing horribly, he drew back his head and disappeared.

*Turn around and walk forward slowly and carefully, with your hand out. When you feel a stone wall, reach to your right. Turn the handle you'll find there.*

"You seem to know this place rather well," Taerith murmured.

*Yes, I do seem to, don't I?*

And Taerith had to be content with that sarcastic reply. The darkness around him now was impenetrable to whatever seeing-magic Blackgult had cast on him; he had to grope blindly. When he found and turned the handle, something large, unseen, and stony grated right in front of him as it moved—the wall, sliding to his left on rollers of some sort?—and a faint breeze touched his face.

*Now wave your hand around in front of you, but DON'T step forward.*

When Taerith obeyed, a faint amber radiance sprang into being high in the air before him, revealing a small, square, high-ceilinged room. Narrow archways like the one he was gazing through pierced all of its walls, and a waist-high cylindrical stone plinth stood in the center of its otherwise bare floor. Atop the plinth lay a few fragments of what looked like shattered and twisted metal, the pieces of something that had once been rounded, like a helm or bowl. The

shards of silvery metal were discolored a vivid blue and purple, apparently scorched, but bore not a trace of rust.

"What is—or was—that?"

*I know not. The curious little mysteries of this place are
best left alone. The coin that was thrown to you: the wizard
can trace you through it with a simple spell. Get rid of it.
Throw it forward into the room.*

Taerith did so. It bounced once, and then rolled a little
way on its edge and fell over, shimmering to a stop.

*Good. The room is safe to pass through. Go to the arch-
way directly across from this one, but touch nothing except
the floor.*

"Couldn't you have used a rat or a war-dog just as easily
as me?" Taerith asked aloud, as he obeyed. The archway led
into a short passage that opened into another room. From in
the distance, somewhere ahead, he heard the sudden clash of
swords.

Blackgult did not reply.


> *Ah, to be led like a thrall through the House. I know how
> that feels. I know all too well.*
> *At least Taerith's fate was not so cold or lonely as mine.*
> *By the Three and the older gods who flourished and faded
> before them, I am so cold.*


Fire flared a room away, hurling sudden light onto ceilings
and walls, and with it came despairing shouts and a wild, rattling series of clangs and crashing sounds.

Armored men being hurled against unyielding stone, by
the sounds of it . . . or rather, *pieces* of armored men. Taerith
frowned and went down the passage like a procurer on the
prowl.

He came to a stop when he saw something silhouetted in a
sudden burst of bright blue magical flame, in the room beyond. The something was large and serpentine, and in its
pain flung up two arms that looked like those of a brute-

muscled human. When the spell-burst died, the thing slumped to the floor trailing little yellow licks of flame and streamers of smoke. It shuddered and arched once, and then rolled over and lay sprawled and still.

"So should I go on?" Taerith murmured.

*Keep to the wall, and try not to be seen. Whatever slew the maedra may still be in the room.*

It was. A crouching Taerith had a brief glimpse of a tall, dark robed figure. Its dusky brown head was surmounted by a rack of black antlers as splendid as those of any stag-head he'd ever seen mounted on a Sirl tavern wall—and such trophies of hunting prowess are popular in Sirlptar. There was a flash of red-rimmed yellow eyes as the stag-headed sorcerer peered in Taerith's direction, and the procurer shrank back.

As he did so, Taerith became aware of a faint murmur at the corners of his mind. He couldn't hear any words, though he knew it was speaking some—in floods and waves of entreaty and sly suggestion—but was suddenly reluctant to withdraw.

WHAT IS THAT? he tried to ask, thinking his question rather than daring to mutter it with the stag-headed sorcerer so near.

*(The Whispering Mind of Silvertree House. The lure that drew so many here to make war on the Omntharr.)* Maretta's voice sounded grim.

*Or, if you prefer, the Curse.* Blackgult's tone was more brisk. *More, we cannot say—because we do not know.*

SO WHAT DO I DO?

*Creep forward again. Is the Omntharr sorcerer still there?*

Taerith crawled this time, moving very slowly and stealthily, peered into the room where the maedra lay dead, and was thankful to be able to breathe, "No."

*Good. Keep crawling. Go to that far archway and look out. The passage beyond it runs almost straight to the Orblarum.*

The procurer did as Blackgult directed. He was in time to see two maedra scrambling to melt *into* the passage wall before—more bright blue mage-fire blasted them, leaving their sagging, blackened bodies half-in and half-out of the solid

stone wall. A little way farther along the passage, several
men in robes lay sprawled and dead, one of them headless
and one of them apparently a-crawl with tunneling, flesh-
devouring snakes.

The stag-headed figure was striding away down the passage, past a man who sat frozen in death, staring forever at
wisps of dying, crackling lightning that sprang lazily from
one of his hands to the other, and back again.

"I seem to be intruding on a battle," Taerith muttered,
crawling forward. "Do you have any more of those secret
doors or passages handy?"

*None that my spells reveal to me,* Blackgult's mind-voice
said wryly. *You'll just have to do this the old, reckless way.
I'd crawl and creep, if I were you.*

"Have my thanks," Taerith murmured with sardonic for-
mality, starting down the passage.

The stag-sorcerer had disappeared into a large chamber at
the far end of the corridor by the time the procurer edged
cautiously past the body that was sprouting wriggling
snakes. By then, Taerith barely cared about that Omntharr;
the whisperings in his mind had grown stronger and more
strident, and now seemed to include his own name.

It was as if the Curse, the mysterious *something* that was
cajoling him, had recognized him. As a Silvertree, presumably. Recognized him with a sort of delight, and was now
taking an eager and personal interest in getting him to hurry
ahead to the Orblarum, or presumably—if that wizard's
words could be trusted—the room beyond it, where the stag-
sorcerers had their gate.

As he thought about it, the whisperings in his mind rose
into almost shrill excitement and swirled up into brightness,
a scene growing swiftly larger in his thoughts as both Blackgult and Maretta murmured in surprise. Taerith couldn't
think, couldn't look away, could only stare helplessly as he
beheld a small, square, high-vaulted room like the one with
the plinth—only this one had no central cylinder of stone,
but an arch of flickering white fire shot through with flames
of silver, floating upright in the air at the heart of the room.

Four stag-headed figures stood motionless, facing outwards, two flanking either side of the arch, and their hands were cupped above and below—whirling sparks and motes of blossoming magenta and emerald light, magical bolts and bursts that whirled around and around between their fingers, only to race endlessly up their arms and leap to the arch of fire behind them.

And out of a green glimmering within that archway, Omntharr after stag-headed Omntharr was striding, appearing out of nothingness to march out into the room. A few wore leather armor and bore great saw-bladed swords in their hands that ended not in points but in pickaxlike horns or barbs projecting wickedly from either side of the blade. They were given orders that involved pointing out the various doorways of the room from the majority of the Omntharr: the taller, slenderer robed sorcerers.

And then the vision abruptly faded, and Taerith felt a compulsion—a surging, tugging yearning—to reach that room, and the gate itself. To strike down those four sorcerers and hew aside whatever whirled within their hands, to bring down the gate in collapse and ruin . . . and to await those who'd try to rebuild it, and fell them, too.

Taerith erupted from his crawl into a headlong run down the passage, ignoring Blackgult's mind-shouts and Maretta's frantic spell-weavings . . . until her magic took hold of him, warring with the excited whispers to bring the procurer to a trembling halt on the threshold of the room at the end of the passage.

Which was a good thing, considering how many Omntharr were flooding into it, those sawtoothed blades flashing in their hands as they strode across a battlefield of pooled blood and sprawled corpses towards Taerith.

*Get back, you fool! Run!* Blackgult's mind-voice was almost deafening; Taerith cowered and shuddered, clutching at his head and shaking it to be rid of the painful mind-thunder. He was still doing that when claws reached out of the walls beside the foremost stag-headed warriors and dragged them hard against the stone, ripping out throats and gouging eyes

while they were still struggling to bring their blades around
to hack at . . . solid stone. There were shouts of alarm, and
then orders cried in the strange fluid tongue of the Omntharr,
and as maedra boiled forth from the walls to tear and rend
the stumbling, shrieking stag-men, sorcerers appeared at the
far archway of the chamber.

The world erupted in green fire, drifts of ravening green
fire that melted and twisted Omntharr and maedra alike,
leaving blacked, twisting things to gasp and writhe out their
agony on the chamber floor.

By then Taerith was fleeing back down the passage, weeping in pain, his head still a pounding battlefield. He never
saw the bolt sent to reap his life by a stag-sorcerer—but
around him, in bright flame, the world suddenly went away.

He ran on in blinded, brilliant silence, shielded by a desperate spell wrought by Garlen Blackgult, and stumbled
back out into the chamber that held the burned body of the
maedra—which he promptly tripped over—and crashed
onto his face. A second slaying bolt sizzled over his head
and smashed into the far wall, sending shards of stone tumbling in all directions ere it died away.

The next spell was no ravening bolt, but a mind-scrying
that rolled into Taerith's pain-wracked mind like cold surf
flooding up a beach. It brought with it a new, unfamiliar
mind, so cold and clear-edged that its thoughts felt like the
edges of slicing knives. Omntharr thoughts, full of plots to
open additional gates to secure their hold upon the great
palace, and suspicions as to who might be spying for, or
marshalling, the maedra . . . in a mind that saw Taerith's
own quailing thoughts, and pounced.

Here was a human ridden from afar by sorcerers who
were using him as a spy—sorcerers who once mind-thralled
could serve the Omntharr as agents outside this Silvertree
House, in the river-vale kingdom beyond, preventing its
armies and sorcerers from riding against the Omntharr.
*Yes* . . .

The stag-sorcerer plunged into Taerith's mind like a burrowing worm, reaching for the mind-link, seeking to race along it and grapple with Blackgult and Maretta.

Taerith felt their astonishment and rising fear, Omntharran glee, frantic spell-weaving ... and then, like a great whispering wave in his mind, the awareness that dwelt in Silvertree House and in his mind rose up, vast and terrible— and smote the stag-sorcerer with force enough to make it scream.

The procurer had a brief mind-glimpse of several Omntharr roaring in agony and clutching at their own heads, as eyes sizzled and popped, smokes gouted from ears and mouths ... and then more Omntharr joined the mind-fray, many and cold and mighty, and struck back.

The Whispering Mind snarled and ... *sank,* descending deep into Taerith's memories as mind-spells stabbed at it, lights flashed and hissed, and Taerith Silvertree clawed at his head again in sobbing agony, tumbling and falling into endless red mists of pain.

*He'll be mind-blasted, for sure,* Blackgult snapped, from somewhere far away, and Maretta replied, *(And then they'll come through him, to us! Take us to him, while he still has some wits left!)*

Taerith had a mind-glimpse of the Koglaur's flesh parting to jet out blood as Blackgult grimly cast a powerful but swift spell—wiping two of his fingers through the shape-shifter's gore as he finished the casting. Blue-white fire spun swiftly around both Koglaur and Sirl wizard and took them from his view.

He was alone again with the whisperings, now welling up once more, and the cold, stabbing scrutiny of the searching Omntharr as they ravaged his memories, bewildering him with a flashing succession of phantom images and half-remembered mental scenes. Soon the whisperings blocked their explorations, and they struck out at the Whispering Mind, driving Taerith screaming back against a chamber wall, though the whisperings seemed to rise up and thrust back against them with glee, and he was ... he was ...

Torn out of the struggle and able to see once more, standing sweat-soaked and blinking in Maretta's arms in Silvertree House with both whisperings and Omntharran rummagings banished to faint mind-echoes. The shape-shifter stared anxiously into his face, every inch a beauteous human woman—save for her breath, which smelled like fresh-cut herbs and long-grass—and murmured an incantation.

"They're *coming,* Blackgult!" she snarled, voice sharp with apprehension. "Spin the strongest shielding you know, or—"

Emerald flame roared through the room, pierced and sent roiling by bright silver beams of magic, piercing lances of sorcery that numbed Taerith's hand as two of his fingers were simply—gone—and sent him sprawling with the Koglaur atop him, screaming a long, wet wail of agony.

And then a milky-white radiance rose up all around them, and the tumult was cut off as sharply as if severed by a vicious blade. Maretta's cry of pain ended in a gasp as she fell away from Taerith, who rolled over and stared up at Blackgult.

The Sirl wizard was standing with his arms raised in the last gesture of raising the great shield-spell that now enclosed them, looking down at the shape-shifter with a face that had gone the color of old cheese. His eyes were as dark as if the light behind them had been blown out.

"Wizard mine," Maretta breathed, rolling over. "This is what you must do."

Taerith reached out a hand that lacked two fingers to wipe away the dark blue blood that was welling from that tortured mouth . . . and then drew it uncertainly back, even before Blackgult's arm stabbed down to try to stop his. More blood welled, and for a moment the pain-wracked face seemed to sag into something else.

Then Maretta quivered, spat blood to one side, and spoke more strongly. "Garlen, spin the spell of lightnings, but unleash it not. Hold it in your mind, and as you let your shielding drop, say thus: *Sembril avaunta marezma.* The Whispering Mind should hear, and drink the force of your wardings; give her also the lightning-spell, letting it float intact into her mind. You'll see how. I'll show her the gate, and how she can flood the lightnings into it—not seeking to burn it, for the Omntharr have guarded against that, but to make it so large so swiftly that it will be overwhelmed, and collapse. Heed you?"

"Lady, I hear and shall be guided by you," the wizard said quietly, and rose from bending over her to weave the spell of lightnings.

When he was done, Blackgult carefully spoke the incantation Maretta had given him, and the shield fell as if someone had severed the cords of a milk-white curtain. It winked out ere it could reach the floor, and like a great, roaring storm wind, the Whispering Mind howled with exultation around them. Ere any of them could draw breath, wizard, Koglaur, and Silvertree were all mind-dragged along the flood of power it poured into the Omntharran gate.

That fiery arch burst apart in a shower of sparks and hurtling, helplessly tumbling stag-sorcerers—and maedra howled out of the walls, joining their deeper voices to the keening song of the Curse, and fell on the Omntharr like hungry hounds. The stag-headed men were overwhelmed and furiously torn apart in a shockingly brief time.

The Sirl wizard snatched their linked minds from that slaughter to the chamber where the shape-shifter lay with an abruptness that left Taerith bewildered and blinking, and said urgently, "Maretta, we must heal you, before . . ."

Feebly the blood-drenched Koglaur shook her head. "I am . . . too spent," she gasped, body quivering as he spread his hand and poured healing fire, tiny threads of white flame from every finger, into the ghastly wet blue ruin of her collapsing form. "Even with all your magic, fresh and untested," she panted, shuddering under the flow of his sorcery, "you'd not have enough. I lent too much power to this Silvertree of ours, to keep his mind from being ravaged by the Omntharr contesting with the Curse inside his head."

"No," Blackgult snarled, his voice almost a sob. *"No."*

*"Hear me,"* she snarled back, her voice fierce with urgency. "You must hear this, ere I die, both of you. Someone

must know." She struggled to turn her head, her eyes burning into Taerith's for a moment, ere she gazed back at the most powerful wizard of Sirlptar.

"When I die, something more important than Maretta perishes with me. I've been alive for . . . a very long time. Yuesembra Silvertree has helped in that, for her mind rides mine, and she lives on in me. My kind—most of my kind, still—sees humans as cattle. Our birthright . . . our power . . . they hold, gives us the right to rule all. I . . . uhhh . . ."

Blood choked the shape-shifter then, a bubbling froth that would not end. Her limbs quivered and sagged into lax, rubbery things, but her eyes blazed up brightly, and she flung a loop of what had been an arm around Taerith's burned hand. Blackgult bent forward to support her shoulders, cradling her gently, and though she said not a word, her voice rang strong and clear in both their minds.

(*Yuesembra has worked on me, as she's worked on all Koglaur I've birthed or she's had dealings with, down the years. She made us see Aglirta as something to be cherished . . . protected . . . preserved. She's made me do something I've come to take pride in: to stop my kind from striking down or impersonating every Aglirtan of note, and establishing a tyranny. Yuesembra drove me to convince other Koglaur of this view, though many hate me or flatly disagree, remaining convinced they should use their own power as they see fit. We'll die together, she and I, but you two must share this secret with wise humans, so someone will know not all Koglaur are monsters—and everyone else know the danger they offer all Darsar. Promise me this, I beg of you. Please?*)

With the Omntharr slain, a great silence had fallen on Silvertree House. The maedra had stolen back into the walls, and the Whispering Mind seemed to be . . . listening to Maretta intently.

All the barons and armaragors of Aglirta could have been bare-skinned and set aflame and dancing to merry tunes as they diced each other enthusiastically with warblades all around him, for all that Garlen Blackgult would have noticed them—or cared. He drew the dying shape-shifter up into a sitting position, until he was gazing closely into her weeping eyes. His mind-voice trembled with fierce emotion.

*Maretta, you know I've loved you these many years. When I learned your true nature, I loved you still. Lady, I am beyond that now. I am awed.*

Taerith watched the beautiful features of the Koglaur melt away as her strength ebbed, going pale and smooth. As death claimed her, she was becoming truly Faceless.

Garlen's mind-voice rose until it was like thunder behind his eyes, almost audible. Taerith shrank back from its intensity.

*Lady, the breadth of your vision for Darsar, and your deep understanding of it, humbles me. I am but a grasper after power, a storehouse of stolen and honed spells. You are SO much more. I need you. Darsar needs you. Live on!*

*(Garlen . . . love . . . I can't. I am too burned and blasted inside. Your magic has dulled the pain, but I . . . I fail.)*

*Come into my mind. Share this body of mine! Live on in me!*

The dark, dulling eyes caught fire and became Maretta once more. *(No, I cannot! I carry Yuesembra's sentience with my own—your mind will be overwhelmed. Blackgult will pass away!)*

*I hope not, yet it is a risk I'm willing to take. A risk I'll be proud to take. Three claim us all, Maretta, a risk I MUST take for all Darsar!*

*(I . . . oh, my love, I . . . there's no time left . . . I must not . . . )*

"Do it!" Taerith cried, digging his fingers into the cold, dead flesh of the sagging thing that had been one of her arms. "Go into him!"

"Yes," Blackgult gasped, leaning forward. "Please."

He bent his head and kissed the little bleeding wound that her mouth had become. A few motes of light danced around their joined lips—and then the wizard stiffened and reeled, and the shape-shifter fell back, boneless and slithering.

Taerith stared at Blackgult, now shuddering on his knees, mouth spasming and eyes wide and unseeing, and then at the puddle of flesh on the floor that had been Maretta, and could not think or speak.

In some dark and distant corner of his mind, the whispers said one distinct word delightedly: *Yes*.

And Garlen Blackgult lurched, threw out a hand to clasp Taerith's shoulder for support, and clawed his way stiffly upright. Then without a word or a backward glance, he strode away across the room.

The procurer watched him go, still stunned and silent.

At the door the wizard turned, smiled lopsidedly at Taerith, and struck a pose, hands on hips.

Curving, feminine hips. Those hands grew smaller and more slender, losing their hair. Shoulders and height diminished together, and the wizard's robes swelled out as breasts arose. Hair fell away from the narrowing, shifting face as Taerith stared, and he found himself looking at . . . a woman. A tall, regal woman clad in the ill-fitting robes of Garlen Blackgult.

"So I win my life and lose my love, all at a stroke," she whispered bitterly. "I've never liked the jests the Three play on us! Oh, Garlen, love, how could you hope but be overwhelmed?"

Tears glimmered in her eyes—but she tossed her head, drew in a deep breath, and slashed one shapely hand dismissively towards the floor, as if casting aside all that concerned her.

Then she strode back to Taerith Silvertree.

"Come," she commanded, holding out her hand. "We must away from this place, the two of us, and breed. We'll found our own noble family, Taerith *Blackgult,* and abide across the river until we or our descendants uncover what fell thing lurks in this place, and the Silvertrees can reclaim their own."

Taerith gaped at her, and said the first thing that came into his amazed mind. "But—but the lands across the river belong to the barons Mramaun and Thelver!"

Maretta, or Garlen, or whoever she was, gave him a wry smile.

"That's why you're going to become the greatest, most loyal warrior King Naegrath Snowsar has ever seen, and unmask them both as traitors," she said archly. "As my magic holds their Koglaur abilities in abeyance, of course. Come, Taerith! Your next few summers bid fair to be rather busy."

It was Master Vuhuhaum who first saw the disused palace, when farscrying the far continent of Asmarand seeking lore and goods that could enrich our family. We at first knew nothing of Aglirta or its noble families— and knew not even a hint of the shape-changers who rule that land as covert tyrants.

Forays by the Firstheir and the Secondheir to the coastal city of Sirlptar, where I am less than proud to record that they posed as humans afflicted by a spell-curse to explain their horns, revealed to us something of the fell history of Silvertree House, which most in that port (a bustling and trade-ruled place akin to our great ports of Ithduoul and Maersangh) knew by the name of "the Silent House." Many were the fanciful tales and obvious embellishments told of it, but the slumbrous magic therein was clear enough, and the senior Masters of the family were swift to agree that the palace should be explored and scoured to our benefit.

At the time, ignorant of the existence of the shape-shifters beyond some dark tales about "the Faceless," several Masters were of the opinion that Aglirta could be covertly conquered, subverting a barony at a time with our mind-spells, once we held the House. A pleasant-seeming, verdant land, its uplands alone could yield far more food, timber, and fodder than we could ever need, and would serve to enrich our family above all others, by giving us surplus goods in plenty to sell.

And so it was agreed that Master Vuhuhaum's most able students, under the spell-scrutiny of himself and our Master of Battle Arhandros, would essay an exploration of the palace.

They found it deserted for a good reason: a monstrous race of intelligent worm-creatures hight the maedra dwelt within its very walls, having the power to both to shape stone and to pass freely through it. These fell beasts devoured humans of Aglirta as well as any of our folk they could overcome, and contested our every foray and intrusion.

Though Silvertree House had been disused for some centuries, and was largely bare of lestal goods, much of it was newly built, for the maedra built and rebuilt it constantly, expanding it greatly, in particular in the direction away from the river and possible floodings.

Yet Master Vuhuhaum's estimation of the value of Silvertree House was proved over and over again. As time passes, the stones themselves exhibit ever-increasing magical properties, and sorcery betimes seems to build within the House to near-storms of rackling energy, eagerly seeking discharge. Enchanted items and books of lore have been accumulated from intruders and hidden throughout the House by the maedra, who seem fascinated by magic. This apparently continues practices of earlier inhabitants of the House—at least one of whom seems magically bound to the structure, existing as a sentience heard in the mind but lacking, so far as we have been able to discover thus far, any surviving body.

Master Arhandros is of the opinion that this sentience, which is known to Aglirtans as "the Whispering Mind" or "the Curse of the Silvertrees," is marshalling forces against us, mind-influencing treasure-seekers and local wizards of little accomplishment to journey to Silvertree House and attack us, but others who have spent much time in the palace believe these attacks arise out of fear of the maedra—who demonstrably herd and goad humans to do battle against us—and out of self-interest. Apparently the vast fortress-ruin has always been a goal of those hungry for treasure and items of sorcery.

Despite these perils, it is my recommendation and the common opinion of the Masters of this family that we persist in the exploration and exploitation of Silvertree

House. In the words of the great Phrestal: "One does not turn one's back on great opportunities without grieving for the spurning of the few gifts life freely offers."

We have established a gate in a small way-chamber adjacent to a great hall known to the Silvertrees as the Orblarum, which was apparently at one time a venue where trophy-magics were displayed wrought or collected by the apprentice wizards in service to the Silvertree family, who were known as "the Orblar." The life-forces of some of them were sacrificed by their fellows to craft certain lasting magical effects which prudence demands we explore only when resistance to our presence is lessened, so we have not crafted gates that draw on the sorcery of the Orblarum, or explored it in any detail. Our primary focus at this time is to control the passages and chambers in the opposite direction from the Orblarum, keeping these free of maedra by spells that send slaying waves of disruption through solid stone. My own researches are concerned with perfecting such sorceries, but progress slowly. Capture and study of maedra is vitally necessary, but has thus far not been accomplished.

Nevertheless, it is only a matter of time and persistence. The forces that contest against us surpass us only in superior numbers. They cannot hope to destroy our gate or inhibit our inevitable victory for long.

Thorlaunt forever triumphant.

> Malyvur Thorlaunt
> Lord High Sorcerous of House Thorlaunt
> First Turning, Wanesummer, Seventh Year of the
> Wyvernrule

# BOOK FOUR

---

*Helbara Silvertree*

1029–1048 SR
Sorceress of Sirlptar
And of the Time She Was Hunted Across the Realm

# 1

## Love and Lightnings

"So why, old man, didn't the Silvertrees just hold this place with hireswords, or their household cortahars? 'Tis big enough!"

Dlanazar Duncastle waved a hand ahead of them, at the hall where three passages met, running off at angles, their lofty vaultings lost in cobwebbed darkness. Dust swirled around their boots, the silent fortress still seemed deserted . . . and there was still no treasure to be seen. Every one of these passages was taller than the houses he'd roomed in, back in Sirlptar.

"You've not heard of the Curse, lad?"

"Hah! Even in Coelortar, we knew about the Curse! Something big and ghostly that settled like a cloak around the heads of Silvertrees, and drove them mad!"

"You don't believe that, then?"

Dlan snorted. "I . . . I think there was probably a spell or something, yes—but why didn't someone *else* take this place as their fortress?"

Horl smiled. Yes, this Dlanazar was what he seemed: a strong, smart-mouthed and greedy youth who thought all Darsar will soon be his, because the Three had smiled upon him too often. Too handsome and always right—Dark One take him!—life seemed a simple enough business to Dlanazar Duncastle.

"Well, there were the maedra, and lots of roaming outlaws and beasts—longfangs, for example—and wizards who wandered about here, too, blasting folk they wanted gone from here."

"Wizards? Like those fat, high-nosed buffoons of the Guild?" Dlan sneered. "I can't see any of them bringing their behinds down here, to trudge about in the dark looking for ghosts and longfangs!"

"Well, now," Horl said mildly, as he set off down one of the passages in his slow, lurching manner. "Well, now . . ."


"Helbara?"

For a moment he thought he was seeing not a young and beautiful sorceress of Sirlptar, but a carved tomb-figure, she sat so still in the darkness, gray cloak drawn close around her.

Imlur Pherember was nothing if not bold. After that query on the threshold, he strolled forward into the tomb as if he were daydreaming in a garden rather than attempting something that was sure to enrage both of the two most powerful wizards in the city.

"Yes," Helbara Silvertree murmured when he was less than an arm's reach away, " 'Tis me."

Three, but she was beautiful! Dark eyes under dark brows in a face so smooth, her lips and figure lush, her limbs as long and strong as his own. Her gaze smoldered, not half as calm as she was trying to pretend to be. "It seems morbid, Imm, to be meeting in this cold place of death."

The young apprentice smiled his handsome smile as he swung his lean height down into a crouch, to gaze at her nose to nose. "This is so, Hella. Yet the wards on these crypts make them our safest refuge against . . . our masters, who'd be less than pleased."

Helbara nodded. She knew as well as he did that neither his master Gorold the Mighty, nor hers, Lormondal Lord of Lightnings, should be named aloud, even inside these wards. They were the most powerful archmages in Sirlptar, and had not achieved that status by being less than shrewd, or unwise in the ways of the world. And being bitter rivals, they were ever alert and attentive to each other's doings and affairs. Which is what had allowed Imlur and Helbara to take notice of each other in the first place, and look upon each other more than once, and then covertly leave talking-stone messages for each other . . . and now meet like this, the fires of love flaring in their eyes as they regarded each other.

Imlur casually waved a hand that held a short, almost toy-like baton behind him, and the faintest of shimmering, ring-ing sounds told them both the tomb-wards had been re-sealed. To Sirlptar, the tomb was once more a thing of solid, cobwebbed, moss-girt, long-undisturbed stone—rather than a stone room with its door ajar, bringing soft fingers of sea breeze in through the sorcery that cloaked all sound. "You know what we risk," he said gravely as he set the baton down on the floor by his boot. It was not a question.

"Yes," Helbara replied softly, showing none of the fiery spirit that had caught his eye. "Oh, yes." Her hand went to her shoulder and undid the clasp of her cloak. "You truly wish to do this?"

"Yes," he told her, eyes smoldering, as he reached for his own belt. "You are—protected?"

"Of course," she breathed, shrugging the cloak aside. Im-lur's eyes gleamed as he saw that beneath it she wore only over-the-knee boots. She bent forward and reached out to him. "Let me do that."

Imlur smiled and spread his arms. "Of course, Hella."

Warm fire was stirring in Helbara. She'd never dared do this before. When Lormondal had espied her and plucked her from among the dozens of Silvertree lasses in Sirlptar, he'd told her that her body was now his, and his alone. Not that he'd ever done anything to fulfill that claim beyond grab her chin to glare into her eyes and snarl curses when she dis-pleased him . . . but she saw the looks men gave her on the streets, when she stalked past, cloak swirling, on her mas-ter's always-urgent errands. She knew she was beautiful.

She also knew she'd never seen such a . . . a *beautiful* man as Imlur Pherember, who was also often sent striding about Sirlptar on his master's business. A swirl of sand-hued hair, large ruby eyes, and a face fairer than those of the best statues . . . and he somehow seemed a trifle *more* beautiful whenever she was close, and they regarded each other. Sor-cery, perhaps, she'd thought with a wry smile.

Helbara wasn't smiling now. She was on fire, burning with a hunger that every successful spell-weaving had made a little stronger. No wonder so many archmages were so arrogant and cruel; they must either be satyrs or frustrated beyond belief. Imlur's hot gaze told her that he was feeling the same as she was. He was large and smooth and well-formed, his stomach even flatter than her own, his sleek-muscled body so close now, so touchable. . . .

He growled as his arms went around her, as his mouth came down on her, as skin slid on skin. In a trice their tongues were dueling and they were grinding against each other. Helbara was moaning in her need, a sound that was almost a purr, and arching herself as wantonly as some of the Silvertree women who sat in Downhill windows beckoning to passing men and mentioning just how few coins they were in need of . . . and she cared not.

This was—oh, his invasion! *Yes!*—this was wonderful, this was—

And then Imlur's bare foot touched his baton, and everything changed.

A spell that had been cast and left ready raced over Helbara like an icy blast of winter sleet, *through* her, clutching at her heart and fingertips and mouth, leaving only her loins afire. She struggled, she sought to break free of his lips and push at him . . . but the chill had hold of her, leaving her weak and shuddering, and it was he who broke away from her, taking her throat in one hand and bending her helplessly back to gloat at her.

"Ah, yes. Every bit as sweet as I'd hoped. Helbara Silvertree, you are *mine*. Now and forever, bound to my will."

Helbara tried to shriek at him, tried to snarl out her swiftest incantation. All that came out of her mouth was a strangled mewing sound.

Imlur smiled his handsome smile at her. "No, I'm not Gorold the Mighty, wearing Imlur's face. Oh-so-haughty Gorold has served his purpose, I'm afraid. By the time he wins free of the little mindmaze trap I left in the spell I presented him with this morn, he'll be a mindless husk, and I'll be long gone—and you with me."

He was like fire inside her, sickening fire. Helbara panted in his grasp, devastated and furious. Imlur bent himself against her and bestowed a gentle kiss on her throat. "Such a beauty," he murmured. "A good choice. You, my dear Helbara, will be my key to the riches of Silvertree House—yes, you shall live rich and idle in a great castle in upland Aglirta. For a little while. Until the maedra or some of my rival kin get you."

Helbara stared at him, struggling vainly to speak, struggling until she choked, and a thin trickle of blood dripped from her trembling mouth.

"Don't harm yourself, my pretty prize. To answer the question you can't ask, I am indeed Imlur Pherember, when I want to be. I'm also many others. You see, I'm one of the Koglaur. Yes, the very same Faceless that mothers—even unwashed Silvertree mothers, in the back streets of Sirlptar; Three Above, there're a lot of you! Your folk have certainly mastered the act of breeding!—warn their children about. And yes, to speak to the fears of most of those tales: I've eaten human flesh, in my time. And yes, again: I can be whomever I want to be."

That handsome face slid sickeningly into the likeness of her own, body trembling with need, eyes hot, kissed her throat once more . . . and then grew his wide, bright smile again. And winked at her.

"Of course, in matters of loving, I can be all you desire— or more." He grew inside her, a delightful pulsing that left her gasping and shuddering despite herself, and then retreated from her entirely and added, "Regretfully, such pleasures must wait. First, I must—"

"You must die, foul Koglaur!" The bolt of ruby fire that struck Imlur Pherember in the midst of those cold words rocked the tomb, bringing down clouds of dust and small shards of stone.

The shape-shifter reeled with its force, even as the flames that were meant to consume him clawed vainly all over still-unseen shieldings that surrounded his bare body, splashing here and there. They scorched Helbara even as their roilings flung her bruisingly off the stone tomb-top onto the floor— where she discovered she could shriek, and did so.

"Be still, wench," her master told her without sparing her a glance. "Your well-deserved death awaits, the moment I'm finished with this—this *thing* you've been so treacherously foolish as to dally with!"

And from all the fingertips of Lormondal Lord of Lightnings burst humming, blinding-bright stormbolts of the force for which he was named—a volley of crackling, leaping fires that raced across the tomb like a cloud of striking arrows to engulf the Koglaur and drive him—it—back, in a shapeless, writhing cloud of desperately growing tentacles and great wings of flesh that fetched up, quivering, against the far wall.

"Still uncooked?" Helbara's master's voice held more astonishment than she'd ever heard in it before. "Well, now. Let's see how you fare against—"

A tentacle shot out, snatched the baton from the floor, and drew it back behind the shielding wings of flesh again, as swift as the lightning had leaped.

"I'm *not* a mere apprentice wizard, old fool," Imlur replied, as sorcery of his own awakened around him in sparks and chimings. "*I* was mastering mountain-shattering spells when your father was kicking in the womb."

"You're slower to achieve mastery than the worst of my students, then," Lormondal told him bitingly, as emerald flames swept across the chamber and broke over the Koglaur in a roiling that left the shape-shifter twisting and crying out in pain, the ruins of his collapsing shieldings raining down on him like dark tumbling fires. "I've been observing your unsubtle dalliance with this disloyal she-cat for some time. Talking stones, indeed. You listen to too many bad ballads, both of you."

The next flood of fire was bright amber, and made the Koglaur shriek as his baton burst in his hand, leaving behind a bloody ruin. Blue gore streamed down the stump ere he subsumed that limb and staggered forward, snarling, "And *you* spend too much time in clever I'm-so-much-mightier taunts, wizard—and too little slaying foes you really should respect more!"

Silvery spheres flew from him then, seeming like empty-air things of filigree or spun silk as they expanded, rushing at the archmage.

Helbara thrust her shoulders back against the floor, arching desperately and drumming her numbed hands on the flagstones, seeking to banish the last weak numbness of the Koglaur's spell. She had to get away from this place, or—

The spheres struck, and one side of the tomb exploded with a bright flash and roar, taking the Lord of Lightnings with it.

The Koglaur shouted in triumph as the roof came down, huge slabs of stone shattering. Helbara watched one shard slice its spinning way across her burned thighs, and went on trying to find the strength to use her limbs again. She was . . . she was . . .

Whatever Lormondal's next spell was, it slammed across the chamber like a fist, and Helbara distinctly heard the snapping of bones as the Koglaur was flattened against the remaining wall—which acquired cracks that spread slowly outwards behind the ruin of the sobbing shape-shifter's body. Tentacles writhed and flailed in spasms of pain, and more stones fell from above.

Helbara managed to roll over. There was a healing-stone in one of her boot heels, if she could somehow get clear of this fray before the rest of the tomb collapsed and crushed her. These two might well go on blasting each other until half of Sirlptar—

Imlur snarled something, and sent what looked like a red mist billowing hungrily across the shattered tomb.

Lormondal swept it aside with a simple spell, shaking his head. "I'm not sure how you bested even a dolt like Gorold, but surely 'twas with better sorcery than *this*. You're not out in the wilderlands now, Koglaur, you're in the only grave-yard Sirlptar has; surely you can show some trifling care and control!" And he leveled his arm at Imlur, who was resuming his handsome human form behind two great wings of flesh, extra limbs busily weaving spells like a busy thicket of tentacles, and sent forth a rushing stream of blue sparks.

"*Your* trouble, wizard," the Koglaur snarled back, as those

sparks struck another unseen shield and streamed harmlessly away along the tomb walls, to wink out and fade in
their dozens, "is that you misjudge everyone around you.
Helbara here is disloyal because she wants to taste a man before you remember her and come to steal her life-force when
she's fifty summers old, or more; Gorold who clawed himself up from less than you to craft more intricate spells than
you ever will is a dolt; and I, you mistake for someone who
cares a whit about this overcrowded dungheap of Sirlptar!"

His counterstrike was a howling flood of crimson lightnings, bolts that drove the Lord of Lightnings once more
from view and burst the walls of the tomb apart in all directions. Imlur shouted with laughter as his foe was driven back
between a burial plinth and another crypt—which promptly
exploded into shards—and the vines that cloaked every
tomb of Sirlptar's burial ground burst into crackling flame.

"*There,* wizard!" the Koglaur laughed. "*Those* are lightnings—unlike the pretty little bolts you toss around like toys!"

Lormondal's next spell blew apart a house overlooking
the burial vale. It collapsed with a roar, the shape-shifter
shouting taunts as he wheeled aside on the wings he'd been
growing, untouched and busily weaving his next spell.

Helbara started the long, slow crawl across the scorched
and smoking leaves and vines. Tilted and toppled tomb-
markers jutted out of the burning chaos ahead of her like
wayward teeth—as Imlur's latest sorcery toppled a building,
too, spinning the mightiest wizard in Sirlptar around like a
child's rag doll in its passing.

The numbness was fading now, and handing her the pain
of her burns and the deep slash across her legs. Helbara
crawled grimly on, towards the edges of the burial ground,
and the staring wall of people there. That ring of watchers
sported a few frightened Sirl guardsmen, the boldest folk of
the street—and what seemed like every last wizard of Sirlptar's Guild of Sorcery. Many of the watchers stared back at
her, and their faces were neither welcoming nor happy.

\* \* \*

There came a soft, scuttling sound from somewhere far away, down a side-passage. Dlan whirled to face Horl, sword flashing up. *"What's that?"*

The old man listened calmly to the echoes, and then said gruffly, "Something not much larger than we are, with claws, and far away. We ignore it, unless it comes looking for us."

*"Ignore* it?"

"Lad, as I recall you took ship away from Coelortar to escape a life of backbreaking stonecutting with your father, in search of an easy fortune in Sirlptar—and ready feminine companionship that wouldn't involve blood feuds, public floggings and censure, and being chased away over rooftops by night, yes? And now you want to turn lion on me, and go racing to embrace trouble?"

Dlanazar gave him a look of mingled disgust and anger. "I'm not a fool, Lord Whitehair."

"No, you're just having fun playacting like one. Still, there're plenty of folk down the years who've done the same, and gone seeking danger . . . and, thank the Three, found it, too."

"Both dead? Are you absolutely sure?" Halarondar's mellifluous voice was sharp with anger and worry.

"High Mage Halarondar, I am neither careless nor blind in the ways of sorcery. Both blasted and dead, so little left that none can say for sure that one was a dreaded Faceless— only that one of them wore many spell-spun shapes during their battle."

"So the woman must be blamed."

"What? Why, exactly?"

"Feiraun, have you forgotten why old Alamaunt started this guild in the first place? We can't have mages battling mages in the streets! Nor can we countenance any wizard wreaking public destruction unpunished, or the commoners *will* rise up against us, and all who work magic! Do you want that? Do you want to live out your last few days as a hunted exile? We above all others should know what it is to be feared and struck down, whenever we're found out!"

Feiraun's face changed subtly, so that it more closely resembled the long-dead Koglaur who'd sired them both, and he said grimly, "Two gone-rogue mages destroying each other isn't neat enough an ending for you? After we of the guild valiantly protected the rest of the city from their wild sorceries?"

"But we didn't, Feir," the older Koglaur said heavily. "Six citizens dead, four buildings thrown down, dozens of tombs despoiled and the kin of the buried seething about it . . . We must be seen to find, pounce on, and punish the cause: that she-cat of an apprentice, who drove her master and her lover mad with her spells to set them at each other's throats so she could plunder both their stores of magic and win her freedom, to boot! It doesn't matter one whit that in truth she's a softhearted lackspell wench who couldn't do such things if she wanted to; our needs in this matter must make her so, or *we'll* pay the price she doesn't."

"Well, then, we have a problem," Senior Sorcerer Feiraun said just as heavily. "She's gone. Broken free of the four wizards we set as guard over her, somehow—all of them capable, experienced mages, but none of them were of our kin, mind—and fled."

"What? Claws of the *Dark One!*" Halarondar roared, bringing his fist down on the table hard enough to make the great ornamental copper platters hanging on the far wall rattle. "Must I do everything myself, just to avoid *basic* blunders?" He sprang out of his seat with force enough to send the splendid old high-backed chair crashing back to the floor, and strode down the room. "Well, we'll just have to cry her hitherto-unsuspected, astonishingly mighty dark powers to the skies, and announce our mage-hunt! She must be found and slain in torment before the entire city—and soon, before any rumors of our weakness and blind blundering have time to spread!"

"Easier ordered than done," Feiraun muttered. "She's had half the day to flee, and all the spells in Lormondal's study. She could be anywhere on Darsar by now."

Halarondar wheeled around, dark eyes glittering. "She could be, yes," he replied, "but she won't be. She's a Silvertree, like all the rest of them our oh-so-wise brethren settled here, to make sure of an endless supply of puppets to conquer that accursed ruin of a palace. She'll be on her way to the Silent House."

The people stood in the overgrown graveyard and stared around in bewilderment. They'd all heard of the wizards' duel in the burial ground, of course—the purple and yellow smokes were still curling lazily up into the sky, for all Sirlptar to see—but these weren't the tombs of Sirlptar around them, and the roofs and spires of the city, colored plumes of smoke and all, were . . . gone.

This was somewhere far from the great city by the sea, somewhere out in the woods, in rolling countryside, with a river that could only be the Silverflow glimmering downslope and mountains in the distance beyond it, and the largest castle or fortress or palace any of them had ever seen rising like a frowning gray wall in the other direction, with even-more-distant mountains beyond *it*.

The great, sprawling fortress looked deserted, and disturbing, and yet somehow familiar . . . and the wide-eyed people stared around at it and each other in silent amazement. No one wandered.

One moment they'd been cooking or washing or shuttering shops in the familiar noisy, stinking, crowded confines of Sirlptar, and now they were . . . in this other place. Sorcery, to be sure. One look around told them how many folk had been similarly treated, all at once.

Mighty sorcery.

Then there was a flash atop a weathered crypt in the midst of a field, and a stooped, stout, motherly woman in a ragged gown was standing atop it, where no one had been a moment before.

*Be welcome, folk of Silvertree.* That kindly voice sounded in their minds, and left them gaping in awe . . . and fear. *What befell in the burial ground of Sirlptar this dayheight will spark much trouble in the days ahead—trouble that will fall most heavily on those who bear the name of Silvertree. As all of you do.*

*I know this because I am of the same blood as those who will slay and enslave you, if you return to Sirlptar. I am Druthaea, of the folk you fear as the Faceless. I offer you a new life, a better life. You have only to step away from the ruins of Silvertree House—yes, this is the high house of your ancestors—down to the barge that awaits you at the river's edge. It will take you downriver to a ship docked just above Sirl city, that will sail past Sirlptar to far places, where I'll see you settled, a family here and a family there, in various locales and under new names.*

She pointed down at the river, and amid shimmerings, a great barge appeared on the apparently empty waters, clinging to the shore without benefit of moorings.

"And if we go, what then?" one of the bravest old Silvertree men called, squinting up at the crypt. Some of those standing nearest shrank away from him, as if they expected him to be blasted by the Faceless witch.

*I shall visit you,* Druthaea's mind-voice told them, *and teach you of the Faceless and poisons and herb-lore, and of the Arrada. You'll be known as the Wise in time to come, if you can keep yourselves—and especially your lineage—secret enough in the seasons just ahead to avoid being hunted down and scoured from the face of Darsar.*

And then she was gone, and the roof of the crypt was as deserted as it had been a moment before.

The Silvertrees blinked at each other for a moment or two, and a murmur of bewildered talk arose. Why had some of their Silvertree kin not been brought here? Why was such-and-such missing? Where was so-and-so? Some folk turned to look back at the deserted palace, and others at the barge. Many heads turned to survey the roof of a particular crypt again, almost wistfully.

And then, as if they were cattle at feeding time, they began to make their various ways down through the tombs and markers to the waiting barge. Every last one of them.

# 2

## Great Evil Awaits Within

*H*elbara came awake very suddenly, jolted out of a slumber of sheer exhaustion by the blast of a spell causing the felled tree she was lying on to bounce and shudder, bruising her face and almost breaking her nose.

"Got her!" an excited male voice called, as crashings and rustlings approached her swiftly through the bushes.

"Well, let's hope you left enough of her to be revived, or at least identified," another, more sour man's voice said, from much nearer at hand. "The High Mage wanted her *alive*, remember?"

"Well, we may have to do a little fleshcrafting, but as long as her face is—"

As the two young mages burst out into the little space just cleared by the spellblast in front of the larger space cleared long ago by the falling forest giant, gold-thread guild badges flashing bright on their breasts, Helbara gave them a brittle smile . . . and fed them both death.

Lormondal's best fleshmelt spell. It blinded them first, but as their faces dripped down off their chins to leave wet, red-washed bones behind, they had time for bubbling screams. Their brains foamed out of their slack mouths a moment later, as they started to collapse towards the patiently waiting ground.

Helbara muttered a few barbed and impolite words, and set off through the forest again—upriver, as always. The mages were probably all around her by now. She'd given up trying her former master's unfamiliar and complicated translocation spell; every time it whisked her, weak and shaking, to a new hilltop, someone was there to burn or blast her, or someone had seen her from afar and was now calling down lightnings on her. So it was back to running like a stag in the woods, harried by young and ambitious guild wizards hungry to earn the status and promised guild spell-rewards of being her slayer or capturer.

This was strange country. Beautiful, but . . . she could hear faint, very faint *whisperings,* in her mind, as if the land itself was talking to her. She'd never been this far from Sirlptar before, and she'd never thought she'd get much closer to Aglirta than a good view of it from some high east-facing Sirl balcony, but . . .

The trees and rolling ridges seemed vast and dim and endless, and she was hungry and tired and . . . and scared. She was glad she'd slept through the first night and never known it, but what might lurk in all these trees and *go hunting* when darkness fell?

And her healing-stone was almost gone, dwindled away to a tiny pebble closing those gashes and banishing those ugly, rippled burns. She hadn't had time to snatch more than her work-breeches and the burnt and much-patched tunic that went with them, either—if hedge-wizards and desperate apprentices hadn't shown up by the score to fight with the guild mages over the stripping of Lormondal's tower, she'd never have gotten away, spells or no spells. As it was, she'd had to cast the statue disguise on herself a dozen times before reaching the garden-gate—and waste a rolling lightning on the guild mages waiting outside it to pounce on anyone who emerged.

Little streams were everywhere, running across her way down to the mighty Silverflow, so she could drink often, but if she didn't get food and sleep and a chance to study the spell-scrolls enough to memorize the runes and gestures and incants, she'd run out of magics to fight these hounds chasing her long before she found someplace to hide. She didn't even know a good disguise spell beyond that statue trick, and she doubted Lormondal had known any. After all, what need had he of such things? He used his name and face like a weapon to move folk to his bidding, and if he needed a spy or not to be seen doing something, he'd had half a dozen apprentices to send on such tasks.

She was stumbling in her high boots, which had been fashioned more for looks than for sturdy walking, and she was hot and dirty and just ... so ... *tired.*

She half fell down a steep streamside, splashed through its tiny trickle, struggled up the far bank through a tangle of thorny canes, and—reeled against a tree. *What was that?*

It was as if a window had suddenly opened in her mind, a vivid scene flooding its light in front of her eyes ... of three guild-mages, one of them with a face she knew slightly from doing her master's business, standing together on a high hill pointing at various stretches of woods. And then down at a broad stream that flowed below the height on which they stood, where their gesturing arms made it clear they intended to cast some sort of spell as a barrier or to sniff out her presence, when she reached it ...

And then the vision was gone, quite suddenly, leaving behind only the whispering, which was louder now. Helbara strained to hear it, but could recognize none of its words ... yet it seemed to sense her attempt, and surged still louder, showing her a few brief glimpses of things, more mind-pictures. A vast stone fortress, stretching away seemingly as far as all of Sirlptar did, looking down from Lormondal's tower. *Safe. Refuge. Hidehold. Safe.*

The whispers were as loud as hammerblows in her mind, and she stumbled forward, almost dazed. Another mind-picture: the High Mage of the Guild conferring privately with another senior guild wizard, the both of them stretching their arms out like tentacles to point at places on a map that the vision just wouldn't show her clearly, beyond the central dark snake that must be the River Silverflow ... like Koglaur tentacles ...

Another scene, very suddenly, accompanied by a warning: *Close.* This one was a guild mage daring to cast a were-spell on himself in the depths of this unfamiliar forest, and sink down into wolf shape. He was unfamiliar with it, she saw, and loping awkwardly, raggedly—but his nose came up, and he turned his head sharply, and he was—

Just over there. As he gathered himself for a charge that should carry him in a rush along a little ridge and across a gully tangled with dead branches to pounce on her, Helbara spun a swift airspike, and then a see-behind, swift little spells that used very little of her dwindling magical energy, and sat down to wait with her back to her pursuer, feigning dejection and weariness. If only he pounced first, and didn't stop to change shape or confront her. . . .

He didn't. She sat watching him with the eye conjured in the back of her head, the invisible spear of the airspike projecting up and out from her backside—and when he sprang, paws spread so as to be sure of coming down on her back and smashing her flat to the pine-needled ground, he impaled himself on it and vomited blood all over her back and head as the force of his landing bowled them both over.

He had a healing-stone at his belt, but she plucked its pouch from between his dying, feebly fumbling fingers, and ran down to the nearest stream to rid herself of all the gore. With the flies already buzzing all around her.

The moment she hit its foul, scum-covered coolness, her mind showed her a mage aloft as a hawk, drifting lazily to peer down at the trees below, waiting for any glimpse of . . .

She sighed, stripped off all of her clothing, put the healing-stones into her cheeks, and cast the most powerful spell she knew.

Had the hard-running mages who'd heard the crash and shriek of the dying wolf been just a sprinting breath faster, they'd have seen two shapely bare human ankles projecting up from the waters of the stream into a dense cloud of mist. . . .

But as it was, all they found was a messily disemboweled guild mage, discarded clothing that made them shout excitedly enough to draw a hawk down from the sky, and a misty, deserted stream that defied their every spell to scour it. The fish plucked leaping from its shallows by their magic remained fish, and gasped and wriggled their lives away on the forest loam while their slayers stamped up and down disappointedly and then reluctantly crossed the stream and went on east through the endless wood, peering and sighing and peering some more.

And the mist made its own slow and silent way down the stream to the banks of the great river, and decided to wait until dark to travel.

It quivered from time to time, as it lingered in the gloom under some overhanging trees. Even mists find dream-visions and whispers startling.

"So she got away from the hounds sent out from Sirlptar," Dlanazar said impatiently. "Is this supposed to be some sort of lesson for me, Lord Whitehair? Do the right thing and go hide in the Silent House and I'll find my fortune?"

"No," the old man said gruffly, turning back to the younger man to point at a particular flagstone, his useless hand dangling at his wrist. "Mind you don't step there, or 'tis death you'll be finding, not riches."

Dlan peered down narrowly. "Oh? I see nothing to be wary of."

"Trust me," Old Horl said dryly. "About another sixty paces along here, if nothing's been along to root around and clean up, you'll see the results of someone not being wary enough."

Dlanazar stepped around the flagstone with exaggerated care and walked along in Horl's wake, the twinkle back in his green eyes. "Ah, some adventure at last," he murmured almost happily.

"Well, no. More like viewing a dug-up corner of a Sirl burial ground," the older man replied, pointing ahead. "Look yon."

The block that had fallen from the ceiling was of impressive size—about as large as the biggest wine cask that a Sirl wagon could carry, or about half again as tall as Dlanazar. It had fallen on an angle, one of its corners crushing the stone floor and sinking in several feet deep. Bones were splayed out around it. Human bones.

Dlan looked down at them silently. Limbs reaching vainly for escape, forever—but the bones of one arm had been gnawed at and strewn about. He glanced up at Horl. "Are there any other traps just hereabouts?"

"No," the old man replied, his eyes glinting in the lantern-glow. "This one was enough."


"They're not finding her, aren't they?" Halarondar's voice was still sharp.

"No, High Mage, they aren't. Yet." Feiraun's voice was both calm and weary. "Though there have been several, ah, sightings. She's heading for Silvertree House, just as you said she would—and overclever for a green apprentice or not, she can hardly hope to elude the dozen-some veteran wizards of the Guild who await her there."

"Elude, no," the High Mage of the Guild of Sorcery of Sirlptar replied, toying with a decanter that had held much more when Feiraun last glanced at it, moments earlier. "But as to who's being overclever . . . that remains to be seen."


It was getting harder and harder to just drift. The whisperings were ever-stronger, their beckonings almost physical tugs now, pulling her closer to the Silent House. Visions whirled into her mind, of this or that comely person doing thus or so in well-lit, luxuriously furnished chambers in that vast palace . . . visions that were more terrifying than reassuring.

She could almost see it now, in the pale mists before dawn, rising like a great dark prow out of the trees, looming above the riverbank. Where the guild mages were waiting for her, alert, shieldings dancing around them almost as brightly as their scryings.

It was time to go belly-down among these tombs—tombs? Was her life to be spent doing spell-battle amid tombs? Probably, and spent soon, if she took part in too many such frays—and drift up the slope even as most of the mists were scudding down the slope, and out over the river. Slowly and stealthily, oh-so-slowly . . .

Parts of Silvertree House were in utter ruin, roofless and overgrown, pillars of stone reaching like fingers into the sky amid tumbled rubble and clinging vines, and other parts looked almost new. It was even larger than she'd thought it was, now that she was this close to it, slipping like a floating serpent past these unfriendly, half-asleep men as they shifted restlessly. One of them almost relieved himself all over her as she ghosted past, and another lit a pipe and then shook it out almost right through her when older mages snapped at him to desist. . . .

And then she was through. Past the mages, past the overgrown, ruined outer wall of the Silent House, and stealing oh-so-slowly up to the nearest gaping doorway, an arch as tall as a Sirl back-alley cottage that had lacked doors for a long time by the look of the gnarl-rooted trees growing on its threshold, and—

Torn out of mist-shape and back into her own bare body in a single sickening instant of fire in her veins and breath seared from her, to twist and arch helplessly in midair, bonds of fire crackling around her limbs.

"Hah! Drace, you've caught her! Our little spell-witch at last!"

There were roars of approval, and laughter, and—a bolt that would have slain her right then and there if its smashing arrival hadn't made her swallow both healing-stones involuntarily as her sizzling limbs were slammed into those trees in the archway and—splinteringly—right through them.

"Corbar, you *idiot!* Halarondar wants her *alive!*"

"I know a sorceress who's starting to spin something *awful* when I see one! If I hadn't blasted her—"

"She'd still be caught, you utter fool! Now she's free, and *in* there, and we're going to have to go and get her out again!"

"Well, so?"

"Well, clever young Corbar, *you* can go first!"

"B-but I've cast my best battle-spell, just right now, and—"

"And you should have thought of that *before* you let fly in hopes of snatching a little glory, stonebrains! There she goes—blast her! Down her now, before she can get inside!"

Shaking with agony as the healing-stones did their soothing work from her innards far too slowly outwards, Helbara Silvertree staggered to her feet in the rubble-strewn, thorn-choked courtyard inside the gate and stumbled blindly off towards the darkest openings in the frowning walls all around her. Shelter, any shelter . . .

A vision of a yawning pit warned her away from one archway, and a forest of falling spikes made her whimper back from another—and by then, the guild mages were in the archway or standing on air above the courtyard, and bolts of lightning and webs of force and jets of flame were all reaching for her.

Helbara ducked desperately aside, running along a crumbling wall towards the next opening and panting out a shielding-spell as she went. She stumbled on loose stones and went down hard, winded and helpless, the moment she finished the incant.

Bouncing in the rubble, she slid down it in despair. This was it, these were her last few moments of life, before . . .

There were shouts of surprise and alarm, and a spellburst went off somewhere close by, showering her with small stones and clods of earth. Helbara lay still until the ground slapped her to her feet.

Literally slapped her, as it rose in a great stony wave to fling a dozen mages off their feet. Statues and merlons shattered and fell on them as they rolled, as if a great guiding hand was using the House itself as a weapon against them.

But that's just what *was* happening, she realized in astonishment a moment later, as a stone wall momentarily grew a great wolflike stone head that lunged forth to engulf a bewildered guild wizard and draw back again an instant later, leaving only severed legs to totter and sag bloodily to the ground.

Her stomach heaved, and Helbara tried hard to be sick—as statues strode off their plinths to crush and hammer mages into the ground with their stony limbs, showers of stones buried wizards or sent them sprawling to where pillars could topple on them, and wizards started to flee, shouting in terror.

And then an eerie silence fell, leaving Helbara alone on her knees in a courtyard of death.

Or rather, not quite alone.

A grim ring of wizards were rising into the air well outside the walls, standing together on nothingness with the flickering shimmering of shieldings ripplingly strong around them. Deliberately that ring advanced, high in the air, until it crossed over the ruined outer wall—and when stones sprang up at it or towers toppled towards it, the wizards coolly blasted those hazards to dust and smoke.

When nothing else could touch them, they faced Helbara Silvertree and cast tangle-line spells. Old, and slow, and simple magics, anchors to a foe rather than translocations that could go wrong or snatches that some geyser of stone could intercept or sever. They were tethering her in the courtyard until they were ready to come to her.

Not that Helbara could have done more than crawl to get away from them. Her head swam with weariness and despair, and she went from her knees to her face on the rubble-strewn ground and lay still.

Her last shielding-spell was flickering on the verge of failing, and the wizards—under the curt commands of Drace—were carefully and thoroughly destroying every bit of stone around her, leaving only dust.

She was doomed.

She let the visions take her and drifted in a sea of memories that were not hers, and whisperings she could not understand.

It didn't seem long before painful throbbings of lightning jolted her awake and upright again. The guild wizards were pelting her shielding with lightning bolts, slashing at it until it collapsed and they could take her.

Tears trickling down her face, Helbara did nothing but watch and gasp in spasm after spasm, as the lightnings struck.

"Three Above, *what's* keeping her shield up? Not even all

the Masters, working in a circle, could hold against this much lightning! She must be as strong as the younglings were shouting, after all!"

"No, Nalgar," Drace's voice cut in. "Someone is bolstering her shields, aiding her somehow, and when I find out—*there!* Strike right there, with all you have!"

Asmarand seemed to crack apart under the lash of a score of lightning bolts, in a white-blinding flash that sent fortress towers thundering down and made the ground heave and smack Helbara's well-bruised face again.

And then silence fell again, broken a moment or two later by the heavy, wet sounds of many bodies falling onto stones from a considerable height. Human bodies.

"I always find," a pleasant male voice commented from somewhere very near, *inside* the faint singing of her wards, "that letting foes slay themselves by dashing their own spells right back at them is particularly satisfying. Justice of the Three, perhaps."

Helbara rolled over, opened her eyes, and peered up at—a tall, black-bearded, hawk-faced man clad in light armor. He was helmless and wore no war-gauntlets, but there was a warblade scabbarded at his hip. His war-harness looked well-used. He was extending a gallant hand down to her, keeping his eyes on her face rather than surveying the bared rest of her.

"I mean you no harm, Lady. I am Baron Ezrym Blackgult, at your service. I am, as you can see, a mage of sorts, and my lands lie across the river, yonder—beyond the royal isle of Flowfoam, wherein the king is probably cowering right now. As for your name, I know it not, but I can tell from the way the House defended you that you are a true and rightful Silvertree—*the* Lady Baron Silvertree. Will you accompany me to chambers where you can rest, and bathe, and be healed? I promise me that you will be as safe as my magic can make you, and free to walk where you will."

The visions showed her the depths of the ruin around her. *Safe. Home. Refuge. Here. No Other.*

"I . . . Lord sir, your offer is . . . very kind, but I must enter this House of mine. Something bids me. . . ."

Blackgult looked grim. "I know. Yet if you would live, you must cleave to me rather than enter this palace. As you're a Silvertree, Lady, great evil awaits within. Great evil that will break your mind and leave you mad, whereas all I'd have to fear in yon halls would be talons striking at me out of the stones, and the spells and warblades of the greedy. Lady, go not to your doom. I offer you the protection of my spells and my house—by the Three, I beg of you not to go in there."

He drew her to her feet, and Helbara leveled her gaze at him along their joined arms and whispered, "Release me. Let go of me, or you're no different from all these others." She gestured around at the courtyard full of dead wizards.

Blackgult stared into her eyes sadly, and then sighed, let go of her hand, and stepped back. He made a swift gesture in the air as he did so, and muttered something that had to be an incant, so Helbara hissed a sword of the air back at him, striking out with all the feeble magic she had left—but he stepped back out of its reach, saluted her, and then backed away, never taking his eyes off her, until she turned and ran barefoot through the nearest archway.

No more would she trust wizards. She was home now, home at last, and the whisperings were welling up welcomingly all around her. . . .

The air in the great upper hall of Blackgult Keep shimmered and disgorged Baron Blackgult, who ignored the startled servant's low bow and strode to the balcony that looked out over the river.

With the bright morning breeze sending the mists marching away over the Silverflow below him, Ezrym Blackgult gazed at the distant dark bulk of Silvertree House and called up the spell he'd cast on the Silvertree lass.

He could still see her eyes—dark fire, gazing back at him—and he knew he'd never forget that pain-wracked, defiant face for the rest of his days. He knew what he was going to see now, and bit his lip to keep from weeping. It would not be pleasant, but he had to watch.

The nude woman was trotting delightedly through the dust and gloom, dancing aside from the traps she knew were there as if guided by something unseen. Which of course she was.

She'd explored seven largely empty rooms and seen her first shaft of sunlight through a shattered roof when she started to giggle, and then make bestial barks and wheezings.

The spell started to twist and swim, as it always did as the Curse ate at the sanity of whomever he was spell-riding . . . he started to shuffle and bark, too, sweating on the balcony. He'd have to break off soon, or go down into madness with her.

Damnation of the Three, this Curse, and . . . and . . .

"Helbara," she whispered, turning to gaze at him as if she could see him. "I am Helbara Silvertree."

And then she thrust her own hands into her mouth and started to gnaw on them, choking as she bit and chewed and the blood flowed, and then thrusting the stumps of her slender wrists into her mouth until the long, rattling choking began. . . .

And Ezrym Blackgult flung himself down through a very expensive chair to break the spell, shouting at the agony in his head rather than at the bloody splinters protruding from his hands, and wept.

"Lord Baron?" The servant was almost screaming in fear and worry, but Blackgult snatched himself up and strode past the man with no more than a curt wave to get out of the way. The scroll he needed was only a room away.


They were just sitting down to a meager nightfeast when the grand-looking, armored man with the white face and the bleeding hands strode into the room, having passed somehow through a locked door. He snatched up the wide-eyed young imp of a Silvertree lass from the seat by the corner despite her mother's scream and her father's angry shout, held her astonished face up to his own, and said softly, "You shall be my bride in time to come, Laurea Silvertree."

And then, before the mother could claw her way over the goggling boy-child and the father could lunge across the table to reach him, the stranger was gone, and Laurea with him.

I fear this grand palace of my ancestors will soon become my tomb. As large as Sirlptar itself it stretches now, in some towers nine levels aloft, and everywhere at least four levels beneath the ground. I have lost count of its courtyards, let alone its towers. I have seen cities of Asmarand that its outermost walls could swallow, and as it has been days beyond counting as I write this since I've seen those ramparts, they are now probably altered and built over, with newer walls reaching farther into the forests. Silvertree House sleeps not.

Though Aglirtans call it the Silent House, it is far from that. Not a day passes without the shouts and dying screams of outlaws, lawless freeswords, and roaming beasts—longfangs, greatserpents, and worse—slaying and being slain in these halls. The maedra, of course, win all battles in the end, their talons reaching from the solid stone to rend or choke, if need be when a mighty monster sleeps. I've seen a perching nightwyrm maedra-caught before it could flap free, and torn apart atop its turret.

Yet beast-cries are not what torments me or others of the blood Silvertree who come here. We hear the ceaseless murmurs and whisperings of the Curse.

None alive today that I can find, from highcoin sage to learnéd wizard, can tell me how the Curse was laid, and by whom, but it seems a living thing to me. There was a time, not so long ago, when it seemed to drive Silvertrees into madness nigh-instantly after their arrival, but it now seems to linger in delivering such fates. My uncle Tharlyn, gone to the Three like all of the blood who came here before him, dwelt here for some years before succumbing. He thought the Curse both ancient and lonely, and that it delayed in driving us wit-

less only to learn all it could of Darsar today from our
memories—ere crushing us into drooling and gibbering oblivion.

It whispers in my head. Betimes I think it feminine,
and other times I am not sure. Wise and fell it is without
doubt, and sometimes it seems to chant and hiss in a
chorus of many mind-voices. Tharlyn and Maertel before him thought it ate the minds of those it drove mad,
so their thoughts and remembrances lived on within it,
in an ever-growing multitude. The Curse tells me much
about itself, yet I know not what I can credit truth, and
what is but cajolings.

So much I can say, from the writings of others: the
House feels like rightful home to every Silvertree the
moment they set foot in it, even though they may never
have seen it before. It changes us, mind to mind—corrupts, some say—working thus on all of the blood Silvertree, *and only* those of the Blood Silvertree.

The first sign of its changes is when we begin to be
able to sense—"smell," Tharlyn put it—nearby danger,
or the scrutiny of other beings, or the presence of
magic. With this we gain a driving hunger to learn all
the secrets of the House, a yearning that comes to force
us to stay inside these walls far more than maedra alterations that rob us of known exits. This feeling begins
with the urge to press against the stones of the House so
as to hear its whisperings better.

Then its grip tightens, until nothing else seems to matter. Like Tharlyn before me, I now restlessly stalk these
halls, exploring every trap and hidden passage, and finding them all somehow *familiar,* half-remembered rather
than new. The secrets of Silvertree House have become
the greatest treasures of all, and seeking them out is now
my life-work . . . whatever life is left to me. The visions
that used to slide into my mind when I was weary or
dreaming now come in a ceaseless parade. Long ago the
House revealed to me tables that are magically set with
feasts from time to time, so that I need not starve as I

search, and never need think about the Vale outside and the food it holds. Only dimly do I recall Aglirta ... pleasant green trees and the broad waters of the Silverflow ... and more and more often I hear in the whispers a word that may be a name, or may be an incantation: *Sembril*.

Sometimes, too, a deep growl seems to echo through the stony vastness: *Arau*. I know not what these mean, or anything, anymore. . . .

I am becoming a mad ghost, like those of the blood who came here before me.

The halls are dark and endless, the whispers unceasing.

The Whispering Mind seems ever closer, more affectionate—and I am leashed to it.

It will not let me out. Three deliver me. It comes for me, and will not let me flee. Three deliver me.

Pray for me, you who read this, and do not let all Darsar forget utterly the name of:

Argaunt Silvertree
Lord of Silvertree
Highsummer, Ninth Year of the Reign of Ammarandar

# BOOK FIVE

———◆◆◆———

*Phelmar Silvertree*

1157–1188 ? SR
Lord of the Wartalons
And of How Serpents Tried to Enthrone Him Baron

# 1

## In the Service of the Serpent

They came out into the sixtieth or seventieth chamber, and Dlanazar looked around a little wearily. "Where are we now?"

Horl was definitely lurching along more slowly, and seemed to welcome the excuse to sit down on another stone block—after a lantern-assisted glance up at the crumbling ceiling to see if any adjacent stones looked eager to follow it down to the floor anytime soon—grunt his way into some semblance of relaxing, and sigh, "This was where Lord Phelmar used to roam . . . until some Serpents came a-plundering, and hacked him to dust and shards."

Dlanazar looked around the room as if expecting to see a skull rising up in one place and skeletal hands in others, clutching a crumbling sword. Nothing but empty, dusty stillness met his gaze.

He sighed. "All right, then," he said wearily, feeling for his water flask. It was fighting for space about his waist with an unknown number of daggers and the thick coil of stormbraid rope that encircled his hips. "Why don't you tell me about Lord Phelmar Dusty-shards?"


" 'Tis the Master Cellarer, Lord Baron—with the new wine."

Baron Halgryn of Cardassa frowned at his steward for a moment, his storm-gray eyes narrowing. "New—? Ah! The ithqual! Good, good, let him in!"

Narmandur Halgryn's most trusted servant inclined his head with a silent smile and returned to the door, leaving the most able baron of Aglirta frowning down at the map on his desk once more. Halgryn had been much concerned with tardy sailings of late, which had twice caused a fleet that was supposed to make him staggeringly rich to bring goods to market well past the time when prices were high and takings best.

Yet if this ithqual was of the best—black, thick, salty, and fire-strong, from far southern Dethtyl beyond Sarinda—then the Three were smiling upon Cardassa at last, and Halgryn's sure march to becoming the richest man in all Asmarand was back on full stride. Why—

Master Cellarer Ormond set a silver thirst-platter before him, the decanter and full-flagons set in its ornately sculpted hoops clattering slightly. Halgryn sat back as the ithqual was poured—yes, black as night!—and smiled, stroking the tiny point of beard that adorned the very center of his chin.

The cellarer bowed and presented him with the first flagon, the ithqual winking and sparkling at its flaring lip.

Halgryn inhaled its scent, and his smile broadened.

"Have my thanks," he declared, and sipped appreciatively.

In the manner of ithqual-lovers everywhere, the baron then threw back his head to savor the slow, fiery slide of the oily vintage down his gullet—and his steward stepped forward from behind him with a hook-knife at the ready, and slit open Halgryn's throat in a savage instant.

The most able baron of Aglirta gurgled and stiffened, wild-eyed. Then the poison in the ithqual met the venom that had been on the blade, and his futile struggles abruptly ceased.

Holding other weapons at the ready, the steward and the cellarer watched him die. They did not relax until his body slumped into a rubbery, faceless mass—a transformation that caused them to exchange satisfied nods.

"Well done, Serpent-Brother," Ormond murmured. "Another Koglaur gone. We'll have them all purged from the realm soon."

The steward shook his head. "We're just eliminating the most brutal and lazy, and driving the more clever ones into hiding. D'you really think every last Faceless in Aglirta is posing as a baron or tersept?"

The cellarer shrugged. "I care not if they lurk, so long as we control the baronies, and soon, the throne."

"How soon? Ammarandar Snowsar seems able to *smell* the faithful—he had Onglas slain last month, Rethil back in spring, and dozens more—Nlarga, Ultost, and even Hammaert, with all his spells, this past year alone!"

"He has his wizards, as we have ours. Yet as the years pass our gold hires more and more, however weak their spells, whereas his aren't replaced when they fall. The weight of might in Aglirta will change soon."

"There you use that word again. How far off is this 'soon'?"

"That, good Dremenaus, is very much up to you and me," Ormond replied softly. "And to whether we can install a puppet-baron not here in Cardassa, but within sight of Flowfoam itself: in Blackgult or Silvertree."


The Lord of the Wartalons turned his head, the sharp point of his broken nose thrusting forward like the beak of a falcon, and silenced his slavemaster with an impatient air-slicing wave of his hand.

"I don't *care* how prettily she pleads," Phelmar Silvertree growled. "She's a backcountry farm lass, she's too riddled with rotboils to take pleasure with or to sell as a slave, and if we keep her alive, she'll need to be fed and watered! Do any of these facts escape you?"

The slavemaster, a tall brute in tattered leathers, hung his head and growled a slow and reluctant *no*.

Phelmar sighed loudly, got to his feet, strode over to the tent where the trim backside of the rotboil-ridden prisoner could be seen stretching the fabric—and drove his sword unhesitatingly through the tent wall just above it.

Her death-scream wasn't much of a shriek at all. It came out as a sound more akin to a short, bubbling bark.

The tall, dark-haired mercenary commander withdrew his dark and glistening blade, wiped it clean on the side of the tent as the body inside slumped over, pointed at the fabric with it as he stepped back, and snapped, "Ungmar, burn this *now!* I'm not aching to come down with rotboil this day. I might be of a different mind on the morrow . . . but I doubt me that."

"Lord?" The hesitant voice belonged to Marrlel, the youngest blade in the Wartalon band. Phelmar swallowed a silent curse and whirled around.

To find Marrlel standing with two stone-faced, death-eyed men in gray battle-leathers. They bore no weapons that Phelmar could see, but their cold, fearless manner told him they believed they could kill everyone they might meet about as easily as they could breathe. Both wore tiny pendants at their throats, of green stone carved into the shapes of coiling serpents.

"Phelmar Silvertree, we would do business with you," one of them said gravely. "In private."

The Lord of the Wartalons measured them both for a long moment, his face as cold as theirs, and then pointed across the camp to a rockpile where the bodies of the dead had been piled for burning. "Private enough?"

One man turned to regard the place while the other kept a level gaze on Phelmar, and then said without turning, "It will serve."

He strode off towards it without waiting for a reply, and his fellow followed. After a moment, Phelmar shrugged, caught the eyes of two of his band who held loaded crossbows, and went after the two gray strangers.

Behind him, the two bowmen strolled off to find the best vantage points for slaying unwanted visitors on the rockpile.

A distant, eerie howl arose, and echoed strangely through miles of empty, high-vaulted rooms. Dlanazar Duncastle looked up from where he sat against the block of stone and hissed, "What's that?"

Old Horl shrugged. "Must be getting dark outside. They'll be starting to prowl, now. We'll have to keep close to walls, and be ready to use our blades."

The young procurer gave him a sour look. "I haven't seen any treasure yet, old man."

The weather-beaten old man lifted one eyebrow. It was the only part of his thinning white hair that still held a trace of its former brown, Dlan noticed. Horl's eyes were brown, too.

"That could be due to your lack of eyes in your backside," the old man rumbled.

The young procurer frowned. "And what does *that* mean?"

"Get up, and tell me if there's a mark on any of the flagstones you've been sitting on."

Dlan frowned again, but did as Horl had directed, peering closely and then reaching down. "This one he—"

"*Stop!*" Horl snapped. "I thought you were a little past being a witless child!"

Dlanazar looked up at him, a dangerous expression settling over his handsome face. "Meaning?"

"Witless children look with their hands before thinking," Horl said gruffly. "The rest of us use our eyes first."

Dlanazar nodded slowly. "I grant your wisdom, old man. Well, then: this flagstone has a tiny mark along one edge: two lines running side by each, with a third curving across them. That curve can't be a wear-scrape; it's deliberate cutting-work."

"Indeed. Look across the flagstone, to its other edge, right in line with that mark. What see you there?"

"Nothing. Oh . . . a tiny scalloping, just here."

The old man nodded, his scars catching the lantern-glow. "Drive your swordpoint down into the seam between that stone and the next, right at that scalloping. Straight down, and pull towards you whilst keeping it that way, until you hear a clicking."

"I'd prefer to keep my blade unmarked," Dlan replied, reaching out a dagger.

"*I'd* prefer to keep you alive," the old man snapped, folding his many-scarred arms across his chest. "Yon dagger's blade is too short to move both triggers. There'll be an upper one that releases the stone, but not the trap—so as to slay overeager thieves who just use daggers. You need to reach them both; 'tis the lower trigger that halts the trap."

Dlanazar gave his guide a long, level look, and then

resheathed his dagger and used his sword, slowly and carefully. Sweat sprang out on his brow ere he sat back on his heels and announced, "I heard two movements, almost as one."

"Then you've done it," Horl said. "Get back clear of the stone, put my sword upright on it, lock the guard of your blade with that of mine so as to give you a handle—and push the stone straight down. It should sink about the width of your hand."

The younger procurer did those things, and the stone clicked once more.

"Let it rise," Horl said gruffly—and when Dlan did, the stone rose right up, standing proud about a handspan higher than the surrounding stones. Shallow grooves could be seen in its newly exposed edges.

"Handholds," the old man said, pointing. "We'll use the sword-guards rather than our fingers, if you want to make quite sur—"

Dlanazar gave the older procurer a contemptuous look, laid hold of the block, and snatched it up and back, moving hastily.

Nothing sprang out or fell from the ceiling or erupted in sorcery.

After a tense, warily peering moment, Dlan set down the block, snatched up the storm-lantern, and cautiously approached the opening, sword in hand once more. Horl sat patiently on the block, making no move to look into the opening or rise to reach it.

"A . . . a stone coffer, sealed with . . . pitch, I think," Dlan said slowly. "About this big." He moved his hands to frame an imaginary box about as long as his body was wide, and about two handspans high.

"Use your sword to push it sidewise, and keep a firm hold on the lantern," Horl commanded. "Be ready to leap back *very* swiftly. Watch under the coffer."

"I've stolen things before, you know, Lord Whitehair," Dlanazar said sourly.

"And, if the Three notice not your refusal to bow to prudence, may even live to steal more things again, young Duncastle," Horl replied mildly, and gestured at the opening like a courtier politely bidding a lady to go before him.

Dlan dispensed another dark look and did Horl's bidding. The heavy coffer grated as it shifted, revealing—an empty hollow beneath it. The young procurer reported as much, and asked acidly, "You were expecting?"

"Poisonous gas, sometimes. Tomb spiders—their bite has an even deadlier poison—most often, in this older part of the House. Very rarely, a spell . . ."

He broke off abruptly, and made a swift, urgent "back away!" gesture. Dlan scrambled back, raising sword and lantern.

"What?" the young thief demanded . . . and then he saw it.

Rising out of the empty shadows of the hollow beneath the coffer was something that looked like thin mist or smoke, a darkness that was almost invisible in the lantern-light, but rose like a dark cloak in the gloom beyond its direct radiance.

"What is it?" Dlan hissed, stepping back as the mist—or whatever it was—rose higher, looming up over him.

"If we're lucky," Old Horl said calmly, "a harmless wraith."

The mists grew a head, an eyeless helm that regarded Dlanazar Duncastle coldly with the eyes that it did not have, shifting its shoulders to raise a shadowy blade to menace him.

*"And if we're not lucky, old man?"* Dlan shouted, as the wraith started to drift forward.

"Then we'll die here, as bold heroes, not slashed to ribbons in some dirty Sirl alley," Horl said gruffly, not moving from his seat on the stone—as the wraith rolled forward like a wall of darkness, with sudden speed, to engulf Dlanazar Duncastle.

Who screamed, hacking wildly and beating at the air with the flickering lantern, as cold darkness swirled around him, searing past his ears and up his nose—and was gone, leaving him shivering and bewildered, blinking at empty darkness.

"Wha . . . where'd it go?"

"Through yon archway," Horl told him. "To report to something more dangerous, if the Three aren't smiling on you with their usual bright fervor. If they are, of course, it'll do nothing at all—because it can't do anything more than what you saw. A word of advice, youngling: If you ever meet with something like that in here that's wielding a *real* sword or ax or the like, be prepared to die fighting. Swiftly."

Dlan stared at the old man, emerald eyes bright with rage, and snarled, "You were just going to sit there and watch me get killed!"

Horl shrugged. "My strength is failing, lad. If I didn't need someone swifter, stronger, and with a greater reach than I have, I'd be here alone right now . . . and you'd be dead with the flies crawling all over your eyes—unless those eyes were floating in someone's backalley stew-bowl, that is. Save your fury for some beast, lad; you did very well. Most treasure-seekers drop and break their lanterns, the first time they get a scare. 'Tis time to take out yon coffer, and find out how rich you are."

Dlanazar Duncastle stared at the older procurer for a long moment before he mouthed a long and heartfelt curse, and started back towards the coffer.

"I mistrust these snake-worshippers," one of the wizards muttered.

"Astute of you," another replied sardonically.

"So why are we taking their gold? Why serve them?"

"Because it was that, my dear Nalgryn, or be destroyed by them. They made that very clear."

"What—*destroy us?* A few chants and poisoned daggers against *our* spells?"

"Did you see that corpse, on your way in? Purple, bloated, eyes swollen up into the size of fists, lots of foam?"

"Yes. Varthyn's been casting transformations on slaves. That's the third 'experiment' he's left by the stair."

"Well, that particular experiment was 'can my spells shield me against a wingéd snake flung by a Serpent priest.' And that unpleasantly dead result was Varthyn."

*Ah, but there's nothing so deadly as a wizard with a sense of humor. Unless it be a wizard who lacks a sense of humor.*

* * *

The wind softly ghosted over the rockpile. Phelmar Silvertree took up a stance that put a heap of sharp-tumbled stones between him and the two cold-eyed strangers, and waited, saying not a word.

The slightly taller of the two smiled thinly. "I am Larayel, and this is Tharsarn. We want to make you an offer."

The young, ruthless mercenary warlord shrugged and waved his hand in a directive that they should do so. "Make this good," he warned. "I see your snake-pendants. Worshippers of the Serpent do not enjoy a good reputation."

"We slay those who cross us, yes," Tharsarn agreed expressionlessly, "as you do. We treat well those who work well with us—as I trust you do. That's merely sensible trade-conduct. Dark rumors we can't be responsible for."

"I do not regard the use of poison as sensible."

"That's because you aren't immune to it, Silvertree. We employ only snake-venoms, which are sacred to the Serpent."

"Why worship *snakes?* What's wrong with the Three?"

"We don't worship snakes. We revere *The* Serpent, the most mighty wizard Darsar has ever known," Tharsarn said flatly.

"Who ascended unto godhood after crafting the Dwaerindim," Larayel added, "and took the shape of a gigantic snake. If treating with us offends your piety, think of him as the only mortal to achieve divinity by his own deeds."

"By being the greatest sorcerer in Darsar," Tharsarn added. "And consider also this: In our reverence of him, we of the Church of the Serpent strive to achieve the utmost mastery of sorcery."

"Which means," Larayel put in, "we can destroy your entire Wartalons band in a breath or two, with a spell that's a simple casting for us. If you'd like a demonstration, we could eliminate both of those fools now aiming crossbows at us."

"They're just a trifle obvious, Silvertree," Tharsarn murmured, leaning closer. "A mistake in technique, in fact."

Phelmar folded corded arms across his chest and growled, "If you two are done trying to impress me—and *no,* I don't require your little demonstration—suppose you unfold to me this offer of yours."

"It's more of a choice," Larayel purred. "Phelmar Silvertree now knows more about us than he really should—which means he must die forthwith, *unless* he becomes our trusted ally. Here in Aglirta, our most valued allies are all barons—so we'd like to raise you, Phelmar, to your rightful place as Baron Silvertree of Aglirta."

*"Baron?"* Phelmar lifted an eyebrow in disbelief. "Aha. And your price?"

"You must do as we say. Not as a slave, mind you. Consider us clients who'll give you precise and exacting orders while we achieve your barony . . . and polite policy suggestions from time to time thereafter."

"I see," Phelmar grunted. "Death or servitude." He looked them up and down with open contempt. "Magic! You'd swagger a little less, I wager, if all you wielded in life was a sword."

Tharsarn shrugged. "Perhaps."

Larayel said and did nothing at all.

Phelmar regarded them both for a moment, and then said calmly, "I'll agree to this servitude on one condition."

"Which is?"

"That you explain to me just how being a baron of Aglirta is my 'rightful place.' "

Larayel smiled. "Now *that*," he began, "is easy. . . ."

---

*And **that** lure is stronger to some than raw power itself. The desire to know where one stands, to lay bare the secrets of one's lineage and past.*

*Prudent, for some. After all, it's always best to know if Darsar holds a bastard brother or two, who might come seeking one's life so as to claim a name, and with it land, titles, coins, and perhaps a wife or two.*

*A wife or two. I'd welcome such lasses now. Anything to warm me as I drift, caught in this endless, tireless cold.*

\* \* \*

There were murmurs of mistrust and wary fear from the men
of the Wartalons when they strode into the room—and saw
the row of coldly capable men in robes. Even had the wands
and glowing finger-rings not shouted, "Wizard!" to any
watching eye, the gold eye-and-hand badge of the Guild of
Sorcery of Sirlptar shone bright upon every breast.

Swords sang out, but Phelmar snapped, *"Easy!"* back
over his shoulder even before Larayel could do so.

"These gentlesirs are under hire to us," Tharsarn announced calmly, "just as you are. Sheath your blades; this is
*not* our idea of a trap."

Phelmar turned to add his nod to these words, and caught
dark looks from even Raldro and Gaunter. Some of the other
men of his warband gave him glares in which utter terror
warred with murderous thoughts. Thoughts of their betrayer
Phelmar.

He turned back to the two Serpent-worshippers. "Suppose
you tell us why we're here," he suggested curtly. "Before any
*accidents* occur."

One of the wizards spoke. "For you to have any hope of
surviving the perils that lie before you, Phelmar Silvertree, it
is necessary that your Wartalons be utterly loyal to you. I
think you'll agree that such devotion is not a hallmark of
mercenaries."

There were mutters of alarm from the Wartalons. The
wizard raised his voice and continued, "We know of no way
that a man can be enspelled to obedience and still be able to
fight. I'm sure you've all heard tales of the lurching, shuffling hulks that result from mind-mastery."

"And so?" Phelmar snapped. Behind him, various
Wartalons spasmed, reeled, or acquired alarmed
expressions—and then returned, for the most part, to their
former common state of stoic suspicion.

The wizard of Sirlptar turned to his fellow mages. "Kaerest? Nalgryn?"

"The mind-bond is done, Korcelyn."

"And those who fought against it?"

"Those two only," Kaerest replied, pointing. The Wartalons whirled around . . . to regard two of their own. The tall Southerner, Telblud, and the short, dark, grim Ieiremboran, Nantyre, were reeling, white-faced and staring.

As their fellow hireswords gaped at them, the two men started to shudder violently, and wisps of smoke curled from their eyes. A moment later those wisps had become greasy tongues of flame, and smokes were issuing from the ears and mouths of Telblud and Nantyre—as they toppled soundlessly to the polished floor. The bodies crumpled like empty sacks when they hit, and lay still.

"There. Simple enough," Larayel commented, "and, look you: a *very* small price to pay for trust among your ranks."

Phelmar drew in a deep breath, let it out again, and asked heavily, "And what small and simple thing is next?"

"Your ancestral home—that vast palace known to all Aglirta as 'the Silent House'—is overrun by monsters, and exists in a state of trap-filled ruin," Tharsarn announced almost happily. "To be recognized as the rightful Baron Silvertree, you must cleanse it and make it your own. Korcelyn?"

The Sirl wizard nodded gravely, turned to his fellows, and began a long and complex spellcasting that involved an eerie, droning incantation, the tossing of many pinches of aromatic substances into guttering braziers, and the drawing of dozens of runes with very coarse powders that seemed to be shards of copper and of silver.

It seemed to the sweating and suspicious hireswords to take a very long time—and when it was done and the guild wizards stepped back, two tongues of flame arched slowly up into the air, curving towards each other . . . and then rushed together to form an arch of flame.

The view of the back of the room framed by that arch flickered, blurred, and became a sunlit scene of a hill overgrown with tall, gone-to-seed grasses, saplings, and clinging vines. Here and there amongst the scrub, an ancient stone crypt or leaning burial marker could be seen.

"A graveyard," Raldro of the Wartalons muttered darkly. *"That's* a good sign."

"A gate," Larayel announced, "leading to the Silvertree burial ground, that lies before the gates of Silvertree House." He raised his hands and cast a spell on the assembled Wartalons—who felt nothing and could see no alteration in themselves or their fellow blades . . . and regarded him with hard-eyed suspicion.

Tharsarn smiled. "You have now all been endowed—for a time—with the ability to see in darkness." His voice changed, rising to ring with eagerness. "Phelmar, lead your blades through—and take what is yours!"

Phelmar Silvertree shrugged, turned to his Wartalons, raised his sword with his usual rallying yell—and his men yelled back, their own swords flashing out, and as he ran towards the arch, sprang to follow him.

The flames threw off no heat as the hireswords plunged between them. For each man there was a sickening moment of twisting innards and feet falling through nothingness—and then grass was crumpling underfoot under bright sunshine, with the River Silverflow behind, overgrown tombs all around, and a great bulk of stone walls, towers, and gateways ahead.

"It seems," Phelmar muttered to no one in particular, as he led the rush, "that we fear monsters and traps a good deal less than wizards and Serpent-swine."

"Wise of you," Tharsarn's voice purred in his ear, though there was no sign of either Serpent-worshipper among the men now charging up the hill towards the largest grim fortress Phelmar had ever seen.

Phelmar snorted and made a rude gesture. It was either that or shiver.


"I feel . . . ill. Not just uneasy, but . . . riven inwardly, and . . ." Nalgryn's voice held more distress than his guild colleagues had ever heard in it before.

"It's these *surges,*" Kaerest said sharply. "The ruin has

strong magics. If you think hard about Silvertree, and dwell on his thoughts and what he's seeing, the sick feeling fades."

"And if you do that," old Harakthar said sourly, "you fail at precisely what we're trying to do: see everything we can of conditions inside Silvertree House. If we all simply ride this Phelmar, there might just as well be only one of us."

"Well said," Larayel of the Serpents said firmly, his cold, emphatic tone a quiet reminder to the wizards of who'd hired them, and why.

Korcelyn, the most powerful of the seven guild mages, asked suddenly, "Have any of you managed to make out any words in all this whispering? I—"

"*Don't,*" Tharsarn said quickly. "Set your mind on anything else, but do *not* try to hear and heed the Whispering Mind. Unless you intend to go mad well before sunset, of course."

"Raldro, come out of there!" Phelmar snapped, trying to watch five doorways at once. "We haven—"

"Hah!" Phelmar's trusted swordlord shouted, and there was a sudden clang of warsteel from the room he'd stalked into.

"*Get in there!*" Phelmar roared, waving a dozen Wartalons towards the door Raldro had taken. "I don't want to lose anyone else—"

Raldro trotted back into view, waving a bloody blade. "Just a few outlaws. All dead now."

"'Just a few outlaws'? Three Above, who *else* is wandering around this place?"

"The Great Serpent?" Gaunter offered innocently.

"No more such jests!" Phelmar growled, feeling the two Serpent-worshippers linked to his mind stiffen in unison.

"That makes, now, four outlaws before Raldro's 'just a few,' two outlander adventuring bands, a pack of wild dogs," Gaunter muttered, counting kills off on his none-too-clean fingers, "and a spider as big as my head."

"Huh," Phelmar snorted. "That'd be one big spider. I'd be happier if—'ware! *Get it!*"

Something that swooped and darted like a river-swift flashed out of an archway and arrowed amongst them. Blades flashed as men ducked and struck at it, cursing and slashing and whirling. Dangerous when so close together, but this was an—

"Ondrakh!" Ungmar roared, from somewhere across the chamber. "Blades out, all!"

"Three void themselves!" someone else shouted. "Down it *now!*"

Marrlel sprang high into the air and hacked at the darting thing. There was a thick, wet sound like a goodwife chopping a melon in half, and black wings spun crazily, one lopped half-off. The deadly flying spider tumbled to the floor, where three blades diced it so enthusiastically that sparks flew and abused swords rang loudly.

Phelmar sighed. "Save your steel," he growled. "We're going to be needing it, I'm thinking."

He shook his head as if to clear it, and Gaunter eyed him frowningly. "Are you all right, Phel?"

The leader of the Wartalons tossed his head as horses do, winced, and said, "Yes. There was a . . . pain in my head, suddenlike. . . ." He looked at the familiar faces all around him and snapped, "Do you hear a voice? Whispering something?"

A silence fell on the chamber as hireswords exchanged grim looks.

It was Raldro who said almost gently, "Yes, I do. We all do."

And as if that had been a signal, the whispering voice swelled up in triumph, loud and swift and exulting, words bubbling out as if a dozen excited folk were chattering, all at once, in an unknown tongue, a flood of chatter that every Wartalon strained to hear more clearly, to understand . . . but could not make out more than a single word: *Silvertree . . . Silvertree . . .*

The three-headed snake had time to glide into the room and rear up taller than Ungmar, who was standing near, before anyone noticed.

"'Ware! A treth! Get it, you motherless backsliding bone-brains!" Gaunter roared, pointing with his sword.

Wartalons leaped eagerly at this new foe, seemingly relieved to have something to hit out at.

Phelmar Silvertree did not leap with them. He was too busy reeling, as the Whispering Mind swelled in his head, red and savage and gleeful, and reached *through* him. . . .

And there was a sudden shock, a sickening feeling, an echo of incredulous and hurried despair . . . and then profane, fear-riddled anger, from many minds.

*What was that?* The mind-shout was deep and grand and shaken.

(*That, Mage Korcelyn, was your colleague Kaerest dying. I warned you to guard yourselves appropriately.*) The mental voice belonged to the Serpent-worshipper Tharsarn.

*This, this . . . whispering thing can slay through a MIND LINK?*

(*Evidently.*)

There was another surge of whispering, and another shock. In the wake of a stomach-wrenching emptiness that made Phelmar stagger, almost dropping his drawn sword as he clutched at his head with both hands, the flare of fear in minds linked to his mind grew. There was one fewer mind than before.

(*Yes. I would say "definitely."*)

# 2

## A Surprise for the Serpent

"*P*ull out!" Nalgryn shrieked, as sudden fire swirled around the heads of the Sirl wizards. He slapped wildly at the faces of his fellows, causing some to blink and back away. As they did so, their haloes of fire collapsing into nothingness, one of their number—Rarhavyn of the Red Cloak—stiffened, clawed blindly at the air, and toppled floorwards.

Guild mages gasped curses and backed away as if Rarhavyn's sprawled body had plague-maggots leaping from it.

"Korcelyn!" Larayel of the Serpents snapped, his voice like the crack of a whip, "rally your men! We paid you to keep mindwatch—"

"*Gold that shall be returned!*" the most powerful Sirl wizard bellowed in the instant before a roaring wall of flames sprang up at his bidding, encircling the guild mages and forcing the two Serpents back.

The fire died as swiftly as it had come—leaving only fitful blazes behind, rising from the sprawled bodies of the dead wizards—but took the surviving guild mages with it.

Larayel and Tharsarn exchanged glances and then sour shrugs. Tharsarn struck a gong on the wall and stepped back to let the warriors of the Serpent rush into the room.

They were not long in coming. Three bald-headed, cruel-faced priests of the Serpent strode hurriedly into the room in their wake.

"The wizards of Sirlptar fled, as expected?" one of them snapped, barely waiting for Tharsarn's nod ere he flung an arm out to point at the flaming gate arch, and shouted, "Hasten! You are to find and recapture the one called Phelmar Silvertree—the mind-images are clear? Good! Bring him back alive. Here. Swiftly."

Serpent-warriors shouted obedience and charged through the gate in a well-ordered stream, venomed blade after venomed blade flashing in salute.

The three priests joined Larayel and Tharsarn, folding their arms in frowning unison as they bent their gazes on Larayel's hastily cast farscrying whorl.

Its slowly whirling oval showed them Serpent-warriors rushing up the hill of tombs, blades at the ready, leaping through the gaps in the crumbling, outermost wall, and plunging—to the ground, dying. Swords flashed from behind the weathered stones, thrusting deep into hurrying warriors. Those blades were hauled hastily free, blood spraying, to reap the next face or throat.

"Helms, next time," one of the priests murmured. "Serpent-headed, of course. See to it."

The youngest priest nodded. "For the glory of the Serpent, Ghaelen."

Neither Ghaelen nor the other senior priest, Brenthur, so much as flickered an eyelid as the slaughter went on.

"A few deaths, yes," Brenthur murmured, after watching for a time, "but this—this incompetence . . ."

"Is unexpected, yes. It's as if Silvertree and his hireswords knew our force was coming," Ghaelen replied softly, watching men die.

"They did," Tharsarn said tersely.

"The mind link still holds," Larayel added.

Ghaelen whirled as if the two had drawn blades on him. "*End it,* you dolts!"

"By your command," Larayel said swiftly, making an intricate gesture.

Brenthur regarded him with narrowing eyes. Had there been more than the merest hint of mockery in that soft, swift response?

The last Serpent-warrior fell, and Phelmar Silvertree tugged his bloody blade out of the corpse, held it aloft in a meaningful salute—for all Asmarand as if he knew the Serpents were watching—and then turned and led his men back into Silvertree House. There was a stillness in the chamber as the Serpent-worshippers watched those silent figures vanish into the great gloom of the ruins.

"So," Ghaelen remarked in bored, idle tones, "the Wartalons lose three blades, butcher ours to the last, and retreat into a place where taking the battle to them will cost us many, many more lives."

"They must *not*," Brenthur said furiously, "be allowed to go unpunished. Every last one of them must be hunted down and slain before they can leave the ruins, so not a word of this defiance can spread!"

"Agreed, yet a small practical matter arises. Your zeal and devotion to the Serpent makes you quite capable to lead such a force, Brenthur, and I'm sure Ombryn, Larayel, and

Tharsarn, here, will prove both loyal and competent, but four men, however gifted, is too small to provide more than a passing amusement to yon hireswords . . . and to waste worshippers of the Serpent needlessly is to sin against Our Scaled Lord."

"And what of *you*, Ghaelen?" Brenthur snapped, seething. "Would not your mastery of sorcery make our force that much more formidable? That much more likely to achieve a glorious holy victory for the Serpent?"

"I must remain here," the elder priest said serenely, "to report what has befallen to the Great Serpent hims—"

"An unnecessary duty, as it happens," rasped a thin, cold voice that made everyone in the room stiffen into nervously swallowing silence.

The Great Serpent had not rushed into the room. He was just suddenly *there,* his ever-present dark hooded cloak curling around the coils of an emerald-hued, serpentine body that was entirely covered in scales, from the bald, fork-tongued head to the humanlike arms and hands. Seventy feet long or more, with eyes like bored winter ice in a viperlike face, he towered over the men gathered around the scrying-whorl.

Out of a swirl of his cloak, while they still stood awed, spilled a gout of thick mist—that sank floorwards to disgorge half a dozen Serpent-priests, powerful sorcerers all. They stood in its calf-high roiling with carefully expressionless faces . . . and the men around the whorl, even Ghaelen, started to tremble.

"You will *all* go into Silvertree House," the Great Serpent ordered, his voice silken with menace, "while I remain to watch—and report your achievements to myself. Through the Thrael *I* shall link to you all, and guide you, so that none of you will waver under . . . mere whisperings. You are to seize control of the mind of Phelmar Silvertree once more, and discover what's happened to him—and just what lurks in the ruined palace that can snuff out the minds of Sirl wizards like doused torches. Moreover, I am close to one of the missing Dwaerindim now. I can feel it, and that feeling centers on that whorl—so the Dwaer-stone lies hidden somewhere in the Silent House. It must be found and brought back to me. Do not bother to return without it."

"A handful of coins—old, and badly corroded," Dlan reported, peering closely but not disturbing anything with the dagger held ready in his hand. Yet. "I don't recognize any of them."

"And?"

"Two stones," the young procurer said disgustedly. "Not gems, or anything cut or mounted—just two lumps of stone, such as you'd find by a roadside."

"Touch them," Horl said. "One at a time, and with a finger, not steel."

Dlan shot the older man a swift look, and then did that— recoiling with a gasp as both stones began to glow with a soft, steady light.

He looked up at Horl, who grinned and asked, "Better than lanterns, no?"

"Are . . . are these what wizards call glowstones?"

"Indeed. Pick up one of them, and will it to go dark."

" 'Will it to go dark'? How do I do that?"

"Look into the darkest corner of this room, gaze at the darkness there, and imagine it getting deeper, and spreading everywhere . . . see?"

Dlan looked down at the now-dark stone in his hand—it was firm and hard and cool, seemingly just a stone—and asked, "And to make it glow again?"

"Think of light."

The stone kindled into radiance once more. Horl nodded. "Now give it to me."

Dlanazar rose, took a step towards the old man—and then frowned. "As I recall, our agreement was that all magic things we found were mine, except that copper hand you're seeking. Is this not so?"

Horl's face was unreadable. Not for the first time, Dlan cursed that. It *did* look like a piece of old barn-board, rough and wrinkled and lined. . . .

"Of course it's so, Dlanazar," the old man said gruffly. "Both stones are yours, and I'll freely surrender this one to you the moment we're out in the sunlight again—but use your wits, lad: If you've two magical lights, shouldn't we douse the lantern for now, and each carry one? So we can *both* see traps, and battle beasts? Hey?"

"Oh. Uh, yes," Dlanazar said grudgingly, and held out the glowstone.

Horl took it, willed it dark, and then made it flare up again immediately. "Right. Mind you try that, several times, until you can make it dark swiftly. In case we have need to hide."

"What would we have need to hi . . . oh."

Dlan fetched the other stone, and the coins. "You want these?"

"You carry them for now, lad. They may do as my handful later, but these were your first. Now close up that coffer, put it back, and set down the block just as before—and mind: the trap *will* rearm."

"So why do all that?"

"Lad, you now have a hiding place, here in the House. If you leave it thus, anyone knows right where it is, and how to get it open. You may have need of it, in the years ahead. And the moment you have secrets in your life, you can never have too many hiding places."

Dlan nodded, and returned the coffer to its place. "You knew where this was, and exactly how to get it open. Who else does?"

"Well, many caches in the older rooms of the House have such marks—but on the other hand, most folk who come exploring here find death, one way or another. So . . . the Three know, and old stones like me know, too." Horl hefted the glowstone in his hand, and added, "There are a *lot* of these light-orbs in the House, mind. You'll probably have a handcount or more before we leave. They command a good price, if your buyer doesn't know you've any swift and pressing need for coin."

Dlan looked at him thoughtfully, and then said, "Well, let's be up and sharp and finding them, then."

\* \* \*

In the third chamber three Wartalons dropped down from a door-lintel, groaning as the shieldings of the Serpent-sorcerers made their blades blaze up in fire in their hands. Yet they slit three Serpent-loving throats ably enough, and their kicks as they plunged down had felled three more men; Marrlel, who was the swiftest, managed to plunge his knife into the eye of one of those fallen, struggling sorcerers.

By then the others had found time enough to spin spells. The Wartalons died horribly, torn apart by unseen hands whilst they frantically stabbed themselves, over and over again.

Yet when the butchery was done, eleven Serpents had become seven, and the anger of the Great Serpent lay like a cold, heavy sword in their minds, a leaden weight among the faint, ever-present whispering.

A scuttling thing, like a centipede but with fur and taloned arms, was accordingly blasted to a few flaming scraps of fur when they saw it waiting on a ledge in the fifth room—but their satisfaction was savagely curbed by the Great Serpent. Moments later his anger flared again when a section of floor suddenly gave way and spilled a screaming Brenthur into unseen depths—depths that held some sort of pivoting stone block that crushed the Serpent-priest like an egg, bringing an abrupt end to his sobbing attempts to cast a spell.

In the seventh room Ungmar rushed at them, a great charging giant who staggered, reeled when Ghaelen's snapped spell burst his head apart like a hurled fruit, and then fell—but by then he'd come close enough, and drawn so many slaying spells into him, that Raldro and two others were able to launch themselves from behind him at the Serpents, and slice bloody ruin through Ombryn and two of the Great Serpent's upperpriests before they were killed. If they hadn't been trying so hard to reach Larayel and Tharsarn before all others, they might have spilled even more Serpent blood.

As it was, only four sorcerers stalked reluctantly into the lone passage that led out of that seventh room. It was a long, narrow way, and before long a deep rumbling overcame the incessant whispering in their minds, and they caught sight of a huge, irregular rock—a carved head, broken off some gigantic statue—rolling towards them. It was so large as to scrape and shriek its way betimes along the walls, and it was coming fast.

The Serpents blasted it into shards, in a spell-burst that slew three of the men pushing it. The other five Wartalons, however, sprang over the bloody ruin to strike enthusiastically at the intruders—and although the Serpents' spells were swift and well-aimed this time, they were also enthusiastic enough in their unleashings to shred the last failing shieldings of the sorcerers as they burst forth . . . and a narrow tunnel does not permit much dodging of sharp warsteel, for men who have no armor to withstand its bite.

The last of the Great Serpent's upperpriests went down with a broken blade in his face—in part because Tharsarn's desperate shove had made the man take a thrust intended for Tharsarn himself—and left just three panting Serpents staring at each other.

The whispering was loud around them now, loud and confident. Ghaelen stared fearfully through the sweat that was streaming down his face at Larayel and Tharsarn . . . and they looked back at him, faces just as empty of hope.

And then the Thrael hummed with fury all around them, the Great Serpent seething in their minds, and they were frantically trying to remember just how many men Phelmar commanded.

"There can't be many left," Tharsarn gasped aloud, his voice flat with self-doubt. They were going to die here, they were all going to die.

Lashing their minds with the whip of his will, the Great Serpent goaded them upright like so many stiffly stumbling puppets, and drove them on down the passage.

Horl lurched forward—and then dropped into a sudden crouch. Dlan didn't need his warning wave to do the same.

"Darkness," the elder procurer commanded gruffly, extinguishing his own glowstone. Dlanazar made his go out, too, and in the resulting sudden blindness, heard the old man mutter something.

Then light blossomed in the room beyond—and Dlan saw that it was coming from Horl's glowstone, as it tumbled end-over-end towards the floor. Three passages branched off through grand arches on the far wall of the room, there were mounds of rubble on the floor . . . and something low and dark moved swiftly along behind them.

"What'd you—you *threw* the glowstone! You threw my glowstone!"

Horl didn't bother to turn his head as the beast—something low and scaled, like a great lizard, but built like a forest fangcat, and moving about as fast—raced around the end of some rubble and charged at them. "Of course, lad—that's what they're *for*. Unless, of course, you think you'd have time to slay yon rocktail if it came at you out of the darkness, with you all lit up so it can see just where to pounce!"

Dlan was already snarling curses and plucking out and hurling daggers for all he was worth—two, three, four . . . most of them glanced away harmlessly, but the fifth caught the thing's eye, causing it to roar and shake its head in pain—and the sixth went into that roaring mouth and made it rear up, choking . . . just about at the time when it crashed into them, its charge spoiled.

Horl had dropped into a kneeling position that made his old sword into a sort of grounded lance, so the rocktail would have to turn aside or run right onto it and impale itself.

As Dlanazar sprang to one side and started hacking at the thing desperately with his own blade, not knowing if he'd get a chance to drive home the dagger in his other hand . . . the rocktail, still squalling and choking, did just what Horl had hoped it would: slammed into the old man and hurled him back, wrapped around his own sword . . . with its teeth raking at his scarred arms, and his sword buried to the guards in the roof of its mouth.

It thrashed in agony, taloned limbs and razor-edged tail whipping and flailing around the walls and bowling Dlan

painfully off his feet and along the floor . . . and then it vomited a great gush of gore and bile, spasmed once or twice, and
sagged limply, sliding half-off Horl's battered blade.

"Youngling!" the old man barked. "Look into yon chamber, and if you see no more perils, retrieve the stone I threw!
Use your glowstone to look closely at the floor, and don't
hurry. If you see *anything* moving, no matter how small,
come right back!"

Dlanazar was four strides out into the chamber before he
slowed, frowned, and looked back. Aye, of course he'd agreed
to do Horl's bidding . . . but when had he settled so unthink-
ingly into following the old man's orders?

Was the old man using magic on him?


In a far tower, a wizard whose name was unknown across
Darsar because he so carefully kept to himself shivered all
over, and almost dropped the book of spells he'd been trying
to study.

His pet arhaunag flapped its tiny leathery wings restlessly
and switched its tail, feeling its master's mood.

The Thrael had never blazed up like *this* before. His carefully layered wards, built to keep him alive by preventing the
Great Serpent from finding him, usually kept all hint of its
use from his mind, but . . .

Some mighty working must be afoot. Either someone formidable was trying to slay the Great Serpent and he was
having to fight hard, or the Serpent had abandoned all prudence to craft some mighty magic or other. Which in turn
meant either doom for someone that he'd best know
about . . . or the Serpent was hurling aside all else to find
him at last.

The time for hiding and cowering was over. He ran along
a passage in such haste that his flowing robes upset a precious crystal and swept a floating chime-sculpture of precious gems to the floor.

He spared them not even the briefest of regretful glances.
It was time for the Dragon to fly.

\* \* \*

The next Wartalon was easy to slay. They found him dancing
alone by himself, capering in a room where three passages
met, sword in hand but eyes bright and merry as he sang—an
aimless, keyless, wordless idiot's moan. Larayel's lip curled
in distaste as he felled the man with a simple fangfly spell.
One's blade does not have to be envenomed to slay in a single thrust if the target mounts no more defense than grinning
and beckoning.

The three Serpents stood over the feebly writhing corpse
and exchanged grim glances. The whispering was a pulsing
shout in their heads, now, almost drowning out the fierce-
with-rage coldness of the Thrael . . . and if it somehow
drowned out the Thrael, they'd be left blind in the darkness.

Almost as if in demonstration, a man stumbled blindly at
them along one of the passages. Tharsarn recognized him as
one of the Wartalons by the snarling wolfhead painted on his
battered breastplate, a trophy he'd noticed earlier. The man's
head was engulfed by a long, gray, snakelike beast that
seemed to have no fangs. It was *sucking* obscenely at what
was in its mouth, its long, heavy body trailing down from the
man's shoulders to be dragged behind the weakening hiresword like a tail.

Ghaelen's mouth tightened, and he blasted both beast and
victim with immolating fire—a spell that left behind only a
clatteringly collapsing tangle of bones. Larayel and
Tharsarn gave him looks of respect mingled with surprise.

He silently waved at them to precede him down the passage the man had come from, and they obeyed.

After only a few paces it opened out into a great high-
ceilinged hall, a vast expanse of bare floor interrupted only by
two things: the mold-and-dust-covered ruins of what appeared
to be a collapsed table . . . and a giggling man in armor.

Phelmar Silvertree shuffled staring-eyed but unseeing
around the great chamber, wandering aimlessly as his mouth
bubbled forth foaming mirth. He looked like an empty husk,

as if someone had plucked his mind and his verve out of his body in one swift plundering, to leave this ruin behind.

The three Serpents exchanged looks and then moved forward to cast a lesser shielding that would give them a leash on this body. None of them particularly wanted to try a mindchain with such giggling insanity.

Ghaelen gestured to Larayel, who said uncertainly, "Your spell will be stronger than mine, Masterpriest. . . ."

The Great Serpent stirred in their minds, as if he was going to comment or more likely issue an order. And then something slumped, sickeningly, and—though the hall remained right where it was, in front of their eyes—the world seemed to plunge into an endless void.

Falling and fading, the three Serpents had time to see the darkness steal in and realize the Thrael was collapsing before a shrieking rush of bright-swirling magic came racing into their minds, so loud and vast and terrible that everything just . . . went away.


The Thrael's customary hum was a roaring shriek that made the diving Dragon wince. It was foolhardy to work a spell this close to the greatest sorcerer of Darsar, but it was either that or be slain crashing into the great domed roof of stone and slate that was rushing up to meet him so fast. . . .

He risked two spells. First, a farscrying keyed to the scrying-whorl that he could feel already at work in the great chamber under the dome. If he just clung to its fringes and let himself be carried around the chamber, seeing what little he could without gazing at the Serpent . . .

There were a few silently cowering Serpent-priests standing against the walls of the hall, but his great serpentine foe was standing alone in the center of the room, arms spread as if frozen in the act of clawing the air, eyes fixed on nothing like two dark swordpoints. The sorcerer's attention was fixed entirely on the ruined mind of a man in Silvertree House, and whoever—or whatever—was controlling it.

The Dragon abandoned that spell so fast that its collapsing tangles made his head burn inside, and shouted the incant he needed only just in time.

The stones of the dome melted away an instant before he would have smashed into them, leaving his claws and jaws free to slash and shred the Great Serpent.

Collapsing spells seared and scalded him, but even if his jaws hadn't bitten the great man-snake into blood-drenched gobbets, the mighty crash of his landing crushed all that remained to a bloody pulp against shattered stones—as the floor of the chamber gave way and crashed down into the cellar beneath it, spilling mindblasted Serpent-priests to broken-bodied dooms.

The Dragon fought to roll over and struggle out of the wreckage, but great pains flooded through him, and a web of spells was collapsing in ruin on top of him, many small explosions spitting fire in all directions, and oblivion was so near and so welcome. . . .

All over the shattered citadel of the Serpents, priests roamed mindlessly. Those few who'd been asleep and unattuned to the Thrael were jolted awake, heads aching, into utter confusion. They snatched up robes and weapons of magic and stumbled out of their chambers to investigate— but found only death.

Servant after slave after guardian beast shifted shape into humans who grinned like eager wolves and delivered those dooms to the bewildered Serpents. One of them had time to gasp, "W-who—?"

And the face of his slayer bent close to smile very unpleasantly at him, and said, "We're called the Koglaur, or 'Faceless' if you prefer. And we've had quite enough of Great Serpents or anyone else lording it over Aglirta. If I were you, I'd thank me for giving you so swift and easy a passing. We're going to enjoy hunting the last few of you down."


Priest of the Serpent Ilmarr Maertryn stiffened in front of his high window in Sirlptar. A tallglass of very expensive dragondream fell from his slackening hand, to shatter like a spray of blood on the tiles at his feet.

"The Thrael," he gasped dazedly. "That can only mean . . ."

There was an evil chuckle from behind him, and he turned slowly towards it, aware in his stunned state only that it was a sound that shouldn't have been there.

His wine-wench was standing right behind him, clad in the net of fine chains that was all he allowed her to wear. There was a broad smile on her face that shouldn't have been there—and she was lacking the platter of decanters that should have been in her hands.

One of those hands had stretched out to an impossible length—and was, in fact, just parting fingers that were growing into talons, to encircle Maertryn's neck.

The priest blinked at her, too overwhelmed by the horror of the Great Serpent's passing to react to this . . . this impossibility.

"Such a disaster for the Church of the Serpent," she purred, as her smile grew fangs and her eyes grew hungry. "Yet such a relief for Sirlptar—and such a triumph for us Koglaur."

And she tore out his throat without waiting for Maertryn to think of a reply.


Outside the window, sheep made their usual sounds—and smells. Lord of the Serpent Alphaer Chonthul curled his lip in distaste, but turned back to the bared and bound female on the table and painted particular areas of her flesh with the glowing powders his spell would need.

Upland Aglirta offered primitive conditions indeed—but the results of his transformation spells needed a lot of space, even when nothing went wrong. If this wench could be twisted into a nightwyrm, the Church could soon have many such, aerial battle-steeds that could conquer even Sirlptar with ease. . . .

And then something in his mind flashed up and struck him hard behind his eyes, and Chonthul reeled, tasting his own

blood. There was a sickening feeling, a falling, in his head
rather than his gut, and in slow disbelief the Serpent lord
whispered the only thing this could mean: "The Great Serpent is dead!"

And the maid on the table laughed lightly and said, "*Well,
then . . .*"

Chonthul turned back to her in time to receive the bony
spears her hands had suddenly become right through his
chest.

He grunted helplessly, unable to breathe, as she lifted him
as if he weighed no more than a handful of feathers, her
bony blades wrist-deep into and through him, and grinned
into his astonished and dying face.

"Fare you well, Lord Alphaer Chonthul. You weren't as
bad as some of them—except for these little matters of
working transformations on the unwilling, and what you
liked to do to lasses. It might amuse you to know that none
of your shape-changing spells have worked . . . the changes
you saw in us were wrought by our own powers. You see,
every last one of us is a Koglaur."

Deep in the Silent House, the shambling thing that had been
Phelmar Silvertree hefted its sword and shuffled silently into
the darkness, seeking the darkest alcove wherein to await the
next intruders.

This Silvertree House that men fear so much is large
and plentifully supplied with nasty death traps, to be
sure, and roamed besides by monstrous strange beasts.
I myself have seen taloned hands reach out of solid
stone to crush a man's skull as easily as a cook puts her
thumb through an egg above a fire-fry.

Yet for all the whisperings, which that ring I found in
that archmage's tomb in the Windfangs seems to keep
at bay, and these perils I've noted, the so-called Silent
House is nothing more nor less than a series of plun-

derable crypts, scattered through a labyrinth of largely empty halls and passages the size of Teln or any other city of the Asmarandan coasts.

I'll admit this much: the House does seem to *grow* by itself, as if invisible builders work whenever no one's watching, to throw up more wings and turrets, and the maps of one season do not always serve as safe guides in the next.

North of what some old maps call Galard's Hall, I judge to be scoured out. The wings beyond the Banner Gallery, and the underways beneath the Long Hall, all were plundered by the Blackfalkaun Band, out of Gloit, before Daers Blackfalkaun made one too many forays into the beast-haunted ways beyond Flaertrumpet Hall.

I doubt me the new sprawl southwards can hold much treasure; methinks going deep under the old part of the House, by taking the stair off the South Forehall, will offer the richest yields. I found that stair all choked with mens' bones last season, but they are all gone now (carried off by unknown hands or claws). So some creatures at least have been before us, or travel that way habitually.

Duth of Duth's Blades, the Sirl band, was busy in Ghostwynd Tower last season, and his blades set upon us whenever they saw us, as if guarding great wealth. Yet I hear they were for hire in the Sirl backalleys all winter, which tells me their bellies were empty. So whatever trail they follow is false or lost, or their wits cannot unravel it. I'd be unsurprised if the plundering of the wizard Maurauvan's tower turns out to be their work, for word in the city has it that all his maps and books that were not spellguarded are taken.

Our best road will be to find another way down to the old deeps besides the South Forehall stair, so that neither Duth nor prowling beast nor a simple fall of stone can entomb us.

For that is the fate the Three intend for me, methinks:

for Silvertree House to become my tomb. I must take care to keep them waiting for its befalling for many long and coin-filled years.

The Plunderer of Tombs
Deepwinter, Fourteenth Year of the Reign of Kelgrael

# BOOK SIX

---◆◆◆---

*Joszgar Silvertree*

1212–1241 ? SR
Lord Baron of Silvertree
And of the Dream of His Lady,
and How Talasorn Wizards Saw Ghosts

# 1

## A Dream of Two Baronies

*H*is instructions were quite clear. The Lady Baron
Narembra Blackgult was to die this night, to remove
a great evil from the land.

The short, slight, nimble man with the sly good looks
hung in the darkness, feeling the magic take hold of him,
and stared across the dark waters of the moat. His shoulder-
length brown hair was held back out of his eyes with a brow-
band, and his agile body wore dark hides crisscrossed with
lacings to keep the achingly tight leather from creaking
when he moved. There were other men who dealt in stealthy
deaths for a living, but as far as he knew, he was the best.

Joszgar Silvertree was of Sirl stock, and had been a busy
slayer-for-hire for a dozen years and more; he accorded but
little regard for the pretty words of clients. Anything a handful of Serpent-priests regarded as a "great evil" would be at
best an impediment to the greater glory of the Serpent. However, their coins had been real enough, and he'd insisted on
full payment in advance, knowing full well that any attempt
to collect a remaining half-payment after the deed would put
him into their hands—by which time he, too, would have
somehow become a "great evil" better removed from the
face of Asmarand.

It was no secret that the Serpents desired to openly rule
Aglirta, and then turn their venomed daggers and snakes-
out-of-sleeves spells to conquering rich Sirlptar itself. It was
also no secret that something bad had befallen the Great Serpent, years ago, and thrown these schemes into disarray.
Many Serpent-priests had been slain all over Darsar in the
wake of that happening, as many scores were settled.

Now the Serpents were feeling their strength again, at

least in Aglirta, where barons fought like snarling dogs over meat scraps, and needed but paltry excuses for making war upon each other. Elsewhere, the Church of the Serpent was either outlawed or harshly kept down . . . so it was "elsewhere" that Joszgar Silvertree would have to go, in haste, the moment this night's deed was done. He would need a new life, new looks, and many smiles from the Three Above to disappear from their notice.

If he could find a wizard he could trust, he could "switch faces" with a Serpent-priest, slay "himself," and let word get back to the snake-lovers . . . but there was a small flaw in that plan: the complete lack of anyone in all Darsar who might accurately be called "a wizard he—or anyone—could trust."

Enough of such night-wasting thoughts. The task at hand, first.

Castle Blackgult was old and impressive, with side-turrets aplenty sprouting from its massive, frowning towers. Its black stones had been smeared with Silverflow mud and then fire-fused by mages to seal the lower reaches into a surface like black glass . . . but that had been done centuries ago, and at such cost—wizards again—that the treatment extended perhaps only six man-heights above the green, still waters of the moat. The fondness of castle owners for stocking such stagnant moats with flesh-eating Sarindan eels made the purchase of a lofting spell a necessity for any would-be intruder; Joszgar had murmured the word that awakened his moments ago, and then fired the heaviest crossbow he could carry away into the night while bounding into the air. The recoil, as he dropped the weapon, had flung his temporarily floating body across the moat to the wall. The spell was now protecting him from a fall as he methodically scaled the wall. Above the fusing the stones were old and crumbling, and afforded many ready handholds. The night was cool and dark; moonless, just as Joszgar preferred. If the information he'd bought was correct, the side-turret thrusting out from the wall directly overhead contained the Lady Blackgult's chambers . . . and even evil and rapacious

Aglirtan barons had to sleep sometime. Moreover, if one was single by choice and a lover of books and solitude rather than of lusty men, why not sleep at night, when the light for reading was at its worst?

Not that he professed to understand *anything* about Aglirtan barons. This was the only female one, out of the whole brawling, cutthroat, nose-in-the-air pack of them. King Kelgrael Snowsar had been on the River Throne but *not* on the throne—gone and vanished; the bards said he wasn't dead, but rather "asleep" somewhere hidden—for years, since shortly after misfortune had befallen the Great Serpent. It hadn't taken long for the barons to squabble and then erupt into open war. So many had died since then that their successors, the barons of today, had never known any other state but ruling their own tiny corners of the realm like so many rival warlords.

Which left beautiful Aglirta a war-torn, nigh-lawless land . . . and offered slayers-for-hire like Joszgar Silvertree plenty of employment opportunities.

Too many, in fact. He'd made his coins and worn out his luck, and 'twas time to say farewell and slip away. Just this one last job . . .

The underside of the turret had the usual privy-chute, its door thankfully closed right now, and its walls were pierced by two smallish windows and, on the side that looked south to the Silverflow, a large balcony embrasure with both a window and a door with a man-high window in it. When he'd last peered at them, just before dusk, there'd been no sign of war-shutters. It remained to be seen if the door had locks, edges, or bars.

Joszgar Silvertree paused just below the lip of the balcony to check his blades. There'd be no time to fumble at the ties of laced-against-loss daggers once he was in the bedchamber beyond, or to reach for a second knife if the first one proved to be missing.

All accounted for. Three Above, keep smiling. Like a dark wind he boosted himself up and over the lip in one smooth movement, vaulting the smooth-carved rail to land on his toes against the inner wall, knees first to kiss the stones and keep his body from touching the glass above and making any sound that might warn or awaken someone within.

He stood motionless, listening, and heard only a night-croak from some far-off creature below, carried on a rising breeze. No lights, no clamor of alarm. Joszgar turned away from the window and whispered the second word, as softly as clear and precise speech allowed.

He half expected the door to be glowing warningly when he turned around again, for the spell had certainly worked, banishing his lofting but showing him the flickering glow of its dying as it did so. Far inside the glass, across the darkened room within, there were two small, motionless glows—enchanted items of some sort—but all else was dark. No warning-ward upon the door or its threshold, nothing on the window or balcony.

Could it really be this easy?

Joszgar put his fingertips to the door, to test the strength of its lock, and pulled gently . . . and the door slid open, soft on a well-soaped wooden runner. Three bless!

Not even locked. Either the Lady Baron Narembra Blackgult was supremely confident of her defenses—overconfident of her defenses, rather—or there was some sort of trap awaiting, something nonmagical. A falling gate of spikes, or a prowling beast. Joszgar stood smelling for the latter, and then plucked up a small wooden table that sat beside an empty chair on the balcony, and extended it through the doorway.

Nothing. No slamming-down portcullis or opening pit. He put the table gently on the floor inside and reached out with his reaching-claw to put all the weight he could on it. Even when the metal shaft of the claw was bending warningly, nothing happened.

So Joszgar returned the table to where he'd found it, and stepped boldly inside. After another few moments of silence, he slid the door closed again, and waited for his eyes to adjust to the darkness of the room.

Slowly they did so, and he became aware of an open expanse of floor, covered by the largest Telnan white-fur rug he'd ever seen, right in front of him, with a closed door that must lead into the rest of Castle Blackgult facing him in its far wall. There were sideboards and a man-high looking glass and wardrobes to his right—crowded alcoves of them, in fact—and a gigantic canopied bed to his left, with what must be a spiral stair up to a second level beyond it. And on that bed, propped up on pillows in the darkness, lounged . . . a barefoot woman in a revealing gown, an open book in her hand and her long, unbound hair spread out over her shoulders and breast like a great dark wave.

"Fair evening to you," the Lady Baron Narembra Blackgult said politely. "Will you take wine?"

Though she did not seem to so much as lift a finger, brief blue fires raged around Joszgar's every weapon. Even the well-concealed ones.

Rather than trying to use any of them, he whirled to dive at the glass door, to hurl himself through it towards some slim chance at safety—but found himself rooted to the spot, his frantic exertions succeeding only in making his body shake.

Rage and fear mounted in Joszgar's throat as he stood helpless, watching a silent parade of his weapons stream away from him. The boot-heels she left to him, but the belt-buckle knife tore itself free and darted across the room towards her, leaving his breeches to sag. Had they not been skintight, he'd have been standing before her with very little dignity indeed.

And if she could read a book in this darkness, she could see him breathe, see his eyes shift, see everything. He was helpless in spell-thrall. Joszgar swallowed, to see if he still could, and then tried to speak.

"Uh . . . ah, yes, Lady Baron, I *would* like something to drink about now." He tried a smile, but it came out rather lopsided. He settled for swallowing instead. Several times.

"No doubt," the Lady Baron replied dryly. "The most comfortable chair is that one. Bring it over here beside the bed. We must talk."

Indeed. The Serpents had said not a word of Lady Black-gult being a powerful sorceress. Perhaps the hiring had been their contemptuously adroit way of getting rid of him. Josz-gar turned towards the chair she'd indicated, and found that he could move freely. He hitched up his breeches and fetched the chair.

When he set it down, she said, "Closer." When he moved it to where she was pointing, he found his belt buckle floating in the air waiting for him. "My apologies for the indignity," she said, without the slightest hint of mockery—and a full flagon of calamanta floated up to join it.

"Lady," he asked gravely as he reached for it, "will drinking this harm me?"

"Unless you happen to hate fine calamanta," she replied, "no."

"You know who I am, and why I came here?" he asked as he restored his garb and sat down with the flagon in his hand.

"Yes," she replied, setting the book down to lean forward on the bed and provide Joszgar with a view that was most distracting, "and that's why you're still alive. I know you were hired to slay me, and by whom, but I don't know your own feelings in this matter. Do you hate me, or bear a grudge against me?"

"No, Lady," Joszgar replied truthfully, daring to sip his wine. He felt a tingling, but when he hastily lowered the flagon to stare at her, it remained in his head.

"Could you come to trust me?" she asked, face very serious.

"I—yes, Lady. I . . . I like you, thus far."

A thin smile came and went around her mouth. The tingling grew stronger.

"Good. If you feel anything untoward, that's my rather clumsy truth-telling spell. Call me Narembra, and answer me this: Could you live with me, as my wedded lord?"

"I—*whaaat?*" Joszgar tried hard not to sputter very fine and fiery calamanta all over her white-fur rug, choked, coughed a few times to clear his pipes, and regarded her through swimming eyes. "Lady, this is a strange way of toying with me!"

"I'm not toying. I'm asking you a fairly clearly worded question. And the name's Narembra, Nar for short." She waited, and then asked, "Well?"

"Uh, ah, Narembra . . . well *what?*"

"Will you marry me?"

Joszgar blinked, and then regarded his wine suspiciously. "I . . . that's what I thought you were asking. Lady, are you serious?"

The woman on the bed leaned forward enough to sit up on her knees, her face—her throat—close enough for Joszgar to reach, and said with some asperity, "Joszgar Silvertree, I'm not in the habit of spending restless hours waiting for hired assassins to steal into my bedchamber so that I can bandy clever tricksy words with them. If I wanted to slay you or addle your wits, 'twould have been a simple spell to work as you crossed the moat—so your body would have just dropped down to feed my eels when your lofting spell ran out, and I could have enjoyed a good night's sleep. And Nar am I, *Nar,* not Lady Baron anything, while it's just the two of us here in this chamber. Do you know how *long* I've been spying on you? How many oh-so-subtle spells it took, delving into those sewers of Serpent-priest minds, to manipulate them into hiring you to come here?"

Joszgar blinked. "Uh . . . why?"

"Because you're the only Silvertree heir of age right now, and I quite like what I've seen of you. Slayings and all."

She drew her feet out from under her and sat on the edge of the bed, so their knees were almost touching, and added more softly, "My question stands."

Joszgar licked his lips, and then, very carefully, drank the rest of his wine. She pointed at the glass, and it promptly refilled itself.

He regarded it thoughtfully, rather proud that his hand wasn't visibly shaking, and then said, "I . . . quite like what I've seen of you thus far, too. What . . . conditions will you place on me? I'm not to touch you, I presume?"

"Oh, no," Nar replied, her eyes large and dark. "You presume wrongly. There is one condition, yes: you must work with me to reclaim your lands and title."

"My—? Oh, you think I'm one of *those* Silvertrees," the Sirl assassin said in a rush of enlightenment—and disappointment. "Ha-huh, Lady . . . I was born and raised in Sirlptar. Legendary haunted palaces have nothing to do with me. Why, there are dozens of Silvertrees in Sirlptar, and a few in Gilth, too."

"Yes, and all of them are of the same lineage. You are indeed one of 'those' Silvertrees. I've traced your lineage directly back to Taerith Silvertree. Mine, too, though we're not so closely related that we cannot wed. The legends do not lie: if you can dwell in Silvertree House without going mad, you *are* the rightful Baron Silvertree, and every commoner of Aglirta will believe it. Of course, there is the small matter of mustering an army to hold your lands—or being swept away by every greedy baron, tersept, and wizard in Asmarand."

Joszgar shook his head and laughed a little incredulously. "Lady, Lady—*Nar*—even if all this is true, I'm a dead man if I accept your offer. I dare not betray those who hired me. If you truly know who they are, you'll also know very well why. So what would you have me do? Die by your hands for refusing me? Or accept, and be slain on the morrow, or the next day, or the next?"

Narembra gave him a brittle smile, waved her hand—and there were suddenly eight pale-faced, empty-eyed men in robes floating upright in a half-circle behind Joszgar, heads lolling, like so many cloaks hung up on pegs of empty air.

Joszgar looked around at them, recognizing a few faces, as they dripped and drizzled blood onto white fur below.

"As you can see," the sorceress said softly, "there's no one left to come after you for failing to kill me or falsely keeping your slayer's fee. Thanks to a few spells I spent some time crafting, their superiors will believe they died fighting each other. And as for your lack of future fees . . . I've plenty of wealth here."

She gestured again, and the corpses vanished. Joszgar blinked at the empty darkness, and then down at the little puddles of gore on the rug. He swallowed again.

It was some time before he turned his gaze reluctantly back to the woman in the dark gown. Their eyes met in silence, and Narembra's eyes dropped first.

"So," she asked, her voice almost a whisper, "will you be wed to me?"

She reached out her hand to his.

He took it in a sort of disbelieving dream, and found it smooth and warm and real enough.

Lady Baron Narembra Blackgult did something with her other hand that made the front of her gown fall open.

Eyes on hers, Joszgar Silvertree reached out, fingers spread, and whispered back, "Yes."

"We're nearing the Long Hall," Horl said, peering through another archway. "Near the place where Joszgar Silvertree . . ."

"Yes?"

"Ne'er mind, lad. Tell you after we get at whatever treasure awaits under yon statue."

"Treasure?" Dlan started forward eagerly.

"Hey, there! Saying is easy, doing always harder. Start striding towards a statue or what's left of one in this House, and you're usually hurrying to your own grave."

Dlanazar stopped dead and gave Horl a look of disgust.

The old man shrugged. "Know this, overeager youngling: Just about every statue in Silvertree House can be shifted, and there's treasure or at least a hiding-hole under bebolten-near every last one of them. There's also traps on most, of the poisoned spring-dart sort. So . . . go warily. Patience is the mark of the successful procurer, lad. Patience, not greed."

"A trap on *every* statue? So this place was built like some sort of death trap, or slaying-amusement parade?"

Horl shrugged. "No one knows why all the features of the House were built, lad. All I can say is that centuries of adventurers have learned—the hard way—that statues here usually have both treasure . . . and traps. At least they did last year, and bid fair to do the same next year, too."

Dlanazar's eyes narrowed. "And how is it that you know all this, old man?"

"Well, now . . . see these scars? I've been around for a long time."

"Yes, yes, you're terribly old and wise," the handsome young procurer snapped dismissively. "Suppose we sit down over there—that block is safe to sit on, isn't it?—and you tell me about *yourself* before you wag your jaws about dear departed Baron Joszgar Silvertree. Just so I know whom I'm walking through this death trap with, you understand."

Horl grinned, rubbed his grizzled old chin, and said, "*Now* you begin to ask what you should have, back when we were trudging along the forest trails to get here. Telling you just a handcount of the things I've done would bore you to snores, I can see, so let's just say I hail from . . . somewhere in Aglirta, and down the years I've been a warrior and a shepherd, a dock-loader, a drover, a merchant's hand and a score of other things, besides. I've spent most of my days either in Sirlptar or in Aglirta, mostly in the lawless time of the Sleeping King, and I have one great talent."

He fell silent, but Dlan merely waited for him to continue rather than asking what it was, so the elder procurer announced, "I like to hear a good tale, I remember what's said to me . . . and I long ago learned to sit and not be noticed and *listen*. You might like to try it some time."

"So I try it for sixty-some winters, as you have, and I somehow remember that much rumor, downright lies, exaggerations, and embellishments, and I gain . . . what?"

Horl grinned. "A lot of scars, colorful tales to keep folk interested around tavern-fires, and the wits to drag along eager young procurers to reach and lift and slay when you no longer can."

Dlan stared at him expressionlessly. "And a little magic to move said young procurer to your will, perhaps?"

Old Horl gave his younger companion a disgusted look. "If

I had a little magic, lad, what would I need you for? And why wouldn't I have cozened the wits of a lovely young lass, hey?"

The ceiling of Nar's bed-canopy was a magical window, into a beautiful daytime scene of a deep, sun-dappled forest through which a stream flowed, the faint laughter of its waters almost lost amid the gentle rustlings of leaves. There was a ruined castle in the background—and as Joszgar gazed at it, a stag walked into view amid the trees, lifted its head to stare in his direction, and then moved unconcernedly on.

"It must be nice," he said slowly, "to be a sorceress."

"Sometimes," Narembra purred, from close beside his ear. Joszgar lost all interest in the distant forest, wherever it was, and turned back to her.

He still couldn't quite believe. . . .

She smiled a little ruefully as their arms went around each other once more. "Afraid this is all a dream?"

Joszgar nodded.

"Well, you're now part of *my* dream. I want to refound Aglirta—a strong, fair Aglirta—around our linked baronies. I expect we'll die trying to make that dream real, and die failing, too, but I very much want to try."

Joszgar sighed. "The Three gather us all, in the end. I—I can think of no better company to die in."

The sorceress kissed him, and he responded . . . and at some point they both drifted off to sleep lying in each other's arms.

Joszgar cursed as a crossbow quarrel glanced bruisingly off his ill-fitting armor, snatching him out of his saddle. Gods, he hated wearing armor, but . . .

Narembra did something to slow his crashing fall, and cried, "Betrayed again! It seems Cardassa's word means nothing!"

As Joszgar struggled to his feet, he saw the banners of the

barony of Cardassa coming into view out of the trees on their flank—their last remaining flank. They'd have to move like the wind, or be—

"Surrounded!" he snarled. "They're trying to pen us in and butcher us!"

Lady Baron Blackgult stood up in her stirrups and announced, her soft voice carrying to every armaragor and cortahar around them, "All of you turn upriver. We'll be riding back to Silvertree House."

"But look you!" a veteran knight protested, waving at the bright-armored wall that was the army of Baron Tarlagar. "Those lances will spit us like penned cattle! And they're four or five to our one!"

"None of which will give them a fighting chance against me, Tarlorth," Narembra said calmly, shaking off her chained-to-her-waist war gauntlets to lay bare her hands. "Up shields, all! *Arrows!*"

Her warning came but moments before a thunderous rain of shafts, arcing down from the Wolfhammer mercenaries. Someone screamed as he fell, and many others pitched over silently into death—but at the height of the tumult Lady Blackgult's voice rang out as clear as a trumpet, "Ride! Spurs hard and *ride!*"

And with a ragged shout of defiance, what was left of the tattered armies of Blackgult and Silvertree spurred their mounts into a gallop, some horses limping and some arrow-adorned men reeling in their saddles. Straight at the ready cortahars of Tarlagar they rode, a desperate charge that made many of those bright-armored, waiting men smile in grim anticipation of the slaughter they'd do, with Cardassa closing in behind their foe, the Wolfhammers readying another volley of shafts, and the huge host of Maerlin already moving to harry the fools of the Lovers' Baronies.

The charging men were barely a handful of the mighty muster that had seized the Silvertree lands from brigands and petty lordlings and tersepts loyal to Maerlin and Phelinndar. Sixty-some blades, now, no more . . . and no wonder.

For month after month hired mercenaries and armies

raised by barons up and down the Vale had struck at the
forces of the Lovers, gnawing at their strength as do hungry
wolves who return again and again to a snow-trapped herd in
a hard winter. They held but this small patch of trampled
ground now . . . and not even that for much longer. It was all
going to end in red slaughter here, one more foolish dream
of taking the throne of Aglirta. . . .

Armaragors on three sides of the doomed, hard-galloping
warriors leaned forward in fierce anticipation, to be there at
the bloody ending.

And if the faces of some of them slipped into strange
forms inside their helms, or their limbs lengthened just a bit
to let them lean farther, who was to notice but other Koglaur?

*This is* our *land, fool of a sorceress. Try to foist your dupe
somewhere else. We Koglaur rule here.*

*Squabble we may—but thrust yourself into our nest, and
we'll unite against you.*

The Lady Baron Narembra Blackgult stood up in her stirrups again amid the full rolling thunder of the charge, arms
spread, and cried something high and harsh.

And a wind that was all unseen talons and driving hammerblows blasted into the Tarlagar lines, rending men and
metal with equal buttery ease. Bodies flew high into the air,
broken and tumbling, or were dashed to bloody ruin . . . and
in the heart of one shouting, screaming moment, an army
ceased to exist.

*Gods, but there's a sort of sickening glory in such might! Be-
holding it thus, in the remembrances of others, I can feel the
fire and fury and hunger of mighty sorcery, and what drives
those who seek such mastery!*

*And then it passes, and I'm alone again in the cold and the
shadows, remembering something else: what becomes of all
such mighty wizards.*

*And then I truly feel the cold.*

\* \* \*

The tattered few who bore the colors of Blackgult and Silvertree raced through the ruin while bodies were still falling from overhead, and men all over that field were gasping in awe.

One of them was Baron Joszgar Silvertree, who gaped at his white-faced, reeling lady and hastily caught at her, to keep her in her saddle. There was blood running from her mouth, and her eyes were half-closed.

"Nar? *Nar!*" he cried frantically, clutching her hand as their frightened mounts pounded along flank to flank.

Wits swam back from somewhere onto her pale face and left her wearing the wan ghost of a smile. Dark eyes glimmered back at him, wet with tears. Tears of pain.

"I live, Josz . . . for now."

They pounded on, holding hands, as Joszgur looked into the face of the lady he had come to love, into the future, and saw . . . nothing.

Death was rushing up to meet them, or they were galloping hard to reach it.

Better than a spell blasting him off Nar's balcony, on that soft night that seemed now so long ago.

Better, but harder. They'd tasted defeat after defeat, these last days—so much death—as hireswords from distant lands had come crowding up the Silverflow on barges, the armies of rival barons marching on both banks. All, Narembra had snarled to him, one night when they were too tired to bury the dead, because of the Koglaur.

It was dream-time again for Joszgur; weren't the Faceless nightmares out of the nursery and hearthfire tales?

And now they were riding hard for Silvertree House, fleeing to a deserted ruin to sell their lives dearly. Where he was going to learn if another nursery-tale nightmare was true or not: that any of the blood Silvertree who tarried for too long in the Silent House went drooling-mad, forever. . . .

Or until merciful death claimed them.

Arrows were thrumming down among them again, now, and men were gasping and falling, twisting out of their saddles in dying agony to be trampled underfoot. Along the riverside road they were pounding, with three armies on their tail. Thick woods guarded one of their flanks, now, and the Silverflow the other . . . but every last shaft that could be set to bowstring was howling at their backsides.

The towers of the vast and sprawling House were just visible in the distance, beyond a gentle shoulder of hillside and over a lot of trees.

And all that hard-riding way, with horses beginning to stumble with exhaustion, armaragors of the Lovers' Baronies died, saddles emptying one by one. A horse fell, and others crashed over it to be ridden down and left dying in the dust. An armaragor turned in his saddle to raise his shield against arrows—and had it torn away, and the arm with it, by a flung lance that spun him out of his saddle to the road and his doom under a thousand hooves.

And seven—six—four riders struggled up the tomb-studded hillside into the palace, and clottered across a court-yard to dismount in frenzied haste and run through archways, into the waiting gloom beyond.

"Whither?" Joszgur shouted, seeing a familiar helm crash to the ground ahead, freeing a swirl of dark hair. He flung his own away delightedly in its wake.

"This way," Narembra panted, pointing along a passage. "To the Long Hall, and beyond!"

"You'll have to give me a tour, some time," he called back, his ill-fitting armor clanging—and giggled.

Narembra and the two grim armaragors running with them all turned to give him sharp looks, but Joszgur Silvertree exploded into mirth again.

He couldn't seem to stop giggling.

Behind him there were shouts and clangs as men in full armor strode into the darkness, hurriedly readying torches and bows.

Joszgar turned to watch—in time to see snakelike things with sharp-taloned but otherwise human arms boil out of the solid stone of the walls, floor, and ceiling to clutch and rend and, yes, devour cortahars and armaragors and hire-swords.

Heads rolled, blood sprayed, and men screamed and died in his front hall.

It was all very amusing, and Joszgar Silvertree's giggles broke into wild peals of mirth.

# 2

## Ghosts in the Castle

"Thank the Three," the mightiest archwizard in all Sirlptar said gleefully, turning away from his scrying-crystal, "for this foolish sorceress and her dreams. It all comes to a bloody finish for her, now—leaving the rich heart of Aglirta bared for *me* to seize. As is only right."

Osprur Talasorn spoke these last words with satisfaction, but surprisingly little pride. His father and forefathers before that had been mages of power and fame, and the Talasorns had risen to wealth and prominence in Sirlptar and Coelortar over a century ago, now. Tall, white-haired, and masterful of manner, he was now patriarch of the family. For such a personage as himself, acquiring the rulership of a backward but verdant country would be . . . only proper.

He passed out through the enspelled doors that would part for him alone, and into the polished marble hall where his apprentices were busily instructing young Talasorn mages in the intricacies of subtle sorceries. "Attend," he said, almost casually, and listened to instant silence fall. As was proper.

"In accordance with my earlier orders, you prepared battle-spells. You are now to use them." Osprur glanced at the ceiling, and the great oval archway of spell-worked rock crystal began to descend, sparks and phantom flames of awakening magic racing and dancing along it.

"On the other side of this gate lies a great, nigh-deserted fortress: Silvertree House in upland Aglirta. You will find many warriors entering it, with armed strife ensuing inside.

Slay all who offer you resistance, save two: you are to seize the Lady Baron of Blackgult and the Baron of Silvertree, and bring them alive to me. Any magic you find in that palace—and there is much to be found—you may keep for your own, so long as none of you fight each other over it."

The gate erupted into blue flames, and the view of the room within it started to darken and change. Eager to gain the enchanted items he'd mentioned, the Talasorn wizards and apprentices hurried forward.

With a smile, Osprur ushered them through. It took only a few moments for the chamber to empty. He smiled at its glossy emptiness and returned to his scrying-crystal.

"Yes, hurtle into battle, my witless kin, and learn some competence. And when you deliver those two barons to me, I'll gain two useful mind-thralls who'll crown me King of Aglirta—and commence conquering the rest of the Vale in my name. As is only proper."

"More coins than we can carry," Dlanazar said triumphantly. "Three willing, we'll be finding gems to replace them with, soon!"

Horl chuckled. "That's the spirit, lad! By the maidens' moon-drenched shoulders, I'm relieved, I don't mind telling you! I'd started to think every last hiding-hole had been found and plundered already, and you'd start to think I'd been leading you here just to run you into a lonely, starving grave."

"Well," Dlan said, losing his smile suddenly, "I *am* low on water."

"Not to worry, lad—that's the Long Hall ahead of us, and I know where there's a well, two rooms beyond it."

"And would its water be safe to drink?"

Horl shrugged. "We'll know when we get there, hey? If not, the Silverflow lies in that direction . . . through about thirty rooms just bristling with stonefall traps."

"Wonderful," Dlan grunted. "My throat feels dry just thinking about it."

"On, then," Horl said cheerfully. "I grow no younger."

\* \* \*

A ball of flame erupted in the darkness, and two Talasorn mages shrieked as they were flung, flaming, against a wall. Behind them, another three more burned like torches in terrible, hissing silence, and died.

"Who *dares*—?" the senior Talasorn apprentice snapped, not knowing he was echoing the words of his distant master Osprur, bent over his scrying-crystal in a high tower in Sirlptar.

"*I* do, as it happens," a dark-eyed, sharp-featured man in robes replied, stepping out from behind a pillar to transfix the Talasorn apprentice with a conjured lance of cold, sharp stone, that bit right through the older wizard in its haste to join the stone wall behind him. "I am Harlvur Bowdragon, of the Bowdragons of Arlund," he told the gagging, dying man. "A name your master Osprur has for too long considered unworthy of notice—to his cost, it seems."

"Hah!" A fat, bearded wizard in robes that bore the gold badge of the Guild of Sorcery of Sirlptar called. "Die, puppy!" His spell of dark fires sent Harlvur Bowdragon screaming in flames across the room. "After a few more battles, you'll learn not to gloat over one foe while others lurk beneath your notice!"

Three snakes sped across the room like arrows to sink their fangs into the guild mage's face, and he staggered, making horrible gargling shrieks as he tried to tear them away from his face. "A common failing, it seems," the Serpent-priest who'd sent them sneered.

He was still sneering when a sword burst out of the breast of his robes from behind, and his gloating stare went glassy.

"Three, but it's getting crowded in here," the tall, scarfaced armaragor Tarlorth remarked, shaking the dead priest off his sword. "So many greedy folk trying to plunder the fabled magics of Silvertree House to get its store of magics before yon hireswords and baronial blades do . . . We'll be having the adventurers next."

As if his growled jest had been a cue, blue fire flashed

across the Long Hall, and a motley band of armed men sprang out of its heart with triumphant roars, swords flashing out.

"Well, now," Narembra Blackgult hissed, staring at these new arrivals. "The magic of this place allows gates from outside to open just there, hmm?"

Another brief blue star blossomed beside the first, and three young men tumbled out, fire-spells rolling from their hands as they came. "Bowdragon! Bowdragon!" they called, as their magics seared the startled adventurers.

Another guild wizard ducked out from behind a distant pillar to fell one of the three Bowdragons with a lance of lightning. An instant later his head exploded as three Serpent-priests stepped out of a side-chamber chanting something.

"Claws of the rutting Lady!" Tarlorth swore, staring in amazement. The two surviving Bowdragons came sprinting down the chamber, spitting curses of their own, but before they could get anywhere near Lady Blackgult—who stood protectively in front of a giggling, vaguely stumbling Lord Silvertree—the foremost Wolfhammer hireswords ran out of a side-passage to confront them.

The floor promptly erupted in maedra, slashing and clutching legs and ankles with their talons, and men shouted in fear and went down, hacking wildly, all over the Long Hall.

"I thought we were running from too many foes," Tarlorth said slowly, "but this . . . this beats all."

Spells flashed, here and there in the crowded room, and with a thunderous rumble that shook the floor beneath their boots, a nearby pillar shattered and began to topple.

"Tarlorth! Brammar!" Lady Blackgult cried. "Help me with Lord Joszgar! Back! Back, out *that* door!"

"Men of Talasorn! Stand *together!*" a mighty voice rolled out over the chamber, coming from everywhere—and nowhere. "Look to the southeast door! Blackgult and Silvertree! Don't let them flee from you! Take the—"

The voice fell abruptly silent, as Osprur Talasorn staggered back from his scrying-crystal in Sirlptar, blinking in astonishment. Something had been prying at his mind, trying to *twist* it . . . something ancient, and fell, and—not a wizard-foe known to him. "Three Above," he muttered, "what can that be?"

Dust and a fine rain of stones fell from the ceiling of the Long Hall in Silvertree House as spellbursts occurred here and there in the many-taloned fray of maedra and screaming, dying men. A guild wizard died shrieking as a fallen shard of stone was whirled up from the floor by a furious Bowdragon, to pierce through him—and elsewhere, a great shower of ceiling-stones flattened a running group of Serpent-priests.

Wizards vanished all over the chamber, winking out as spells whisked them to faraway safety. They were the fortunate few who had the means to flee. The maedra swarmed over the struggling men left behind—until mages grimly sacrificed fellow warriors, and let fly with blasting spells that tore apart maedra and men alike.

The shouts, clangor, and rumbling explosions of that battle faded behind the hurrying, panting Lady Blackgult, as she led two weary armaragors and the drooling baron between them deeper and deeper into the Silent House. A faint glow clung to her limbs, and gave Tarlorth and Brammar enough light to see by, up short flights of stairs and down others, along dank and dripping passages and across rubble-strewn, dust-choked halls. Light appeared far ahead of them, and they soon reached it, in a square, high hexagonal room with a domed roof of many windows, and balconies running around its inner walls.

"The Sunshaft, this is called," she said briefly. "A place I often used, down the years, when whisking myself here— and away again—with spells." She smiled weakly. "And no, I never found any treasure, fabled or otherwise. Just a lot of traps, and a lot more maedra."

She turned to face the two armaragors, and said, "Have my thanks, loyal blades. Here is where it ends for us; the dream is done. I'll not waste your lives, for Aglirta will have need of you in the years ahead. Find someone just and good—and wiser than I have been—to serve, and rear strong sons, and . . . and think of Joszgar and me, betimes."

"Lady, I—"

Tarlorth got out that much of a protest before her magic snatched him away, and Brammar with him. Back to whatever was left in her bedchamber in the ravaged halls of Castle Blackgult. Which had to be safer than here.

She could snatch herself there, too, of course—but not Joszgar. The House had its hooks in him, whispering magic rising in a warning murmur even now, as she thought about translocating him away.

He broke off gibbering then, and looked up at her, suddenly purposeful. Hope leaped in her, just for a moment, until she saw the blindly staring blue radiance leaking from his eyes. Whatever it was that inhabited the House—the Curse, the Whispering Mind, whatever it was truly called—was doing this.

Her Joszgar was almost gone.

He shuffled past her, pointing at one of the dark archways that led out of the sunlit room, and an armor plate fell off his shrunken frame with a crash. Its straps had been tightened about thews much bulkier than he now was . . . skin wrinkling and shrinking, he was growing old in front of her eyes.

Narembra followed him as he led her through that arch, and along a dark and narrow passage beyond, that turned abruptly into a rising stair. Steps glowed briefly blue so her feet could find them, and they climbed with surprising swiftness, emerging at last in a small bedchamber, furnished with a canopied bed that looked very much like her own, back in Castle Blackgult.

*Very* like. Narembra's eyes narrowed.

But Joszgar was turning to her, some of the wrinkled age fading from his face, and his eyes were his own again—wry but merry and bright.

"So, Nar, the Three have played their tricks on us this time. Never mind—the dream was glorious while it lasted . . . and your love has been the brightest flame in my life."

His arms went around her, and he kissed her . . . and despite her wariness—this *must* be the work of the House—she kissed him back, weeping inwardly.

Her tears burst forth in earnest as he grinned at her, stroked an errant lock of hair away from between them—just as he always had—and led her back to the bed, tugging at armor straps all the way.

She laughed, despite herself, and helped him shed his iron shell, whilst he clawed more enthusiastically than expertly at hers.

Through glimmering tears she saw his crow of triumph when the clasps of her sweat-soaked undertunic parted at last, and he drew her down onto the bed.

It was warmer than she'd expected, and neither moldy nor clammy, with no hint of dust at all. The House again . . .

Feebly Joszgar clutched at her, caressing eagerly but too weak to hold himself up, so she rolled them both over and rode him, his delighted laughter welling up for the first time in days.

Stronger he seemed, now, and more ardent, holding her to him, and Narembra felt her own strength ebb. She tried to rear back, and found herself both weak and slow. . . .

Of course! He was feeding on her vitality—or the Curse was, as it fed on him. For a moment Narembra Blackgult froze in horror and revulsion, and then she glanced again at her lord's eyes, and bent to kiss him, and thrust herself against him, locking her lips to his. Let him have what he needed of her, a few moments longer, while she drifted into him, deeper . . . and deeper. . . .

A fell sentience lurked in him, yes, and throughout the House. It was aware of her scrutiny, and ready to lash out at her mind, but she offered it no hostility, only curiosity and wonder, and in its startlement at that, it let her see much.

This mind . . . *Arau* it thought of itself as, sometimes, and *Sembril* at others . . . dwelt in the thousands of enchantments enshrouding Silvertree House, and manipulated its traps and rebuildings through mindbound maedra. Whenever it could, it worked to expand, defend, and consolidate itself . . . but that took force, life-force, vitality—and when its energies grew too low and its sanity grew weak, it fell asleep for long periods.

Until times like this day, when the Whispering Mind used the greatest magic it had ever crafted, and renewed itself by feeding on the wits and life-force of any of the blood of Silvertree present in the palace. From them it stole memories, and thoughts, and sanity itself, just as it drank life-force alone through the maedra, from victims of the stonewyrms. This, then, was what drove Silvertrees mad. . . .

And had already made Joszgar an empty thing, a shell that regained his words and gestures only because the Curse had his memories to guide it. . . .

Narembra tore herself free of her lord's failing husk desperately, spinning a mindweb to duck away from the searing bolt that sought to slay her, and tumbled from the bed, calling on all the magic she had left even as she rolled.

No time for incants or gestures, none for weaving a spell properly, as the walls themselves burst forth stony hands to reach for her, maedra boiled up out of many stones to clutch and howl—

And she was elsewhere, in a place she thanked the Three Above that she'd taken the trouble to study in some detail on her only other visit there . . . when its owner had sought to prove just how much more important he was than some up-river Aglirtan baron by keeping her waiting for a long time.

He wouldn't have the chance to do that now. Harriburth the Sage was seated at his study desk, gaping up at her in utter astonishment.

"The Lady Baron Narembra Blackgult-Silvertree," he said slowly, as if he was a herald proclaiming the titles of guests arriving at a grand feast.

Floating above him nude, wasted in flesh and mind, and trembling in the sickening aftermath of her great teleport, Narembra struggled to speak, desperate to deliver her warning ere she died.

Her magic gave out first, sending her crashing to the floor. Purely by a whim of the Three she landed upright, rocking on bare feet, and leaned against his desk to keep from falling.

"Write!" she gasped, leaning forward over the desk, breasts thrusting at the bespectacled nose of the old man until he recoiled. "Write this down, ere I die! The Curse of Silvertree House . . ." Breath failed her, and she clawed at the desk to keep from toppling and fought to find the strength she needed.

Fearfully the greatest sage in Sirlptar snatched up a quill and speared it into his best ink. All he had in front of him at this instant was the priceless map he'd been studying, but he hesitated not a moment.

He was still frantically scribbling, some agonized moments later, when Narembra Blackgult-Silvertree's strength gave out, and she gasped out, "Joszgar!"

Then Aldron Harriburth's none-too-clean tiled floor rushed up to meet her, and all Darsar went away, forever.

*I weep again, just watching that. Such valor, struggling to stay alive long enough to send a warning to those who might come after.*

*And yet, are those who warn ever heeded enough?*
*I know they are not.*
*And soon, so will you.*

A twitching tail and a severed talon tumbled down the room to fetch up against a far wall. A fearful Talasorn apprentice watched them narrowly to make sure they didn't grow back into the beast they'd come from again—or even two new stonewyrms!

The wizard whose spellbolt had slain the maedra straightened out of his tense crouch, rubbed his hands in satisfaction, and said, "There. That's the last, it seems. Hundreds, I've slain. *Hundreds.* To say nothing of a lot of mercenaries and baronial blades who should have known better than to chase anyone in here—or defy a Talasorn mage. Now, let's see about plundering this place."

"Rarlynd, do you think that's wise?" a younger Talasorn asked nervously, looking around at all the carnage. "I think just getting out of here alive would be achievement enough, about now."

Rarlynd Talasorn gave him a cold glance. "And having done all the bloody-work to gain us our chance to search, you'd throw it away? I hope you're personally ready to justify such folly to Himself—because I'm quite certain *I'm* not."

"Himself" was the term by which Osprur Talasorn was known in Tower Talasorn—never to his face, of course. Several Talasorns paled at the thought of facing his wrath, and the one who'd questioned Rarlynd—his sister's son Taeruld—visibly cowered.

Rarlynd smiled. "I thought so."

He turned back to survey the room and decide which of its several dark, open doorways to take. There seemed to be—

Something gray and ghostly swooped out of a doorway and came to a halt facing him. It was the head and shoulders of a man, no more, and it hung in the air at about the right height for it to have an unseen body beneath it, reaching down to the floor in the usual way . . . but no running or even leaping man could *swoop* like that.

Slowly, almost menacingly, it advanced on him, floating silently forward, *glaring* at him even though its eyes were merely holes that he could see the glowing smokes of his spellburst curling through.

Rarlynd Talasorn took an uncertain step back from it, and then, conscious of the other Talasorns watching him, stood his ground, lip curling contemptuously.

And the ghost-thing drifted *into* him. He felt a chill so sharp that it took his breath away, and as he doubled up, gasping, memories started to flood through him, in an ever-quickening stream that left him bewildered, and sick, and *empty. . . .*

Rarlynd sobbed, or thought he did, and then clawed his way up from his knees blindly to run, run desperately, howling in his terror.

The other Talasorns watched him race into a wall, stagger back from it, and then plunge through the door beside it. He managed three running strides along a hallway beyond before there was a rumbling crash—of a portcullis descending heavily to the floor . . . or as close as it could get to the floor with the impaled body of a Talasorn mage transfixed on it.

Two more ghostly things promptly drifted out of doorways to face the remaining Talasorns, and there was a general murmuring and backing away.

The ghosts did not hurry, but as they drifted forward, a third and a fourth joined them. Several Talasorns spun hasty spells—a warding, a fireburst, and a phantom blade—as they retreated.

The ghosts advanced patiently, until there was a sudden, startled shout and the slamming sounds of a floor tile collapsing downwards, to plunge a Talasorn into a hitherto-concealed pit.

More ghosts appeared as the mages from Sirlptar started to curse and back away more swiftly. Then there was another cry—of alarm, this time. The Talasorn who'd uttered it, studious Naeron, was pointing at the archway in the back corner of the hall . . . or rather, at the figure lurching through it: Baron Joszgar Silvertree, white-faced and drooling, stalking forward into the room with glittering eyes.

As the Talasorns ran out of room to retreat into and depart the chamber down various passages, the fireburst went off with a flash and roar that seemed to have no effect at all on the drifting ghosts, and the phantom blade sliced at its first ghost and seemed only to make its wraithlike body larger, Naeron Talasorn reached his limit, and with trembling hands wove a spell-sending to the head of House Talasorn.

Osprur Talasorn's voice erupted out of the air beside his head with an alacrity that scared Naeron more than anything else. "I've been farscrying your . . . performance," he said, his dry voice pitched loudly enough for everyone to hear. "These wraiths are manifestations of the House itself, and can drain you of wits and life-force . . . but if you flee from them in overmuch haste, they'll hound you to various demises in the Silent House traps. Withdraw. Now. In most places, attempting a gate or translocation will be a fatal disaster; it's best if you physically retreat back the way you came—if, that is, any of you sharpwits remembered your route to reach where you are now. I will recover Lord Silvertree myself. There's much to be learned from him."

The voice ceased. A moment later, empty air flashed and flickered across the chamber, and Osprur Talasorn appeared, flaming wand in hand. He traced a circle in the air with it, an oval of flames that hung crackling—a gate—and then held the wand inside the oval, stretching out with the other hand to snatch at Joszgar Silvertree's arm.

The drooling baron seemed not to notice him—but even as Osprur drew him stumbling sideways, something rushed out of Osprur's gate, sending him staggering.

He whirled, wand out to destroy. A dozen Serpent-priests were crowding through his circle of flames. One of them snapped, "You're not the only mage in the world who knows how to farscry, grasping old fool!"

Osprur Talasorn drew his lips back from his teeth in a snarl—and triggered his wand, right in the face of the foremost priest.

The Serpent's shield flared from flame-orange to deep red and then black in an instant, and then collapsed with a sound like a thunderclap. Half-melted bodies were flung wildly across the room, the gate exploding in their midst and wreaking further havoc. The handful of surviving Serpents scattered, hurling several previously prepared spells at the Talasorn patriarch rather like children hurling fruit in a market.

Osprur staggered back, the rings on his fingers winking wildly, but the ward-shield he raised was no match for the trio of spells that tore into it. With Joszgar Silvertree vomiting forth ghost-wraiths in his very arms and spells snarling towards him seeking his life, the head of House Talasorn desperately triggered all the powers of his wand at once.

The wand-flash blinded Naeron Talasorn. *It's like looking into the sun,* he thought, in the brief moment before Serpent spells slammed into the unleashed wand-magic, and the hall in front of him exploded.

He was plucked off his feet, and landed hard, ears roaring . . . which was when the shock wave that ripped up floor tiles in a great, enthusiastic shuddering, and flung pillars over like toys, reached him—and Naeron Talasorn was flung helplessly boot-heels-over-fingertips through the air.

A Serpent-priest, still frantically hissing spells, landed hard atop him in the next moment . . . and in the one after that, something very hard came down on them both, bringing black oblivion.


"Ran like a scared child, he did! Bawling and tripping on his own robes and rolling back up and just running on! Never seen a *wizard* that scared before!"

"Three of 'em got out, I heard. Just three. Babbling about serpent-headed men and ghosts and wands going off and the roof falling . . . well, now."

The old shepherd had reached the crest of the hill, and fell silent as he surveyed the smoking wreckage of the Silent House. Not far from the riverfront entrances was a great hole or gulf where a squat fortress tower had always stood. He gave vent to a long, liquid whistle of amazement.

The younger shepherd who'd been walking with him shifted his boots restlessly. "So, do we go down there? Mebbe find some plunder? Bodies and such?"

"Not if you've brains, boy," the old man growled—but he was talking to the younger man's back, as young Branad descended the far side of the hill, striding eagerly. "What're you *doing?*"

Branad swung around. "Nothing ever happens to us. To me. All *we* ever do is watch things happen, and talk. The same old jests, the same nothing. Well, I want more than that. I want to be *part* of things, not just watch them!"

Old Lorgul opened his mouth to protest—and then shut it again, and went after the lad. "I'll be hauling your bones away after 'things' happen to you, sure I will and see if I don't!"

"That's fine," Branad said cheerfully. "Glad of the company."

He strode down the last grassy slope to where the tombs began, Lorgul hurrying to catch up.

"Careful, now, boy! They say there's *traps* here, and lurking beasts, and—"

He fell silent abruptly as Branad wheeled around warningly, and then turned back towards the ruin and pointed.

Between two tombs lay a sprawled body in grand robes. It was fresh, and the gorcraws were at it—but not plucking and squabbling. Instead, they were perched silently all around, atop various tombs, watching the carrion intently.

Or rather, watching something gray and ghostly, that was rising from the staring-eyed head to hang like a darkly drifting cloud.

It started to move, quite suddenly, floating towards Branad—who came to an abrupt halt, swung up his staff uncertainly . . . and then turned and ran, the ghost-thing drifting after him.

Lorgul swallowed and hefted his own staff as the lad came panting up past him, but Branad did not tarry to do battle. "Run!" he gasped. "Run!"

Lorgul turned his old legs and ran after the scampering youngster, growling, "Be a part of things! Bah!"

He managed three strides before something as cold as winter ice seized the back of his neck, and his scalp. Memories started to flood, and grass rushed up to meet him. Lorgul groaned once, but he'd lived a long time, and some of his older memories were far more pleasant than the more recent ones . . . so he was smiling by the time Branad noticed him, and started to scream.

* * *

"So, do we have to worry about yon wraith and a lot more like it drifting merrily around Darsar from now on, draining everything to make the Curse stronger?"

The faceless being who asked that exasperated question was as young and as restless as the shepherd Branad, but knew it, and was quite prepared to wait in silent patience for an answer.

The older Koglaur looked up from the scrying-whorl. "No. The farther from the ruin it flies, the more force is needed to hold it together—energy the Curse, as you call it, cannot spare."

The younger Koglaur turned its expressionless head as if to glance at its elder with the eyes that it did not have. "As I call it? So if what's in the Silent House isn't the Curse, what is it? And how much was it hurt by—that?"

"Likely not at all. Joszgar Silvertree was probably crushed, but it had drained him already. It lost the chance to drain Osprur and most of the Talasorns, and a lot of Serpents, too."

The older Faceless passed a hand over the whorl, ending its magic; slowing, it started to go dim. "The so-called Curse," it added, "is some sort of sentient being, quite old, that's either linked to the Silent House or unable to physically move out of it. It has some blood connection to humans of the Silvertree bloodline; them it can drain until they die—collapsing, crumbling husks like Joszgar Silvertree. It can make them walk again, after death, as it pleases, but if the body is too damaged to walk, the Curse can somehow send forth something of the dead intellect as a 'silent shadow': the apparition you termed a wraith. They serve to drain wits, memories, and life-essence, which feed the Curse, but also to lead or lure intruders to traps or treasures or exits, serve as warnings, or merely to terrify."

Two eyes appeared in the smooth flesh of the younger Koglaur's face. "And do we know how to destroy these wraiths, or the Curse that sends them?"

"Not yet," the other Faceless replied. "There's no need, so long as shunning the place serves just as well. Which is why

yon sprawling fortress, for all its busily building maedra—
and yes, many of them still live, in its far reaches—is probably doomed to be a haunted ruin forever."

"Just like Aglirta's future," the younger Koglaur muttered.
"Forever haunted and ruined."

The older Koglaur grew a smile. "Ah. You begin to grow
up. And learn *our* doom."

In reply to yours, just received:
Since you hired us, lord, I have warned that the plundering of Silvertree House would be both long and perilous, and that we should confer regularly as to your
willingess to continue. The palace enjoys a fabulous
reputation as a treasure-house, but my opinion, then as
now, is that if you desire wealth and magic, it would be
easier to openly assault the towers of a dozen archwizards—and suffer all consequences thereby—than to
venture into the Silent House.

Even its exploration is fraught with difficulties. With
the passing days it continues to grow and change, seeming to me to become *darker* within, and more menacing, even as the walls crumble. Several of my blades
swear that the House itself is alive, and I cannot find it
in me to disagree with them. Ceilings that should collapse, given the deteriorating walls beneath them, do
not. Gliding ghosts—wraiths, if you will, drifting shadows—are everywhere, and at our every foray come
closer to us.

Of traps, we have found three-and-forty, including
divers examples of floor-stones that drop a foot or so,
allowing blades to sweep out of the sides of the cavity
thus created, to sever feet at ankle-height; ceilings in
crawl-tunnels that descend to crush and smother; drop-
hammers and portcullises; and doors that drive blades
into those closing them. To list for you the deaths and
maimings my hirelings have suffered would be merely
wearisome; let it be said only that I will now have to
travel as far as Sirlptar's hiring-fair to find any blades

willing to join us. Three handcounts of men have fled, abandoning all wages.

Of treasure, thus far, we have gained the following: sixteen swords, much rusted; two-score daggers, some of them very badly gone; a dozen coins of divers mintings, none worth much; a key, probably to a lock not in the House; and sixteen belt-buckles. All of these listed were recovered from corpses.

Yet I do believe that treasure is here to be gained, if we but find where it is hidden. Four tombs outside the walls we broke open, in hopes of finding burial-goods, but it seems Silvertrees laid the dead to rest unclad and with nothing but a shield atop each, on which their names and deeds were writ. So unless every last bauble has been looted from this death-trap by mightier men than we, in times past, or the Silvertrees achieved their fame and power in lasting penury, wealth must lie hidden here somewhere.

I leave it to your wisdom, lord, to decide if either of us will live long enough to achieve any of it.

Annar Fendelmer
Fendelmer's Forays for Coin
Wanesummer, Five Hundred and Seventh Year
of the Reign of Kelgrael

# BOOK SEVEN

———◆———

## Thaulon Silvertree

1689–1736 SR
Lord Mage of Blackcastle Keep and Lord Baron of Silvertree
And of How He Ascended from One Title to the Other

# 1

## Spell Trap

"*I* know men beyond counting have died there, mage, and I know the place reeks with magic and is roamed by beasts galore! I grew up hearing all the tales, too!"

The baron set down his massive, flared flagon with rather more force than was necessary and growled, "I *also* know that I feed and house and pay you, mage—much good coin, season after season! Aye, the task is a long one, and to do it clumsily is to find disaster—I know this, too. I don't expect you to fling wide the gates of Silvertree House for me on the morrow, or on the day after."

Not bothering to refill the flagon, the great bear of a man plucked up the decanter and took a long pull of saal from it. "I *do* expect you to tell me, from time to time, how your work fares, and if you've uncovered anything of interest that I should know. I am, after all, Baron of Silvertree—and your spell-chamber and yon palace both lie within the lands of Silvertree . . . or did, when last I looked, before this evening's feasting."

Barangar Silvertree was a big, florid bull of a man, as wide across as many doors, with hands as large as Thaulon's head, an impressive collection of sword-scars, and a warrior's impatience with subtleties or any whiff of prevarication.

And as he'd just oh-so-gently reminded Thaulon, he provided the mage's living, their achievements bound one with the other. Moreover, Barangar's very fair daughter sat at his side, her hair as black as midnight against her father's brown bristles, but her skin smooth and moon-pale where his was brown and hairy. Her eyes were downcast, as they usually were when Thaulon—whom she detested—was near.

Three Above, but she was beautiful! Thaulon had full

cause to know; in a house where he was the only wizard, the
only defenses against prying spells were ones he'd put
there—and each and every one of those had unseen windows
that opened only to him. He'd idled away a month or so of
pleasant hours by now, watching the fair Asmurna disrobe of
evenings. Her shoulders, and those long, long legs . . .

Thaulon swallowed, both to quell such thoughts and to
master his irritation, and said pleasantly enough, "Slowly,
Lord Baron. Very slowly, but proceeding step by step towards opening the first important door to greater things."

He held up a hand to forestall Barangar's growl about
over-clever words and just what *this* fistful of them was supposed to mean, and added, gliding closer and lowering his
voice, "To speak far more specifically: in examining the
House with my scrying spells, I've discerned a fell intelli-
gence therein, who is aware of my scrutiny. It—for I know
not its true nature, yet, though I know it is very powerful—
does not yet know who I am, or where I scry from, only that
betimes my spells pry into its lair. I am working on spells
that will cloak my identity and whereabouts completely . . .
for I dare not risk your safety, to say nothing of your daughter and the other ladies of your household—"

Asmurna did not look up, but her lips thinned with distaste.

"—by giving this entity, whose powers are yet unknown
to me, a clear foe to lash out at. However, I can say that I am
very close to weaving the spell-cloaks I require. The moment that is done, I shall inform you, and begin extensive
scrying of the palace, until I know its rooms and hidden
ways, and what lurks therein."

He stepped back, bowing to Barangar's daughter—who
turned her head slightly away from him in revulsion—and
saw that the baron was smiling.

"Well said, and a prudent path. I am pleased. Have our
thanks, mage."

Barangar made the opening-his-hand gesture that gave
Thaulon leave to depart, and Thaulon bowed deeply to
him—my, how swiftly and thoroughly we forget our days as
a rough warrior, and the wizard who helped us to snatch this

grand title—turned in a swirling of dark robes, and with un-hurried dignity strode out of the high chamber.

His soft slippers sped down his private stair, however, as swiftly and angrily as any thunderstorm. Had any servant of Blackcastle Keep dared to listen, they would have heard Thaulon muttering to himself, mere fragments of words and curses.

Inwardly, he was bitingly reminding a chastened and kneeling Barangar Silvertree of a few recent and pertinent historical facts, to whit: King Kelgrael Snowsar had been missing and "asleep" for centuries now, and barons brawled up and down Aglirta as often as the seasons changed. So weak had all their strife made them that just one capable out-lander mercenary captain, growing tired of being ordered about by a brainless oaf with a title, had been able to con-quer most of upriver Aglirta. This Heldahar had needed a wizard to safeguard himself and his warriors of the Flame Sword against everyone assailing his grand new barony, and had hired a wealthy Sirl wizard by the name of Thorongal—who'd promptly double-crossed and slain him.

That left Heldahar's second-in-command, one Barangar Silvertree, scrambling to escape a short, unpleasant life of servitude. He'd hired a certain Thaulon Talasorn—not the most evil mage in Sirlptar, but not the most shining, either—whose hatred of the wizard Thorongal drove him to dare al-most anything. With luck, cunning, and some desperate spell-work, he'd managed to slay Thorongal.

Barangar then took over both Thorongal's wealth and command of the Flame Sword, proclaiming himself Baron Silvertree and conquering a few more terceptries, until he held all of Aglirta east of Lake Adeln.

Leaving Thaulon as his overworked pet house wizard—who was still grumbling as he shouldered through the warded curtains into his spell-sanctum to get back to work on his assigned task: taming the Silent House to make it safe for Barangar to dwell in.

\* \* \*

"Unless I'm mistaken," Thaulon breathed, hardly daring to speak more loudly for fear he was wrong, or would cause something to burst into sparks and nothingness, "the working is now perfect. I've created a spell trap."

He stepped back as delicately as any layer-of-tiles working on a palace floor, and studied the humming webwork of spells. *The capture enchantments here, linkage to the farscrying eye out here, the life-draining aumglora there, and the whistlestar just here.*

*See the mage, snatch and hold the mage, drain his life away, and store the energies in the whistlestar—holding any items to be imbued with those forces in yonder clamps, by means of which they can be thrust into and held within the open heart of the spinning whistlestar, and through this simple spell written out ready here, caused to enter the item, charging it. Remove item, cast its activation magic, and . . . bury one wizard.*

*Or—no—hmm . . . ah, a fireburst into the hearth, let the smoke go up the chimney, sweep up the ash, let the smell like roast boar clear away, and all I'll have to trundle off to the rubbish shaft is a sack of burnt bones.*

Thaulon Talasorn smiled a truly evil smile, checked on the bolts and bars on the door once more, and strode to the farscrying eye. There was no better time to find a victim than—right now.

A lackspell wizard first, someone whose handling will be no challenge at all. One of those doddering upcountry hedge-wizards he'd found in the barony last season, while securing Barangar's precious demesnes for him. That fat one with the miserable excuse of a beard, in Leaningtree . . . Aumhallow? Arhallow, that was it, Omdur Arhallow!

The eye flickered under his hands. Still smiling, Thaulon leaned into its glow and said gleefully, "Omdur! Omdur Arhallow!"

And the gold and flame-orange swirls in the eye swam into a scene of a crowded one-room cottage, and a stout man looking up sharply from his stool by the hearth, something small sizzling on the end of his blackened firefork. "Who—"

"Baron Barangar Silvertree has need of his esteemed friend Omdur Arhallow, and sends this greeting. . . ."

That was the beauty of his capture spells. A glowing gate as a lure in front of the quarry, and a second, invisible gate that he could move about. If he kept it behind Omdur, and the fat old man scuttled away from the glow, he'd run right into it and be taken anyway.

But no need; he was marching forward into the glow, pride conquering astonishment in his lined old face. Ah, Omdur, the world is a cruel place.

There was a flash of golden radiance in Thaulon Talasorn's spell-sanctum, and an old man hung blinking in humming chains of spell-radiance.

He knew Thaulon's face, and frowned. "Milord baron needs me? How—?"

"List and learn, old man, list and learn," Thaulon told him merrily, making the gesture that started the aumglora flickering. "This," he announced smugly, "is a spell trap—the very first spell trap in all Darsar, ever. *You* have the honor to be its first subject. It serves to whisk unsuspecting wizards into my reach and hold them helpless while it drains your life-force, which I can transfer into various items to enchant them."

"Drains my . . . life?"

"Precisely," Thaulon said delightedly as the aumglora started to pulse, and the whistlestar started to turn . . . very slowly at first, but quickening. . . .

Omdur Arhallow struggled, then, like a rat caught in a tail-clamp trap, actually clawing the air and whimpering as the aumglora really took hold. Thaulon doubted the man had any useful spells ready even if the sickening draining had left his aging mind clear enough to cast anything, but old Omdur, in the end, did nothing. Nothing at all.

He'd been sicker and more feeble than he looked; when the old wizard's last breath rattled out, the whistlestar was spinning steadily but not swiftly. Barely enough to create a glowstone, if that. Thaulon regarded it with a curled lip, spoke the word that released the capture magics, and rolled the husk of Omdur Arhallow onto the floor and then across it to the hearth.

No, "husk" was the wrong word. The corpse was surprisingly heavy, its skin more wrinkled than before, yes, and the eyes sunken skull-pits of darkness, but Omdur was no bag of bones. Yet.

There was a faint moaning in the chimney, which meant a wind coming past the end of the Windfangs and down the Silverflow. The smell of cooked Arhallow would reach overgrown and deserted Flowfoam and perhaps the Silent House on the far shore, ere wafting downriver into the streets of Telbonter, where if anyone smelt the faint wisps at all, they'd merely think the baron was enjoying boar this night. What the smell wouldn't do was drift throughout the rest of Blackcastle Keep. Thank the Three that this part of the Keep—once Castle Blackgult's sentinel tower—had tall chimneys that drew well.

When the corpse lay right in the hearth, the grate kicked aside and the disturbed ashes of the last fire settling back down on top of it, Thaulon shook back his sleeves and cast the fireburst, still smiling.


"What's that?" Dlan asked, coming to a sudden halt. A spider the size of his head scuttled away through the dust, but both he and Horl ignored it.

The young procurer was pointing at a symbol on the wall. It hadn't been visible at all before the light of the glowstones had touched it, but it was glowing brightly, now: a small cluster of curving, crisscrossing lines that weren't a letter in any script Dlanazar had ever seen or a badge he knew.

"That, lad," Horl said gruffly, "is the sign of Thaulon, who began as a Talasorn but ended up a Silvertree. He put most of the magic into this place that folk find today—like these glowstones we're holding. He wasn't a . . . nice man."

"So is yon mark . . . safe? Or a warning?"

"On that point, lad, my wisdom ends—and the learning begins for the both of us. If you want to delay just possibly being blasted by fire or lightning, or turned into a puddle-toad, we can sit down on that bench in the last room, and I can tell you something of Thaulon's deeds."

"But that bench had another of those wraith-things sitting on it!"

Old Horl shrugged. "If we both leave our glowstones on, we can see each other right through it. It hasn't moved, and it probably won't. After all, it might want to hear the tale, too."

Dlanazar Duncastle looked at the white-haired old man, from his weathered old face down to the gnarled arms covered with crisscrossing, knotted white scars and back again—and shivered.


"I don't like him, Daer. He scares me."

"Hush, lady-love. Stop trembling. He's a wizard, and as twisted as all of them. The magic softens their brains, see, making the women utter storm-queens and the men leering fusscocks. Thaulon'd no more know what to do with you, if he had you as bare and beautiful as I do now, as how to dance that—that thaerillyon the bard showed your father last night."

The Lady Asmurna giggled at the memory of her father's red face and near-tumble—and then broke off her mirth with a gasp as the most handsome guardsman of all her father's blades stopped talking to bury his tongue, applying it with deft skill. She arched, shuddering in rapture, and forgot all about Thaulon Talasorn's glittering gaze. For a time.


"Talasorn, I'll tear out your heart for this! I'll curse you to the Doom of the Three! I'll—"

"You'll *die,* Indeszar," Thaulon told him sweetly. "Leaving all of your threats mere words that fade with you!" He chuckled gleefully as the aumglora throbbed again, and Morith Indeszar's ragings ended in a gasp. Ah, but this was heartening success upon heartening success. The whistlestar was living up to its name, spinning so speedily, it was a shrieking blur, *almost* a whistle—and the spell trap was easily holding someone who could really struggle against it. Spell after spell Indeszar had tried, only to feed the magics holding him more swiftly, and now he was visibly weakening, his effective battle-magics spent. Left to bluster as he slid inevitably into death.

So the spell trap could break highly capable Sirl sorcerers. It was but added richness that Morith Indeszar happened to be one of Thaulon's most hated enemies.

Indeszar's next curse was weaker, and ended in what sounded like a sob. Thaulon chuckled again. He'd be pleading next.

Indeszar of the Four Vows disappointed him, though. Rather than begging for his life, he fixed his dark and beady eyes on Thaulon and mouthed long and detailed curses. Curses that made Thaulon Talasorn more than a trifle uncomfortable—not for the threats they contained, but for all the words in them that he'd never heard before, and couldn't understand. Could some of them be wyrmtongue, or another lore-language, and be successfully weaving a future doom for him?

Well, all of us find our doom, sooner or later. Thaulon consoled himself by deftly emplacing Indeszar's life-force into a wand he knew to have very little magic left, a glow-stone, and an enchanted belt. The enchantments on the latter would need testing to make sure of what he'd wrought, but the wand fairly hummed with power.

Thaulon thrust it into his belt and started rolling Indeszar's corpse towards the hearth. He was glad his foe had no eyes left to glare accusingly with.

He was also glad the rubbish-shaft wasn't far away. Draining mages was tiring work, and it was almost morning.

Thaulon laid his hand on a certain stone and whispered the word that would make this little part of the Keep wall swing outwards and let him in.

The scepter in his hand was still crackling with power from the testings he'd just finished—spectacularly success-

ful transformations, every one. He grinned at the last, faintly
glowing wisps of smoke curling from it as he stepped into
the secret way. Why, if he could craft a sufficient number of
items—eliminating potential rivals with every enchanting—
before any mage outside the clutches of his spell trap noticed what was happening, he could very well become the
most pow—

A ring on his finger winked into sudden life in the gloom
of the passage, and Thaulon Talasorn stiffened.

Someone was scrying him from afar. This was an old and
long-disused secret way, and upon discovering it, he'd thoroughly explored the few fading enchantments clinging to it,
so this couldn't be someone alerted by his use of the secret
door. Nor was it someone seeking Thaulon Talasorn, or he'd
not have fallen under scrutiny until in his spell-sanctum or at
least within the walls of Blackcastle Keep.

So unless it was mere mischance, he was now being
watched because someone had noticed, by whatever means,
the outpourings of magic from his experimentations of the
scepter.

And he was leading that someone right to his greatest secret.

He hesitated in midstride, his hand almost on the panel
that opened into his chambers—and then reached out and
touched it, awakening the enchantment that caused it to slide
aside. Minor spells on the tapestry beyond would cloak any
sounds he made from any intruder into his rooms, and keep
the tapestry from moving, too . . . and the spell-ward he'd
cast around the spell trap should keep its specifics, though
not its powerful presence, hidden from the spy.

Which meant that there was a very good chance that he
could snatch his mysterious watcher here to him, and drain
this sudden and dire threat away. Thaulon strode along the
spell-frozen tapestry to where it ended at an ornately carved
pillar, and peered out one of the spying-holes afforded by
the carvings. The faint blue glows of his wards showed him
his chambers quite clearly. The entry door was closed, there
were no lamps or torches glimmering that shouldn't be
there, and—

A man was standing motionless in front of the door to his
strongcloset. Very motionless, and familiar, too: Dru, one of
the Keep servants. Alaunter Dru. Very much too curious for
his own good.

Thaulon gave the frozen figure silent thanks. Dru had
given him a lure—Dru himself—with which to draw his spy.

He stepped around the pillar, dusted off his hands in satisfaction, and announced, "You've been gathering dust too
long, Alaunter. It's time to do our little dance together, as
promised."

Thaulon stepped through the wards he'd set up around the
spell trap, leaving them intact and unbroken behind him. He
was the only being who could do so, of course. Working
swiftly, he cast a second ward-ring, just inside the first, leaving a gap in it closest to Dru, and just enough room between
the two wards to set down his dagger, when he was done
with it. That in turn befell after he'd used it to lever up the
loosest flagstone inside the ward, used the scepter to trans-
form it into a door, and bound it into the gap in the wards. He
now had a stone door in his inner ward, and—setting down
the dagger as he stepped through his wards, leaving them intact once more—a dagger between them. Many mages did
this, enspelling a dagger to fly like a stinging wasp, point
first, between two wards. Thus someone with the power to
force the first ward could be struck—and harmed by any
spell carried by the knife blade—ere they could shatter the
second ward. He hoped his spy would recognize this common defense.

Thaulon did not quite touch Dru. Rather, he made contact
with the field left around the overcurious servant by his immobility spell, and moved it to his bidding. The still-
unmoving Dru glided past him to the wards and Thaulon
caused the outer one to collapse. His hand was already
clasped over the rings of his other hand, to conceal the tell-
tale flash as he made the dagger dart into view—and
promptly halt and fall to the floor as he flung up one hand.

"Step into my greatest secret, Alaunter Dru," Thaulon said

pleasantly, opening the stone door for the frozen man. His eyes met those of the servant, and found them wide with terror. A perceptive and wise reaction, to be sure.

He closed the door firmly behind them, and spun a swift link between it and the capture magics of the spell trap. Then he shoved Dru aside and leaned on him to wait.

His spy was more bold than patient. The first flash of a probing spell came within a breath or two. It flickered out, only to return more strongly, twice, the last time accompanied by the high singing of a *very* powerful ward-key.

Anchored as it was by no less than six of Thaulon's newly created enchanted items, the ward would probably withstand any magical attack short of a concerted effort by every last wizard of the Guild of Sorcery of Sirpltar. And one of those items was tracing the source of the probe.

With luck, its work wouldn't be needed. With luck, the spy would be just overconfident enough to arrive in person and touch the door. For a mage able to directly launch a battle-spell, shattering the door would be a simple matter. Touching the door directly could also deliver a powerful scrying that would reveal all that went on inside the wards to the spy, even if he translocated back to his distant elsewhere. Yet it would take an overconfident fool to dare to intrude into Thaulon's chambers, when a more prudent watcher would simply wait until Thaulon emerged again, or break off scrying to renew scrutiny later.

Yet the lure had been set. He'd called it his "greatest secret," and the ward and its closed door would mock the spy henceforth. No matter how much time he spent scrying, he couldn't see inside th—

Cautiously, someone touched the door.

And Thaulon, face tight in silent glee, willed the link to do its work.

The flagstone flew inwards as the capture magics snatched the spy and whisked him into the spell trap like a streaking arrow.

The man was still struggling for breath as the aumglora

started to pulse . . . and Thaulon finished closing the gap in
the ward and came smilingly around from behind the helpless Dru to inspect his victim: a Serpent-priest.

"Well, well," he murmured, scepter held ready. "No
snakes up your sleeves, Klarsyn?"

He knew full well the priest Klarsyn had been dead since
last winter, but perhaps his misidentification would goad
the man—

"My name is Ghelcont, and Fangbrothers of the Serpent
do not go about with snakes in their undergarments save in
drunken mens' tavern-tales," the man said coldly. "Release
me, and end this magic, or the Church of the Serpent—"

"Will know nothing at all about your fate, Fangbrother
Ghelcont, just as they remain serenely ignorant of what befell Masterpriest Klarsyn."

Thaulon strolled past the trapped man and said back over
his shoulder, "You snake-lovers are all so proudly overconfident and so bound up in your own private feuds that you care
nothing at all for the strength of your so-called church.
You're just a disorganized cabal of inferior mages who share
a rather grand collective delusion as to your own skills and
importance. You can't even *sneer* very well. Observe how it
should be done." And Thaulon broke off gloating long
enough to favor the Serpent-priest with an expression of
haughty scorn.

Ghelcont spat at the Mage of Blackcastle Keep in such
gobbling fury that he struggled for some breaths to find the
right words to hurl . . . and partway through that battle for
self-mastery, his face went pale and his eyes widened in apprehension.

"Getting weaker, are we? *Such* a pity," Thaulon murmured. He checked his ward once more, to make certain that
no determined Serpent-priest was following on Ghelcont's
heels, or had sent unwelcome beasts or bladesmen to disturb
the spellbound peace of Thaulon's chambers.

The ward held strong, and the Mage of Blackcastle Keep
left it undisturbed until Ghelcont of the Serpents had left
off his weeping pleadings and was quite dead. Then

Thaulon expanded them cautiously—just enough to give him room to roll the body out of the spell trap and force the servant into it.

Dru's paltry life-force followed that of the priest into the racing of the whistlestar, and Thaulon dropped the ward to fry both corpses in the hearth before unhurriedly setting four finger-rings on a succession of clamps to be imbued.

He left the bones to cool and went to decant himself a drink—calamanta first, then a smaller tallglass of dragondream, in fitting celebration—ere he put the scepter in his strongcloset.

Nothing was missing from it. Thaulon sipped as he studied the pale glows within. Ranks of wands, a gauntlet set with enchanted rings at every joint, three wicked-looking daggers that did various nasty things beyond merely wounding, and . . . all manner of ornamental gewgaws. Ornate lamps that glowed upon command, rather than the usual smooth, pouch-sized glowstones; boots whose wearer could walk in utter silence . . . and many less useful things. That one might even impress the lovely Asmurna, when he gifted her with it at the next high feast.

His flagon was empty. Time for the waiting tallglass of dragondream. He had an armory that had to surpass what most mighty archwizards could muster, by now. So, which of his wizardly rivals to eliminate next?

Larmatlur of the Seven Curses . . . or wary old Melgurt of the oh-so-puissant Guild of Sorcery, who'd once ridiculed him in the streets of Sirpltar . . . or Ondrevvo of Teln.

Melgurt. Yes, let all Darsar applaud: 'twas time for Ansiah Melgurt to die.

If Thaulon Talasorn had become sleek and self-satisfied, he considered he had good reason. Six wands that would erupt at his command alone rode sheathed to a belt that harbored powerful warding and flight enchantments of its own, and that belt was clasped about his own waist. An ornamental half-cloak rippled away from his back as he strode, conferring a constant magical shielding that he was particularly pleased with; it was such an *elegant* use of Melgurt's life-force.

At least three extremely powerful mages had now graced his spell trap—Ondrevvo of Teln, Hoel of Ragalar, and Niiyreszm of Carraglas—and others were sure to follow. Practice was even making him adroit at luring them. He walked through the wards that now walled his chambers off from the rest of the Keep, twisted a ring on his finger, and a scrying-eye sprang into being in front of him.

As he'd expected, Asmurna was bathing in scented oils this evening. There was much satisfied sighing and languid arching of limbs and giggles from the servant-girls doing the pouring. Thaulon watched with simple pleasure for a time.

Thus at ease with the world, he banished the eye, drew down a hoary war-helm from a compartment hidden in the carvings of his high-backed chair, and settled it on his head.

The spell trap—or rather, the life of the wizard Hoel—had augmented the failing enchantments of this Blackgult tomb-yield. It could see thoughts, not so much as clear words that could be followed—though it sometimes afforded that—but rather as bright clusters of will, showing one mind as more powerful than another. Using it was very tiring, but also—fascinating, and occasionally very useful indeed.

He quested across the wide Silverflow with it now, finding no sentience on wooded and abandoned Flowfoam, but . . . some rather dim thoughts just where he wanted them: clear across the river, in the hills just west of Silvertree House.

Thaulon drifted closer and became aware that a simple shepherd, one Elgrest Thamsheir, was "irritated proper" at old Harstag for getting so drunk as to fall and break his foot, and leave Elgrest to wrestle with dogs that were of a mind to ignore his commands (Harstag's dogs), when "every jack knew" that things as came for sheep (with claws and jaws or with clubs and knives and stealthy hands) came at night (Harstag's time), and, more yet, were "as thick as bite-beetles" around the haunted Silent House.

Thaulon smiled a cold little smile, did things to two of the rings on his finger ... and slid like a sly dark cloud into the mind of Elgrest Thamsheir.

Elgrest bellowed in alarm, startling several sheep ... and then startled the dogs far more by staggering around in a wild circle, clawing at the air and slobbering liquid and slack-jawed snatches of words—only to straighten and stride off without a backwards glance, but with some purpose, towards the great stony gloom of the palace.

The shepherd had dwelt in these hills all his life, worrying about nothing worse than occasional armed and desperate outlaws—and the large, well-armed desperate sort of outlaw that rides under the banner of a baron and hacks at anything he sees rather than slinking furtively like the first sort of outlaw. Both of these perils were best avoided—and if necessary, led on a scrambling chase through bogs and sinkholes and breakneck gullies until they grew too bewildered, tired, or injured to keep up pursuit. In all his days, however, Elgrest Thamsheir had never been so desperate or so foolish as to venture into one of the dark, gaping archways of the Silent House. On the other hand, he'd never hosted the heavy weight of a mind sharper and stronger than his own before, that had seized upon him so as to ride him, however inwardly quailing, into Silvertree House.

Like any shepherd, Elgrest wore an old, much-patched woolen coat, and several seldom-washed vests for warmth beneath, and a smock and breeches beneath those—and in divers pockets of the vests were several battered flasks that held fiery courage against the cold. Elgrest would never have dreamed of doing off his coat in the chill of dusk, dousing it in the contents of several flasks, and igniting the result with his flint and fire-steel, but the mind riding his wanted this done, and—moving stiffly, like a man lost in someone else's dream—he did it.

The light was fitful, even when raised on a branch, but the stone ceilings were lofty enough that Elgrest could raise it high and peer past it, half expecting roaring monsters to pounce as he took his first few steps.

What he saw instead was dust here, damp there, a few

fallen stone blocks scattered about, silence whenever his
own boots weren't making echoes . . . empty, deserted darkness. Room opening into room giving way to long, straight
passage, doorways without doors in them beyond what Elgrest had ever learned to count. Which meant more doorways than the largest herd he'd ever had charge of, which
was a lot of doors. All dark and empty, like so many holes—
so many eyes of the Dark One, coldly watching. . . .

And then, so suddenly he shouted and almost dropped his
flaming light, something moving. Something gliding in the
darkness, or flying, like an owl slowing over a field just before striking—but not there when he fearfully raised the
flames to reveal it.

When he lowered his bundle, though, he could see it
again, a silent shadow in the gloom: the outline of a head—a
head with no face!—and shoulders, turning towards him!

Elgrest screamed then, raw and hoarse and helpless,
trapped into shaking immobility as the thing swept down on
him, cramping and spasming legs rooted to the spot as he
fought the mind riding his, suffering a thousand defeats, his
heart like a thundering thing in his throat. . . .

A coldness swept over him, and into him, thrusting through
him like soft talons, and a new mind came with them. Old it
was, and fell and wise, whispering things to him that Elgrest
couldn't understand, but wanted to—and was afraid at himself for wanting to.

The mind already riding him recoiled, drawing away
swiftly, leaving him with a last flash of excitement . . . leaving Elgrest, as his flaming coat fell to the floor and started to
go out, alone in the thrall of the older, colder mind. It let him
use his limbs, let him howl and run and crash into unseen
stone walls as much as he desired—or could manage—but
ever it burrowed deeper, whispering. . . .

Whispering . . .


Thaulon Talasorn snatched off the helm, breathing hard.
Even if the Whispering Mind had sensed him, he'd now bro-

ken contact, vanishing from the shepherd's mind as abruptly as if a falling knife had severed the bond between them.

The fell sentience in the Silent House had sensed him in that last, flickering moment—but it couldn't have had long enough to learn who he was, or where he was. Whereas he, thanks to the augmentations of all this new magic of his own making, had learned something of what the Curse was.

It was mad, that was what it was. A madness born of years—centuries—of loneliness, something that had once been a woman and yet had always also been a monster . . . at war with itself, long ago . . . at war with itself in a different way now, as creeping, gnawing madness left its reasoning in tatters.

That ghost-thing had something to do with a Silvertree who'd perished in the House . . . and there were others . . . and the Whispering Mind could command them. They could drain lives, like his spell trap, but also memories—wits. Silvertrees now gone had called these ghosts "silent shadows" and fled from them . . . they could not go far outside the House, and lost power the farther they drifted outside the roofed areas of the vast palace.

The mind that marshalled them, now. It was a deep and dark mind, a mighty mind, and he would have been a mere candle to its gale without his magic . . . but now, knowing what he did of it, and having that magic to link into great webs of enchantment that could be at once armor and weapon against it, Thaulon could measure that mind, and stand against it. If he did the right things, using the right magics and crafting just a few more items of particular inner fires, he could defeat it.

He could conquer it and Silvertree House together, something no arrogant archmage could manage.

Yes, he—Thaulon Talasorn, little-known mage to a back-country baron—was truly the mightiest wizard alive!

He fetched and donned his battle-gauntlet of many rings, and buckled on two belts of the knives that flew to strike as he willed, and laughed in exultation.

Then he sat on the edge of his bed, put the helm back on,

and drove his thoughts not across the river again—to where that shepherd must be a drained and lifeless husk by now—but rather down from the far side of Blackcastle Keep to the handful of twinkling lanterns that marked the village of Blackcastle.

"Yes," he snarled, alone in his chambers with his spell-glows, "feel the hand of Thaulon Talasorn! Feel the *might* of Thaulon!"

Like a hunting owl he sped through the night. He knew the cottage he sought, and the mind sleeping within it. Not the mind of the smith Dunkath Yardro, snoring on one side of the great bed, but the mind of the sated woman who lay tangled in the covers on the other side of it, sleeping but lightly after his lovemaking.

Janthra Yardro was by far the most beautiful woman in Blackcastle—and an honest, loyal one, too, as Thaulon discovered as he pounced on her mind and plunged deep into it, not caring what he tore.

She came awake in mewing, violated outrage—but in utter silence. Moving with a stealth she'd never have considered, she did the unthinkable: rising from her husband's side without a stitch of clothing on her magnificently muscled body, she slipped out of the back door of the cottage and stole off through the dew-wet grass, keeping close to the bubbling laughter of the little brook to avoid setting any dogs to barking.

Halfway across the Long Meadow, Thaulon laid a flight spell upon her, and whisked her around the Keep like a great bared-to-the-moon bird . . . and in his window.

She landed on her knees before him—his doing—and kissed his feet, trembling with inward fury and fear. He made her sit back and offer herself to him, pleading to be allowed to touch him. Her eyes smoldered even as she begged—but his control was sure and strong, strong enough to make her dance briefly before she flung herself on the bed and beckoned him.

As Thaulon let fall his robe, he caught sight of one of the rings on his gauntlet, and then another. The first flared into life and clamped down on Janthra Yardro like a cold mind-vise, keeping her frozen before him. The second winked as he spun a link between it and the aumglora. Because all of its enchantments were keyed to him, he couldn't be drained by his own spell trap, so he could safely link himself to the aumglora, through the ring . . . thus.

Which meant that whenever he desired, he could drain a little of the vitality of Janthra Yardro. Three Above, but she was beautiful, spread out to his gaze and offering herself so beseechingly . . . with such rage seething in her eyes.

"Worship me," he whispered as he claimed her. He soon lost interest in forcing her to say things—after all, she said only what he willed her to say—and let her gasp. Those gasps turned a little wild as she felt her strength begin to flow out of her.

Thaulon chuckled, reflecting with a thrill that this was just what the Curse did, back in Silvertree House—and he grinned in genuine pleasure when she began to pant, "Yes! Yes! Yes!" of her own accord.

It was only later, while he was tipping the bones down the rubbish-shaft, that he abruptly stopped his satisfied humming as he realized just what she'd been welcoming.

"Oblivion was too good a release for you!" he snapped into the darkness, but the tumbling bones made no answer.

# 2

## A Triumph in Silvertree House

"My Lord Baron," Thaulon said with a smile, his eyes bright, "I can report success at last. Small success, but a sure step towards our goal. I now know how to bind the Foe and the great number of monsters that serve it. In time, Silvertree House *will* be yours."

Barangar Silvertree's gaze was cold. "How much time?"

The pale-skinned wizard bent his head. "A very long time yet, Lord. I must ask you to be patient. Silvertree House is the size of Sirlptar, or even larger, and is home to as many fell beasts as Sirl city has people."

"I'm not growing any younger, mage," the baron growled. "Still we crowd into this keep—while you make *your* chambers ever grander—when we could all have room upon room upon a good dozen of rooms, yonder across the river! Everyone says the Silent House is deserted—heh, that's why it's called *Silent,* see?—and any fool can see it has no doors in most of its doorways. So if it's a-boil with all these monsters, as you say—why don't they come tumbling and winging and slithering out of it, day after day, and roam the Vale making menaces of themselves? Hey?"

Thaulon almost snapped back an angry reply—Three take this bull of a man; how could he be so *stupid?*—and seethed even more when he saw a smirk playing about the mouth of the Lady Asmurna.

"If my Lord will permit me a small demonstration—?"

"Demonstrate anything, mage!"

"My thanks. Guards, please be ready. There may be swift danger."

A few of the cortahars of Silvertree standing at their posts along the walls unfolded their arms from across their breasts and gave Thaulon looks about as loving and trusting as those their master had been dispensing. The Mage of Blackcastle Keep was not loved.

"The answer to your very astute point about roaming beasts, Lord Baron," Thaulon said silkily, "is the nature of the monsters of Silvertree House. Most of them are bound to the palace, and cannot go outside it. In fact, some of them dwell inside it—*right* inside it. Within its very stones, in fact."

As Barangar frowned at him in puzzlement, Thaulon linked his hands in front of him and awakened no less than six of his rings at once.

Some of the baronial guards stiffened and put their hands

to sword hilts. Thaulon gave them a brittle smile and spell-snatched a maedra out of the distant East Forehall of Sil-vertree House.

The baron's high hall was suddenly full of—an eel or a snake, the hue of dark stone, with a serpentlike head whose jaws offered a forest of fangs to the cursing guards. It was as long as a large horse, or longer, all serpentine body but with the shoulders and arms of a giant human smith—though its hands ended in huge sharp talons.

A guard shouted something derisive about wizards and their illusions, and darted forward to slash with his blade at the great beast. His warsteel clanged off—stone, by the sound of its ringing protest—and it reared up over him. Several cortahars were hacking at it now, one blade shattering into spinning shards, but it lunged suddenly, striking down at the first guard who'd challenged it.

Its bite left one severed leg swaying alone above a cloud of gore that spattered the flagstones and made the Lady As-murna whimper. The beast chewed as it swung its head to-wards a pair of cortahars—and then, without looking, swept out a talon on its other flank and raked open the guts of an-other guardsman, armor and all.

"Fall back!" Thaulon ordered. "Form a ring, blades out—but strike it not!"

Cortahars, arriving at a run in response to shouts from their fellows, looked to the baron for orders, and he snapped curtly, "Heed the wizard!"

No sooner had the men with drawn swords drawn back from it, the maedra turned in a swift circle to be sure no menace was about to be hurled—Thaulon had already swept his glowing hands behind his back, and kept them there—and then *plunged* down at its own tail. Or rather, at the flag-stones beneath its own tail.

Into them it flowed, as if they mere illusions, vanishing headfirst in a long, smooth dive. Folk gasped, all over the chamber—but Thaulon snatched both of his hands out from behind his back and pointed at the maedra, snarling an impressive and incomprehensible word that seemed to thunder and echo in the high hall.

And all that could still be seen of the great stone-snake shivered, the floor quaked underfoot, and—the great tail and one backswept talon fell to the floor and bounced wetly, severed cleanly where they touched the floor. Which stretched unmarked and unbroken, worn flagstones looking as if no strange beast had ever been there.

Cortahars advanced hesitantly towards the great tail, which still twitched and curled slightly. One of them whirled around to glare at Thaulon. "Is it—dead?"

"Yes. My spell slew it, not diving into the floor. These maedra can live inside solid stone."

Another guard shook his head. "Never seen the like. There can't be many of these."

Thaulon shrugged. "I've seen scores at once, gathered together, in my scryings. There are a *lot* of stone walls in the Silent House."

The Lady Asmurna's head was buried in her father's chest. Barangar looked up from her and said rather shakily, "Lord Wizard Thaulon, you have our leave to take all the time you need in this matter."


The first basket had been the worst. Even pebble-sized glow-stones weigh something, and several hundred of them are *heavy*. He'd begun weaving the linkages well before stepping inside the Silent House, so he was always surrounded by spell-strands in a growing, humming web that would immobilize any creature but him. Any creature touching it would be—should be—lock-limbed and frozen in an instant, and feeling Thaulon's thoughts and will, many times magnified, crashing into its own.

Cautiously tossing a few stones into the darkness, he'd willed the linkages to them up to full, shining strength before placing more, his belt keeping his feet well up off the floor as he walked. He'd seen many a talon reach up out of floor to snatch or slash. He'd been sweating by the time that first room was his . . . but his it was: one chamber of Silvertree House now belonged to *him*.

Room by room Thaulon had proceeded, in agonizing slowness, anchoring the growing spell-web to the many gewgaws he'd created, and placing said items, from glowstones to flying platters to threshold chimes, all over the Silent House. Many he'd hidden on high ledges, in niches, or behind concealing panels, working slowly and carefully to avoid giving the Curse—or the maedra it commanded—a good chance to lash out at him.

Days had become months, months had become a season, and then a second season, as Thaulon Talasorn grew ever more grim and silent. The work made him thinner, his eyes blazed, and folk of the Keep avoided him as he stalked the halls, barely noticing them.

It was growing harder to find and lure lone mages, and he dared not openly confront large cabals like Sirl's guild or the Serpent-priests or the sorcerous families of Carraglas or Gloit. They all knew something was stalking mages, by now, and were watching each other, seeking to discover who.

The enchantments of the Silent House concealed the growing magefire of Thaulon's web from their scrying, and the spell trap was no larger than the wards about many a tomb or throne chamber . . . but he had to work carefully. Moreover, there was not a single hedge-wizard left in Aglirta, so far as he knew, nor any mage of more power—and drinking the lives of both brutish beasts and commoners made the whistlestar turn so slowly as to not be worth the trouble; he'd die of old age before they yielded him enough power to craft anything useful.

And the Silent House was huge. He'd lost count of how many thousands of enchanted gewgaws he'd placed there, the newest of them being scores of the simplest glowstones . . . and he needed at least as many more, even if all he intended to do was wrest command of the ground floor nearest the river—the area bounded by the four towers of Ghostwynd, Hawkheron, Stonelion, and the Candletower, say—from the Whispering Mind.

It watched him as he worked, always, hissing angrily and

mustering maedra by the dozens to slither and crawl watch-
fully around him, prowling as close to the web as they dared.
Time and again it had tried to disrupt the web by having
maedra collapse floors, hurl down walls, and reshape the
chambers of the palace when he was back in Blackcastle
Keep wearily crafting more glow-stones . . . but the entire
spell-strength of the web flared to guard each individual
gewgaw from being crushed or spell-blasted, the web itself
drank and was strengthened by attacking magics, and the
gewgaws remained anchored to the web by links the Curse
had as yet found no way to break. Moving them, even to
places Thaulon couldn't reach or discern, served only to expand the web faster and farther than he could have dared to.
The Whispering Mind had soon ceased open attempts to
ruin the web—for now, at least.

If he succeeded in capturing the Mind and its servitor
maedra within the confines of the web, and then awakened
certain enchantments to flow into the web, he could force
both Curse and monsters into stasis.

And this, now, *at last,* might be the day.

With dusk fast approaching, Thaulon Talasorn floated down
through the web to the undercellar that maedra had been
busily expanding these last few days—to delay him for as
long as possible, he suspected—and placed another gewgaw.

And the stones above and below him snapped together
like great maedra jaws, crushing—nothing, as he smiled like
a wolf and triggered both of the wands clutched ready in his
gauntlet, together. One was aimed above him and one below,
and the sorcery they spat burned right through the Whispering Mind's trap of linked and bonded maedra.

Cooked maedra bodies tŭmbled. The shrill, liquid wails
of the dying were brief—and Thaulon took the last few
stones from his pouch and lashed the shuddering survivors
with the spell-whip he'd made of them back at the Keep,
linking them together in a long chain whose ends could easily be added to the web here . . . and *here.*

Done.

Thaulon soared up out of that cellar, too wily to risk

awakening the stasis spells while he was under a roof the Curse could collapse on him. There was a crumbling tower near the river entrances where his web extended out to give him space enough—and he hung there in its cradle as he cast the last great spell . . . and felt his creation thrum into full, awesome life around him.

The task is done. Live or die, succeed or fail, Thaulon Talasorn had done this. The greatest sorcerous construction ever crafted on Darsar.

Even the Three ought to notice this.

The spell-web glowed more brightly, its rushing energies a muted but ceaseless roar—and several chambers away, a tower broke into sections and toppled, a domed ceiling cracked and fell, dust rose in clouds, and the endless whispers soared up into a frantic scream.

Thaulon Talasorn clenched his fist, every ring on his gauntlet winking warily, and hefted the scepter of transformations in his other hand, waiting. . . .

And the Curse of Silvertree House squalled helplessly, securely bound.

Thaulon threw back his head and bellowed out his exultation, brandishing his achievement at the sky.

This had been no sly trickery, this no good fortune sent by the Three—this had been work, long and hard and his. His striving, and his victory.

He closed his fist again. A ring winked and he was elsewhere.


"So you see, my Lord of Teln," Barangar Silvertree was saying heartily, waving his flagon, "that Silvertree is a rich and well-governed holding, a land at peace, a—"

The air in front of the glittering feast table erupted in sudden fire, causing the rich, haughty Telnan trade envoy to drop his own flagon with a clatter. Paling with fear and rage, he felt for the warding-token at his belt as guards in glittering harness, his own and the baron's, cursed and tried to draw ceremonial blades.

A man in dusty robes was standing in midair, a sparkling wand in one hand and a gleaming metal gauntlet afire with the blue sheen of strong sorcery—and studded with winking enchanted rings at every joint—on the other.

"Lord Baron," he said triumphantly, "my task is done! I have *triumphed!* Silvertree House is yours!"

Barangar Silvertree came out of his great chair with a roar. Then he drained his flagon, flung it high into the rafters, and bellowed, "Cortahars of Silvertree! Ready a war party! Make ready, here—without delay!"

Thaulon Talasorn laughed, and the baron laughed with him, the two shaking their fists in the air like excited boys. And then the mage said, "One warning: physical traps aplenty still remain. It would be less than prudent to just rush across the river, in too great haste."

Baron Silvertree fell silent in midchuckle. He stared up at Thaulon for a moment, and then called, "Halt! I renounce my last command!" Glancing sideways at the mortified trade envoy, he added, "I—I was overtaken by the excitement of this great achievement!"

He looked up at Thaulon. "Lord Wizard, will you dine?"

"Gladly," the wizard replied, smiling down at the Lady Asmurna, who sat openmouthed in amazement, regarding him with awe and favor for the first time.

The baron waved at his seneschal to leave his place at the table. As that stout personage scrambled to do so, trying to hide a scowl, Barangar Silvertree turned a trifle ashamedly to his Telnan guest. "Pray pardon, Lord Lzurellan. Uh, may I get you a fresh flagon?"

Khelt Lzurellan of Teln was unused to being so vigorously interrupted at feasts, but he had not become one of the richest men in all Darsar by being a fool. He nodded, thin-lipped, and replied, "I would like that. It seems a new hero needs toasting—and a wizard at that. Now *there's* a rarity, by the Three."

\* \* \*

Barangar Silvertree smiled out at the vista below. The Silverflow sweeping endlessly past, its waters briefly gold now in the lowering sun, Flowfoam a long, dark hump of forest in its waters before him, and the dark turrets of Blackcastle Keep just visible beyond. It was a pleasant evening on the riverside battlement of Silvertree House, with the soft lamps lit to greet the coming sunset, and the dragondream in his flagon was good. The gardeners had all gone in to let Thaulon's slaying mist settle and clear the air of all stinging insects, so the neatly tended gardens were deserted.

It was all his.

"Somehow," the Lord Baron of Silvertree said, waving his drink at the view, "the river looks grander from this side. I've thanked you many a time, mage, but have my thanks once more; I can never say it enough. You delivered Silvertree House to me, after centuries of Silvertrees before me could not have it."

Thaulon Talasorn raised his own glass with an easy smile—and made the lazy gesture that raised a long warblade up from concealment beneath the merlons, where it had been thrust into a banner-socket in a carved stone gargoyle.

Still smiling, he watched it thrust through the baron's back, and burst out the splendid salander-weave breast of Barangar's ornate tunic. One of his rings kept the baron's death-cry a soundless thing, and another held up the blood spraying forth, in a motionless midair cloud.

Thaulon chuckled, and made a ring on his other hand flash. The air flashed in answer, and suddenly the guardsman Daerent, tall and handsome and beloved of Asmurna, stood on the balcony, blinking. He beheld Barangar, and his jaw dropped in astonishment.

Thaulon took great pleasure in mind-blasting the grandly muscled guardsman until Daerent's brains bubbled out of his ears in a froth.

Then the Lord Mage of Silvertree rose, put his own flagon into the guard's nerveless hand, and used sorcery to make the man clutch it and Daerent's other hand take firm hold of his sword.

Strolling around the scene, Thaulon whisked the scabbard of the blade he'd stolen earlier from Daerent's distant chambers into his grasp, belted it in place around Daerent's hips, and arranged both bulging-eyed dead baron and empty-eyed, mindless guardsman just as he wanted them.

Aye, perfect. Daerent and Barangar had been drinking dragondream together here, and the treasonous guard had stabbed his master fatally from behind, thus. Whereupon the baron's *most* loyal mage had been alerted magically, and had translocated himself here in haste, to discover the horrific deed—and frantically mindblast the guard, *thus*.

So the bodies, slayer and victim, had fallen so, and Thaulon Talasorn had but one thing more to do before frantically raising the alarm: use two of his rings to weave the strongest mind-master spell he knew . . . on the Lady Asmurna, from afar.

She was dozing, and to awaken her mind enough to seize control of it took a fierce effort.

One of the rings turned black and crumbled off Thaulon's finger, but he gave the pain it left behind a wry smile. 'Twas worth it. Worth it indeed.

Assuming a look of shock, he drew in a deep breath and cried, "Guards! Guards! *A rescue!*"


Easily six-score of the two hundred or so folk now crowded together on the battlements were cortahars, armaragors, armsmen, and longtime servants of Barangar Silvertree, and many of them ringed the seated, white-with-shock Lord Mage with dark frowns of suspicion on their faces and hands clenched on sword hilts. Old Ardanath of the guard had gone so far as to demand that Thaulon remove his rings into the seneschal's keeping, until "What must be decided is decided."

The Lady Asmurna was grimly sent for, the older men agreeing that the senior ladies of the household—the chate-

laine and the head chambermaid and Asmurna's old nurse—
be the ones to gently rouse her.

Thaulon slowly and carefully removed his rings and set
them, one by one, into Ardanath's upturned helm, and then
sat in an apparent daze, murmuring betimes, "Oh, Barangar.
Oh, old friend. What a way for your dreams to end."

And then the silent crowd parted as if by sorcery, and the
Lady Asmurna came walking, her face as white as marble
and as set as a statue. Tears ran down her cheeks like a waterfall, but she did not sob when she beheld the bodies.

She looked down at them for quite a time, and seemed to
be struggling for control—but as her old nurse reached out a
hand to give her steadying comfort, she lifted her head and
said clearly, "So what I foresaw in my nightmares has come
true at last. Forgive me for doubting you for all these years,
Lord Mage—and please accept my thanks for slaying the
traitor who wooed me to get at Father."

She raised her voice to let it ring out from end to end of
that silent assembly and announced, "My father's wishes
were that this most loyal of men, Thaulon Talasorn, succeed
him as baron, and take me to wife. I am both sad that this
day has come, and glad that I welcome my new Lord—and
yours—so eagerly. Lord Baron Thaulon Talasorn Silvertree,
will you wed me?"

The Lord Mage looked up at her and managed a weak
smile. "In memory of my friend and master, Barangar, and
in love of you, dear Asmurna, I can do no less than accept."

There was a stir, then, and a halfhearted cheer—and in the
heart of it, Thaulon claimed Ardanath's helm full of rings
with one hand, and the Lady Asmurna with the other.

Folk slept but poorly in vast Silvertree House, on the nights
when the Whispering Mind raged. Whisper, and send
dream-visions, and twist the occasional enchantment of the
House were all it could do; its fell power was securely
bound.

Yet it knew when Thaulon slept, and it fell silent often, in his chambers alone, to tempt him into deeper slumbers. His mind-chain to Asmurna kept him on the verge of wakefulness, most nights—but when he was too exhausted to hold it longer, one or twice a season, he took her to a remote tower of the House, spell-sealed the doors, and bound and gagged her so he could let his control slip and find true rest.

And whenever he did so, the Whispering Mind sent horrific visions to any guard whose post was too close, and sent them panting with terror a few rooms away, to gasp and stare into the dark and not see what it was doing.

And in those brief moments of privacy, the Whispering Mind gathered its strength at one or other of the magical gates scattered across the House, and covertly altered their destinations.

It left an echo of its whispers behind, to make sure the unwitting beasts who blundered through the gates to wander the back chambers of the House did not become a flood. It did not want to goad Lord Baron Thaulon Talasorn Silvertree into seeking gate after gate and trying to seal them.

Not when it could in time goad him into trying to destroy a gate—and so bring down his great web, releasing the Whispering Mind to act as it pleased.

It would be *very* pleased to act upon Thaulon Talasorn, energetically and at great length.

"Seneschal! Where's Skorntar, and why does he not answer my summons?"

The stout, grandly uniformed official turned from the muttering throng at the door of the Long Hall to make reply, and his face was grim. "Word's just come from the North Forehall, Lord. Skorntar was found torn in half there, at his post, with *this* dining on him."

He stood aside to let four cortahars trudge forward, carrying a shield full of monster between them.

Baron Thaulon Silvertree surveyed the untidy mass of slimy jaws and bony necks—like oversized, plucked turkey necks, only jointed, with swellings of bone occurring at about the length of his forearm along them—twice, thrice. . . .

He glared at the yellowish ichor dripping from the shield onto the floor and snapped. "Take that outside, and burn it in the bonepit—now. I don't know what it is, and I don't want to."

He glanced at the Lady Asmurna, who never spoke. She kept silent, and it was left to the seneschal to say nervously, "My Lord Baron, that's the third beast-slaying these last two days! The household—"

"Are beginning to feel as under siege here as I am, no doubt," Thaulon snapped, wondering if he should cross the river and step inside the humming wards he'd left in the Keep, to use the spell trap to hunt down the prowling beasts by their minds.

No. No, he'd not leave the House. That was a journey he dare not make with someone—but didn't want to make alone. He'd have to take Asmurna, and bind and gag her somewhere in the Keep . . . and what if the Curse somehow broke free while he was away? Or whispered into the wrong mind, and goaded the seneschal here, say, into mustering the household against him? Mightiest mage in all Darsar he might be, but if he didn't stop every last arrow his oh-so-loyal cortahars might send his way . . . It would take only *one,* after all.

No. Here he'd bide, and here make his stand. On the morrow he'd mount a hunt, using his cortahars to flush out the wandering beasts and travelers from far lands—there'd been a bard from Ultharn beyond Sarinda, a few days back, completely lost and bewildered at how he'd blundered here!—and then he'd pounce on what they found with his magics.

The Curse and its maedra were still bound, of that he was sure, but these intruders were becoming an increasing danger and annoyance. They'd probably always come to the House—it was riddled with gates, after all—and been devoured by the maedra. Hmm; perhaps he could starve those stone-wyrms yet. . . .

He glanced at Asmurna on her throne beside him, and she

gave him a loving smile and reached for his arm, to lean forward and kiss him.

At his bidding, of course. He loved to watch her magnificent breasts swing free in her low-cut gowns as she thrust herself at him . . . but it was still there, in the depths of her sparkling eyes. It was always there. A deep flame of agony and hatred, searing darkly through the mind-thrall to tell him she knew exactly what he'd done to her father and her lover.

He almost shivered at the intensity of her gaze, this time, but contented himself with taking hold of her chin, kissing her, and forcing her to moan with need and nibble at his mouth hungrily.

"Ah, such a distraction," he purred to the seneschal, as the man reddened to the roots of his well-oiled hair. "I'd best take the Lady Baron to our chambers, or she'll be mounting me right here on the throne. Though that *would* be the sort of siege I'd welcome."

When the six robed men stepped out of the trees to form a silent ring around him, Halduth knew things had gone very wrong.

He swallowed, but tried to keep his voice calm as he turned to the man who'd brought him here and asked, "These are your business partners? Seven ways you split things? I'm afraid I don't trade in anything valuable enough to be worth splitting sev—"

"Your name is Halduth Silvertree?" one of the Serpent-priests snapped. "Of the Silvertrees of Sirlptar?"

"Aye, but—"

"Come. We have need of you. Which may keep you alive. Trying to flee, or disputing with us, will not."

The Serpents closed in tightly around the traveling merchant, snakes swaying up into view from various sleeves as they strode. Halduth Silvertree, his innards suddenly as empty and as loose as water, strode with them. He was going to die, no matter what befell, he was going to—the Serpents never left anyone alive who knew their secrets—he was a dead man already, but if he was careful, might not spend his last moments with a snake actually *gnawing* his eyeball. . . .

He whimpered before he could stop himself, and one of the Serpents almost smiled. Then they were ducking under a low tree branch in turn, and turning sharply to the left—two Serpents stepping back to flank him with raised hands that crawled with glowing sorcery, presumably to prevent him trying to bolt. Halduth followed the line of priests and found himself staring at an upright, oval ring of blue flames that was floating in the air between two trees.

He blinked at it. Well, of course, everyone knew the Serpents used sorcery, but he'd never seen anything more than a hedge-wizard twisting the flames of a bonfire into images to tell old tales, before this. This was—frightening, that's what it was.

"Step through the ring. Take care not to touch the flames, if you'd prefer to stay alive."

A lit lantern—a sturdy metal war-lamp, that could take falls—was thrust into his hand, and a second one, its stout candle unlit, hooked to his belt. Another Serpent put a long wooden staff into his hand.

"You will step into a dark place. We will be with you—in your mind—to converse with. Tell us what you see, as you walk, and bear this always in mind: to shout, or scream, or make loud noise as you move, will be to doom yourself. Not from us, but from those who dwell where you'll find yourself. It is *not* as deserted as it may seem."

"What is this place I'm going called?"

"There's no need—"

"Oh, yes," Halduth said quietly, "there is. I'm going to die there, and I want to be told. Or I'll just swing this staff at some of you, and die *here* instead."

"He's a Silvertree, all right," one of the Serpents muttered.

Another priest regarded Halduth with a smile and said, "Silvertree House."

"Ah," Halduth replied, turning to face the flickering gate. "So I'm going to be driven mad. Well, why didn't you just say so?"

And he bent his head and lowered the staff carefully, and stepped through the flames.

*Ah, that Silvertree spirit. I admire it still, despite all the blunders and messes so many of them have made of things.*

*After all, 'tis not like they're alone in striding swiftly into error after error.*

*I've done that far more than once too often, myself, and have this cloak of cold to remind myself of that.*

*For every last chilling moment of eternity.*

"Empty," Halduth murmured, holding the lantern a little higher. "So what exactly do you expect me to find here for you, anyway? Treasure?"

"Nothing so crass. We seek lore. The ache behind your eyes is us, seeing out through them."

"Oh." Halduth became aware of a faint sound then, and came to a halt. It was a whispering, faint and distant. He listened hard, and then asked, "Do you hear? Do you know who—or what—that is?"

"No, but it's been heard for a thousand years, if we can trust certain writings. It seems . . . we cannot discern the direction of its source."

"You, too?" Halduth asked mockingly. "So—do I go on?"

"Yes. Along this passage, and stop when you reach a door, or an arch, or a crossway. We'll listen again there."

The whispering was louder, more insistent, and Halduth thought he could *almost* make out the words. Yet it still seemed to be coming from—everywhere. All sides of him, equally strong. There was a thrumming now, too, and it grew louder as he peered through the archway.

"Go towards that sound," one of the Serpents said, "but do not touch whatever is making it."

"Tell me something," Halduth murmured, as he obeyed. "Why did you choose me?"

"You are of the blood of Silvertree. You can serve to un-lock the secrets of Silvertree House."

"I see. Are these secrets likely to bite me? Or swing swords at me?"

"If we knew that, talkative merchant, they—"

"Wouldn't be secrets," Halduth finished in chorus. "Of course." Something like a glowing white beam of light—or the vibrating string of some gigantic, unseen harp—stretched across the passage before him, from something tiny on a high ledge to his right down and through a crevice on near the floor on his left.

"Don't touch it!"

"I wasn't eager to," Halduth replied, eyeing the thrum-ming magic. He had a hunch that if he extended the tip of his staff into that beam, the tip would simply vanish . . . but he wasn't aching to prove himself right. Why—

The whispering suddenly swelled, becoming almost a chant, a murmuring that he could pick words out of at last. Those words brought a flood of visions to Halduth, like scenes in a vivid dream, of serpent-things with human arms that could plunge in and out of the stone walls of this place, of men shouting and fighting with swords and dying, of other men whose faces slipped into melting facelessness as they grew tentacles and tore apart screaming women, of— the whispers swirled up into a scream, a great howling shriek that swept through Halduth and rushed out of him, to pierce and sear and rend . . . he heard the Serpents scream-ing as they died, praying vainly or trying to stammer incan-tations, and—and then they were gone from his mind, and flowers were speaking to him under a pink sky, and his name was crumbling away from him no matter how desperately he clutched and clawed at it, and . . . and . . .

The insane husk of the unfortunate Halduth strode pur-posefully along the passages of Silvertree House, staff in hand and lantern swinging. When the first Silvertree guard swung away from the wall with drawn sword to bar his way, he stopped, hefted his staff, and announced crisply, "I have a

message for the Lord Baron Thaulon Talasorn Silvertree—
words for his ears alone. Conduct me to him, or I shall be
forced to destroy you with my spells."

The guard stared at the stranger uncertainly.

The man looked like a peddler who'd lost his pack, but he
strode along like a king . . . and that staff looked like it had
been a sapling this morning, but then again . . .

Well, wizards did conduct themselves like madmen, the
Lord Silvertree included. He plucked his buckler from his
belt and rang it with a tap of his blade.

When two cortahars came bustling up, drawn swords
flashing, the guard told them this stranger wanted to be taken
to speak with the Lord Baron. Halduth repeated his words
obligingly—and the two cortahars exchanged glances and
then waved at him to accompany them.

The road through the palace to reach Lord Silvertree was
a long one, with several challenges and frowning parleys—
but there was nothing of Halduth Silvertree left to be
amazed to hear himself say, over the seneschal's shoulder to
the black-clad, thin-lipped man on the throne beyond, "My
name is Halduth Silvertree, and I am come to reveal what
should have been said to you long ago, Thaulon Silvertree. I
know the great secret of our family curse, and how to take up
the peerless magic that underlies it."

Thaulon frowned at the stranger, and then awakened a
ring on his finger and launched a mind-delving to reach behind the mild blue eyes of this Halduth.

He found himself falling into flowers, a pink sky whirling
overhead and then around beneath him.

The seneschal's shout of, "Lord? Lord Silvertree!"
seemed to come from far away, and so did the cold graze of
stone as he stumbled down off his throne and staggered
against a wall.

He was abruptly aware of the talons of a maedra lurking
just beneath it, smoldering in bound hatred, and flung himself blindly away from the wall, fighting to drag his mind
back out of the babbling, whispering insanity—and a flag-

stone abruptly gave way under his boots, and he plunged—
onto something very solid and sharp.

The shrieking pain brought Thaulon abruptly back to himself, in time to see the seneschal desperately hacking the
fallen body of the stranger, the staff rolling towards him. He
was in an ancient pitfall trap, armpit-deep in a pit, on a spike
of some sort that had run up his leg and into his rear, on up
into . . .

Thaulon swallowed, sweat almost blinding him, and
clenched a shaking fist in front of himself. The Whispering
Mind had done this, had lured him into a trap that must have
been here for centuries—

The ring winked, and he was abruptly back in his chambers.
His precious enspelled wine of healing was just paces away,
yon statuette of Barangar Silvertree its concealed decanter. . . .

Three Above, the *pain!*

Thaulon lurched towards relief, reaching out desperately,
trying not to sink down into agony.

Someone shapely and familiar glided into his path and
gently pushed his trembling hand aside. Someone who wore
a smile that promised murder.

Asmurna drove the tiny dagger he used to trim the can-
dlewicks into Thaulon Talasorn's left eye and hissed, "For
my father!"

Then she plucked it out and drove it into his other eye.
"For Daerent, you spawn of the Dark One!"

Those panted words seemed to Thaulon to echo from a
great distance across his new darkness, as he tumbled down,
down. . . .

It had taken so little time to reduce him to a dark huddle
on the rug at her feet.

The wizard's moments of insanity had broken his mind-
thrall over her—thank the Three!—and now the revenge that
had burned in her for so long was done.

Weeping, Asmurna reeled, and then fell to her knees as
Thaulon's death brought a wave of thrumming light crashing
into her mind. Blinded and lost, she whimpered as it

whipped and tumbled her along, on and on into endless-
ness . . . and when at last the fury of the collapsing spellweb
died away, the Curse thundered in like a racing dark cloud
and claimed her.

The Lady Asmurna Silvertree straightened, ignoring the
ribbons of blood—and one glistening eyeball—that marked
her diaphanous gown, and stole away into the shadows on
soft bare feet.

Her eyes blazed with a dark fire that matched her terrible
smile—and shadow after shadow became her refuge as she
padded from chamber to chamber, using her little knife with
stealthy skill.

And at every death she kissed her victim, and the Whispering Mind gathered in their thoughts and failing life-force.

The sun rose and set and rose again before Asmurna was
done, the last and most isolated guard choking out his last
breath at her feet.

She stepped over him, the dark whispering loud in her
head, and strode alone to the center of a chamber where
scores of stone-snakes twice as tall as she was glided around
and around in a circle. They parted smoothly before her, until she came to the upright shadow at their heart, a tattered
pillar of darkness that betimes seemed a thing of talons and
whipping jawed tentacles, and betimes seemed to have the
shape and face of a tall woman, a woman whose face
seemed almost familiar. It was a Silvertree face.

*Little one,* the shadow said in Asmurna's mind, *come to
me. Come to Sembril, and know peace.*

These things I saw in visions in the Silent House, in
those last moments when the whispers began to make
sense to me, ere I fled forever: a pale young woman slaying guard after guard at his post with a dagger, flitting
barefoot from one to the next until all are sprawled and
dead. The madworms come out of the walls to feed, devouring corpse after corpse but touching not the barefoot
slayer. She walks on as one in a dream, into a great
chamber where madworms circle a tall shadow and the

whisperings are shouting-strong. The slitherers-through-stone part for her, and she embraces the shadow that seems to take woman shape. It gives her death.

The madworms feed and feed, until naught is left but bones, and then they go back into the walls. Silvertree House falls silent, deserted as the winter winds blow, and then the spring rains, that in turn give way to the summer sun.

So it follows, seasons chasing seasons, the House empty but for the fleeting footfalls of bold adventurers after plunder, who fall to traps or madworm jaws and talons, and wanderers who blunder through the gates that shimmer unseen in many rooms and passages of the House.

I was one of those adventurers, lured by the bright, cold fire of enchanted things. The House is filled with them: glow-stones placed upon high ledges as though by a child, wands and scepters to delight any battle-mage, and oddities such as boot-scrapers that cry alarm when intruders pass. A handful of these things I have brought out of the House, a mere handful out of a mountain of glowing sorcery.

It calls to me, it lures me, yet I dare not venture into Silvertree House again. Swift spells and the lives of friends and the luck of the Three let me escape the last time, though I felt it, and knew it like a dark shadow in my mind: the House was alive and aware and watching *me*.

It lives still—sprawling, ruined, but somehow still growing. Its very walls pulse with life around every one of the thousands upon thousands of scattered enchanted items. Its gates draw life-force from their "other ends" into the House, and it seems to me that this powers its continuing growth.

It lives still, and watches for me.

So I've laid aside the hurling of spells and the faring forth on adventures to turn to the tomes of a sage of spell-lore, out of nothing more noble than fear. Fear that I shall be drained, and my mind conquered, by the ever-growing Curse that lurks in Silvertree House.

And if I and too many others fall, soon it will become able to reach out across Aglirta after all mages—and then across the rest of Asmarand, and Darsar, until no place is safe. Could this be the curse of the Three, come upon us at last?

Aundramus Varandthorn
Sage of Sorcery
Second Turning, Wanesummer, Eight Hundred and Thirty-sixth Year of the Reign of Kelgrael

# BOOK EIGHT

---

*Brungelth Silvertree*

2008–2062 SR
Lord Baron of Silvertree
And of His Kinslaying and Doom

# 1

## No Dirtier Profession

The chained man in the hacked and battered armor started to sob. "*Please,* Lord Brungelth!" he pleaded from his knees, a thin line of blood running from his lips. "Spare my life! I'll be a servant in your kitchens—an exile—*anything!* I—"

The burly, brown-eyed baron in only slightly-less-battered armor clanked over to him, bent to give his prisoner a sneering smile—and brought his long-hafted war ax around in a vicious, slaying blow.

Its wetly solid bite threw the man over on his side in a rattling of chains, his head almost severed. Dark blood flowed.

Baron Brungelth Silvertree grinned down at the light of life fading from despairing eyes. When it was entirely gone, he turned to face the ring of watching warriors and brandished his ax. "So passes the last; Aglirta is mine! *We ride!*"

The warriors roared back, *"We ride!"* and scrambled for their saddles.

"See, lad? Yon wraith did nothing to us at all. Now, if it'd been one of those hunting wraiths they call silent shadows, that would've been a different thing. . . ."

Horl was leading the way along a passage that turned twice and ended in a blank wall, his left hand with its ever-curled fingers dangling uselessly.

"Our doom?" Dlanazar asked, a little wearily.

"Indeed, by the maidens' moon-drenched shoulders," the elder procurer muttered almost absently, his attention on certain stones on the wall beside the dead end. He did something to them with his right hand, fumbling his sword into the crook of his left arm to manage it—and the dead-end wall slid aside with a deep rumbling, revealing a large, dark space beyond.

Dlan regarded it with deep suspicion, and made a throwing motion with the hand he was holding his glowstone in.

Horl nodded. "Do it, lad—but keep it low. There're things in yon room we don't want to hit."

The younger procurer opened his mouth to say something—and then, without uttering a word, closed it again and tossed his stone into the chamber beyond.

It proved to be large and grand. At its heart stood a massive stone chair with a high, ornate back, a thick coating of dust and cobwebs that couldn't quite conceal the cuts and cracks in it that made it look like dozens of swordsmen had chopped at it like madmen, not caring what happened to their blades, and . . . gems as large as Dlanazar's fist sparkling along its arms.

"Ahhh," the young procurer gasped, stepping forward eagerly.

"*Easy,* lad," Horl said gruffly, putting a hand on his shoulder. "Yon's the Throne of Silvertree. They say Brungelth Silvertree died sitting in it."

"And? So?"

"So there's supposed to be a curse that falls on anyone who disturbs those gemstones. Two curses, actually—a swift sorcery of some sort, here and now, and a slower, weightier doom that blights the rest of the, er, blasphemer's days."

Dlanazar pulled free of Horl's grasp. "Blasphemer? The Three *smile* on me, old man! Remember? Now, these're the first gems we've seen—look, enough of them to make us both as rich as kings—and you want me to *walk away from them?*"

"Lad, lad—there're lots of jewels to be had, hidden throughout the House, but none of them are worth spit if you die before seeing the sun again, and have no chance to spend them!"

Horl lurched sideways to stand before Dlanazar again, and added sternly, "Before you stride angrily in and start trying to wrest those stones out of the throne, consider this: The far wall of that room—see?—holds a dozen or more cupboards set into the stone. All of them—look you—stand empty . . . and if you close one or two, you'll soon notice that they're all hidden: close the swivel-blocks, and they look just like every other block in yon wall. So a thief who was good at his work, or knew this place very well, or both, has been through this room. And look you: he emptied a *dozen* hide-holes—yet left yon throne untouched! Now, does that tell you anything?"

Dlan let out a snarl of anger as he shrugged and waved one hand in exasperation, and then burst out, "All right, Lord Whitehair! You're right again! Right, right, always wise and right! I should trust you in all things!"

"Sweetly put," Horl said. "Now, bridle your temper, lad, and look about. See the wall I made to move—and note: no handles or pull-rings to move it back again. These are the things you should be noting, hey? And don't think of moving the throne, either—it spits killing lightnings at all who try. Now try to keep your hands—and your behind—off the throne. If sitting somewhere in this House is going to change you into some horrible monster, this would be the seat to do it."

He lurched forward on his uneven legs, leading the way into the echoing throne chamber. "Our first move is to make as sure as we can that the way is safe, and that nothing's up on the ceiling or lurking behind yon pillar to pounce on us . . . and then we recover your glowstone. *Then* we look about."

Dlanazar did as he was told, and was soon gazing about at a flight of stairs ascending into darkness above, a stone table in a far corner, a single stout pillar rising from the floor to the ceiling, a rotting row of tapestries along one wall with a huge gap in them that looked as if someone had torn handfuls of them down . . . and at a selection of closed doors in various walls. Most of the rooms he'd seen thus far were square or rectangular, but this one had walls running inwards and outwards at irregular angles. It also had a high but flat ceiling— bereft of monsters—rather than the usual curving vaulting. It was a strange room, and Dlan said as much.

"So 'tis, lad, so 'tis . . . but they were strange folk, in those days. It was a rare baron that knew more than a season of peace at a time . . . a far cry from these days of Regent

Castlecloaks, and peace at last, and the Guardians not even needed again yet. Back then, no one had much time for grand building."

Dlan arched an eyebrow and waved a hand all around, indicating the enormity of the Silent House around them. "Oh, no?"

"No, lad, much of this was built and rebuilt by the maedra, pursuing their own whims—not by men at all. There were some Silvertrees who feared to take to their beds for worry over whether they'd be walled in alive by night."

"Oh, come now!" Dlan sneered. "That's *got* to be a fireside longtongue tale! And I know the maedra—madworms, inside the walls!—have got to be, well, highly embroidered from someone remembering an illusion spell some wizard used to scare off intruders here, once."

Horl lifted his useless left arm and pointed at Dlanazar with the fingers that never quite uncurled, his face serious. "*No*, lad. That sort of scoffing will get you killed here faster than anything else short of blindly running through the halls. Maedra *do* exist—and they eat humans, when they've a mind to."

Dlan looked at him incredulously—and then cast a quick glance down the room. Had that been something stirring, in the stonework, there?

"Let's be up and sharp and moving, old man!" he snapped. "So I can't touch these gems and the crawling monsters will get me if I don't believe in them! Fine—so let's be off to wherever we *can* get jewels, yes?"

Horl nodded and lurched forward. "There's just one more thing you should see, first." He pointed at a flagstone in the floor near Dlan's boots. "See the little arrow mark? That's warning you that there's a thrust-blade trap on the side of the stone where the arrow's pointing."

"A sword blade that shoves straight up from the floor?"

Horl nodded, and without a trace of a smile added, "So we'll step around it, and go out *that* door."

They both glanced back, just before they stepped through the doorway, but it was a long breath later before the shadow that looked like a sad old man faded into view on the hacked and battered throne, got up from it, and started walking after them in utter silence—so neither of the treasure-hunters saw it.

"Richest spice importer in all Sirlptar, and here I sit, camped outside an Aglirtan baron's gates! Hah!" The man in leaf-green salamite spat wryly into the crackling fire.

"And you're somehow more important than the rest of us?" another merchant asked from its far side, looking up from warming his hands.

"Huh," commented a third, inspecting the plume of smoke streaming from the nut wedged in the tines of his firefork. Burnt, definitely. "We're none of us too grand to go chasing coin, are we? We'll await trade audiences on beaches piled high with dead fish in the Isles and on rat-crawling docks in the stinking sewe—ahem, canals—of Urngallond, won't we?"

"Now *there's* a truth spoken," another Sirl merchant agreed, striding up out of the night-gloom. "I've never waited in a graveyard before, though."

"I have," the man with the firefork and the nuts said briefly, but volunteered no more. Several of the others around the fire exchanged glances and chuckles.

"Ah, but this place is pleasant enough. Our dogs'll keep off wolves and outlaws, there's the river handy, and the closed gates of Baron Brungelth Silvertree are as welcoming as anyone else's shut gates, hey?"

The man who was warming his hands cast a quick glance up at the dark, frowning towers above them and murmured, "They've been saying for centuries that ghosts that slay folk lurk in Silvertree House, you know."

"Aye," said the man with the firefork, waving it, "I *do* know, and I was hoping we could avoid trading curl-your-hair tales with each other for once. Let's talk about this baron we're all so anxious to fleece, shall we?"

"Agreed. So they say Ulthorth's doomed, and Silvertree'll be back here in triumph late on the morrow, or the day after."

"Who's Ulthorth?"

"Three Above, man, you dwell in Sirlptar and trade upriver and don't know who Ilangh Ulthorth is? He's just the last warlord of Aglirta, that's all! If 'twasn't for Brungelth Silvertree, he'd have been storming our gates a season ago!"

"They're *all* warlords! What does one matter more than another? I don't trouble over their names. Wait until one—this Silvertree—wins out, and deal with *him*. Anyone care to enlighten me as to why he's won it all? Sheer brutes' luck, or low cunning, or do the Three love him dearly?"

The fire crackled and spat—and several of the merchants spat thoughtfully right back at it. The one with the firefork was the first to stir himself. "Well, now," he said slowly. "Baron Stoneheart . . ."

"Baron who? How many bloody barons does Aglirta have?"

"Dozens, lad, and they're all of them bloody," came the reply, amid many mirthless chuckles from around the fire.

"They call Silvertree that," the man with the fork explained, "on account of his ruthlessness. Baron Brungelth Silvertree—just one more hiresword, out of all the Silvertrees who swing swords for coin in Sirlptar because they've never learned to do aught else—but a good one. The most wily and swift to strike . . . even knows a little sorcery, too, they say. Perhaps the fiercest Baron Silvertree yet."

"The Terror of Aglirta," someone murmured.

"And well named. He's pillaged his way down the Vale. Blackgult yonder, across the river—down the years the two baronies have been rivals, see?—he burned every keep and village and barn of, leaving it little better'n a beast-roamed waste; if there are any Blackgults still alive, they're living outlaw, in hiding, in the Windfangs or beyond. We came here because here is the only place to meet Brungelth without a sword in your hand and your own grave ready-dug behind you, but he never sleeps a night in Silvertree House—it's just his palace. For show, I mean."

Several men peered up into the darkness. "For a place he never sets foot in, he's spent a lot on it," someone muttered, all the usual Sirl scorn for money wasted in his voice.

"A grand gatehouse and a few banners, no more," was the

reply. "He rather needed yon gates, too: when I was a lad I took a barge past here, bound for Tselgara, and 'twas all gaping empty archways here then, with bears and the like roaming in and out."

"Huh, such improvements," someone else commented. "The roaming beasts put on armor and airs here now."

"So's it true? The place is haunted, and any true Silvertree who dwells here falls under a fatal curse?"

"Mayhap, and mayhap not. I've heard the baron mistrusts its nigh-endless secret passages and creeping creatures, but I wasn't planning on asking him. It's not as if he lounges around anywhere, lad—when he isn't exploring its cellars and far-off rooms with a small army, like any adventurer, he's in the saddle up and down Aglirta, slaughtering every capable ruler or petty warlord in the Vale."

"*I've* heard that the High Houses of Sirlptar are trying to buy prayers with priests of the Three so flood and earth-gulf and lightning will rid them of Brungelth Silvertree."

"Huh. See how well it's worked? He's a season away from tearing down our gates and coming in to empty all our coffers!"

"And that's why our highest and mightiest are scared. They don't want a king to rise in Aglirta at last and come to conquer *them.* I'd believe it, about the prayers—why not, after you've openly sponsored any mercenary who desires to try to carve out a barony for himself in the lower Vale? And offered coins and aid to any wizard who offers to slay the Baron Silvertree?"

"Some of 'em have come close, too, I hear."

"Aye," said the man with the firefork, in a dry voice. "Which is why Brungelth is now hiring mages of his own. And why I asked all of you for as many coins as I did. That bound and hooded cargo under guard in my tent isn't a pleasure-lass: it's a Sirl city sage who just happens to owe me a *lot* of money—and who just happens to be an expert on magic."

* * *

As the hood came off, Brungelth Silvertree gave the startled, blinking man who'd been under it a hard look and asked, "You're the sage Darvult?"

"Uh-ah, yes, Lord."

The Baron turned to the watching merchants. "I agree to your deal."

Three servants strode forward, one holding out a contract, and the others bearing open chests of gold coins.

The delighted Sirl merchants inspected both, found the baronial signature and seal on both columns of the former and a cursory but satisfyingly numerous count for the latter, and turned to load both onto their waiting barge.

The Baron Silvertree gave them a cordial farewell and moved one finger in a signal as he turned away—and from behind the carved gilt of his balconies bowmen rose up with ready shafts and turned the Sirl merchants into so many arrow-festooned, blood-drenched pincushions. Other servants hurried to reclaim the gold and plunder the bodies and the waiting barge.

Brungelth watched them for a moment, a thin smile on his lips, and then put a firm hand on the terrified sage's arm and guided him deeper into the great domed forehall. "I'm glad you came all this way to see me, Master Darvult," he said pleasantly. "I just need answers to a few questions. . . ."

The sage fainted.

Darvult could see only one door out of this room, and he'd heard it being locked earlier. Fear-sweat was almost blinding him. It dripped from his very nose as he stared across the table at Baron Silvertree.

Who was asking, "And the most capable independent wizard of Asmarand just now would be—?"

"Kalanth Bowdragon," Darvult stammered eagerly.

Brungelth Silvertree nodded and smiled, and the sage almost wept with relief. Perhaps he'd manage to keep his life, after all.

Still smiling, Brungelth glanced at the burly cortahar

standing behind the seated sage—who stepped forward, blade aimed at one of the gaps in the carvings of the high-backed chair, and smoothly ran the man through.

Anstan Darvult stared at the baron in horror, gargling blood deep in his throat as the glistening sword tip retreated back into his guts . . . and then he pitched forward to crash face-first onto the table.

The baron turned away from the dying man and reached for the goblet a servant had been holding ready on a platter.

"Consultation at swordpoint is so much faster," he murmured, "and they speak so *eagerly,* too. Even more remarkably, they've all agreed on the same man. This Kalanth Bowdragon must be the best." He turned to another cortahar. "The hedge-wizards are here?"

"Yes, lord." That assurance was firm, but the knight's next words were hesitant. "Lord? Are you sure this is wise?"

The Baron gave the man a long look. "Wisdom is for old men who look at things after they've befallen. I'm not afraid of any foe, greatest wizard or not. Bring them in."

The lackspell wizards looked fearful enough as they shuffled in—and openly cowered when they saw the dead man at the table.

Brungelth Silvertree gave them all a hearty smile. "The coins I've offered are satisfactory, I trust?"

They all stared at him, so he let his smile start to fade, and then they almost stumbled over their tongues to assure him that yes, yes, the gold was handsome, Lord, yes, handsome!

When he held up his hand, they fell as silent as if he'd made them mute with a spell, and he smiled into the restored stillness and said, "Fear not, masters of magic. I stand by my bargains, and you've nothing to fear from me unless you betray me—as, regrettably, Darvult of Sirlptar, there, did. Sages are an untrustworthy lot, come to think of it; Bartapan Helder crossed me before Darvult, and Yundreth of Gloit before Helder, too."

Baron Silvertree scratched his chin thoughtfully, and then rediscovered his smile and waved his goblet. "But that's of no matter to us. We must be concerned only with what I need

you to do for me right now: farspeak the wizard Kalanth
Bowdragon. Yes, the great Kalanth. I've a little magic of my
own, but not that spell—and if this goes well, I believe you'll
be as useful to me as I can be to you, in the days ahead. Once
I rule all Aglirta, I'll need a mage at the side of every one of
my tersepts, so we can speak back and forth speedily."

"King Brungelth," one of the old men gasped, and tried
unsteadily to go down on his knees.

"No, no," Brungelth forestalled him laughingly, waving
the man to his feet. "Let's not be having crowns before
swords here! Come, farspeak me Kalanth Bowdragon!"

As the wizards hastily began their castings, he hummed a
tune, clearly pleased. The cortahars along the walls regarded
his wide smile with carefully expressionless faces, and fore-
bore from comment on the lyrics of the air their Lord Baron
was recalling: "The best wizard's a dead wizard, the best
sage has no tongue. . . ."


"He suspected nothing. So far as he knows, he made firm
pact this day with the real Kalanth, at a price lower than he'd
thought he'd have to pay."

"Ah, but if I were Brungelth Silvertree, I'd not think the
former barony of Tarlagar was all that low a price. After all,
he'll now have the man he thinks is the most powerful wizard in the world sitting in a castle at one end of Aglirta, judg-
ing just when having a brawling self-proclaimed king
around is become too much of a nuisance. Were I Omngluth,
I'd expect poison or a nasty trap of some sort, soon."

"True enough, yet Omngluth chose to play Kalanth for that
very reason: he loves matching wits with these brutes. 'Tis
our brawling Brungelth that'll receive the nasty surprise."

"Oh, not we craven hedge-wizards? I'm thinking he'll be
sending cortahars through secret passages with their daggers
sharp to slit our throats before morning."

"Not yet. The sages could do him more harm selling word
of their dealings with him, and what they saw, than they
could aid him with their learning. He needs us for the very

purpose he revealed to us—and he'll probably start handing us wands and the like, just one or two baubles each, to keep hidden for him, in case he has to run from Kalanth, so he can turn and deliver his own surprise."

"And what of the *real* Kalanth? Won't he come down on us all like a summer storm, once he gets word of someone pretending to be him?"

"Of course—eventually. The warring nobles of Carraglas have been claiming his support for this faction or that for some seasons now, so he deals with such problems only when he has nothing more pressing. And when he does come, we have another little deception to play."

"I'm glad you can keep all of our little deceptions straight. *I* lose patience with it all and start killing people."

"And thereby make the Koglaur ever more hated and feared. We're going to rule here openly someday, Arauntras—and it'll be harder to find pleasure in doing so, and more dangerous for us all, if common humans hate and fear us right down to their toenails and their great-grandsire's toenails."

"Three Above, you should be writing ballads, Nornthear!"

"I'd much rather do the deeds the bards sing about, Arauntras. Writing ballads is hard work, whereas wenching and betraying and deceiving have an undeniable element of fun. As far too many kings and barons discover."

"Adroitly done, fellow Faceless!"

"*Don't* call me that! I hate that word!"

"What, 'adroit'? It's a per—"

"*Faceless,* as you know quite well, Nornthear! Some of us object to—"

"Yes, yes, yes! How many centuries have we heard you huffing upon this matter? Sheathe tongues, the both of you! I agree, Nornthear, this was adroitly done. Brungelth is smarter than he pretends to be, but I believe he suspects nothing—and I had the lightest of mindtouch spells going, when he spoke to us. That was genuine delight and surprise."

"Yes, surprise because he really had decided to slay us

rather than keeping us in his service, Arauntras. This ploy succeeded because he was *expecting* a Sirl-wizard-led attempt on his life. I'm more worried about what he'll get to thinking after he starts puzzling about how his doddering old hedge-wizards could possibly have the sorcery or the wits to defeat a dozen guild wizards."

"Well, we won't be repeating this 'ploy,' as you call it. A dozen more of us can easily be brought into play, but I'm not denuding Darsar of moderately competent wizards just to get us into the good graces of one more grasping, ruthless backcountry Conqueror of All. We may need those wizards when we embark on our next grand scheme—because the Great Serpent is rising again, and the Serpents are on the crawl!"


The Koglaur standing by the upright oval of cold blue flames snarled and thrust out a small forest of tentacles, a sword or a wand in each one—but the man who'd staggered through the gate, one broken arm dangling and trailing blue blood, snarled right back at him and struck the nearest wands aside with a sudden tentacle of his own.

"Some astute gate-guard *you* make, Thaalor!"

"What're you *doing* here, Nornthear? We're never supposed to use this gate to get from the baron to—"

"Human hedge-wizards aren't supposed to bleed blue, either, are they? Too many Aglirtans know that about us, thanks to some overtalkative bards whom we left alive too long. Now get Arauntras! I need healing, or I need someone else to go play at being old Gluth the foolishly loyal hedge-wizard!"

Thaalor turned and scuttled away, growing a small forest of legs for speed in doing so. As he ran, he called back, "But what *happened?*"

"We've been having so much fun mounting false attacks on our beloved Brungelth and foiling them," Nornthear replied sourly, watching Thaalor almost run right into Arauntras and a trio of hurrying fellow Koglaur, "that we weren't ready for more than the most feeble real attack on him."

"Well?" Arauntras demanded, growing hands to begin weaving a healing as he came trotting up to the bleeding, half-transformed Nornthear.

"Sirl wizards again."

"Three Above! How many throw-my-life-away fools does the guild have *left?*"

"A plentiful number yet, probably, but these were out-landers—from Ravander, hired here to Asmarand by a *lot* of Sirl coin."

"Ravander? I'll bet. Takes a powerful mage just to fars-peak from Sirlptar to there. So they were good, hey?"

"They were adequate. The Serpents were worse, much worse."

"The *Serpents?*" Thaalor's gasp sounded outraged.

"Yes. They waited until the full spell-fray was raging, and then appeared in force and well-organized, with well-chosen spells—which means they've been watching us as well as Brungelth Silvertree—and . . ."

The rest of Nornthear's words were lost in the stunned swearing of all the Koglaur, including another two who'd just appeared down the passage.

One of these newcomers promptly hissed severely, "Si-lence! Unless you want nigh a dozen Silvertree infants awakening, seeing all the tentacled monsters, and running around screaming! It's bad enough holding the Curse at bay, without all of you playing at being idiots!"

"Apologies, Laumthrara. How goes it with the Curse?"

"We still hold the entire wing, but she hurls maedra at us the way your baron beheads folk who stand in his way! She's had them digging beneath us, these last few says, trying to make everything fall in on our heads."

"Our spell-web is more than a match for her."

"Says the bold Koglaur who's just had a nasty surprise courtesy of the snake-lovers, and so thinks Darsar holds no more nasty surprises for him, ever."

"Peace, Laumthrara," said the other most recently arrived Koglaur. "The truth stands thus: Our magics against the Curse hold, and I've woven them several layers deep—if she pierces one barrier she gains a few rooms, not free passage to our vitals. The Silent House around our little refuge is become a battlefield of shifting passages and roaming beasts, both maedra and worse. She certainly wants us destroyed, though not enough to reveal herself to Brungelth Silvertree."

"Who still takes care not to come within reach of her whispers," Laumthrara added.

"Indeed. The gate you just came through, Nornthear— healed yet, by the way? even brutish barons can count wizards; he won't not notice your absence forever—lets me weave grasping spells to drain life-energies just as the Curse does, to help hold her back."

"And all for a handful of squalling Silvertree brats," Thaalor grunted. "Why are we doing all this skulking and playacting, anyway? Why not just slaughter them all and *take* Aglirta, if we want it so much?"

"Because then we'll be just another brutish baron, awaiting the flood of would-be replacements itching to bury swords in us. We'd not last. Moreover, the Curse can't last forever, and when we find the way to take her down, we'll be able to accomplish what was left unfinished when Ravengar Silvertree built this place long, long ago. This palace, and all its magic, would be a fitting Koglaur fortress—*the* fitting Koglaur home."

Thaalor shook several heads, which had been noting the expressions of various Koglaur during the converse, and asked, "Again, why must we skulk? Why snatch children and rear them here in hiding, under siege?"

"This way," Laumthrara explained patiently, "we rear some protected, hidden Silvertrees under our teaching—and so do something no baron or Serpent-priest knows how to do: conquer Aglirta's future."

\*　\*　\*

*Ah, a noble goal, ruling the future. A pity no mortal—and, most days, the Three themselves, I think—can master that.*

*Or a blessing, more likely. What joy could life hold, if someone—anyone—could leash and command the days ahead?*

*Had I managed a shred more authority over my past days, though . . .*

*Ah, but I did not, and so find myself drowning in endless cold.*

*Yet who save the Three can say that I'd not have found the same fate, whatever mastery of my days I commanded?*

*Some say the Three know our ends before we're born, and—*

*No, I cry them wrong, those who believe that. If 'twere so, how could the Three find any entertainment, in watching our strivings?*

*And if they seek no amusement in observing us, why let so much chaos reign in the world? Why not order things better?*

*But enough of such thinking. The cold claws at my thoughts. Better to drift, and just remember.*

*Remember thoughts and memories not my own.*

Omngluth made it a firm rule never to let his mask as Kalanth Bowdragon slip, not even for an instant. This was once more proved to be a good thing, as Brungelth Silvertree flung wide the doors of Bowdragon's tower without warning, nine armaragors at his back, and strode in on the wizard—who merely raised an eyebrow in query, put a hand on his spell-tome to mark his place, and remarked, "There's ithqual in yon decanter, my King."

"I'm not king yet, wizard," Brungelth snapped, "and the priest tells me I'll never be, unless I 'break the prophecy' without delay. Yet the fool refuses to tell me what he means, or what this precious prophecy is—says it's blasphemy in the face of the Three for him to do so!"

"Ah. That's so. For him, it is. I hope you didn't have him slain."

"No. Not before his own altar, in front of priests and a

score of praying folk, no. If he ever strays out of his temple, though—"

"No, lord, you must not! The displeasure of the Three has swept empires away before this, and he was but doing his holy duty—and yet trying to warn you, as best he could. He deserves thanks, not a blade."

Brungelth Silvertree glowered at the tall, white-robed wizard, and then said shortly, "You know best, which is why you're here. So, can you tell me this prophecy?"

"Yes. Shorn of all the pretty titles of the Three and priestly verbiage, it stands thus: In time to come, you will be slain by your own offspring unless you scour them all from the face of Darsar by your fortieth summer."

Brungelth's jaw dropped, and the wizard gravely repeated his words.

"You're . . . you're serious," the baron growled, studying Bowdragon's face. "Oh, Three look down!" He cast a wild glance back at the nine gleaming-armored knights standing with their hands clasped on grounded swords behind him, and then shook his head. "I . . . I'd best be at it, then!"

"I'm afraid any heir you name can't be of your own . . . making," the wizard murmured. "I know you find this distressing, and—"

"Three Above, it's not that, Bowdragon! I've rutted up and down the Vale for *years!* I might have scores—hundreds—of children!"

"Then you've said it rightly," the wizard said sadly. "You'd best be at it, then."


There was laughter. "*I* hear he hunts them through the forests, like stags!"

"Poor bastards," someone growled.

"Ah, that they are! That they are!"

More laughter.

"Ho, innkeeper! More calamanta!"

"Aye, and more saal while you're at it!"

The innkeeper gave them a smile and the merry call, "As swift as the wind, lords of Sirlptar!"

Yet as he turned away, to his casks, the smile fell off his face like tumbling stone. Two nights these Sirl merchants had graced the Silent Forehouse Inn, and he was heartily sick of their jests and their boasts and their open contempt for Aglirta and Aglirtans.

It was almost a taunt in itself, their gathering here, in an inn built just outside the gatehouse of Silvertree House, to toast their successes.

For three years these Sirl dogs had grown fat feeding on the Lord Baron. For three years they'd been free to make trade deals that beggared the Vale, filling their own pockets whenever they desired, by selling Brungelth Silvertree news that this or that kin of his had been seen in this or that remote hamlet—and three years the baron had spent riding up and down the Vale like a madman, hacking down his sons and daughters, and employing spies galore to ferret out any hint of kin to him or a surviving woman he may once have enjoyed.

For all that, he set down their decanters of saal and calamanta with gentle care and more smiles, for their coins were good.

And when he was gone a safe distance from the table, a Sirl merchant with dusky skin and a long, arrow-straight nose leaned forward and muttered to his fellows, "For my part, I thank the Three that so powerful a warrior seems to have gone as mad as the rest of them—all the other backcountry barons of Aglirta, I mean—and devoted himself to terrorizing his own lands, and not Sirlptar."

"Aye, but mad he is, and I'll not want to be sitting here when he finishes devouring his own young and looks up, bloody jaws a-drip, for someone else to savage."

"Well said, and there's this more, lads: The supply of living Silvertrees must be running very low. It will be more than prudent to take barge down the Silverflow and depart the Vale on the morrow."

"*After* we finish this excellent wine!" a younger merchant put in brightly, a suggestion that was greeted with a relieved roar of laughter.

Coldly amused eyes watched that mirthful table from a room away, in the darker, more simply furnished chamber reserved for outlanders whose coins were not quite as freely given as those of plumply successful Sirl swindlers.

"Time to depart," one of the watchers murmured. "It would be best to be well gone before the dying starts."

"The Great Serpent will be pleased."

"Indeed. The innkeeper's been sipping, I've noticed, as he fills their decanters—and why not? After all, they're paying for it."

"Paying for it now, and paying for it before this candle burns out," the first watcher muttered. "Let's begone."

And the priests of the Serpent went down the room to the side door, and slipped out into the night, well satisfied. They'd poisoned every keg of wine, and even the precious decanters of dragondream—in case a thirst befell the Lord Baron Brungelth Silvertree when he came to view the shocking crime, later. Only a truly stupid man would take drink in a house of death by poison, so the doom of the Serpent would fall—fittingly—only on the truly stupid.

The Serpents knew where they'd spend the night, but many houses hereabouts were open to them, should they call softly by the windows. Prayer to the Great Slitherer was strong in the Vale these last three seasons, as Aglirtans came to hate and fear the Butcher Baron and looked elsewhere for guidance and protection.

And as every Priest of the Serpent knows: Venom Is the Best Protection.

# 2

## Faceless Fury

There was a flash in the room behind him that Omngluth knew could only be trouble. Powerful sorcery was *always* trouble. He shape-shifted his face, hands, skin, and all as he bent and took up the water-ewer he always kept ready, and turned smoothly to face—

A tall man in sky-blue robes, with simmering eyes and hands aflame with deadly magic, whose face was the one Omngluth had been wearing moments before. This was the real Kalanth Bowdragon.

As he let astonishment flash over his features, Omngluth hoped his own shield-magic would prove powerful enough— and hoped even more that he wouldn't have to use it.

"Oh, Lord Wizard! You startled me! I was just coming to water the flowers."

"You know me?" The question was as sharp as the gesture that swirled flame and warned Omngluth to approach no closer.

"Of course, Lord. You are Kalanth Bowdragon, the greatest mage in all Darsar. The Lord Baron Silvertree has often told me how grateful he is to you, for coming to help him rebuild Aglirta. I know I'm not to be in these rooms when you're weaving sorcery, but—forgive me—I presumed you were gone to Silvertree House, to greet the baron this day. I saw the guise you wear when out among the people, here in the scrying-bowl." Omngluth pointed gracefully at the flared bowl of water beside Bowdragon, hoping the mage wouldn't notice that its enchantments were linked to his thoughts.

Kalanth Bowdragon studied Omngluth for a moment and then stepped back, waved at the bowl, and commanded, "Show me. This guise, and the baron."

Omngluth let a puzzled frown flicker across his face for the briefest of instants, set down his ewer, and walked to the bowl. "Of course, Lord Wizard. Here—this is you." He looked back at Bowdragon, and added in awe, "Your power is even greater than I imagined. Here you stand, yet that spellspun body obeys you from afar. I've always thought it was you, in person, disguised by spells."

Bowdragon studied the image in the bowl. A gigantic serpent with a man's eyes, towering some sixty feet above a ring of Serpent-priests. The Great Serpent himself, awake at last. So where was the Dragon?

He looked back at Omngluth, eyes narrowing, and asked softly, "Why do you think this is me?"

Omngluth gave him another startled look. "I know this is kept secret from the people, Lord, but I and all of the household were there when you and the Lord Baron agreed that you'd appear as a great snake. So that none would ever see your true face, you said, so you could walk the Vale freely in your own shape whenever you desired, without fawning folk and spies or blades at your back. You insisted on it—or did the baron insist it would be best, now? So much was discussed that day."

"And it *was* three years ago," Kalanth Bowdragon murmured, with the merest hint of sarcasm. "Show me the baron."

Omngluth passed his hand slowly over the great bowl, and the waters rippled and became a scene on a riverbank, where a great barge was docking before a huge stone fortress, amid horns and banners and many folk crowding excitedly forward.

"The Lord Baron doesn't think much of the inn built right in front of his gatehouse," he remarked, pointing at an angry gesture from the broad-shouldered, splendidly armored figure at the heart of all the activity. "I thought he'd hate it. I wager it'll not be there for many days longer."

"Show me the S—my snake body again," Bowdragon ordered. Omngluth did so, and watched the archwizard's nostrils flare as a slow smile grew across his face. "Water the flowers," he added—and was gone. Just suddenly not there, leaving empty air where he'd been standing.

Omngluth swallowed carefully, and went to pick up the ewer. He walked without taking his eyes off the scrying-bowl. This promised to be good.

The Great Serpent was casting a complex weaving, his priests chanting and echo-drawing his runes in unison, to re-double his power with their own. Omngluth wasn't familiar with the spell, but it was definitely designed to do harm . . . and it was definitely aimed at the baron.

And then there was a flash, and a figure in sky-blue was standing on the ramparts of the Silvertree House gatehouse, hands moving in a great casting that left sizzling lines of fire in the wake of their gesturing.

Omngluth awakened his own shielding and took a prudent step back from the bowl.

And then there was a bright flash from the scrying-waters, and a thunderous roar—from outside the tower. The bowl showed a startled Great Serpent and dumbfounded priests suddenly enmeshed in a net of fire—and then abruptly gone, torn from their surroundings, runes and all.

Then the bowl showed Silvertree House again, and a huge serpent surrounded by many robed Serpent-priests being slammed down out of nowhere, onto the stones of the House foreyard where the Lord Baron Silvertree and his gleaming armaragors were standing. Or rather, had been standing. There was much blood and writhing broken bodies there now, and many folk shrieking and running.

Then a great serpentine body reared up out of the blood and dust, crackling fires of sorcery ringing its head, and grew a small forest of human arms. They looked ridicu-lously puny against the Great Serpent's scaled bulk, but each pair of them was busily spell-weaving—and Kalanth Bowdragon's face looked distinctly startled as he traced his next great casting.

"Ahhh," Omngluth said aloud delightedly. Such entertain-ment comes but once in a lifetime. . . .

Aye, but whose? The deception had worked, thus far, sending Bowdragon to attack the Great Serpent in the belief that the Eroeha had been impersonating him. If the Three truly smiled on the Koglaur, Bowdragon would destroy both baron and Serpent, but . . . he was only a powerful wizard, and the Great Serpent had been a very powerful wizard, worshipped and aided by other powerful wizards, for thousands of years.

Two flashes burst blindingly from the bowl almost in unison. Omngluth snarled in pain and flung up his hand—the water in the ewer tracing a graceful arc through the air—to shield his eyes. Too late, of course.

The scrying-waters calmed at about the same time his watering eyes could see again, however blearily.

It seemed the Great Serpent's strike had come first—and the Baron of Silvertree was now short one gatehouse. Its collapse had taken care of the inn he hadn't cared for, and most of the crowd, who were now so many bloody smudges under fallen blocks of stone. If the baron still survived—or any of the Serpent-priests—Omngluth couldn't see them.

What he could see was much of the upriver front of Silvertree House being smashed apart by the Great Serpent in its writhings of agony.

And no wonder. Its innards were laid bare to all Darsar, purple flames of sorcery still burning here and there amongst its scales, and its lower jaw was quite gone. Steaming innards seemed to be sliding forth from its ruined mouth as it twitched and thrashed and arched, its wildly lashing tail toppling towers and shattering walls.

There was a flicker of golden radiance amid the tumbled stones by the half-sunken barge, and Omngluth leaned forward, trying to blink his way back to sharp vision, and willed the scrying-bowl to seek that flash of gold.

The scene rushed in to peer closely at that glimmering. It was the struggling radiance of a feeble spell, woven by a broken and pain-wracked man . . . but Kalanth Bowdragon still spoke and gestured, despite the blood all down the tatters of his sky-blue robe.

Omngluth murmured a simple incant, and the room was suddenly full of a great howling, and the crashes of falling stone. From out of the din came a voice thick with pain, snarling, "Enough . . . of this. Back to Arlund—forever!"

And the golden light flared up into flame and was gone, taking the sorely wounded Kalanth Bowdragon home.

Omngluth pulled his sorcerous scrutiny back to the wider view of the ravaged shore. The Great Serpent was moving slowly now, mere twitchings and slitherings that meant the Eroeha had abandoned this snake-body, stealing away like smoke to possess some unfortunate Serpent-priest or other, and rebuild his strength.

Thank the Three there'd been no sign of the Dragon, or there might have soon been no Aglirta for anyone to conquer. Or had the—

But no matter. Where was the baron of Silvertree?

He'd been in the foreyard, just before the gates . . . where the tumbled and shattered stones of the gatehouse and the inn were now strewn deeply, and—*there!*

Brungelth Silvertree was lying almost against the frowning walls of Silvertree House, in the lee of a tower that had been shattered by the now-motionless Great Serpent. He looked whole, and as Omngluth stared at him, one of his hands moved. He seemed to be rolling over, and groaning.

Which was about the time a Serpent-priest came around the curve of the tower, venomed blade in hand—Omngluth stiffened, knowing there was no spell he could send that far, in so short a time—and saw the baron.

The priest's cowl had fallen back onto his shoulders, and Omngluth could see his bald, scaled head turning to peer alertly in one direction and then another, as if to ensure he wasn't being observed.

Then he raced over to the stunned baron, and—grew two long, ropelike tentacles that slid in under the sprawled Terror of Aglirta and lifted him gently from among the tumbled stones. Brungelth turned his head and moved an arm, as if in feeble protest, and the Koglaur whipped a tentacle across his eyes and grew four or five more to cradle him in a fleshy sling—and then extended new legs right over him, to make of itself a large walking-beast with Baron Silvertree slung under its belly. A beast that set off purposefully back around the tower, in the direction of the wing of the House secretly held by the Koglaur.

Omngluth relaxed, allowing himself a smile. Victory snatched from all this, after all. He turned away from the scrying-bowl and went to refill the ewer. The flowers did, after all, need water.

His smile would have quite vanished if he'd seen what befell when the Koglaur carried the baron through a gap in the House walls and down a tunnel. The Koglaur sentry guarding that tunnel mouth greeted the arrival warmly, offered his congratulations—and then, when the baron's carrier was past him, turned and drove no less than a dozen blades through his fellow Faceless.

Brungelth Silvertree bounced heavily along the tunnel floor, flung free of the writhing tentacles. The sentry calmly reached down a cask-sized stone vessel from the rafters of what had once been a stairwell, and emptied most of its contents over its sorely wounded victim. The acid hissed and bubbled as it melted Koglaur flesh, and he was obliged to risk the tips of two tentacles to the acid, to mute dying screams by plugging the mouth making them.

The Faceless was in too much agony to muster the will to grow another one, ere it died.


Tentacles lashed out around a neck, horrified eyes stared at a would-be slayer and snatched down blades to slice and sever, a spell-bolt seared through the gloom, and a Koglaur screamed.

"What's *happening?*" a young and bewildered Faceless demanded, peering out of a doorway. Its head was sheared off cleanly by the whirlwind of spell-spun blades that flashed down the passage an instant later, and the headless body took a swaying, unsteady step out into the passage, gouting fluids from agonizedly opening cavities all over it . . . and then collapsed into a puddle of flesh.

Laumthrara reached out with arms that slid out to some forty feet in length, and firmly closed and bolted the door. Then she spun a warding to keep spells from shattering it.

Indreira had already woven a charm to send the Silvertree children to sleep, but her eyes were dark with apprehension. "At the risk of seeming as brainless as Thaalor: what's happening?"

Laumthrara sighed. "Our rivalries have flared into open strife at last. The younger, more impatient among us have seen a chance—and rushed to seize it, as rashly as the humans they so despise."

Indreira frowned. "Some of us hold grudges, yes, and the young always chafe against the decrees of those older, but I had no idea any cabal had formed among us, that could pursue different aims than those we've all shared . . . for centuries, now. Or am I blind, Laumthrara?"

The other Koglaur sighed again. "I fear so, Indreira. Blind enough not to mark who couldn't be trusted, at least. Yet they've moved *very* swiftly; Thaalor was one of them, and knew not what was afoot."

"So what *is* afoot?"

"The Baron of Silvertree was struck senseless in a spell-battle—that was the tumult we heard and felt—and Nornthear seized him . . . only to be slain by Brazam. His deed was seen by several of us, and Arauntras killed Brazam—which has set them all to fighting."

"But *why?* What rivalry could possibly be strong enough to *kill* for?"

Laumthrara gave up on sighing and fixed Indreira with sad eyes. "The longtime way of our kind is to keep hidden, and work to manipulate rulers and their rivals, to keep Aglirta strong, yes? So in time to come we'll rise to collectively rule a strong, rich kingdom?"

Indreira nodded.

"Well, some Koglaur desire to rule Aglirta openly from

Silvertree House, using the sorcery all around us here to give us supremacy over the Serpents, outlander wizards, and all warriors and merchants who might think to seize the Vale. They want the River Throne now, and they don't care what they do to anyone—including the rest of us, obviously—to get it."

Indreira shook her head. "I . . . see. I *have* been blind, and yet I'm glad of that. What sort of a mind can place such value on power that's so tainted and misused?"

Laumthrara's eyes grew even sadder. "Now you're making the same mistake embraced by far too many of us: thinking of us as somehow superior to humans. Indreira, we *are* humans. And how many humans seek power at all costs, not caring what harm their swords and spells do?"

It was Indreira's turn to sigh. "So what we do we do now, Laum?"

Laumthrara's answering smile was crooked. "Why, we fight. Of course."

Bleeding and gasping, the tentacled thing snatched up Baron Silvertree again and thrust him through an archway. Brungelth was dimly aware of being set down none-too-gently on cold, hard stone, and then of the tentacled body above him whirling away to go elsewhere.

Somewhere behind him there was a brief, wet, savage snarl, a surprised mewing sound, and then a roar of pain. Brungelth tried to roll over and peer at where the sounds were coming from, but the room seemed to be pitching and rolling around him, everything watery, as if seen through a tallglass of eddying wine.

Steel clashed on steel, and rang off stone—as if two warriors who cared nothing for the state of their swords were clumsily crossing blades.

Brungelth narrowed his eyes and found something he could see more clearly: a pair of tentacles, behind the back of the nearest shape-shifting half-human, that had grown dainty human hands that were spell-weaving.

He thought about hurling something to break that casting, but his hands were empty—and just lifting himself off the floor enough to bring one arm forward made his head and guts both swim sickeningly.

Brungelth gave up, sinking back to let his chin rest on the floor, to watch what befell next.

The monster finished its spell and pressed forward, driving its foe back with a wild flurry of slashes. Shards of blade spun away to ping and clang off stone and fall floorwards, the other monster staggering back through the doorway—'twas a Faceless! They must both be!—and then the one that had cast the spell murmured a single sword and hurled itself back and to one side of the door.

And in the passage outside, its spell-burst blossomed with a roar right behind its foe, ravaging that Faceless and hurling its broken body into the room and right past Brungleth's face, to crash heavily and wetly into the far wall.

No sooner had the rolling echoes of the spell died away than there came the sound of running feet in the passage outside—furiously approaching footfalls.

The Faceless who'd cast the spell launched itself from the floor to the ceiling above the doorway, flinging down its tentacles on either side of the door like pillars, and folding the rest of itself into a cantilevered, awninglike mass above the door. As Brungelth stared at its transformation in awe, its hue lightened and turned gray, to more closely match the stone of the walls.

A Faceless appeared in the doorway, long tentacles stabbing across the room with swords clutched at the ends of them. They slashed and stabbed wildly, and Brungelth pressed himself flat to the stone and hoped he'd not be sliced.

Then the body—like a man whose face was a smooth, featureless mass of flesh—followed the tentacles into the doorway, and Brungelth saw eyeballs surging down the tentacles towards their ends, like swiftly rowed skiffs cleaving the waters of the Silverflow.

Which was when the Faceless above the door disgorged

its notched and bloody sword, point downwards—and impaled the newcomer from above, falling with all of its weight behind the sundering steel.

Blue blood fountained as the body of the struck Faceless opened up—and fell apart, innards sagging even as they flowed and raged and struggled to take on new shapes. "Arauntras!" it shrieked, from half a dozen mouths—as its tentacles sprang back from the far corners of the room, racing inwards to drive deadly steel at its foe from five directions at once.

Arauntras sprang out into the passage, still slicing with its blade, which was now so deeply lodged that its movement dragged its foe over backwards and along with it.

Another spell-burst promptly roared past the doorway, searing and sizzling the half-butchered Faceless. Its long, tremulous wail wobbled down into silence, and it slumped and lay still.

"Arauntras?" came a soft call.

"Here, flattened down behind Hanauntyn, whom you've cooked very thoroughly. Have my thanks. I took care of Rezmur; he's in there—with the Baron of Silvertree, who's probably wetting himself about now from seeing Koglaur make brief, bloody war on Koglaur."

"Unless he's still too bewildered to be fearful."

Brungelth Silvertree hastily closed his eyes and relaxed in his sprawl on the stone, but he'd been too slow to escape the gazes of slithering, eye-studded tentacles, and was rewarded by two chuckles.

"Humans," Arauntras observed, "tend to be poor actors."


"Dursil?"

"I used to be. Now I'm just *most* of Dursil. I left three tentacles back there."

"Ah, yes. Ah—uh—I'm Enselnur."

"I'm aware of that. Otherwise you'd be dead now. I do have some magic left, you know."

"Uh . . . ah . . . yes."

Dursil sighed. "Look, youngling, this is *not* a good time to dither. I'm aching to slaughter certain fellow Koglaur, and if you irritate me sufficiently, I'll simply add you to the roster. What do you want?"

"Ah-uh-to know what happened!" the younger Koglaur said in a desperate rush of words.

"It came to open fighting at last, and we lost. The 'watch over and cherish Aglirta' faction has won, for this day at least."

"Well . . . ah . . . what do we do now?"

"I'm going to slip away and go into hiding—and no, I'm not going to tell you where. Find your own fate."

"Slip away? They hold all the ways out—and if we try to go deeper in, the walls come alive with maedra!"

Dursil sighed. "I've spun a spell-cage around myself, so they can threaten me but not—quite—reach me. You're welcome to use it as a shield until we're out of the palace."

"T-thank you! But . . . you're heading deeper in! How can you get out by going—?"

"Through this gate, Enselnur. It's been here for centuries."

"Where does it go?"

"Out of here. Gates always do."

"Y-yes, but where?"

Dursil sighed, but did not slow his purposeful stride. Around a corner he went, maedra scuttling out of his way, towards a flickering radiance.

Enselnur followed hastily, into a high-vaulted, square room. At its center an arch of flickering white fire shot through with flames of silver was floating upright in the air.

"It leads to your future, idiot," Dursil replied, hurrying towards it. "If you've wits enough, that is, to make sure you have one."


"No, no, Brungelth Silvertree, *don't* try to run from us." The deft tentacles of Arauntras plucked the last concealed weapons out of the baron's armor, squirming disconcertingly as they dragged his belt-buckle dagger out by way of his codpiece. "You won't succeed—except in annoying us—and you'll only be running right to your own death."

"You see," the other Faceless said soothingly, sounding for all the world like a kindly wet-nurse, "because you're a Silvertree, the Curse of Silvertree House will drive you mad—and then suck the life out of you, leaving you as a wandering ghost—if you force your way through our ward-spells and deeper into your palace. . . . Oh, yes, the Curse is very real, and you came *that* close to dying that way when you pondered exploring this place."

"And because if you go the other way," Arauntras added, "you'll die of the wasting plague. Oh, yes, the Great Serpent unleashed a nasty spell that's ravaging the Vale right now—so until we find a way to quell it, stepping out into the sun is the same as plunging a sword into your own guts. Only much slower; your fingers and toes fall off, and then your hands and feet, and so it continues, your flesh rotting from the ends of your limbs back to your torso. Show him, Laum!"

The other Koglaur dwindled down from a many tentacled column into a tall, graceful human woman with long white hair and a regal manner—but not before Brungelth noticed two of those tentacles finishing a swift spell.

Beckoning the Baron, she swept out of the room and down the passage—in the other direction from the charred mass of tentacles and entrails that had been Hanauntyn. Brungelth Silvertree followed grimly, eyeing Arauntras uneasily as he passed, and wishing he had a weapon left to hold in his hands. *Any* weapon.

"Here they come; stop complaining and grow a hardcage, or he'll see you breathing," Gelkhesm snarled.

Indreira gave him a rebellious look as he sprawled out on the floor, looking very much like an unshaven human farmer, stripped to the waist, whose arms were shrivelled and blackened stumps at his shoulders, whose empty eye sockets and mouth had the same dark, twisted hue . . . and whose legs were missing, too.

His response was to say, very quietly but very coldly, "Do you really want to cross Laumthrara?"

Indreira shot him a contrite glance and then lost her eyes, swiftly becoming a woman without arms or legs.

Gelkhesm's spell promptly shrouded them both in a glowing, humming aura—moments before Laumthrara led Brungelth Silvertree into the room and said gravely, "Behold. As you can see, our sorceries keep you safe from the plague lurking in these two unfortunates—but out there, where the breezes blow down the Silverflow, you'd have no such protection. Folk are falling dead by the hundreds. Horses, too."

Baron Brungelth Silvertree peered closely at the dead couple and then stepped back and stared down at them, shivering. He was white to the lips when he looked up and said to the Koglaur, "I—I'll stay."


The weary, dusty-haired man rose from his squat by the campfire and darted into the bushes, his fire-blackened sword out and in his hand in an instant.

The woman and the boys stared out into the wilderland gloom, trying to see whatever it was that had alarmed Orstel Blackgult.

Nothing. Silence, but for distant birdcalls.

Then, surprisingly close, they heard him gasp, "Father? *Mother?*"

There wasn't even time to exchange disbelieving glances before Baron Blackgult shouted, "*Stay back!* I don't know who you are—ghosts, or—or—but keep back! *Keep away from me!*"

And he came backing out of the brush, his face pale and his sword held out warningly before him. Two figures came after him, and at the sight of their faces, Lady Blackgult gasped.

"Orstel! What does this mean?" she demanded, arms instinctively reaching to cradle her sons' shoulders.

"Please be at ease," the man who looked like Tarthen Blackgult said gently.

"We mean you no harm," the woman who looked like Orphala Blackgult added, and then looked straight at Baron Blackgult and said, "Yes, your mother's dead, and as far as I know, her bones lie in peace. I only took her shape so you'd not carve me quite so quickly."

"We'd like to talk to you—all of you," said the man who looked like Orstel Blackgult's father. "Would it help if we all sat down around your fire? As you can see, we have no weapons."

Without waiting for a reply, the two strangers sat down across the fire from the Lady Blackgult and her two sons. Baron Blackgult remained standing, his sword trembling in his hand. "Who *are* you?" he demanded hoarsely.

"Have you ever heard of the Faceless?"

"Bah! Drunkards' tales, all . . ." His eyes widened. ". . . mere . . . fancy . . ."

"About shape-changing monsters who kill and eat people, and take their shapes to get close to their next victims?" the woman who looked like his mother asked, a bitter edge creeping into her voice.

"Yes," Lady Blackgult whispered, arms trembling around her sons.

"Bards and tavern drunks have a regrettable tendency to embellish," the woman who wasn't Baron Blackgult's long-dead mother added—and her face slid and melted, the Blackgult boys staring at her in fascination, into the wrinkled visage of the farmwife the Baron had last dared to buy eggs from. "We are both Faceless, or to give us our proper name, Koglaur. We've always dwelt in Aglirta, hiding among Aglirtans by taking the shapes of folk who die alone."

"We aren't here to betray you, slay you, or eat you," the man who wasn't the Baron's long-dead father said then . . . as his face, too, changed—into that of the shepherd whose herd Blackgult had raided when his family was desperate for food.

"We show you these shapes to prove that we've been watching over you for some time, and have done nothing to harm you," the farmwife said. "We do this because we Koglaur—most Koglaur—live to safeguard and nurture Aglirta."

"And you are a part of Aglirta we must preserve," the other Koglaur said firmly. "We prefer never to reveal ourselves, but we couldn't think of another way to lure you back out of the wilderlands to your rightful home in Castle Blackgult."

"And be slain by Silvertree?" the baron snarled. "What—?"

The Faceless who'd been posing as men held up a hand, and Orstel Blackgult fell silent. His wife and sons shot astonished glances at him, but he had eyes only for the Koglaur, who said calmly, "I know you'll find this hard to believe, but the Great Serpent almost slew Brungelth Silvertree, though its reward was being slain on the spot by a wizard. Some of . . . our kind . . . hold Silvertree prisoner in the Silent House. His gatehouse has been thrown down and destroyed, and many of his cortahars lie dead on the riverbank. The face of the realm has been changed, and you're needed—or upriver Aglirta may become a desolate land of outlaws and prowling wolves . . . and worse."

"Will you come back to Castle Blackgult?" the other Koglaur asked. "It can hardly be more dangerous than trying to last another winter out here."

The baron's wife and sons looked to their father beseechingly. He glanced at them, drew in a deep breath, set his teeth, and then lifted his head and said, "I'll trust you two Koglaur. We'll come with you. And may the Three smite you down in shame if you've deceived us."

Baron Blackgult strode hesitantly to the brow of the hill, as if dreading what he'd see. The Koglaur slowed obligingly to keep pace with him; he cast a grim glance in its direction, and then walked on.

And stopped, stood in slack-jawed silence . . . and then started to cry.

His family hastened to join him, bewildered and apprehensive—and beheld Castle Blackgult below. It was no longer the burned ruin Silvertree had left of it. Masons and timberers were swarming over and around it. Castle Blackgult's towers were rising again.

Orstel Blackgult mastered his tears long enough to choke out, "How—?"

"We can change our faces, remember?" the other Koglaur murmured. "So 'tis easy to impersonate certain Sirl merchants and use their fortunes, hirelings, and contacts to get the work done. Behold: busy Sirl merchants and crafters *can* do good work, even in the backlands of Aglirta, if you pay them well enough. No betrayal awaits you; this will cost you nothing, and is your home. Again. As we said, we strive to watch over and rebuild Aglirta—always."

The Blackgults stared at the soaring towers in astonishment—until Lady Emdeeme Blackgult suddenly burst into happy tears and threw her arms around the nearest Koglaur.

The boys let out a cheer, and their father threw back his head and laughed . . . for the first time in a season.

And then, quite suddenly, Blackgult fell silent, and stared out across the river, over wooded Flowfoam, at the distant, brooding towers of Silvertree House. "He's there, isn't he?" he murmured, suppressing a shiver. "I can feel it, that accursed place. I've always felt it, all these years. *Watching* me."


Brungelth Silvertree walked down the passage for what was possibly the thousandth thousandth time, brooding. They'd very neatly raised this prison around him, these Faceless. He was trapped in these endlessly pulsing ward-spells.

He stumbled wearily as he turned away from the door he dare not open and started down the long passage again. He was always exhausted these days, thanks to the horrific visions and whispered threats that ruled his brief snatches of slumber—and always, in the end, drove him awake sweating or shouting or ice-clutched in terror.

It was the Curse that was whispering to him. Straining to get through the Koglaur magics and reach him, haunting his dreams . . . a Curse he'd begun to get tantalizing glimpses of, through her whispers.

Tall she was, and bare but for her long, flowing hair, and shapely face still shadowed but eyes like blazing stars, coming towards him. Closer, these days, ever closer . . .

He turned abruptly and stalked back down the passage, heading for the chamber at its end. He could feel the eyes of the two Koglaur like sly blades slid into his back, watching him, but felt none of the blue-hued foam that swirled around the edges of his mind when they were using magic to pry at his thoughts.

Which was good, because they'd not have been pleased at what he was thinking, just now. He kept his hands well away from his belt, trusting in his cod-lacings to hold the sword hilt he'd slid down the front of his breeches. He'd found it under some rubble days back—it amused the Koglaur to let him dig and scrape around in these few rooms of theirs, or perhaps they thought the diversion kept him more content . . . or more sane—but recovered it only yestereve. He'd no idea where they'd taken his weapons, but this—old and heavy and surprisingly free of rust, with a snapped-off stub of blade not quite as long as his hand—should serve him better.

Idly he tramped around the room, getting the blade out and into his hand, and idly he strolled along that back wall, to the door that opened out into the rest of Silvertree House—*his* house—where the Curse ruled.

Its whispers quickened, coming to him clearly now as he leaned against the door—and then in a sudden frenzy, thrust the blade into its seam where the locked-down latch must be and thrust upwards. Something metallic clinked, deep within the stone. He threw his weight to one side, prying hard—and the door ground open, revealing darkness, a sudden surge of glowing white ward-spells, and a swelling, exulting chorus of whispers. And Brungelth Silvertree hurled himself into the darkness.

One Koglaur shouted behind him, but the other said calmly, "Let him go. He's half-mad anyway, and we have the others."

*Have the others?*

And then, as he ran blindly into the darkness, the Curse's whisperings rose up around him in a triumphant, suddenly deafening chorus, pounding in his ears—no, in his *mind*—and showing him sons slain with sword thrusts and infant daughters being twisted and broken in his hands like stewing-fowl, mothers screaming with beseeching, bloody hands that became warriors shouting in fear as he gave them death and women shrieking as he forced himself upon them, and . . .

He slammed hard into a wall, shrieking pain breaking that flood of madness, and rebounded away from it, shaking broken fingers and turning, turning back towards the tiny rectangle of white light.

Running, running, whisperings suddenly roarings all around him, blades flashing and grim helmed heads blocking his way . . . forcing his eyes shut, Brungelth Silvertree sprinted harder than he'd ever run before, feeling his heaviness bouncing and flopping, muscles gone to fat in this long imprisonment that he now welcomed . . . frantically clawed for . . . found again!

He was back into the light, and rolling hard, right past the feet of one of the Faceless.

"Welcome back, Brungelth," its voice came down to him, a clear thread of mockery running through it. "Feel saner for that?"

He was too breathless to reply—and too mind-seared, as the tall dark nude woman raged at him inside his head, reaching out shapely hands to claw, and leaning forward with a face as vast and dark as the night sky, to bite. . . .

The room rocked, and there was a flash of light around him.

"O-Omngluth!" one of his captors exclaimed in surprise.

"Omngluth indeed, you dolts! *What have you been playing at?* I could feel yon Curse rising to its full fury clear up the river in Tselgara!"

Brungelth lay still, clutching at his head, and then let himself go limp, as if he'd fallen senseless.

"I—we—the prisoner—"

"Realized you were keeping him bound in here long ago, and finally found courage and means to try to break free . . . because you *let* him find those two things. Fools! You're not just endangering one brutal man, or yourselves and all of our kin who might enter this refuge unprepared to battle the Curse—you're dicing with our hold on Aglirta itself!"

"Truly? While you do what?"

"*Don't* fling tart words at me, Gelkhesm! I'm not the one who let boredom conquer! Patience, you younglings, *patience!* You sigh, all sullen, whenever we use that word, as if we misjudge your brilliance by even mentioning it . . . and time and again demonstrate that you know not what it means! We're *Koglaur,* and—to repeat the chief lesson of your childhood—'Patience and stealth are our two best weapons'! Did you know the Curse has been trying to tunnel under this refuge again? Do you want to be here when the floor collapses and its mind-furies flood in?"

"No, Omngluth," the other Koglaur said quietly.

"Aye, be sullen—but *heed* me."

"Yes, Omngluth," Gelkhesm murmured.

"That's better. Now, let me relieve your boredom a trifle. 'Tis best you know that Castle Blackgult is habitable again, and home to the Blackgults once more, though our rebuilding continues. So, too, is Maerlin restored, and the rightful holders of no less than a dozen terseptries dragged out of hiding and set back on their thrones, up and down the Vale—though none so openly as in the barony of Blackgult. Some of our kin have also covertly gathered together this wretch's surviving sons—yes, all the ones he missed slaying—in Sirlptar. They're holding council right now."

\* \* \*

"Of course we want to be part of this," the most richly garbed Sirl merchant said firmly. "Aglirta remains the largest untapped cask of wealth within our reach!"

"And you'd much rather tap it yourselves, and take the dragon's share, rather than settling for whatever dribbles from it as it's shipped down the river and out to sea by others, right past you," commented the loudest of the sons of Silvertree.

The merchant sputtered, but several of the other Sirl traders grinned, and one of them said smoothly, "That's correct. Thanks for the candor, and can we move on, then? I think we all know what brings you here—the fire of revenge and perhaps a small fear that as long as Brungelth Silvertree's alive, he'll somehow find and reach out to reap you. And now we all know why *we're* here. Moreover, we've been getting rich here in Sirlptar for years, and know how it's done. We expect to have to sponsor an army so you can storm Silvertree House and bring the hated Baron down at last. We merely—as sensible mercantile masters—want a return for this costly and risky investment. *Our* problem is with the House itself."

"Aye," another merchant muttered. "How does one fight ghosts?"

"Ghosts?" a Silvertree asked derisively. "Grown men, and you believe—"

"Mind-eating, life-sucking *things,* then, boy. That have slaughtered your ancestors—and treasure-seekers, too—for centuries."

"Ah," one of the Sirl wizards who'd hosted the meeting spoke up, leaning forward from where he stood in the shadows. "That's where we come into this. I believe we can promise to take care of the minor magics and scuttling things that haunt the Silent House."

"Minor magics and scuttling things aren't my worry," one of the merchants muttered. " 'Tis this Curse."

"We're not the overconfident Guild of Sorcery of Sirlptar," another wizard sneered. "We've been studying the Curse of Silvertree House for centuries."

"Centuries? You haven't been *alive* for centuries!"

"Oh, no?" the wizard replied in silken tones, as his face slid into an exact likeness of that merchant's father . . . and then grandsire.

The man gulped as the faces of all the wizards started to similarly change.

"All this work. All for nothing. They gave me a household, and an army, and thrust back the Curse to give me this half of Silvertree House," the man on the throne snarled, listening to the shouts and screams and thunder of rushing boots. "And we broke and hurled back the Sirl wizards and their army of my vengeful sons and every bloody hiresword they could find in every last hovel of Asmarand—only to have Blackgult sneak in up our backsides and bring it all to ruin."

Furniture crashed down somewhere, and from somewhere else came a roar of anger and the skirl of blades.

Then they came back for him. The same close-helmed armaragors who'd ringed him with steel, taunted him . . . and butchered him.

Leaving him to bleed on his throne, arms and legs gone, his own guts glistening in his lap, kept alive in his agony only by the magics he wore. Magics that were, one by one, failing. 'Twould not be long now.

He watched them stride back in and resume their grim ring, blades drawn. Magnificent in their battle-plate, that reflected back the flashing, dwindling light of his own fading amulets. His gorget was crumbling away already, and the crown would soon follow. Of course, death would take him long before all of the enchantments were gone.

"I have no magic left to strike you down," Brungelth told his slayers almost wearily, "and it won't be long, now. You can put your swords away. The rings that could have slain you went with my arms."

One of the men facing him moved restlessly, but the ring of warriors said nothing.

"Well?" he asked them, voice threatening to fail. "No taunts? No cries of 'Blackgult triumphs'?"

"We're not of Blackgult," the man who'd moved almost spat. "Father." He tore off his helm to reveal tangled black hair and eyes that were two dark coals of anger.

An echo of my face, right enough. But give them their taunts, let them tell me all. . . .

Lure them into my trap . . .

Brungelth Silvertree lifted his head to study that angry face, affecting faint puzzlement. " 'Father'? An ambitious armaragor of mine, surely? Or—are you adventurers from outside the Vale, seeking to take a land of your own?"

Men doffed helms all around the circle. Their faces were different, but shared the same smoldering eyes.

"We're all your sons, Baron Silvertree," the first who'd unhelmed snarled. "Your bastards—that is, the ones whose mothers you didn't strangle, or hunt down with your dogs, when you discovered they carried your seed. The ones who've lived all their lives in hiding up and down the Vale, or farther—with mothers who cowered in fear at the very sight of the badge of Silvertree."

"We're the ones you missed," another man said bitterly. "O most brilliant butcher of the Vale."

He strode to the magnificent sideboard, caught up a decanter from the forest of fine drinkables on it, flicked the stopper forth with the thumb of his gauntlet, and took a long swig, swallowing in loud satisfaction. "Ah, but that's good!" He smiled. "Like sweet fire! All ours, now."

"Until you start to fight over it," Brungelth mumbled. Everything was darker now. . . .

"Hah!" the first slayer snarled. "I think not! And even if we do, at least we've lived long enough to taste some of your fine vintages!" He strode to the sideboard and snatched up another decanter. That started a general rush to take up slender silver and crystal.

"That you have," Brungelth Silvertree said softly. "That

you have." His head settled lower, and the patter of blood on the floor around the throne slowed to a gentle rhythm of drippings.

"Your best amberfire, I believe, Father Baron?" another of his sons taunted, waving a decanter in Brungelth's face.

"And I have a fine stagblood, by the taste of it," said another, holding it up to catch the flickering firelight. "Most splendid."

"Have you all drunk, then?" the dying man on the throne asked wearily.

His sons roared out affirmatives, and the Baron said faintly, his words slurred now, "Consider it a toast, then. If you've sipped, you're fit to hear the secrets of my hold before I die. Swift, now . . . I can feel the fading . . . bend close . . ."

Two laggards hastily swigged and joined the wary, tightening ring around the bloody throne.

"Not too close," one son warned. "He may have some last blasting magic."

"No," disagreed another. "I wear a magequell ring—magic or no, there's nothing he can use in this room."

"I need no magic," Brungelth Silvertree said calmly, "to take you dogs down with me into darkness. All of the wines in this chamber are poisoned."

Decanters fell as faces paled, and amid the shatterings of hurled-down decanters and the oaths there was a hiss of swift-raised blades.

"The antidotes, old man!" one son snarled, sword ready to strike. "I know you'll have some! Speak, or lose an eye!"

"Take it," the Baron told him. "I'll not be needing it, soon. The antidotes are all in my bedchamber—not that you'll live to reach it. I had to take them for years, to take the dosages in those decanters you so heartily sampled. Farewell, idiots. Unworthy, all of you, of the name of Silvertree. Have my curses."

And with those words Brungelth Silvertree's eyes closed, and his head fell to one side. There was scarcely time for the shouting and cursing to rise again before the sons of Sil-

vertree started to fall, all around the throne, crashing limply
to the floor in a limp, helpless fellowship of death.

This is a prison I can never escape.

The House is my jailer—and my life, now. Its terrible, brooding awareness is all around me as I write this,
allowing this small conceit to spread fear in any who
might find it.

I'm not one of the countless ghosts of those it
drained of all life, that glide about these shadowed halls
at its bidding, mad phantoms all. My mind is still my
own, and a little of my life remains, though I'm trans-
formed into something little better than a wraith. Betimes I can materialize part of myself, so as to cast
spells.

The House keeps me thus: its trapped crafter-of-
traps. I drift about its vastness, weaving trap-spells,
lofting fallen blocks up off the dead, forcing scything
blades back into their sockets, casting clinging dust-
clouds to conceal the marks of slayings past.

Once a proud mage, now a castellan. And a sometime scribe, making a hand and arm solid for long
enough to pen these warnings to all who stray into the
House. Scattered about this palace you'll find them; I'm
compelled to place each one in a different chamber.
Speculations as to the nature of the Whispering Mind,
and its purposes. Descriptions of the endless expan-
sions wrought by the maedra, some of them far-
reaching indeed.

In fact, some of their tunnelings go for as far as it
takes days for a man to ride on a good horse. I first became aware of the House as more than a mere name in
terror-tales when the maedra extended its crypts as far
as Adeln, in a long tunnel that pierced the sewers and
cellars of Adelnwater. This ever-farther reach alarms
me now just as it did then, for I believe it reveals a sinister purpose of the Whispering Mind (what some folk

call "the Curse"): to dominate, and someday conquer, all Aglirta.

The House taints or breaks those who dwell here, or tarry overlong. Some it slays, or drives forth with minds infested with nightmares henceforth—but two sorts of folk it corrupts and twists. As the tales say, its most important prizes are persons of the blood Silvertree—which it seems to hunger for, above all else, making of itself a lure and home-haven for all Silvertrees, healing them but at the same time drinking their life-essence, seeking to bind them to it, so if they ever leave, they long to return.

The other sort of folk it enslaves are persons who possess an aptitude for sorcery. Three other mages who share my lot I've found here, though it seems to hide us from each other as much as it can. I found them because they, like me, were driven by the House to seek out certain rooms in its depths—wherein burn magical gates to far places. Again and again it compels us to go there, and stare fascinated at the rings of fire it will not let us pass through. Could it be that the House desires to conquer the places those gates lead to?

> Anstelt Sendimarr
> Wizard of the House (formerly of Adeln)
> First Turning, Wanesummer, One Thousand and
> Second Year of the Reign of Kelgrael

# BOOK NINE

———◆———

## Faerod Silvertree

2230–2276 SR
Lord Baron of Silvertree
And of His Alliance with a Darkhearted Mage

# 1

## Spellmaster Rising

"Careful, lad," Old Horl warned. "This chamber—can you feel it?—is awash in spells."

"Careful *how?* Will we be . . . turned into anything?" Dlan was sweating in fear—the glowstone in his hand was flickering wildly, and though he could feel nothing save a faint prickling or tingling in the air around him, he believed the elder procurer. Magic, strong magic.

He peered around the many-pillared chamber. It seemed empty of all but bones—scattered bones, some of them far too small to be human—and a lot of broken stone, fallen from above. One pillar had been blasted to nothing but a jagged base and a stalactite-like roof-fang. "How did this place . . . get this way?"

"Ingryl Ambelter fought someone here," Horl said shortly, lurching forward. "He was the second Spellmaster of Silvertree—and the worst."

He stumbled and almost fell, and Dlan raced forward to clutch at the worn leathers covering his shoulder, and haul him upright. "*Don't* let anything happen to you, old man!" he cried, eyes large and dark with fear. "Just . . . don't!"

Horl was breathing heavily. "Thanks, Dlan," he said, drawing his sword again and leaning on it, just as an old man puts all his weight on a cane. "I'm not as young as you, lad . . . and strange as it may seem, I'm not getting any younger, either."

The younger procurer nodded, darting wary glances in all directions. "Why're we here, in this room? I don't like it—I really don't. This is the first room that's really made me feel . . . odd."

"You wanted gems, did you not? Well, then, feel odd for a few breaths longer, and you'll have them. I hope."

The elder treasure-hunter lurched forward across the room, glowstone held low so as to study the floor as he went. He was heading for the shattered pillar. Face white and set, Dlanazar Duncastle watched him go . . . and then reluctantly followed after, glancing all around often with his sword up and ready.

His boot caught on an uneven flagstone with a scraping sound, and Horl whirled around. *"Back,* Dlan! *Jump back!"*

The young procurer needed no urging; he turned his terrified rush forward into a frantic spring backwards, landing hard on one hip and rolling, rolling as thunder broke forth overhead, a great stony groaning that became a deafening tumult of plunging stone blocks.

They hurled themselves at the floor with all the fury of the gods, plummeting down like hammer-blows that made the floor dance and quiver, bouncing a young procurer into the air as he rolled . . . rolled as frantically as he'd ever done anything before.

The crashes of their landings and ponderous rollings shook the room and blinded Dlanazar with choking dust. He kept rolling across unseen shuddering flagstones, coughing and gagging, until he heard Horl roar, "Stop, lad! *Stop!"*

And Dlan threw himself right up into the air, arching and twisting. He came down bruisingly on his shoulder, shouting in pain, and landed facing back the way he'd come.

"What?" he called weakly. "What is it?" His eyes were streaming, his lungs burning. He coughed, shoved at the floor to get up onto his hands and knees, and coughed again, a rasping, uncontrollable hacking that left him spewing everything in his guts and throat onto the floor, and mewing in pain.

"Is there a beast?" he sobbed, in Horl's direction. "Or am I safe if I stay still?"

"Just *don't* stand up, lad," the familiar gruff voice snapped. "Stay down on your knees."

Dlanazar did that, coughing and crawling crabwise back the way he'd come. His groping hands discovered stones and larger chunks of stony rubble on the floor as he went, and more than once he quavered, "Is this safe?" and "Am I still safe?"

Horl gave him reassuring words, until Dlan found his

hands striking walls of jagged rock. His tear-filled vision showed him looming darknesses.

"Is this where the ceiling fell?"

"Yes, lad, and stop groping about until you can see. I can't think they'd've put two such stonefall traps in the same room, but the one you set off brought down a lot more of the ceiling than it was supposed to—and it might still shed a block or two, down on your head!"

Dlanazar cowered down. "Oh, *great!*"

"Never mind," Horl called cheerfully. "The Three always smile down on you, remember?"

As if in reply to his words, even before Dlanazar could draw breath to curse, something tore free of the ceiling above with a long, low rending sound, and . . . slammed into the floor somewhere not far behind Dlan's boots with force enough to hurl him forward, screaming in fear.

His cries died down at about the time the echoes did, and the next thing Dlan heard was Horl's disgusted voice from just above him.

"Now, lad, can we try walking across the chamber again with a little more care, this time? Remember: saying is easy, doing always harder."

Dlanazar climbed shakily to his feet, vision still blurred and fear still a cold, racing flood in his veins. "T-Three Above," he prayed, trying to look around. "Is it over?"

"Probably not," Horl said grimly. "*That* sort of noise tends to lure things from all over the House. They'll come slithering in hopes of finding something dead they can feed on . . . and that would be us, if we're still here when they arrive."

"So let's get *gone!*"

"What, lad? No gems?"

"Graul, sargh upon, and *bebolt* the gems!" Dlanazar cried. "We can—"

Callused fingers pried open his own and laid something in his palm. Several somethings: smooth and cold and hard. Dlan held them up close so he could see them, and caught his breath in awe.

"Jelzasters! *Huge* ones!"

"Aye, lad—and as you were starting to say, we can come back for more, later. Can you see to walk, yet?"

Dlan wiped furiously at his eyes. "I—I think so. If—*what was that?*"

"Graul," Horl whispered, as the heavy scraping and scrabbling came again. He tugged at Dlan's arm, drawing him off in a new direction.

"What *is* it?" Dlan demanded furiously as he was dragged stumbling along.

The scraping sound grew louder, as if it had turned a corner and entered the room with them.

"Well, lad," Old Horl murmured, real fear in his voice for the first time Dlan had ever heard, "you've heard of nightwyrms, haven't you? And you're not such a brainless fool as to think *they're* just bards' fireside tales, hey?"

"Y-yes?"

"Well, when they hatch—before they can fly, which matters not a whit in these halls—they're smaller than the ones you can see flying, far out at sea beyond the spells the guild mages send . . . but not a *lot* smaller."

"Oh, *gods!*"

"Yes, lad, this *would* be a good time for your precious Three to shine their smiles on us. It would indeed."

Horl had dragged Dlan into a stumbling run by this time, and was ducking around behind what were probably pillars—so the hissing roars of two hungry jaws, when they came, were a little muffled. But not much.

The two young and darkly handsome men looked across the room at each other.

The taller and more slender man had dark eyes, raven-black hair that descended into sideburns as razor-pointed as two daggers, and a long fine-featured face. He wore a grand overjerkin of gold shimmerweave, many rings, and breeches of snow-white sulkoun that proclaimed him to be either one of the richest merchant lords of Sirlptar, or what he was: Baron of Silvertree.

The shorter man in the dark blue robes and cloak gestured graciously to the Baron, indicating that he should speak first.

Faerod Silvertree nodded slightly, smiled, and said, "I desire your firm loyalty. Your sorcerous service is to be devoted exclusively to me, and governed by my commands alone—for the rest of your life. I've no interest in lying to you; 'tis best we understand each other fully."

"That's one of the traits I see in you that pleases me most," Ingryl Ambelter replied unsmilingly. "That, your fearlessness, and your willingness to keep pacts, once made. We've worked together so well thus far, Lord Silvertree, that your offer entices me . . . as a request of servitude would decidely not, were it to come from any other person. So, a life in service to you, as diligently as I know how—and now that Spellmaster Gadaster has been taken, I'm probably the most capable mage this side of Arlund, though two or three of the oldest archwizards in Sirlptar are nearly my equals—in return for—?"

"A rank in my realm, no matter how large it becomes, second only to my own. *You* shall now be Spellmaster of Silvertree. All the castles and revenues of two baronies—Tarlagar and Phelinndar, though I may appoint tersepts, if you agree, to keep law, collect taxes, and scour out monsters therein—plus a third barony in the future, to be mutually agreed upon, but to be neither Blackgult nor Silvertree. If we conquer Sirlptar, its lordship and one-half of its taxes are yours, from the day of our governance on. And I believe you wanted my sisters?"

"All three, their lives and persons to do with as I will." The dark-garbed wizard stepped forward. "All you offer is agreeable to me. Shall we bind with blood?"

"We shall. Now?"

"There's never a better time to begin, my Lord, than 'now.'"


Faerod Silvertree stood on the battlements of Castle Silvertree and stared across the sundering Silverflow at the soaring spires of Castle Blackgult. The tallest was surmounted by a golden griffon device large enough that he could see its mocking smile clearly from here.

A smile he'd soon shred and cast down, now that he was free at last.

Free of his father's shadow, the coldly mocking Gadaster Mulkyn. The Spellmaster of Silvertree, whose sorceries had ruled all Aglirta for so many years. Gone at last.

Gadaster had died in a sorcery gone wrong, Ingryl Ambelter claimed, though many held silent doubts about that, the Baron included.

For days Faerod had expected him to suddenly appear, as gently terrible as always—but as the passing days brought no softly smiling Mulkyn, that expectation had slowly faded. Whatever Ingryl had done to him, Gadaster *was* gone.

Which left him free to rend yon fortress. The abode of the man he hated and feared more than anyone else in the world: Ezendor Blackgult, peerless battlemaster and quick-tongued wit. The most handsome man in the Vale, before whose boots ladies swooned in their energetic dozens and scores and hundreds.

The armaragors of Blackgult ruled every battlefield they rode onto. Only Ambelter's spells had kept Silvertree from being swept right off the maps, despite far too much Silvertree gold going into the hiring of a muster of mercenaries thrice the number of Blackgult's troops.

Faerod Silvertree had hated and feared Gadaster, who'd refused to hurl his spells in battle, instead reminding Faerod with soft venom of prudence and subtle intrigues and Faerod's father's wishes—more than Blackgult . . . but Gadaster Mulkyn was gone, now, and . . .

"The leashes are off all of us," he whispered into the wind, glaring northwest across the Silverflow.

For almost a decade now Blackgult had laughed and brawled his way freely up and down the Vale, from bedchamber to gaming table, and battlefield to merchants' pact-tables—while Faerod Silvertree, constrained by a Spellmaster who wouldn't help him and an ambitious apprentice, Ambelter, who dare not try to, in the face of

Gadaster's cold watchfulness and iron-strong sorcery—had been powerless to do anything but brood and watch. Brood and watch. . . .

Mulkyn had let Faerod enact rightful justice on his traitor-wife, but had even prevented him from wringing the neck of his pale, staring daughter . . . claiming she had "future uses."

Now Embra would have her uses, after all—but they'd not be Gadaster Mulkyn's uses.

Brooding and watching changes a man. Wherefore ruthlessness and thorough attention to details were Faerod Silvertree's own strengths. Yet in the face of Blackgult's daring and jovial fearlessness, that preparedness had for years served for little more than just keeping the Lord of Silvertree alive.

By stealth and Ingryl's mastery of dark monster-controlling magics, he'd only just now taken the overgrown forest of Flowfoam Isle for his own, and claimed the long-abandoned royal palace of King Kelgrael Snowsar as his own Castle Silvertree. That had been no small or easy achievement, and only Ambelter's spells had made it possible at all.

He owed the wizard so much, and needed Ingryl Ambelter for so much more.

Blackgult must be slain—and broken in torment first. Faerod Silvertree must be feared and obeyed up and down the Vale, not the Golden Griffon. Bards like Inderos Stormharp must write ballads to the praise of Faerod Silvertree, not Bedchamber Blackgult. The riches of Sirlptar must be his, and its sneering merchants taught to cower before Aglirta, not laugh at backcountry barons for being loutish farmers who'd given themselves titles.

And this great river-girt island was not enough. He was a Silvertree, and Silvertree House, with all its fabled ghosts and stone-crawling worms and fearsome monsters, *must* be his.

Involuntarily Faerod turned to try to peer over the trees at its great dark bulk, but the height of the leaf-girt branches thankfully hid it from view. The largest fortress in all Asmarand, bigger than most cities. A haunted, deserted ruin that grew, seemingly by itself, with every passing day.

Faerod desired it almost as much as he feared it. A great, afire-with-magic castle, his heritage but beyond his grasp . . . and he knew of no way to close his hand around it, and master it, and dwell there without going mad. Until now.

For this day—barely the draining of a celebratory flagon ago—Ingryl had signed. Moreover, Faerod had used a spell of his own—one of the most powerful magics of the paltry handful he knew, thanks to twisted old Ileendaera—to take some of the mage's blood right out of him during the signing. That vial was securely hidden now, and at last Faerod could allow the excitement singing in his veins to take control of him.

He stood on the battlements, stared north at Castle Black-gult, and allowed himself to laugh. It was not a nice laugh.

"My brother sent me," she whispered, her eyes large and dark, her skin the hue of bleached bone.

Ingryl Ambelter smiled at her. "And?"

"I am to serve you in all things. Henceforth, you are my lord and master."

" 'Tis good you understand this," the mage replied, moving the smallest finger of his right hand. Soundlessly the door behind her sealed itself, and a gentle glow—as of unseen candles—grew in the air above and a little ahead of her, illuminating her in the darkness.

"Undo your gown, and let it fall."

She stared at him, lips parting in shock—and then, possibly because of what she saw in his eyes, she did so, undoing the sash, and the three ornamental belts that crossed the curve of her hips, and then the rich garment, letting in trail down her arms to puddle on the stone floor.

She shivered once under his gaze, standing only in a loin-scarf and high gold-gartered boots of supple leather.

"Those, too. Remove them, but then stand still."

She swallowed, lowered her head, and did so.

Ingryl Ambelter began to stroll around her, almost soundless in his soft slippers, one hand stroking his chin and the other clenched behind his back.

"Smarelda, isn't it?"

"Yes, Lord. Youngest of us three."

"Yes. Your sisters have been here before you, and have been of great service to me. Remove your jewelry—all of it, no matter how private its concealment or dear its sentimental value. You may set it on your scarf there, on the floor."

Smarelda Silvertree did as she was bid, kneeling shyly and daintily to do so, as Ingryl continued his circumnavigation of her.

When he stood in front of her once more, he made no comment on her blushings or where she'd placed her hands in a belated attempt to preserve her modesty, but commanded abruptly, "Follow me. Do not turn aside into other rooms. Come."

And he turned and set off down the smooth stone floor of the gloomy passage. She stepped out of the light—which promptly extinguished itself, causing her a moment of fright—and followed him.

The way was longer than she'd expected, and through two archways where cross-passages met the one she was walking along. Abruptly the way ended at an archway filled with shimmering force that sighed into quiet, empty darkness at the wizard's approach, and he strode through it and turned to face her.

There was a strange, intricate drawing chalked on the floor, which was of smooth black marble, and two dark metal rods hanging down from the unseen ceiling above, converging at angles towards each other.

"Step into the circle at the center of this rune, and stop therein. Step high; do *not* touch any of the chalk."

When she'd done so, he ordered, "Look up. See the rods? Grasp their ends."

By stretching her arms fully, so that her heels were just off the floor and her body was arched, arms back and pelvis forward, Smarelda could just do so.

"Good," the mage told her, and casually waved one hand. Sudden energies awakened in the rods and pulsed through her, setting her to trembling.

"If you let go of the rods, you will die," he remarked calmly—and undid his own sash, tossing his robe behind him.

Then he stepped forward, not caring if he smudged the chalk, and thrust himself into her, bruising her with his long, dagger-thin manhood.

Smarelda gasped in shame and pain, trying to snatch her hands away from the rods and shove at him—but discovered she could not let go. She was bound by the magic, as a thrilling sensation that was both warm and icy flooded up through her, making her soft breasts stand out into straining points, her hair lift from her shoulders and swirl around her like a restless jungle of tiny snakes, and . . . ecstasy come flooding.

"Yes," Ingryl snarled, from just below her chin. *"Yesss."*

He thrust and thrust, and then remarked, as calmly as before—though through her tears Smarelda saw that sweat was dripping from his nose and chin, and his eyes were like two flames—"You are even sweeter than your sisters, tall one. They had more wits, more experience, but *you*—you have the power."

"P-power, my Lord?" she gasped, feeling she should say something.

"You can weave magic, so your life-essence is so much stronger than theirs was. You shall keep me alive more than twenty summers longer than I would have had, and even augment my own aptitude for sorcery."

She felt weak, suddenly, and the dark room was growing even darker. Ingryl Ambelter was the only light in it now, and he positively glowed.

"What," she gasped raggedly, as ecstasy seized her again, "is happening to me, Lord? What are you doing to me?"

"Taking your life, as I did those of your two sisters. Your essences have given me uncommon vitality, strength, and endurance." He thrust into her harder, clawing at her shoulders and climbing her to do so, adding mockingly, *"Thank you, Smarelda."*

Everything was dark now, dark and cold, rushing up and out of her as she fell . . . fell . . .

"My broth—," she gasped, lips suddenly thick and slack.

"Gave his full permission for this. He knows not the truth about your sacrifices, but rather that the 'great spells' I wove to master the Silent House for him all failed, and drove you three—oh, so regrettably—down into madness and death."

But Smarelda Silvertree was beyond hearing him.

When the wizard stepped back from her dark, shriveled body a long breath later, it crumpled to the floor, leaving two clenched, disembodied hands still clinging to the rods.

*So much cruelty. So many malicious thoughts, as dark and slithering as serpents in the night. So petty and so grasping. Let's pass over much of it. No vision had they, either Faerod Silvertree or Ingryl Ambelter, beyond power.*

*Power is a hunger.*

*It gnaws at many who achieve even a shred of it, and so lift themselves out of helplessness and resignation, into its bright web of delusions. Achieving power makes too many men drunk with the fire to have more, ever more. . . .*

*Yet if one mage or king or outlaw hiresword is to gain power, others must lose it—and that losing is seldom willing.*

*Which is why so much blood is spilled in this world, and so much time wasted on forging swords and fleeing in fear and watching hard work go up in flames.*

*It almost makes me turn aside, and care nothing for the doom I see coming down on Darsar.*

*Almost.*

"Yes, wizard!" Faerod Silvertree laughed, from the height of his high-cantled saddle. "Yes, my Spellmaster—you've done it!"

Ingryl Ambelter grinned up at the baron, the green sorcerous fires that had felled hundreds of Blackgult's armaragors and cortahars still raging around him in a circle, and asked, "Did I not promise you victory?"

"You did," Baron Silvertree roared, "and made our pact

the best bargain of my life!" He punched the air with one bloody gauntlet and hauled on the reins to make his great war-steed rear and lash the air with its hooves. For three hills away the dead of Blackgult lay strewn, vultures settling wherever his own men weren't knifing the wounded—and no one had seen the Golden Griffon escape the field.

His mount had no liking for Ambelter's flaming magic, and came down turned away from it and bucking; Faerod Silvertree bellowed with laughter and used the enchantment of his left gauntlet to hold it from bolting. It shivered and shuddered under him as the magic took hold, and he shook his other gauntlet—the one that had the boneshatter enchantment—in triumph once more.

"M-my Lord Baron?" There was more than a thread of fear in the armaragor's voice. "You wanted to be shown this?"

The man was holding up a riven, fire-scarred helm and a half-melted pendant on a great chain—with that merrily smiling griffon still bright on both of them.

"Where were those found?" Ambelter snapped.

The knight blinked at him. The Spellmaster was not the baron, but no man with wits left to him was going to argue with a roused wizard who had his hurl-fire still raging in a ready circle around him.

"O-on a body yonder, Lord Spellmaster," he said hastily, "atop that hill—just there, where you can see four of us turning the dead over, see? There's a great knot of the dead, all charred and intermingled, where your last bolt hit, and . . ." He nodded his head meaningfully at what he was holding.

Faerod Silvertree threw back his head and let out a great roar of triumph that made heads turn all over the battlefield. His steed snorted and lashed out with its hooves again, causing the armaragor to hastily scramble backwards. The baron pointed at him and laughed, "Wrap those in a cloak and keep them safe for me! Get gone and do it!"

The armaragor bowed, nodded, and trotted swiftly away.

Ingryl Ambelter watched him go, and then turned to his master and said softly, "One victory I've managed for you, Lord, but I've thus far failed in another."

Faerod Silvertree blinked at him. "Oh?"

"Despite the deaths of your sisters, I cannot find a way to tame the Silent House—yet. I . . . I have a plan to make Castle Silvertree as alive with magic and obedient to your will as Silvertree House should be, but—'twill cost you a daughter."

"Mage," Faerod Silvertree replied, still gleeful, "She's yours, but I have only the one. She'll have to serve, failures be damned, for I've no more to spare."

Then he leaned his head down and looked into Ambelter's face, and they said in chorus: "Yet."

Then the baron bellowed with laughter once more. "Take my daughters! Take 'em all—I'll set about producing more this very night! You're going to make one of them into an echo of the Curse of the Silent House?"

"An obedient-to-you Curse, yes. Your daughter, Embra, or a later one, will become a Living Castle—*if* she has the aptitude for sorcery."

Faerod Silvertree frowned. "So I have to couple with sorceresses? I know of only three—proper haughty bitches, too—in Sirlptar, and mounting *them* is going to involve three battles to rival this one!"

"Well, as to that," the Spellmaster of Silvertree purred, "I have a plan. . . ."

# 2

## Dark Wizards in a Dark House

"*I* believe the proper term," Ezendor Blackgult grunted, turning painfully over so the Wise-woman could sew more of the great sword-gash shut, "is 'a stinging battlefield defeat.' Handed to us by that wizard of his, not by grand Lord Coldness, for all his gilded armor and enchanted gauntlets."

The armaragor lying beside him chuckled—mirth that

ended in a grunt of pain and caused the crone to say sharply, "I *warned* you, sword-brains! Now lie still, and think less about enthusiastically carving up Aglirta!"

"If it hadn't been for your cunning and those wizards you hired," the armaragor husked, struggling to speak as his mouth filled with blood, "we'd *all* have been . . ."

The Golden Griffon lay still, listening. It was two long and reluctant breaths later ere he asked the Wise One, "Dead?"

"Not yet," was the tart reply. "But you're all working hard to get to your deaths—and they got there out of love and loyalty of you, Lord Blackgult. *You* ordered them to ride to war."

He lay still under her rebuke, and then said gently, "Their alternative—after my death or flight—would have been to submit to the rule of Faerod Silvertree."

"And are there not far worse fates?"

Ezendor Blackgult lay still, looking at the wall. "No," he said after a time. "No, I don't believe so."



"Two expendable assistants should do it? Then hire them!" Baron Silvertree said sharply, still afire with his triumph over Blackgult. "My coffers open for you, mage!"

Ingryl Ambelter smiled and bowed his head. "My thanks, Lord Baron."

"Accepted—and I'll look forward to thanking *you* again soon, Ingryl, when you help me smash barony after barony, until we hold all Aglirta! *The Kingless Land shall have a king again!*"

Faerod was so taken with this phrase that he stood up from his throne and declaimed it several times more.

Ingryl Ambelter was careful to make sure he was well out of the chamber—and the view of any guards—before he rolled his eyes.



"Your obedience to Baron Silvertree is absolute," Ambelter told the two lesser mages, "by pact and by the precautions we all know he took."

He snapped his fingers, and they were all abruptly—somewhere else. Somewhere that featured weathered stone tombs thrusting up out of tall grass, and clinging vines, and thornbushes in profusion, and startled birds whirring away only slightly faster than a great rock-snake left off sunning itself on a tombstone, and slithered down and away into concealment.

"However, the baron is not with us. He'll farscry us, undoubtedly, but he'll not be walking with us when we go in *there*."

He pointed at the great, dark stone wall looming up at the top of the hill. "So in his absence, your absolute obedience shall be to *me*. I am Spellmaster of Silvertree, I have charge over all matters magical in the Silvertree lands—and I can slay you just as surely and as painfully as Faerod Silvertree. In fact, I can begin your slayings considerably faster. Please bear that in mind."

He strode forward, beckoning them to follow, to where a great flat gravestone—despite the cracks that wandered across it, and the heavings wrought by hundreds of Aglirtan winters—offered a fairly level area to stand on. "Cast your spells," he ordered quietly, "and link to me."

Whenever either Klamantle Beirldoun or Markoun Yarynd served as the focus of a mindlink of what folk had begun to call Faerod Silvertree's Dark Three, they winced and staggered as the link formed—but Ingryl stood proudly motionless, his only response to the mind-rush being to arch one sardonic eyebrow as the two glanced at him.

Silent, solid, cold-eyed Klamantle was the elder and more powerful of the two, Markoun the younger and swifter of temper, deed, and ambition. Markoun was almost too handsome to be a mage, and Ingryl knew for a fact that he'd made conquests among the serving-lasses already. In fact, if the Mighty Yarynd left too many more subtle mind-charms behind in feminine minds for Ingryl to go around removing, the patience of a certain Spellmaster was going to wear thin.

"We're entering the Silent House not to sightsee, and not to blast things—though I'm sure we'll find ourselves in a spell-battle sufficient to test your minds and the spells you've stuffed them full of. We're going in to retrieve as much magic as we can, of all those glittering glows our every scrying spell shows us is massed therein, *and get out again,* without lingering to finish a foe or pay back someone—or some*thing*—that struck at us. If you don't agree, I'll be happy to sever the mind-link once we're in there, and leave the one disagreeing with my orders to make his own far-more-successful way out."

Two heads nodded. Neither mage offered comment.

Ambelter nodded back, not quite smiling, and cast a swift spell that lifted their boots a good foot off the ground. Striding on air, he led the way into the waiting darkness.

"Horl," Dlan almost sobbed, as callused hands spun him around and slapped something into his hand, "what're you—what's this?"

"While you were bringing the ceiling down on our heads," the older treasure-hunter said grimly, "*I* was scooping up the treasure—for once. Not the gems; I've left them lying for now, but something far more useful. Keep good hold on that thing in your hands—yes, 'tis a metal stick, and yes, the end pointing away from you is dangerous, so don't point it at *me,* thank you!—and when you can see properly, aim it into one of yon beast's two mouths, and think of fire . . . fire leaping forth, hey?"

"Three aid me! I'm not going to be able to *see!*"

"Oh," Horl panted, as he towed Dlan hastily around yet another pillar, and something that stank eddied around them, "those mouths won't be hard to find. Smell that breath? If you feel teeth closing on you, just trigger the wand!"

Dlanazar frantically wiped · at his eyes, peered . . . and staggered back with a frightened cry.

A purple tongue was whipping and wriggling obscenely not four paces away, in gaping jaws that yawned from the height of his knees to his chest. Jaws that were moving menacingly towards him on a dark serpentine neck as large around as a mule—with a second neck and set of jaws, its eyes gleaming like cold white stars in glistening black scales, coiling up in search of Horl.

"*Now,* lad! Think of fire! This one's a hatchling, still, not full-grown! *Give it fire!*"

While you do what? Dlan swept away that petulant thought unspoken, set his teeth as the long, pointed snout moved in, and thought of fire.

Raging fire, boiling forth, flames racing—

The wand in his hand erupted into white sparks and a stabbing beam of searing, roaring whiteness, nothing like the merry orange-and-gold tongues of flame he'd been thinking of, a beam that stabbed into the gaping maw before him.

The nightwyrm shuddered and threw its head back, a hissing scream of pain arising deep in its reeking throat. Dlanazar's rushing beam of fire was searing away the roof of its mouth, melting soft flesh amid smokes that swirled wildly as the beast sought to shake its head free of this impaling needle of pain.

At the same time, its other head stabbed down . . .

. . . and Horl stepped up beside Dlan with something golden and gleaming in his hands, whispered something soft over it . . .

. . . and the air around that plunging head, its jaws opening to savage Dlanazar, was suddenly full of whirling golden shards, double-ended blades of metal that flashed around and around and through that head in a deadly, razor-sharp cloud.

The head was moving fast, and the whirling blades with it, and Horl barked, "*Stand* your ground!" just as Dlanazar was stepping back to whirl and flee, his fires forgotten.

The nightwyrm's second head fell away into a cloud of blood and tumbling flesh and shredded scales as Horl snarled out an oath and tugged the golden thing across his chest.

And the whirling storm of golden blades raced through the air to slice into the shuddering, smoking remaining beast-head, that Dlan's fires had just faltered and fallen away from.

Dlanazar watched that carnage openmouthed, as the nightwyrm's last head vanished into a cloud of gore—a cloud that it left behind as it snatched its long neck back, to join its other neck in wild flailings of pain that dashed against pillars and spattered the chamber with lines of gore.

"Right," Horl growled, plucking at Dlanazar's shoulder. "*Now* you can flee. This way, through here, before all this noise brings other—"

He hauled open a door, and—sprang back, gasping an oath that Dlanazar couldn't even understand.

In the dark passage outside, something that looked like a great heap of dew-worms was waiting. Many of its wet, slithering tentacles—if that's what they were, studded with handfuls of tiny eyes and mouths, wet and segmented and all the same—had been straining to force open the door. They fell forward into the room with wet slapping sounds, thrusting in through the doors to prevent Horl from closing them again.

"Fire, lad, as before," the old man ordered curtly, raising his golden sphere of many curving handles again. "*This* is even more dangerous than the nightwyrm!"

Dlanazar groaned in fear, vomiting and hardly realizing it as he raised trembling hands and fought to think of fire . . . fire . . . glistening slitherings reaching for him and no *no* no *fire* . . .

His world exploded in a roar that flung him back, trailing white sparks, across a great open space of passing pillars and tumbling glowstones and scattering, bouncing coins . . . into something black and wet and reeking, that heaved and shuddered under him, yielding just enough to take his tumbling limbs and heave them back.

Dlanazar Duncastle hit stony rubble hard with his knees, and rolled. His hands felt like they were afire, more shrieking pain than he'd ever felt in his life before, and . . . and he'd just been saved from a bone-shattering meeting with a pillar by the body of the dying nightwyrm, whose stinking gore he was now drenched in. His fire-thing had exploded, somehow, and old Horl had been standing right beside him at the time . . . he was doomed, they were both dead or doomed to die, he would never—

Somewhere across the room, he heard the old procurer curse heartily, then snarl the words, "Should've known better than to trust in grauling magic!" Dlan thrust his head up, wildly, almost toppling over on the rubble, and saw Horl fling away the golden thing, which was trailing thin streams of smoke, and draw his battered old sword again.

*A battered old man with a battered old sword,* he thought, and giggled at the sheer idiocy of it all.

"Dlan, boy!" Horl roared over his shoulder, without turning, "I hear you! Get up and get over here—I'm too old to be hacking apart corpse-suckers alone!"

Dlanazar shook his head in dazed disbelief and struggled to his feet, falling on his face immediately as rubble shifted under his boots. His shins hurt like Three-sin, and so did his hands, but they both seemed to be . . . intact and usable. He found footing again, and stumbled unsteadily down off the pile, casting a wary glance back at the feebly thrashing bulk of the headless nightwyrm.

Halfway to Horl, he stepped into a hole in the floor that hadn't been there before, and almost went sprawling. Gems rattled and rained down on flagstones all around his boots as he fought to keep from falling, skidded sickeningly, and then trotted on, hauling at his own blade.

The—the corpse-sucker, Horl had called it, yes—was still in the doorway, much of its front blackened, melted, and drooling steaming gore or blood out onto the floor . . . and much of the rest of its worm-tentacles were lopped-off stumps or dangling, shredded things. Their magics had both died, but not before doing considerable harm.

Yet the thing was rearing up, like a great carpet of tentacles, trying to curl the untouched rear of its body up and over its lacerated front to get at Horl, dozens of worm-tentacles reaching forth hungrily . . . and the passage was quite high enough to permit it to do so.

"Can't we just run *away?*" Dlan shouted, as he came. "Through another door?"

Horl turned his head. "And leave your gems behind?"

"*Graul* the gems!" Dlanazar snarled. "Graul the bebolten gems! Let's get the sarghing graul *out of here,* old man!"

Horl shook himself all over, like a dog ridding itself of river-water, and then pointed across the chamber and said briskly, "Yon door. Watch for marked flagstones as you go."

Then he hacked at the nearest tentacles, stepped back, and slipped around behind a pillar, heading for the door he'd indicated.

A tentacle or two reached after him, but then fell away.

Dlanazar swallowed, fought down his trembling rage, and started to peer at flagstones.


It began the moment they stepped over the threshold. The Spellmaster's floatfoot spell kept them from falling down pit-traps and undoubtedly stopped many of the thrusting and falling blades, but the shieldings Ambelter had spun above them were struck by many huge stone blocks—some of them attached to chains that allowed them to be pulled up into place again to await the next intruder.

Maedra boiled out of the walls, clawing and biting, ghostly shadows flew menacingly at the three wizards—and mages that seemed to be little more than disembodied, gesturing hands in the gloom hurled spell-bursts and arrows of lightning and twist-transformations that tugged at the Dark Three.

And there was the whispering. Words that promised love, and wealth, and power, foes cringing and surrendering, women offering themselves, cities piling up chests of coins . . . and wizards turning to them, in awe and respect, proferring tomes of magic unseen save in legend and sought-after these many centuries . . . power . . . matchless power . . .

And with those whispers came visions, a profusion of horrors—armaragors being hacked apart by floating, darting blades wielded by no visible hand, wizards torn limb from limb by snarling maedra, procurers losing fingers, hands, arms, and even heads—bouncing and rolling bloodily down chutes—to hidden blades . . . all befalling in the Silent House, all waiting for the Dark Three.

Behind those whispers and visions, the dark, titanic mind that sent them, towering over their own thoughts, sidling into the mind-link . . .

Ingryl Ambelter found himself reaching out to welcome a spell-burst, just before it ignited. . . .

Klamantle Beirldoun staggered back from smilingly offering his vitals to a rusty blade swung by a skeleton of something that had never been human. . . .

Markoun Yarynd recoiled in horror from the maedra he'd been about to embrace. . . .

And the Spellmaster wiped away sweat that was pouring like a waterfall down his face and came fully awake in horror—it—it—no, SHE—was *in the mind-link with them!* And with every passing instant, his memories were flowing out and away from him, forever, gathered into that dark and looming column that was now very close to him indeed. . . .

"Out!" he screamed. "Get *out!*" And he spun the strongest ward he had left, using its sizzling lines to buy himself time to work the return—a spell he'd almost not bothered with, thinking he'd never have to use anything so desperate, so precipitous—

Three panting, wild-eyed wizards in the tattered remnants of clothing staggered together in the high-vaulted spell-chamber of Castle Silvertree, whimpered or snarled in fear as their style took them, and lurched apart again, clawing at the air and shivering.

Ingryl Ambelter strode down the room, more terrified than he'd ever been in his life before. His mind was ravaged, his sorcery lessened so greatly that he dared not let anyone know. If these two wretches hadn't shared the same doom, he'd have feared either one of them could now humble him with spells . . . and as it was, if Faerod ever learned just how weakened his Spellmaster had become, it would be a simple matter to take back two baronies and save himself a third and a share of Sirlptar.

As it was, Ambelter need not have worried. Faerod Silvertree was sprawled on his throne in his own vomit and voidings, drooling and glassy-eyed, sobbing from time to time, fitfully, as if his mind couldn't remember how upset he was and only gave vent when it dazedly remembered.

What precisely had befallen his Dark Three, he could not recall, only that it had been horrible—*horrible*—and would have been so easily and swiftly fatal—whatever SHE was, she could claim their lives at will, or worse yet their minds but send them back out into Aglirta, to serve her and do harm!—if Ambelter had not somehow snatched them all free of it . . . that he would never dare to order them to enter the Silent House again.

"I . . . I lost my glowstone," Dlanazar panted. "And the lantern, too."

Horl regarded him expressionlessly for a moment, and then ducked a hand into a belt-pouch and handed him a stone.

Dlan stared at it, and then at the already-glowing stone in the old man's hand. "How many glowstones do we have?"

"Four," the elder treasure-hunter informed him gruffly. "As I said, I plucked up the treasure for once. While you were amusing yourself by rolling around the chamber plucking down stone blocks on your head, remember?"

Rage boiled up in Dlanazar, but he let it pass and merely asked wearily, "and what other treasure did you find, besides the fire-wand I broke and that blades-thing you broke?"

Horl reached into another pouch and expressionlessly slapped a handful of green orblouns as large as Dlan's thumbs into the younger procurer's hand. "These," he said briefly. "Seeing as you dropped most of those jelzasters—and rolled on the rest of them."

Dlanazar suddenly felt the urge to laugh. He tried it, weakly, but Horl slapped his arm lightly and growled, "*Enough* noise. Unless you want to fight something else. Now, through here . . ."

Dlan stowed the gems hastily in a belt-pouch, fumbling to get it closed against the coils of stormbraid rope around his waist, and strode after the lurching old man. "How did you know where to find these? And how did you—?"

Horl whirled around. "Lad, welcome to the world the rest of us live in, where the Three don't smile on our every whim, and nothing ever turns out quite the way you think it will. Remember that: Nothing ever turns out quite the way you think it will."

Those emphatic words were still echoing in the small passage around them when a taloned hand as large as Dlan's head erupted smoothly from the stone wall beside Horl's head, reaching—and the old man smoothly tossed his battered old blade from his right hand to his left, and hacked those talons viciously away from him.

There was a muffled shriek from inside the stone, an ululation that died away swiftly as the bloodied claw was withdrawn. The stone rippled once, and then grew still again.

Dlan stared at Horl's calm face, and then down at the old man's sword. Dripping with the unknown monster's gore, it was held up and ready—clutched capably in the old man's left hand.

The Spellmaster's shieldings had exploded at his vanishing, and the unleashed spells of the wraith-wizards had raged around the chamber, shattering and maiming maedra by the score.

One by one, they were sagging to the floor, or slumping over, frozen in death when they were half-sunken in the stone already. Stone blocks fell from the ceiling as if too weary to stay up any longer.

In the heart of the devastation, something large and dark and serpentine swayed in even greater weariness. The Arau was very old, and sheer malice was not enough to keep it alive in the face of ravaging magic. It could never have hidden from the three intruders, or it would not have been the Arau . . . but age had weakened it more than it had realized.

As happens to many a human.

The Arau leaned against a shattered wall, slid slowly down it into an untidy pile of coils, and drifted into deepening slumber. The slow descent into the darkness from which there is no awakening. . . .

The sentience that had long ago been Yuesembra Silvertree was trapped in this silent, deepening doom, and knew it for what it was.

Desperately she drew all the energy she could from the dying body, thrusting it into her senses and her sorcery, to send out a tremulous scrying as far as she could . . . seeking a new host, any host, before the Arau died.

Sought . . . straining . . . sought . . . frantically . . . *found*.

Away at the southern end of the House, where the maedra had been thrusting new wings out into the woods, an old man had scrambled hesitantly into the palace the night before, seeking shelter from a soaking rain.

Fair shelter it had been, and now he was wandering, clambering and peering in the gloom. Would it also serve as a place to dwell? From time to time, as he wandered, the old man's body seemed to slide into other shapes—and where most intruders spent most of their attention on fearing danger ahead, deeper in the House, this one looked most fearfully behind himself, as if fearing pursuit from Aglirta outside.

With the last of her strength, Yuesembra sent forth a thought.

The old man stiffened, raising his head and frowning. Suddenly it was almost as if he knew the way ahead, was *remembering* it. . . .

That couldn't be. He knew quite well he'd never seen these halls before. Yet, confident now, he hurried on to the grander chambers he knew to be there, to the waiting wells and stairs up to balconies, and where laden fruit trees were growing up through shattered chambers.

He came to a place where disturbed dust still drifted, as if a battle had just been fought, and monster-bodies were strewn everywhere. One of them was a serpent so large and dark that at first he thought it was part of the walls and floor.

He knew he should have been cowering in terror, yet everything seemed so comfortingly familiar . . . and there on the floor, beside the pointed end of the great serpent-tail, lay something small and beautiful.

A statuette of a woman—as long as his hand, no more,

and of some dark stone. So smooth and exquisitely carved as to seem almost real . . . if beautiful, happily reclining nude human women had ever existed in so small a form, that is.

He picked it up carefully, marveling at its beauty and its workmanship. She was beautiful indeed . . . and there were tiny words written down her spine: "Yuesembra Silvertree."

No sooner had he finished reading them than the statuette crumbled to dust in his hands, just falling away into nothing in a sighing instant.

And the old man felt sudden sadness, a despair deeper than the mere loss of a beautiful thing, and sat down alone in the darkness to sob.

Like a soft shadow all that was left of Yuesembra wormed her way into this new host, finding him far more than the aging human he appeared to be. Far, far more.

She'd been fortunate indeed to lure him without his sensing her. Carefully she entered into the best place in his mind to hide and settled into quiescence, awaiting the moment—perhaps years ahead, perhaps never—when he'd touch one of the blood Silvertree, and she could pass once more into a proper host.

Time passes, and I lose track of the days. Winter deepens, and I must spend most of my time as a wolf-spider, or perish of the cold.

Going below brings me to lightless levels that are always cold, but a cold warmer than where the winter chill reaches. Yet I hunger.

I try to pay no heed to my yawning gut and weakening limbs, but I can hear whisperings in my mind. The House itself, I think, telling me to go up, and prowl, and feed. It seems a torch-bearing band of men—desperate men, outlaws—has entered the oldest part of the House, nigh the river. Though how the whispers know this, I cannot say.

I have eaten my first man. My mind desperately wanted me to be sick, but my belly told me the steaming blood—a tang like sword-iron—was good, though the meat was meagre for all the gnawing at that metal shell of armor.

I will eat men. I will stay alive, and keep the whispers content. Anything to keep them from spinning more horrors to haunt my dreams.

As if I needed reminding why I came here. To hide. To be less than a man, to be the beasts whose shape I've mastered: a spider and the hunting horror called by some "longfangs," and by others "wolf-spider." To eat humans and beasts—a wolf, yestermorn, all sinew and fur—and keep hidden from all barons, tersepts, and others who'd exploit healers. They'd keep me chained in a dungeon cell, and bring hurt ones to me, drinking my own life on healings until I died. Three Above, how I hate barons. Almost as much as I fear them.

No man will master me. Ever again.

The distaste for eating humans grows less and less. With spring have come deer and wandering lambs and those who come chasing them. Devouring adventurers is a frequent thing, now, and hunting them less a matter of blind blundering and fear. I seem to know where the traps are, in rooms and passages I have never before entered, and the ghosts and other guardians I have begun to see seem to avoid me.

I long to leave the House, and roam in the green trees and hills I can see from the windows and ramparts and out of archways that lost their doors an age ago, but I cannot. This has become my prison, and my jailer is in my mind. Whispering.

There is no Curse stalking Silvertree House now. Which is to say: the Curse is in me. I dimly see memories not my own, sometimes, though I am stronger. This is my life, now, and though I can and have gone prowling, to prey on sheep and encamped outlaws and adventurers well beyond the walls, I always return.

The House is part of me. If the King should come again and law rule Aglirta, and healers be free to walk and live wherever they desire as merchants do, and I went forth and fared to the ends of Darsar, I would return here some day.

No matter where I might go and how far away the place of my death might be, I would return.

Sarasper Codelmer
(passages from fragmentary diaries)
(Divers Years, in the Reign of Kelgrael)

# BOOK TEN

## Embra Silvertree

2250– SR
Lady Baron of Silvertree, Lady Overduke of Aglirta,
and Guardian of Aglirta
And of Her Tasting Freedom, Ascending to Become Dragon,
and of What Happened After

# 1

## One Becomes Four

On the night when his life changed again, Sarasper Codelmer was hunting amid the tangled stones and creepers of what had once, long ago, been the West Forehall—before a great storm had shattered its domed magnificence. The huge chamber had collapsed, its expanse left open to the sky, and for some reason known only to them, the maedra hadn't rebuilt it, but left it in ruins and expanded the House past and around it, so that it became an enclosed courtyard. Later Silvertrees had dubbed it Stormbellow Courtyard, and over the passing years and times in which most of the House was deserted, it became simply "the Stormyard."

No matter what it was called, the courtyard was now a refuge of whirring, squawking birds by day—and a roost for many at night. A man clambering among all the sliding stones in the dark hours couldn't hope to accomplish anything more than awakening sleeping bustards and woodwings into a shrieking, whirling cloud of fury—but a creeping longfangs could with skill and a little luck of the Three snatch and devour three or four birds before arousing the rest.

Sarasper had managed two, and was just reaching delicately for a third, blood still trailing from his jaws, when something large and leathery-winged blotted out the moon, the moaning rush of its wings enough to arouse the birds into cowering, hopping confusion.

*Nightwyrm!*

Even the largest longfangs ever—and Sarasper's wolf-spider form was far from that—would be easy prey for a young nightwyrm, much smaller than anything that could make the air moan like that with its size. And this one . . . this one was diving right at the front of the Silent House!

Then the very sky cracked apart and shuddered in a terrific blast—a spell-burst of some sort, must be—and the air rained down droplets of gore and the stink of seared nightwyrm.

By which time Sarasper Codelmer was scuttling down familiar dark passages, seeking to get as far into the aboveground rooms of the House as he could. He dared not stray deeper, down the many stairs and ramps. Certain things prowled the cellar and dungeon levels, he'd learned, that regarded a longfangs as a pleasant, easily gained snack.

He let slip his wolf-spider form only when he reached a certain room half the House away. It was one of his favorite haunts; a small, roofless, and nameless room where three passages split, one rising upwards in a smooth ramp to the floor above, one descending in the same manner to the first cellar level, and one running onwards at the same level. There was a bench carved into the wall here where Sarasper liked to sit and think, when in his proper human shape. Sometimes he even fell asleep there, and dreamed of the Dwaerindim.

It was also good for catching one's breath when panting in fear, and Sarasper used it for that purpose now.

"Three Above," he muttered, listening to crashings of trampled underbrush and men's voices sharp with excitement coming faintly to his ears from the river side of the House . . . from the burial ground, most likely.

He glanced up at the night sky, saw nothing—clouds or mists must be blotting out the stars—and after a moment took his lesser shape, that of a spider the size of a small lamb, climbed up onto the ceiling of the level passage, and resumed his journey.

Perhaps he was an overcurious old fool of a monster-sized spider, but he was heading for the river-front rooms of the House. Yes, they were the oldest chambers, and his favorite part of the great palace . . . but if those men were coming in here, or chasing something into here, that's where they were most likely going.

On the other hand—or spider leg—if his abode was going to be invaded by hostile, dangerous beings, or potential prey, it would be only prudent to know precisely how many creatures, of what sorts, and where in the House they reached. Traps would reap intruders in some places, and he could seal unwanted or edible visitors into certain rooms by slamming doors behind them, and toppling beams and stone blocks to keep those doors shut. Though he'd as yet heard no barking, men who came exploring the House often brought hunting dogs . . . which were always good eating.

He was seven rooms nearer to the old chambers when he heard the faint echo of what sounded like a woman's voice, declaiming a few swift words in an angry shout. Then the ceiling of a chamber collapsed, somewhere in the House— ahead, near the river entrance. That deep, grating rumbling crashing of stone was unmistakable.

Sorcery? Most likely, given how the nightwyrm had died. It was to be hoped the mage had been buried in a collapse caused by his—or her; that shouting voice had most likely been the weaver of spells—yes, *her* own spell . . . but somehow, in the real Darsar outside bards' ballads, the Darsar where the Worldstones were lost, things never worked out so neatly.

Which meant that for his own safety, Sarasper had to find that sorceress and watch over her, until either the traps of the House took care of her—or he could.

Powerful mages who set boot inside Silvertree House wore one of two cloaks: they were independent would-be plunderers . . . or they did their magic-seeking for sponsors, which meant either wealthy and ruthless Sirl merchants, or greedy and ruthless Aglirtan barons, tersepts, and warlords. Who would all pay staggering sums for a caged or chained healer. If the mighty mage didn't just blast him to bloody cantles first.

Sarasper chose a small alcove in the lee of a hammerstone trap to become a longfangs again, his stomach growl-ing throughout—Three, but he was hungry!—and then climbed the wall, delicately traversed the upperworks of the trap, and continued on, keeping to passage- and chamber-ceilings. The longfangs form was a larger—and more threat-ening—target than a spider large enough to make men curse in astonishment, but luring the sorceress was far safer than blundering ahead trying to find her, when a ready spell might fry him in an instant. And unlike a spider, however large, a longfangs could howl.

So Sarasper stopped in the Hall of the Old Gargoyle—better-known just as "Old Gargoyle" to generations of Sil-vertrees, of course, its towering central gargoyle statue long since crumbled away to an unrecognizable stone fang on a cracked pedestal—and howled.

He'd barely drawn breath after that cry when, as if in re-ply amid its dying echoes, there came two heavy rattling crashes from a passage near the Hall of Knights—trap portcullises falling—followed by the rolling rumble of falling stones. Not a collapse, but loose stones this time, let down between the massive metal grates to bury alive who-ever had touched off that trap.

More than seventy years old, that trap must be, yet not sprung until now . . . and deservedly so: anyone with a good lantern, fair eyesight, and a snatch of working brain could see it, and someone had even marked its presence on the walls at both ends of the passage in which it was located.

So either his intruders were utter fools and had taken care of themselves, or . . . more likely . . . most of them hadn't been caught in the trap, but had taken the other passage from that fork three rooms in from the Hall of Knights, and were now heading . . . right towards him.

The dirty brown wolf-spider flattened itself out along the ceiling, legs tensed to spring, and drew its lips back from its teeth in a mirthless smile.

But then, that was the way a longfangs always smiled.


*   *   *

"So your hand isn't all that useless after all," Dlan said accusingly as they walked down yet another passage. "Are you going to tell me why you *really* want this precious hand of yours?"

"Lad," Horl said a little wearily, "we all have our little secrets. I'm dying, if you must know. More slowly than you almost were, back in the throne chamber, but . . . I'm much closer to death than you've ever been."

"And this copper hand will help you *how?*"

"That's nothing that need concern you yet," the old man said gruffly, "seeing as we haven't even found the bebolten thing."

"Horl, I want to know! I'm *tired* of being led around by the nose in the dark, and—"

"And *I'm* tired of nursemaiding an oh-so-handsome young man who thinks Darsar shines only upon him, and whines and asks question after question after bleeding question like a petulant child—but you don't hear me complaining about it, do you?"

Something in the old man's tone broke through Dlanazar's fury, and he found himself laughing helplessly.

After a moment, Horl chuckled, too.

Which was when Dlan's incautious boot struck some stones littering the floor, sending them skittering away along the passage—and laying bare something that gleamed.

He looked down, and then reached. Horl lurched forward to grab at it, too, but Dlanazar was much closer, and faster.

He turned away from the old man out of sheer habit as he rose out of his crouch, and held up what he'd found: a smooth, beautifully crafted human left hand fashioned out of gleaming copper—gleaming? Ah, yes, magic to keep it that way, of course—with every finger articulated. There were tiny little fangs or barbs like rose thorns on each fingertip, and a stick-and-hollow handle on the back of the wrist, extending up into the back of the hand.

"So who made this," Dlan asked softly, holding it up out of Horl's reach, "and why do you want it?"

"Thaulon Silvertree made it," Horl snarled, "and we had an agreement, young Duncastle. We *still* have an agreement. Give me the hand."

Dlanazar turned cold green eyes on the older man. "And if I do not?"

Down the passage ahead, a tiny radiance winked into being, drifting like a tiny star. Magic, of course. Silhouetted against it, Sarasper saw three human figures. A very tall, muscular man standing beside a tall, slender female, with a smaller, graceful male . . . a procurer? There was something familiar, somehow, about that one . . . in the lead, closest but moving with commendable caution.

Then the star burst, in a flash of light that left Sarasper cringing and half-blind. Through his furious blinking and tearing, he heard a large-lunged man roar in pain, doubtless from the same blinding.

Then a cold, sharply patrician woman's voice—a young woman—said, "If you'll see to your own tasks, armaragor, I'll *try* to deal with the magic. Craer, I'll be needing those clothes now."

*Craer.* He'd known a Craer, once. . . .

Another man's voice murmured something soft and brief, and the scrape of a heavy boot could be heard, as if a large man was sitting down.

Sarasper half shifted to spider form, and then back again. It was tiring and always felt like his guts were coiling inside him with a mind of their own, but he'd learned long ago that he could clear watering eyes, sneezes, and even nausea by starting a shape-change but then promptly reversing it. He didn't want to think about what might happen if he ever tried to reverse a shift . . . and found his body ignoring his will, and doing what it pleased.

His vision was back now, still a little yellow-dazed around the edges, but if he shielded his eyes with one leg as he crept forward . . .

"Lady!" the soft-voiced man hissed. "Are you hurt?"

"My last magic," the sorceress muttered, as he helped her down to the floor where the larger man was already sitting, "is gone. Which is good, since castings seem to be . . . killing me."

More flashes of magical radiance. Sarasper threw up another leg to form an almost complete barrier in front of his eyes, but he could tell that these fast-drifting sorceries were coming not from the woman, who seemed to have somehow lost most of her clothing . . . but from the entrance to the House—or even from someone outside.

On her knees, the bare-shouldered sorceress moaned at the sight of them, tore free of the procurer, and gasped, "Keep away! I've no magic left to fight these, whatever they are!"

The radiances slowed, unfolded into coils of silvery thread—and veered to rush down at the sorceress.

Sarasper raced forward along the ceiling. Fell magic or not, he'd have no better chance to smite her!

He raced to just the right position, halted, and turned to launch himself—and of course, just then, she caught sight of him.

Fear shrieking inside him, Sarasper snarled and sprang, claws and jaws at the ready!

Those silvery tendrils of magic were converging on the sorceress as she frantically kicked off from the wall and tried to roll away from him. Sarasper landed just shy of her boots, the procurer flooding the passage with soft curses, and pounced.

No biting to slay, not yet. A leg across the mouth—must keep that jaw shut!—and two more to twine about her arms, to keep her from weaving spells. Then pin her by sitting on her, and turn to face the other two.

Just in time. With the sorceress held—and silently suffering whatever the drifting sorceries were now doing to her—the large man had drawn a fearsome warblade and was blindly hacking at . . . at nothing, thus far.

Three, but he could slice air! And he was seeking a foe, could probably smell the longfangs he couldn't see. When his blindness passed, Sarasper might have to abandon his sorceress or be cut to bloody ruin. The smaller man was watching uncertainly, drawn dagger in hand—and Sarasper hastily lifted a leg to shield his eyes.

The warrior mastered his rage—or at least his snarling stopped—and he thrust his head forward, as if listening. His slashes became more deliberate . . . and closer.

Which was when, of course, the sorceress tried to free herself, heaving and twisting under Sarasper.

He shrank back, dragging the woman with him, as that long sword slashed the air repeatedly, reaching farther and farther as the still-blind warrior advanced, step by cautious step.

The procurer suddenly sprang past Sarasper to roll under the larger man's feet, sweeping them up and sending the warrior crashing helplessly to the floor, blade clanging as it bounced free.

He found his feet slowly, shaking his head and cursing weakly as he peered blearily this way and that. Which meant that this particular longfangs would keep its hide whole until the warrior found his sword, unless the procurer . . .

The procurer was crouching warily not an arm's-reach away, and he was staring right into Sarasper's eyes.

"Sarasper?" he asked hesitantly. "Is that you?"

Gazes locked.

So this must be Craer Delnbone . . . after all these years. . . .

The sorceress twisted under Sarasper again, making a faint, wordless sound of pain—and the hulking warrior knuckled his eyes and stared at Sarasper, too.

Which left him no choice but to flee, or . . .

A longfangs is a powerful beast. As large as the largest of men—larger even than this lion of a warrior—and spider-like, but with the fur, jaws, head, and lean, rippling muscles of a wolf. Two of its spiderlike forelimbs sported little rending jaws, too. The others were barbed at the joints.

It takes courage to set aside such armor in the presence of those who can slay you—when one of them has been trying to slay you, and you've given the most powerful one good cause to try to harm you.

Courage, or hope to find a release from aching loneliness, or an inner whispering . . .

Sarasper let the longfangs form flow away from him slowly. The long, subtle fading was the most impressive sort of shape-shift, it left him one small secret, and it hurt and tired him the least.

He kept his eyes on the warrior watching him, and saw the man's face go from tense fear to surprise and then to something just shy of disgust, as he took his judgment of Sarasper's own form.

A thin, sad-eyed, elderly man, kneeling naked, on the back of the sorceress. Who wasn't wearing much more than he was—and who was now larger and stronger than he was. To say nothing of commanding sorcery that could rend him limb from limb as effortlessly as a longfangs did to humans.

The warrior espied his sword and swiftly retrieved it. Then he looked over at Craer. "You called him 'Sarasper.' *Who* is Sarasper?"

Sarasper hastily shuffled back off the sorceress, leaving her gasping on the floor. She managed to turn her head almost immediately and say, "Yes, Craer, introduce us. And when you've done that, I'd like my clothes!"

The procurer smiled and turned to where his sack lay fallen. "Friends," he said over his shoulder, "meet Sarasper Codelmer, one of my elder friends. I lost track of him years back, and only learned he was here not long ago, from another old friend."

"So it was Thalver who betrayed me, hey?" Sarasper growled bitterly and wearily, running a hand over his stubbled chin. The one man he'd chased out of the House rather than slaying, because they'd been sword-brothers. "Old Thundersword . . . no better than all the others." His voice was thick and grating from long disuse.

"He was dying on a Brightscar beach with three arrows through him," Craer said gently. "In the arms of a friend. Someone to spill his secrets to, and so find a little ease ere he died. Remember him not harshly."

"Hmmph," Sarasper replied gruffly, retreating along the

wall and trying to watch them all for any sign of a drawn blade or a swift spell-weaving. "How much did he tell you?"

"That you slew the real longfangs years ago, and have dwelt in the catacombs here ever since, hiding from men . . . as a bat, a ground snake, or as the man-eating longfangs of the Silent House."

And that had all been truth, all but the "longfangs" part, which must have been Thalver's embroidery. Sarasper had killed three longfangs in these halls, down the years, none of them shape-shifters. And devoured them all, of course. A man has to eat.

Even twisted-by-the-Three shape-shifting healers have to eat.

"Hiding from all men, or just my father?" the sorceress asked him through tangled hair, still prone on the uneven flagstones, but with her arms planted as if to heave herself upright.

"From all barons, lass," Sarasper told her curtly, trying not to look at the smooth curves of her bared body—and failing. It had been so long since he'd felt . . .

·  He looked away and asked the wall roughly, "And who would your father be?"

"Faerod Silvertree."

Rage and fear can start the change. . . .

Sarasper fought down the fur stirring along his prickling forearms as he glared at her. Embra Silvertree, the Lady of Jewels even Sirl wizards feared . . . almost as much as they feared her father's Dark Three.

"He sent you to find me, sorceress?" He gathered himself to pounce on her, ignoring the warrior's warning heft of that sword.

She shook her head, chin scraping the floor. "We three are fleeing his wrath and reach—or rather, that of his three mages."

Sarasper almost sighed in relief. Almost. She'd not been lying, but their sorcery could still work through her mind, leaving her not knowing she was uttering untruth. He backed a little farther away, until the wall greeted him again.

"So what of your spells, Lady of Jewels?" he asked sharply. He needed to know, and of course a sane sorceress would lie about what she could cast, but the *way* she lied might tell him something. . . .

"Gone in getting us here," Embra said simply, and turned her head to glare at Craer. "My *clothes?*"

The procurer gave her boots and a bundle, and then held up the sack they'd come out of before her, as a screen. It hid almost nothing, and she gave him a sour look as she sat up and started to draw on the wet breeches.

The three men watched her shiver as she struggled to get them over her hips, and the hulking warrior suddenly rose and strode to the candle-lamp. Setting it down close beside the sorceress, he stepped away to sit down against the wall with his sword across his knees, his eyes never once leaving Sarasper.

"So we've an old man with magic enough to take the shapes of three beasts, perhaps more," the warrior rumbled. "He hides in his most fearsome form, and eats folk raw when they come calling . . . why?"

"He's a healer," Embra realized aloud suddenly, whirling around with her tunic forgotten in her hands to look at the old man hunched against the wall.

Sarasper stiffened and stared into the shadows. His nod was so brief that they almost missed it. "Secrets, it seems," he told the ceiling above him with a sigh, "never last quite long enough."

"He can heal wounds?" the warrior asked. "With magic? *That* drives a man to eat human flesh for years?"

"Traditionally," the sorceress told her tunic flatly, as she shrugged it into place and tugged at its wet sleeves, "barons have kept healers as chained slaves, to heal on command. As the healing flows through such a one's body, it ages and wears out the flesh. A healer without the freedom to limit the use of his powers will probably die young . . . bent and broken like an old man."

Silence fell. The three companions stared at Sarasper.

"You were afraid of being captured by Baron Silvertree,"

the warrior said slowly, almost as if offering a greeting. Sarasper said nothing.

"And rightly so," Embra added into the silence, pulling on dry boots. She kicked at the flagstones to settle her feet inside them, got up, and walked to the old man.

Sarasper lifted his head to watch her, his face a weary mask.

"You hid behind the traps in the catacombs whenever my father's forces—or adventurers, seeking tomb-coins—came calling, and hunted outside these walls only at night . . . and only as a longfangs," the Lady of Jewels said slowly, reasoning aloud. Her thoughts brought her to a halt a few paces away from the old man.

Sarasper nodded again. "I've grown very tired of raw meat," he told her—and was shocked to find himself almost pleading. He *ached* to touch this woman. There was something stirring in him. . . . He gave her a look that was almost a challenge, the way he'd have measured a wench in his younger days—and then swiftly looked away.

Three Above, what's got *into* me? What whims are you playing on me, gods?

"Then stop hiding," Craer said urgently, "and live again! Once we rode together for Blackgult—remember, Sarasper? Now, we need healing; Hawk and the Lady both. She was as much the Baron's prisoner as any chained healer. Will you aid us . . . please?"

Sarasper looked at them all. "Hawk," was it? And the Lady of Jewels her father's prisoner? He had to stay with her, had to be with her. . . . What was making him feel this way? Something dark, stirring . . .

Something he was very afraid of. In his mind he looked away from it, whatever it was, and found himself staring at a Worldstone, blazing in his thoughts. As he so often found himself mindthralled, these days.

Sarasper fought his way free of the too-familiar vision of a Dwaerindim, turning slowly and endlessly in his mind's eye, and looked at the three intruders. So alive, just as desperate as he was . . . three sword-brothers. And those dangerous, uncomfortable days as a sword-brother had been the best days of his life.

"I will," he found himself saying, "but there'll be a price."

Not quite knowing how to tell them about blazing Dwaer-stones without being thought completely mad, he bought himself time by opening a hiding-place in the wall beside him that he'd found years ago, and drawing out the glow-stone hidden in it. He set it out on the floor and pinched out their candle-lamp with steady fingers.

"My price," he told the thread of drifting smoke gruffly, "is your aid in a matter that rides me day and night."

"A debt? A quest?" Craer demanded. "Something lost, that must be found?"

"Four things to be recovered," Sarasper told them shortly. "The quest may last longer than the life remaining to me."

"I don't know if I'm hurt that badly," Hawk rumbled, and looked at the pale, pain-lined face of the Lady Silvertree.

"I fear I am," she whispered, so softly that Sarasper barely heard. In a louder, calmer voice she added, "Say more of this quest, healer."

There was an old robe hidden behind a pivoting stone a little way along the wall, and without longfangs fur, Sarasper was getting cold. He got out the old, tattered thing, ignoring its stink of mildew, and said slowly, as if instructing younglings around a village fire, "The patron of all healers is Forefather Oak, mightiest of the Three, and betimes he speaks to we who heal by sending us visions in our dreams."

The warrior shrugged. "I often have dreams that blaze bright—or dark—enough to recall when I'm awake . . . most of them of blood, and battle, and friends gone down fighting. Does the Old One's face appear, or do you just do as most priests do, and sort out the dreams that are to your liking and deem them the ones sent you by the Forefather?"

The derision he'd expected. They needed him; he had to play on that.

Sarasper made himself stiffen, and then drew himself erect, as grandly as any baron, and said coldly and deliber-ately, "Were the Forefather to send you a vision, you'd know it and not speak so. With gold fire he laces about his scenes, and they burn forever, fading not. Trust me in this, sword-master, as I would trust you to correct me in weapon-work."

Hawk nodded, a trifle embarrassed, and waved his hand. "Say on."

Sarasper nodded. "Steep this price may be, but this quest gnaws at me." He gave them all a glare. "It should gnaw at all folk up and down the Silverflow. It should snarl and prowl at the hearts of every warrior and wizard in what was once Aglirta—and must be again!"

*Three defend me, I* do *sound like a madman.*

He was careful to speak gently again as he added, "It has worked on my thoughts these last few years, the visions coming again and again until I prowl these ways endlessly, never able to rest. The Worldstones must be recovered. The Dwaerindim must then be placed correctly to awaken the Sleeping King . . . who will rise, as the tales say, to restore peace and bounty to the land."

"Ah, horns and bebolt!" the warrior spat disgustedly. "That's but legend, a fancy-tale to make childrens' eyes bright! 'But find the Four Lost Stones, and the castles will rise, the mountains fall, and golden age come upon the land, and everyone will grow fat and happy on endless plenty, as the perilous beasts flee afar!' *Nursemaids* prattle suchlike!"

Embra Silvertree nodded. "My shelves back at the Castle still hold three tellings of the saga of the Dwaerindim that tutors read to me, until I could read the words for myself. Those books are *old*. If the Sleeping King ever existed, he'll be but bones and dust by now! Tell me, Sarasper: Just how would you tell, if you'd made some dust come awake?"

Sarasper growled wearily, "I'm neither mad nor minstrel-witted. I can tell you only that I speak of truth, not empty legend. I suppose you think the Serpent In The Shadows is just another pretty tale, too?"

"Some evil mage now worshipped by dabblers in poison and the like?" Hawk rumbled.

"A wizard—," Sarasper and the sorceress began, together, and then fell silent and regarded each other. Sarasper gestured like a courtier to Embra for her to say on. She gave him a narrow-eyed look, nodded, and said softly, "A wizard who had a hand in the enchanting of the Stones, but went mad, or was mad, and murdered several rival mages to strengthen the enchantments he was placing on a Dwaer. When his deeds were discovered, the other mages of the Shaping confronted him. He fled into serpent-form to try to fight his way free of their spells—and they imprisoned him in serpent-shape. He wears it still."

"He's still alive, too?" the warrior asked, his voice just as heavy with disbelief at her words as he'd been at Sarasper's.

So this great ox of a man was his true foe.

"Swordmaster," Sarasper asked, "is there *anything* in all Darsar you believe in, beyond that sword in your hand and the next meal heading for your belly? Or is it all coins and wenches, better armor and a good bed to sleep in?"

"Old man," Hawk replied, giving Sarasper a steady look, "*I* often think all Darsar would be a better world to dwell in if more folk concerned themselves with such things, and less about following gods and raising kingdoms and slaughtering their neighbors. Oh, yes—and dreaming clever dreams, too."

"Well, we've traded clever words," the old healer growled, looking around at one face after another, "and we know your need . . . and my price. You run from a known peril, and fear a known foe. I offer you a dream to follow, in years to come. A dream that shows us a road out of the death and tyranny that now rules what was once Aglirta, wherein outlaws and monsters outnumber farmers, and even honest folk outnumber those who are happy and bereft of fear."

He shrugged. "Perhaps you care nothing for a brighter future, or the land that birthed you. Perhaps you care only for the next meal, and a way clear of all this. If so, know that I can show you other ways out of this House—or devour you one by one, if you offer me violence. I should do so anyway, to keep my secret safe . . . but I've little heart for that, when there's a chance to follow the Forefather's will."

He shrugged again. "The choice remains to you. I cannot make it for you."

Then he let silence stretch.

Craer was the first to speak, looking quickly to the armaragor. "Hawk? I dragged you into this. . . ."

The warrior shrugged. "My will is to stand with you, little man, whatever road you choose. I think this man follows crazed dreams—but we all have to follow something, or drift to our graves having done nothing. Stay or go; you decide."

Craer shook his head. "I like none of our choices." Slowly, almost reluctantly, he looked to Embra Silvertree.

She gazed back at them all and then at the floor, saying nothing.

"Speak," Hawk rumbled, finally.

Her head snapped up, eyes flashing in anger, and gave him a long glare ere she said softly, "I find in myself no stomach for seeking revenge on my father and naught else. I know not if I dare ever use magic again, or what has befallen me, with the bindings broken." Her lips twisted, as if to curse, but then she continued almost calmly, "You dared to aid me, men of Blackgult. I think we should—must—all dare to aid this lonely man. I could not rest easy if we walked away and left him here alone, and I think we dare not fight him . . . nor would I take any pride in doing so, even if by some grace of the gods we defeated him. We cannot treat everyone we meet as a foe to be fought."

Yes! Oh, gods, *yes!*

Sarasper turned his back as quickly as he could, so they'd not see him weeping. He wasn't swift enough.

The warrior's voice from behind him held the false heartiness of embarrassment. "Well, if we're agreed, than we must be a band of adventurers, we four—and we'll have to choose a name, before bards hang something ridiculous on us. Anyone feel clever?"

"Always," Craer and Embra said together, in identically dry voices. Then, reluctantly—there was a stiffness, between the two men and the sorceress—they snorted in mirth, snorts that broke into chuckles, and then into laughter, Sarasper's tears becoming raw guffaws of sheer relief and ringing among them.

Laughter that died suddenly, as four trapped and desperate folk gazed at each other.

"We must be," Sarasper said swiftly, ere he lost the courage to say it at all, "until that cleverness smites us all with something better: the Band of Four."

"Let us be so," Craer responded, and then added mockingly, "Embra, start working on the ballad!"

"You'll be sorry," the sorceress purred in a voice that held both amusement and warning, "and that's *Lady* Embra to you."

The three men all made sounds of mockery, but when she reached out her hand, they slowly stretched forth theirs . . . to clasp hers in a common grasp.

Four fearful gazes met. No one cheered, but no one hastened to draw their hand back, either.

# 2

## Four, Glory, and Far Too Many Serpents

When Sarasper put his hands on the warrior Hawkril Anharu's ribs, the armaragor let out his breath in a long, shuddering sigh—a sigh that became a moan as the healing began, a warm stirring, and spread . . .

"Ohhh. Sargh, but it's good to be free of that!"

Sarasper kept at it, the energy flowing out of him. This man's usefulness lay in his strength, and his acceptance of an old man who could become a monster lay in all his pain leaving him now. . . .

Hawkril breathed a deep, shuddering gasp of relief, and asked, "So why is it that mages hurl lightnings and bring castles crashing down and walk away all nonchalant . . . and healers die if they heal too much?"

"Healing comes from within. The Three grant the gift to a rare few," Sarasper growled, not looking up. The weakness was coming so *fast*. . . .

He hoped they'd not notice how badly his hands were trembling. "Wizards take power from other enchantments to do their work."

"Oh? So who cast the first enchantment that a wizard drew on?"

"Ah," Craer put in, "now *that* question is one that sets priests at each others' throats, in proper earnest! They all claim it was their own of the Three . . . and there are even wizards who revere this or that elder mage for giving his life to fashion an enchantment that all other wizards could draw on." He looked challengingly along the wall from where he was sitting at the Lady of Jewels. "Do your books say anything different?"

"So many different things that I can believe none of them," Embra Silvertree replied—and sighed in utter exhaustion.

"When did you start to feel . . . worn out?" Craer's voice was sharp.

"Not long ago."

A few moments later, the procurer touched Sarasper's shoulder and pointed at the sorceress.

The healer looked along his old friend's finger. Embra sat slumped against the wall, her eyes closed. Sometime in the last few breaths, her face had become as lined as an old woman's.

Sarasper nodded slowly, trying not to show the eagerness that suddenly leaped inside him. Three Above, he wasn't going to lose control of himself when he touched her, and tear at her like a rutting beast, was he? That would bring Hawkril's sword into his back in short order, no doubt. . . .

He wrestled down that bloody image from his mind and managed to tell Craer, "I'm almost done here. The organs within were well torn, beyond the power of your potion, but this warrior is a right bear."

Sarasper glanced up at the armaragor and said gruffly, "Now just lie still, for once, until I'm done with the lady. The longer you lie quiet, the swifter the healing finds every last little ache."

Not waiting for a reply, he got up and crossed the chamber, stiff and unsteady as he fought down the inner darkness that was shrieking at him to pounce on her, hurl himself on her, tarry not an instant longer. . . .

In his stumbling haste, Sarasper slammed into the wall beside the sorceress. Grunting in pain, he swung down a trembling hand and laid the backs of his fingers against Embra Silvertree's cheek.

And the shrieking within him became a soaring trill of triumph as something that seemed almost feminine *rose* in his mind.

A great darkness lifted from his thoughts . . . no, not darkness, just a weight no mortal should have to bear, could bear without all the swirling shadows . . . that were fading now before the bright visions of the Worldstones.

All four of them, revolving slowly, each vision of one slightly different from the others. She'd left him these, in their bright glory.

Light swirled beyond them, reaching back in what was almost a caress, and a voice that would thrill him for the rest of his days said deep in his mind, *Sembril is grateful, loyal old Sarasper. Aglirta needs more like you. Three Above,* Darsar *needs more like you.*

Sarasper rose in rapturous brightness, and found himself back, blinking, in the Silent House, with the soft cheek of Embra Silvertree under his hand. Gods, *She* had gone into this young lass of a sorceress, now. . . .

Embra opened her eyes for just a moment, and then leaned her weight against his hand, seeming to fall into full slumber.

Sarasper frowned at what he felt as his awareness sank tentatively into her, half fearing he'd blunder into that glory—and it would not be so grateful this time.

No rapture brushed his mind, not even a whisper, but there were dark threads here that had nothing to do with Sembril. Lots of them.

"There are spells upon her," he told Craer and Hawkril, his awareness still sinking into Embra Silvertree's mind. "Her own—or some dark work of the Silvertree mages, I wonder?"

"All my magic is gone," Embra murmured against his hand. "These two broke the bindings set by my father's command, earlier this night. I know nothing of what these spells may be."

"Your father never ordered spells laid on you to keep you young, or . . . change your beauty?"

A faint smile touched her lips. "No," the Lady of Jewels told him, her eyes still closed. "All you see is mine own."

"They're the work of Silvertree's pet mages, no doubt," Hawkril growled.

Sarasper frowned. "Then I'll break them."

"You can do that?" the armaragor asked, rolling onto one elbow to get a better look. He was in time to see Embra's body jump once under Sarasper's hands, and then begin to shudder uncontrollably.

The sorceress arched her back. Her eyes opened to show only whites, and then closed again as she sagged into near-boneless limpness.

The armaragor could hear the chatter of her teeth as Sarasper put his arms around her—*Three, which of us is more hurt? My strength leaves me so fast! Will I have enough?*—and snarled, "Of course. Anyone can break a spell . . . if they know how. Unless the spell is on them." He was sweating now, and his skin felt cold. If he looked down, he knew, he'd see that it had gone dark.

"You mean," Hawkril asked slowly, "that anyone who learns enough can be a wizard?"

"Almost," Sarasper snapped, as the sorceress in his arms erupted into shuddering again, shaking him along the wall.

*Three grant me enough . . .*

*Let me not fail her, this young innocent, and Sembril who went into her, both. . . .*

"It requires more patience than most folk have," he almost spat at Hawkril, trembling in the grip of chilling weakness almost more than Embra was spasming in his failing grasp. "An iron will to hold to a purpose—and a certain ruthlessness. That's why most mages act so grand, or mysterious, or sinister. They want others to think only special folk can become wizards, so few will pester them to become their apprentices."

Sudden pain startled him into a grunt and some gasped curses as Embra's thrashings bumped one of his elbows solidly against the stone floor and broke his hold on her. Sarasper rolled away, too weak to even claw at her.

Embra twisted once on the flagstones, like a dog scratching its back on a mat, and then fell still, leaving him the only one shuddering.

Sarasper hugged himself in pain like many a wounded warrior huddled around a campfire after a battle, barely aware of anything around him now.

"Sarasper?" Hawkril rumbled, "Are you—?"

Somehow Sarasper managed to lift his head to snarl, "Fine. Never been better. Must get up and frolic!"

He coughed then, doubling over uncontrollably, and his coughs became retching, spitting . . . and then groaning. When at last—a very long time later, it seemed—his torment eased, Sarasper glared up at Craer and Hawkril. "Neither of you have the slightest idea how healers work, do you?"

He didn't wait for their replies, but turned to Embra. Her face was still and her eyes were closed, but her skin was the right hue, and *smelled* right. She was free of sorcery, well on her way to being wholly healed.

As tenderly as any father, he rolled her into a more restful position, gently tugged her tunic back into place where her convulsions had almost laid bare one shapely shoulder, and then sighed heavily and looked away.

"It seems harder than when she worked spells," Hawkril said reluctantly, waving a hand from her to Sarasper, to indicate that he meant the healing.

After a silent moment or two, the warrior asked, eagerness and a certain apprehension warring in his voice, "Could I cast spells like a wizard?"

Sarasper looked up at him, his hands on Embra's shoulders again. "Someday, perhaps, if the need was great enough. But you'll have to lose something first."

"Oh?"

"Aye. Your good sense. To be a wizard of any power, it helps a lot if you're crazed."

Hawkril made a disgusted sound, and growled sarcastically, "Thanks. I'll try to remember that."

Under the healer's hands, they heard Embra make a weak sound. It was a chuckle.


Far too short a time later, Sarasper Codelmer clawed his way along a wall of the Silent House as howling winds tugged and tore at his worn robes. Stones and dust hissed and cracked around him, and for a terrifying moment it seemed the sucking whirlpool of spellwinds was coming through the narrow doorway, after him!

"Graul, graul, *graul!*" he sobbed, clawing his way along the stones with bleeding fingers, heedless in his haste.

And then the fury of the spell-driven storm slammed the door shut behind him with such force that the walls around Sarasper shook . . . and there was sudden stillness.

Tiny stones clattered to the floor here and there, and he could still hear a deep booming and roaring, but a closed door now stood between him and the fury of whatever the Baron Silvertree's mages had sent after them.

Faerod Silvertree, who'd pay *anything* for a caged healer . . .

"Craer?" he called, cold fear rising. "Anyone?"

There was no reply.

He was alone again, his newfound friends swept away. His healing wasted . . . and worse. The Dark Three must have been spying with their spells to know where to send this storm. So now they knew who and where Sarasper Codelmer was, what he looked like—and all about his long-hidden power of healing.

They'd never stop coming after him now.

"Claws of the Dark One!" Sarasper hissed bitterly into the gloom around him as dust swirled and settled. After all these years of hiding and lurking, more beast than man . . .

his secret was out in a few frantic hours, and the doom he'd long dreaded was here.

Or would be. He should have torn out Embra Silvertree's throat when first she burst into the House. Fled with her head deep into the catacombs, and eaten it down to a bare, gnawed skull so there'd be no wits to spellcall back.

He shivered at that thought, his mind showing him her beauty again, and then snarled furiously, "The Baron's daughter—his *daughter!* Only heir, too, so *of course* he's reaching for her, and me too close. Too close. She could be after me and everything else here as weapons to wield against him, or even to take back to him as his dutiful daughter."

Sitting himself against the wall, he added bitterly, "Who's to say she isn't serving him as wife by now? Silvertrees will do *anything.* Or compelling her with his mages to come in here to catch me? If they're good, she may not even know it! Gods, *gods,* but you're stupid, Sarasper! One glimpse of a pretty face and—and all, and you're fawning and talking and even *healing* them all, bebolt it!"

With a despairing groan, he leaned against the wall and closed his eyes, shaking with weariness. He'd healed them, all right—and drained himself doing it like an utter fool-head. . . . Oh, Sarasper, how could you forget the lesson that shaped your whole *life?*

Too weary to weep, the old man sagged down the wall, and into oblivion.


Shattered bones shifted under her, and Embra slid helplessly back and down on them, shoulder-first into darkness. Well, at least she wasn't upside down struggling for breath as she'd been a few moments back, with the spellstorm howling and whirling above her.

As if that made things any better. All she'd done was amuse her father and pleased his three mages with some spell-practice. She could have just given Craer and Hawkril some gems and helped them back off the Isle as fast as they'd come. She should have asked them to make love to her—gods, how she ached for someone to just *hold* her, with love and not for cruel sport!—and then kill her, cheating her father out of his Living Castle by dismembering her and giving what was left to the river.

She should have killed herself years ago.

Not that she'd ever had the courage to do more than pick up a knife and watch herself tremble in the mirror as she thought about using it. Drenching her fine white rugs with bright blood, staring at the ceiling until everything went dark . . .

No. Three Above, no.

She was no adventurer. Gods above, she wasn't even a sorceress. And here she was in the haunted Silent House, dragging men to their deaths. Men whose hatred of her was held back only by their fear, though they knew her not.

Well, they knew she could hurl spells, and they knew she was a Silvertree. That was reason enough to hate and fear her, was it not? All Aglirta hated and feared Silvertrees, with good reason.

"I will *not* be like my father," she told the darkness around her fiercely. "I will not!"


Even the spells of great fell wizards can be eluded or fought.

Though it seemed like a long and hard time ago, it was not all that long later when the Band of Four stood together again, in a room of the Silent House not far to the south of where the spell-storm had separated and almost slain them.

They were plundering it of magic, to fuel Embra's spells so they'd have something to serve as both weapon and shield against the Dark Three . . . and on their road to find the lost Dwaer-stones, ahead.

Sarasper smiled wryly. After all these years in the House, he'd become a thief of magic, like so many he'd slain or watched die in the traps that were all around them. He—

"Just add them to the sack," Hawkril was rumbling,

swinging it off his shoulder. "If I can carry a dozen or so wet wizard's books, I can haul a few candlesticks, too."

Embra frowned at the faint smell of mildew from the books inside the sack, sighed, and held out a candlestick and a handful of bracelets to him.

Instead of taking them, the burly armaragor went pale and grabbed for his sword, gasping, "Claws of the Dark One!"

"What—?" the sorceress asked in puzzlement as Craer went into a crouch, a drawn dagger suddenly in his hand.

Sarasper turned to see what they were staring at, and Embra spun around, too—but not before snatching up another handful of bracelets.

All around the Band of Four, in a silently tightening ring, floated three dozen half-rotting, half-skeletal figures, their glittering eyes all fixed on her. Nightmares come out of nowhere, without a sound.

Embra surveyed them, hand on hip, as she slid the bracelets onto her forearm. "We've disturbed something, healer," she told Sarasper quietly, "but I see nothing here that can harm us."

"Some ghosts can harm, though, can't they?" Craer's voice wasn't quite steady.

"Yes," Embra replied, raising her bracelet-adorned arm almost defiantly. The ghosts seemed to fall back as she touched a finger to the enchanted bowl she'd thrust into her bodice earlier, and called on a tiny shard of its power to make sorcerous sparks and glows flicker up and down the bracelets. "I met one, once. My father's idea of strengthening my courage."

The ghosts drifted nearer.

"Need we stay?" Hawkril snapped.

"I think we'd best move," Craer said. "What if the Baron's wizards slip some sort of menace against us—a spell, a monster, or even one of them, in person—into this room amid all of . . . these?"

Sarasper nodded. "That's why we must make haste to leave." He looked at Embra and added darkly, "For the first time in years of lurking in this House with ghosts swirling

all around me until they seem old friends, I've begun to feel
as if someone—or something—is always watching us."


That feeling finally faded when they left the catacombs of
Silvertree House behind, days later, and began the long, long
trudge in the darkness that would take them to the sewers of
Adelnwater.

Walking steadily along behind Craer, Sarasper called up
one of his vivid memories of the Dwaerindim, and smiled
happily at its shining, slowly revolving fire.

His days ahead bid fair to be full of danger and discom-
fort, but at least he had friends to share it with, and felt *alive*
again, after far too many years of waiting alone in the
gloom.

Kept alive, through all those lonely seasons of hunting
and lurking, he saw now, by Sembril Silvertree within
him—surviving only because she needed a host to keep *her*
alive, as she waited for a suitable Silvertree to come within
reach so she could enter into that descendant, Embra Silvertree, and . . .

And do what?

Sudden fear brought Sarasper Codelmer to a halt, breath
catching, to turn and stare at the tall, graceful, dark-haired
sorceress coming up behind him in the endless passage.

Just what had he helped unleash on the world?

He should slay her now, he should. . . .

"Sarasper?" she asked, in a voice of soft concern, and
reached out a tentative hand as she stepped past him.

Embra's fingers halted before they quite touched him, but
her hip brushed his for an instant—and the vision of the
Worldstone blazed up in his mind so brightly that Sarasper
Codelmer stared into it, enthralled, and forgot all about
whatever it was that had alarmed him. He was left smiling
silently back at a somehow familiar smile that was fading
with the brilliance, back into his memory. . . .

The old healer looked back into the darkness, and passed

on that smile to Hawkril Anharu, who was the rearmost of the Four at that moment and glancing at him sharply.

At long last, he was leaving the Silent House. At long last, he could try to find the Dwaerindim, and deliver Aglirta—and himself—out of the long darkness.

The House was receding behind him like a dark cloak, familiar but worn too long and so become distasteful.

He was leaving it, heart high—but somehow, Sarasper Codelmer knew, he'd be back in its halls again. Someday. Somehow.

The merest shadow of the ghost of a smile faded, in the depths of his mind.


A season later, Horlbrant shouldered forward with his fellow armaragors, deeper into the haunted gloom of the Silent House. A deep, rumbling crash ahead had just made the stones beneath his boots and the walls around him shudder, and he didn't want to think about what might be able to cause such tumult. His own baron and others were stalking along with the knights, everyone hurrying with swords out, and—

"Blasphemy!" someone shouted up ahead, in a voice both cultured and furious.

Then a huge, high hall opened out before the hurrying armaragors, its floor heaped with rubble and its walls adorned with crumbling balconies already crowded with warriors and courtiers. It seemed as if all Aglirta—Three look down! Serpent-priests, too!—were gathering in this shattered chamber.

At its heart stood a man Horlbrant knew by sight: the Golden Griffon. The Baron Ezendor Blackgult stood over a handful of folk—a woman covered in blood, a half-naked giant of a man similarly adorned, and someone smaller, half-hidden behind them. A fourth man—an old man, stark naked but for a little blood here and there—hung motionless in the air, frozen in midleap. By his pose, he'd been trying to reach Blackgult—for no friendly purpose.

The Golden Griffon's dark armor looked battered, but on his face was the look of a wolf who enjoys bloodshed—and in his hands were three stones that glowed like newborn stars. The mutters of his fellow armaragors around him told Horlbrant that they, too, were gazing on more powerful sorcery than they'd ever seen before.

Blackgult gazed around at all the grim men and said calmly, "As Aglirta seems to be gathering in earnest for the first time in my memory, let us have more room." The three glowing stones—the Dwaerindim, they must be!—flashed in unison and rose up around him in sinuous arcs—and all the rubble rose up from the floor of the room in a swift storm of corpses and broken stones and woody shards, to fly into one corner and there settle again into a great dust-whirling heap.

Into the awed silence, the Baron Maerlin spat, "You as Regent? Blackgult, your villainy is the reason we *need* a Regent! What makes you better than me? Why not Maerlin as Regent?"

"Maerlin! Maerlin!" echoed the armaragors standing behind him.

"Silence!" another baron roared. "I see no need for the great hurry in naming a Regent that you, Blackgult the Skulker, seem to feel—or you, Maerlin the Grasping! Let there—"

Someone threw a dagger, high over the heads of the crowd—and it flashed past a noble ear and sliced open the chin of the armaragor standing behind that baron.

The room erupted into wild, shouting battle. Swords clanged like swift, furious forge-work, men shouted—and everyone was punching, thrusting, hacking, shoving . . . or dying. The air filled with hurled daggers, swords, and even stones. Horlbrant ducked down, raising his sword and dagger wardingly around him, and tried to see what those Serpent-priests were doing, or if there were any wizards readying sorceries.

He saw none of the latter, but the Serpents seemed to be hastening out to the walls, using their magics only to shield themselves in the bloody fray. The floating old man descended from view behind all the whirling, slashing warriors, and then Horlbrant was too busy keeping himself alive to notice much of anything beyond where the next sword blade was coming from, and how best to hew down whoever was wielding it.

"*Nothing* ever turns out quite the way you think it will," a baron snarled disgustedly in the fray nearby. "For which much thanks to the bloody Three!" And then that baron screamed in pain.

Men were screaming and falling all around Horlbrant, now, and he caught glimpses of warriors who had eyes but no faces, just smooth masks of flesh, fighting skillfully in pairs or groups. They seemed to be striking at specific foes, but Horlbrant whirled away from them towards the door he'd come in by, not liking anything about them, and not wanting to die.

More armored warriors were pushing in through that door now—men whose flesh dripped from their jawbones, frozen in grotesquerie. The Melted!

Among them strode a burly robed mage with hair the hue of dirty straw and eyes like gray ice, snapping incantations and orders. This must be Corloun, Court Mage of Maerlin.

Even as Horlbrant shrank aside, trying not to be noticed, Corloun glared across the chamber, smiled triumphantly, and said, "Men of my making—to yon woman!"

And the Melted drove right past Horlbrant in a great armored wedge, fearlessly obedient, hacking and thrusting. They slew a dozen men, more, and then slowed against a determined stand by armaragors of Maerlin—whereupon several of the Melted burst apart, in blasts of flying bone that felled the men grappling and fencing with them. Mindlessly they moved on.

That seemed to unleash the Serpents and hitherto-hidden mages everywhere, and the room erupted with crawling, stabbing sorceries. Chants and snarled incantations could be heard on all sides, and Horlbrant cowered down under a dying Maerlin cortahar and let the man sag floorwards with him, hoping to escape the ravening fires that would soon be leaping across the slaughter.

Bursts of fire blossomed overhead and spun along the walls, tumbling down blazing men and the balconies they'd been standing on—but from under his gasping, dying shield of meat, a peering Horlbrant was more frightened of the darting fang-spells sent by the Serpent-priests: shimmering snakes of force that flew here and there in the fray, melting away living flesh with every bite they took.

Luckily, it seemed that the Melted—and Corloun their master—were the victims sought by the Serpents. Although the shuffling dead men didn't fall until enough of their rotting meat was gone that exposed bones collapsed under the weight of their remaining flesh, Corloun flung them up all around himself in a wall, putting his own safety first, and the flying fangs ate them at will. The Melted swiftly dwindled to a small, embattled ring—which was when a great fresh force of armaragors wearing the arms of Adeln streamed in through the door Horlbrant had been seeking, and started to carve their own bloody way forward into the fray.

The floor around Horlbrant was wet and slick with blood now, and the dead lay heaped and strewn everywhere, so that those still fighting were wading and stumbling—leaving cortahars helpless to avoid being impaled on blades, and wizards with nowhere to flee the desperate blades of those trying to fell them.

Through it all, the armaragors of Adeln, an armored giant of a man at their fore, drove across the room like a great spear, heading straight for Baron Blackgult. A small, slender man crouching beside Blackgult hurled daggers at the slowly striding Adelnan titan, who struck them aside . . . and then the half-naked giant of a man standing with the Golden Griffon stepped forward to confront the champion of Adeln, a long and heavy warsword in his hand.

Before he got there, lightning cracked forth from the Golden Griffon—or no, from the woman at his feet—to snarl briefly around the Adelnan . . . only to lash back at its source, who screamed, tiny lightnings bursting from her eyes, nose, and mouth for an instant before Blackgult did something with one of the Dwaer-stones that healed her. The

Adelnan must be wearing enchanted armor, or some other shielding magic.

The half-naked man and the larger armored Adelnan crashed together, spike-headed ax locking against the warsword, and the two men shoved at each other, snarling shoulder to shoulder, ere their shared whirlwind of hacking and punching began.

Other Adelnans crowded forward to encircle the two men, reaching out with their blades to stab and hamstring the half-naked man, but the sorceress hurled fire at them, and Blackgult used the Dwaer to make it a purple ring of man-high, roaring flames that widened from around the two straining champions to thrust men back nigh the walls—where its heat melted stones and daggers hurled through it. Men soon stopped trying, and a stillness of sorts fell upon the room as everyone watched the two big men battle.

Sword strained against ax, the weapons sawing slowly back and forth with a shriek of tortured steel as the men pitted their now-trembling thews against each other—and one of the barbs on the Adelnan ax broke, causing the warsword to slip and the two men to reel apart.

A roar went up from the Adelnans. Their champion was encased in heavy battle armor, but his foe was clad only in hair, sweat, and now a line of blood, where an ax-barb had opened a long cut along one forearm.

The champion of Adeln stalked forward menacingly, then kicked one boot heel against the floor, took two running steps, and lashed out with that foot as the toe-blade he'd just unleashed sprang forth.

Horlbrant saw the sickly smear of poison on it, in the instant before both men rushed together. The Adelnan would need only the smallest of slices. . . .

But the half-naked man moved like a striking snake, avoiding the toe-steel and crumpling the gorget of the champion of Adeln with a solid punch that could be felt by many of the watching men, even through the shimmering flames.

Gargling and strangling, the Adelnan toppled over backwards, fighting for air. Which was when a Sirl wizard standing almost on top of Horlbrant murmured the incant of a swift spell, and the armor worn by the titan of Adeln winked bright radiance—and exploded with a roar, shredding its wearer and hurling shards of battle-steel in all directions.

Men howled as jagged shards of metal spun through the flames and bit into flesh all over the chamber, singing and skirling off armor, evoking screams—and, as the sorceress reeled and fell, with a cry of her own—banishing the ring of fire.

With a roar, the warriors of Adeln charged forward, trampling Horlbrant and many of the dead and dying around him in their hunger to get at Blackgult.

The Golden Griffon plucked one of the whirling Dwaer-stones out of the air and stowed it as he strode to meet them, snatching the other two a pace later and causing them to create sword blades of glowing magic as he came. They left trails of sparks and snarling fire in their wake as he slashed the air like any master swordsman showing his prowess—and whenever a charging Adelnan or his blade met those radiances, they were hurled back.

The half-naked warrior who'd defeated the Adelnan champion sprang to flank Blackgult, and the procurer took up a stance on his other hand, still hurling daggers. Several found Adelnan throats or eyes as Horlbrant watched, and other warriors, freed of the ring of fire, struck at each other once more all over the chamber.

And then armaragors of Adeln started to reel, curse, and fall all around Horlbrant, causing him to squirm and crawl his way free of the worst of the weight of bodies, and wonder who—or what—was slaying them. Something striking from behind, once more. . . . the Melted! The few staggering dead men were carving up Adelnans again, and—

Horlbrant cursed and scrambled along the floor, moments before a rusting blade would have bitten into his neck. He kept on rolling, away from the reaching swords of the mindless melt-faced men, forward into the close-packed ranks of the Adelnan armaragors, who were frantically trying to hack down Blackgult and his handful of companions so as to get away from the Melted, but failing.

Horlbrant kicked and crawled and swatted aside legs for all he was worth, thrashing his way forward through a rain of blood. Many of the men above him had already been slain, but were too closely wedged together, armor plates caught on the armor of those pressed against them, to fall.

He found himself climbing up a body that had fallen—just in time to duck his head, set his teeth, and take the full crashing weight of a just-slain Adelnan who tumbled down his back to the floor. He risked a glance up, just to be sure no other man of Adeln was furiously stabbing down at his unfamiliar face, and saw instead a kicking, twisting Adelnan warrior snatched up off his feet by the two hairy arms of the half-naked warrior. Shouting, the man waved his sword vainly—and was hurled away, over to Horlbrant's left and out of sight, where he landed on the floor tiles with a loud, shivering crack.

Men roared in rage and fear at that sound—and then fell into stunned silence. Horlbrant looked up as he struggled to find his feet . . . and joined in the mute amazement.

In the air above the half-naked man, a figure of glowing white light was slowly brightening into view: the ghostly image of the Risen King.

There were murmurs, and men started to push forward—but silence and stillness fell again when the voice of the King resounded in every head: "Blackgult, open your mind to me!"

"Of course, Majesty," the Golden Griffon replied, ere silence fell again—and Horlbrant lost his balance amid the limp, blood-drenched bodies and fell forward, sliding helplessly down them into the forest of Adelnan legs. He hastily closed his eyes and feigned death to avoid being hacked by those above him.

Someone kicked him aside, someone else trod on him and cursed, and he slid into a pool of blood, drifting greasily into contact with a soft limb that bore no armor.

The sorceress made a soft sound of pain at his arrival, and moved, pulling herself away from him. She slipped, and planted a firm, long-fingered hand on his shoulder to push herself free . . . and blood—her blood—brushed Horlbrant's cheek.

Whereupon something whispered within him, faint and yet swift and furious, rising swiftly to an almost deafening chant whose words he could not understand.

"I—," Blackgult whispered, through the whispering din, "I am loyal."

And then the whispers swirled up to take hold of Horlbrant, and memories not his own flowered like nightmare visions in his mind. The last thing he heard, as the whispers dragged him down—*if anything befalls Embra, you shall be the one, you shall be the one, you shall be the one*—was the voice of the Risen King echoing through the chamber: "He speaks truth! Arise, Blackgult, as Regent of Aglirta!"


The smooth, long-limbed body beside his arched suddenly and flung out an arm as tense and firm as an iron bar onto the pillows. Hawkril Anharu came awake in an instant, straining to hear any sounds of intruders or things falling or . . . or magic.

Lady Baron Embra Silvertree lay bare and glistening in the moonlight that was flooding through the high, arched window, her beauty as wet as if she'd been oiled. Hawkril ran one large and hairy hand down her thigh. Sweat.

His touch made her flinch, and then she gasped suddenly, and came awake.

"H-Hawk?" she whispered, as his arms went around her.

"Me," he confirmed, holding her. "What's wrong? Are you . . . ill?"

"I—Tongue of the Lady, I'm *drenched*. I . . . I don't think so." Embra moved in his arms, seeking to sit up, so Hawkril let go of her.

When the Lady Overduke of Aglirta was sitting on the

bed, hair cascading around her, she fell silent again, staring intently off across the room until Hawkril was moved to peer in the same direction. The wardrobe, the looking glass with her gown draped across it just as she usually left it . . . nothing of especial interest.

"Embra," he rumbled. "Embra?"

She went on silently staring at nothing, so he thrust one of his hands under her nearest knee and pinched whatever he could reach in the softness beyond.

She flinched again, gave him a playful swat, and said, "My apologies, Hawk. I—I keep seeing the Silent House . . . its rooms, its smells, us walking through it together—the memories are very . . . vivid."

"Just now? Of a sudden, out of nowhere, or—?"

"These . . . last dozen or so days, I suppose, at odd moments when we were awake and about, but more and more each night. I think I spent all last night in dream-thrall—remember I told you how tired I was, like I hadn't slept, but didn't know why?—stalking through the House in my dreams. Going from room to room, roaming as if restless, not as if I was going to uncover a lurking someone, or a something . . . just now, I was doing it again, but there was a sense of . . . alarm. As if something's not right, something it can't show me but wants me to know about. But what?"

"And why?" Hawkril asked.

They stared at each other in the cool moonlight for a few breaths, until Hawkril said quietly, "If you'd like to throw on some clothes, I can fetch our boots and blades, and we can go there now, if 'twill set your mind at ease. Bloodblade is dead, the Serpents sent down—*again*—and Raulin will be fine on his throne for the next few days at least."

"No, Hawk," she whispered, after a moment. "Just—hold me."

Then she put out a finger to touch his lips and added, "I'm casting a spell on you. When you get back to sleep, you'll be in my mind. We'll share the same dream."

"That might be fun," the armaragor rumbled, "but why, exactly?"

"I want you to do something for me," Embra whispered.

"Aye?"

"See if whatever's not right is . . . in my mind."

# 3

## Seedings and Flowerings

*L*ate in a certain evening years later, all was not well in Silvertree House.

The Serpents whirled around and hastened back when the crash came, but needn't have been in any hurry. The stone block was the size of a small coach, and five times their number couldn't have lifted it.

Its fall had crushed and split flagstones—and buried it deep in the floor. Leaving only red smudges, two feet, and a vainly outflung hand around it, to mark where the last man of their rearguard had been standing.

Sarthen glanced around nervously. "Perhaps it would be best if we turned back."

"No, Holy One, it would *not*," one of the guards said firmly.

Sarthen recoiled as if the man had slapped him, and snarled, "Do you forget who I *am*, worm? Do you know the penalty in the Church of the Serpent for such insolent breach of rank?"

He raised a hand, palm outwards—and it erupted in a small forest of flesh-hued serpents, looking like so many angry earthworms. Their tiny jaws snapped as they drew themselves back and struck at the empty air, again and again.

"Kiss my palm," the Priest of the Serpent ordered, "or renounce our faith right now." And a lazy wave of his other hand made a dozen stone-faced Serpent-guards raise loaded and ready crossbows meaningfully. "When we follow the Scaly Way, we live—or die—together."

"Precisely," the guard snapped. "And we do this obeying orders from above, Sarthen—orders given in authority that flows ultimately from the Great Serpent himself. *You* were ordered to plunder the Silent House and bring back something useful to the Church, not turn and run the moment you lost a man. Brethren of the Serpent have known that there were traps in Silvertree House—and strong magic, and monsters, too—for over a thousand years. Losses were to be expected."

"So you persist in trying to tell me my business?" Sarthen hissed, paling with anger. *"Kiss my palm!"*

"No, Sarthen, you kiss the toe of my boot. *Now.* I'm not accustomed to hearing disobedience from mere Priests of the Serpent, in large matters or small."

"M-mere?" Sarthen was almost choking in anger. "Are you *mad,* worm?" Without waiting for a reply, he turned and signaled to the guards with bows, the wave of his hand as savage as it was florid.

Bows twanged, quarrels flew—and whirled in the air, veering past the lone guard and around in a great arc in the gloomy chamber to speed back at the gathered Serpents. Where they stabbed home, all dozen of them, slamming into Sarthen's chest with a collective force that should have torn the man asunder, or hurled him down the room, or both.

Instead, body shaking and shuddering, he kept to his feet, eyes bulging and blood fountaining from his mouth, chest too shattered to even draw breath. Ever again. Only sorcery was keeping him upright . . . and alive.

"Just stand there and enjoy the pain, Sarthen," the lone guard directed, tearing off his helm and casting it to the floor. "I want you to live long enough to suffer. And to know how little the Church thought of your backbone and your loyalty." He drew himself up and added, "Had we expected better of you, I'd not have had to lay aside my own important tasks and duties to serve as your nursemaid."

Several of his fellow guards had started towards the helm-less guard uncertainly, drawn swords in their hands. He regarded them coldly.

"Unless you want to share Sarthen's fate, you'd do well to leave off menacing me, loyal snake-brothers. Masterpriests of the Church aren't accustomed to accommodating defiance from underlings."

The Fangbrothers standing with the rest of the guards swallowed visibly. "M-may we know your name, Lord Masterpriest?" one of them asked tremulously.

"Lulkoun," was the curt reply, a word that made several of the guards gasp, and one of the Fangbrothers moan aloud. Masterpriest Lulkoun was the Scourge of the Serpent, the punisher of small carelessnesses and treacheries among the faithful—and his cold lack of any shred of mercy was legendary throughout the Church of the Serpent.

If the reaction to his identity pleased him, the Scourge did not show it. He lifted a hand to indicate the surrounding gloom and said flatly, "We came here for a purpose. Let's be about it. Caution in our advance is only prudent, and I may in good time give the order to retreat out of Silvertree House—but only after we've seized magic of value, or suffered so many losses that I doubt our remaining strength can accomplish anything of value, or survive to reach Aglirta outside these walls again. I *do* have to make a report."

He looked from face to face of his fellow Serpents measuringly, and added, "Some of you were chosen for this task because you entered the Silent House in the past, however fleetingly, and got out again. Faithful Dreelar, Faithful Ansur, Faithful Thabras, Fangbrother Rhanglan . . . Have I missed anyone?"

There was an uneasy silence, and Lulkoun nodded a little impatiently. "Kelgrael Snowsar hadn't arisen at the time of your earlier forays; do any of you four sense or notice anything different—however small, mere impressions are welcome—about the House around us, this time? Ansur?"

"N-no, Lord. Only . . ."

"Speak freely."

"Ah—uh—last time I felt *watched,* Lord. All the time. Not now."

The others nodded, and Fangbrother Rhanglan blurted, "I don't think the House is growing, Lord Masterpriest. It seems . . . well, not lifeless, but as if the Curse is gone."

All three of the veteran guards nodded. "No *whispering,*" Dreelar put in.

"No scores of maedra boiling out of the stones every pace you take," Thabras added feelingly.

Masterpriest Lulkoun nodded. "All of which leads to greater expectations of success for us, yes?"

No one dared to venture a reply, and he didn't wait for one longer than it took him to glance meaningfully at the trembling, silently screaming body of Sarthen. "*My* superiors, the Lords of the Serpent, urgently expect us to bring back useful battle-magic. Whatever it is that can command maedra, or these gliding shadows—or even one of the fabled Dwaer-stones; the tale of one of them lying hidden somewhere in the Silent House may be pure fancy, but it's been believed in Sirlptar for a very long time. So, fellow men of the Serpent, let's be about our duty."

He pointed at the mouth of the passage they'd been proceeding along when the fall of the stone block had slain poor Nammas, and waved his fellow Serpents forward.

Their route forced them to pass the quivering figure of Sarthen, who'd thought himself in command of this plundering band. They darted glances at him as they ducked past, as swiftly as they could. The face of a man frozen on the threshold of death, caught in roiling agony, is not a sight cherished in memory when one goes on into darkness and danger.

They passed through two more chambers before two stone pillars toppled from the walls like a pair of hammers, and slew the next man.

"Then you'll have broken our partnership, lad," Old Horl said wearily, "and I'll leave you to find your own way out of the Silent House—if you can."

Dlan frowned. "You've let me take all this magic, these coins, the gems . . . but you want this one pretty little thing." He shook it, so that the fingers rattled, and added softly, "Which tells me it must be worth a *lot*."

"Lad, you're not in much of a position to bargain," the older treasure-hunter said heavily. "You—"

"Could be handing my last shred of usefulness to you, if I give you this," Dlanazar snarled suspiciously. "And one thing more, old man: stop calling me 'lad'!"

"Right then, *young fool*," Horl said coldly. "You are very much that, or you'd know that the one thing procurers dare not do is betray their few professional contacts, whom they must work with—or suffer betrayal themselves, and death under torment. *Give me the hand*."

"No," Dlan sneered, giving Horl a cruel smile. "You can lurch and stagger after me for it!" And he turned and ran back down the passage.

Horl threw something, as hard as he could—something small and misshapen, a knot of cloth that flashed by Dlanazar's head. Hah! The old fool couldn't even throw straight! Why—

Horl's missile struck the floor ahead of him, and burst, spewing forth its contents by the bouncing, gleaming, rolling dozens: glass beads!

Dlan tried to swerve in his headlong sprint, but there was nowhere to dodge to, and they were under his racing feet, now. He slipped once, twice—caught himself, and then slammed into the wall, rolled along it wildly, caught his footing again, and ran on, laughing in relief.

Whereupon something very hard struck him in the back of his head, lifting him clear of the floor. He had a brief memory of landing, very hard, bouncing to crack both of his elbows shatteringly hard on the flagstones, but not his head. . . . Three defend him! But no, it was too late for that. . . .

When he could focus again, a glowstone covered in his own blood was being held over him, and the copper hand was being dragged from his grasp.

He kicked out, hard, and was rewarded by a gasp and the

sudden absence of Horl's tugging at him. Three, but his head hurt!

A roaring and bubbling built in his ears like Sirl surf as Dlanazar Duncastle fumbled out one of his daggers—but Horl was there again, drawing back his arm to punch viciously at Dlan's crotch.

Dlan blocked those blows with his own arms, letting go the dagger-hilt—and Horl's not-so-useless left hand came at him like a plunging arrow, slamming hard into Dlan's throat.

All air went away, and Dlan tried to scream but couldn't manage more than a feeble whistle. Gargling and choking, he writhed, clutching at the crushed ruin beneath his chin, the world starting to go dark. . . .

A hard knee landed on his chest, and another one rammed home in his crotch . . . and Dlan ran out of ways to twist and writhe in helpless agony.

Horl ripped the hand out of Dlan's failing fingers, grasped it by its handle, and lifted it up, shaking it gently.

It started to glow, and the fingers moved as if it were alive. Horl watched them, doing something Dlan couldn't see to the back of the hand, and nodding as if in satisfaction as the fingers moved and curled this way and that.

"As I told you earlier, young fool, I'm dying. Just one more old man robbed of his health and swiftness and agility by the passing years. Which is where Thaulon's toy, here—and you—come to my aid. See these little finger-fangs? They drink life . . . and they're going to drink yours, right into me. I'll be young and strong again . . . and Sirl will have one less ruthless, thoughtless young thief to chase."

Horl made the hand spread its fingers, and brought them down towards Dlan's horrified, pain-twisted face. "A good grave awaits," he said softly. "You rude, utterly selfish young man."

Which was when a third face suddenly appeared, in the air between theirs—just a face, floating without head or body behind it, like a dark mist, its eyes fixed accusingly on Horl. Dlan had a glimpse of its sad old male visage before Horl recoiled with a curse of fear and slashed at the apparition with the copper hand.

Those fanged fingers sliced through the swirling mist, back and forth, frantically, as Horl snarled in fear and shrank back from the face . . . which advanced, quite unaffected.

And with every slash of those fanged copper fingers, Old Horl grew slightly grayer, and less solid . . . fading into mist.

The hand glowed more brightly, like an awakened star rising out of the thickening mist.

"So it seems it's *your* life that's stolen away," the floating face said, in a voice of sad, quiet doom. Remember, Horlbrant: nothing ever turns out quite the way you think it will."

"No," Horl gasped roughly, his voice a faint echo. "No." His eyes were fixed beseechingly on the floating face as he shook and waved his fading hands, trying to wave away the copper hand.

Glowing merrily, it hung in the air, unmoving. Dlan stared up at it in mute, frozen terror as Horl faded a little more, and gasped, as if from a great distance, "W-who are you?"

"I was called Sarasper Codelmer, when I lived. Just as you were Horlbrant Silvertree. The Curse got into you through Embra's blood, I see . . . gaining itself a second sword, should she fall. Well, Horl, we seem to have both found death handily enough."

But there was no reply, and nothing left of Old Horl but drifting mist. As Dlan watched, it began to stream to each finger of the copper hand, and vanish therein, racing and roiling into . . . oblivion?

"A prison within a prison," the shadow that was Sarasper mused aloud, watching the last wraith-mists fade. "Just another Silvertree, in too much of a hurry to seize power or wield it against the problems of today to study or consider consequences or take the long view . . . so once again, things got, ahem, out of hand."

He regarded the copper hand, which was twinkling very brightly now, and sighed.

"Rather like," he added, his sad eyes turning to regard the room all around him, "this place."

And then he gave Dlanazar a long, cold glance, and started to fade away.

The raw-throated thief discovered he could still breathe, though he dared not try to talk, or for that matter start to hope that he could speak, ever again, and though pain ruled him, all over, he thought his legs would obey him. His arms might be broken—one of them, the left one, dangled uselessly from where the bones of his elbow thrust out through his leathers— but he could still run. . . .

When the floating face was quite gone, Dlanazar rolled over. His arms shrieked pain at him and his head pounded, but somehow he fought his way to his knees.

The room reeled when he made it to his feet, and he almost fell again, but frantically sidestepped, planted his boots wide, and stayed upright, swaying and panting until he'd mastered his pain. The copper hand glowed right in front of him, just above his left knee, and—with sudden, leaping satisfaction— he reached down with his right hand and gathered it awkwardly against his chest.

He'd need healing, and if he could find some sleeping shepherd and take *his* life, then he could banish this cursed pain and have his arms back, and all, and . . .

"No!" The floating face was right in front of his eyes again, bursting out of empty air. *"Drop it!"*

Dlanazar shrieked in fear, and then whirled around in rage and terror and started to run.

"No!" he cried, his wild voice echoing wildly off the stone vaulting overhead. "No! I'm through with being told what to do by all the world! The Three smile on *me,* and—"

A flagstone with an unnoticed arrow on it sank just a trifle under Dlan's rushing boots—and a blade as tall as he was burst up out of the floor, right up into him.

"—gather you to them, forthwith," Sarasper murmured, watching the copper hand tumble to the floor as the mewing, dying Dlanazar Duncastle, impaled upright on the sword-thrust trap, stared pleadingly at him. "Where I'm sure they'll swiftly grow tired of your ceaseless complaints and demands and 'me first' airs. What a waste."

Sarasper drifted back down the passage, fading into mist once more, his thoughts again full of the rich dark earth of Flowfoam, that had been packed so gently around his bones. "So much waste . . ."

Lulkoun stood calmly and bleakly watching the bloody blocks of stone withdraw back to their former positions on creaking, rattling chains as thick as a man's arm . . . chains that—Holy Fangs Forfend!—bore fresh oil. When they stood as before, he folded his arms across his chest and ordered, "Fangbrother Rhanglan, test to see if this trap springs every time the passage is traversed."

The Fangbrother turned the hue of old Telnan cheese, stared wildly about as if seeking a way to flee from this place, and then swallowed and said briskly, "*Yes,* Lord Masterpriest."

Rhanglan took a few uncertain steps back the way they'd come, into the mouth of the last room, and nodded at something he saw there. He hissed a swift spell, and then turned back to face his fellow Serpents, one hand raised as if pulling an unseen leash.

And a heavy fallen ceiling-block drifted behind him like a reluctantly dragged dog, bumping and scraping along the flagstones every few feet.

Fangbrother Rhanglan came to a halt and lifted both of his hands, as if giving wagging-finger directions to his animated rock. Its bumpings became more measured and rhythmic, as if it were walking . . . like the footfalls of a walking man.

Between the toppling stones the rock thumped. They remained immobile, only the fresh blood on them confirming that they'd ever moved at all.

Rhanglan's large stone block bumped back between them again, losing tiny fragments of itself at its every thump. The pillars stood immobile.

He glanced at Lord Masterpriest Lulkoun—and found the cold eyes of his superior just waiting to stare into his. They were black pools, dragging him. . . .

He shivered and reared back his head from them, as if pulling out of a trap.

The trap still stood silent. Unmoved. He looked again at Lulkoun's steady glare, and shivered. The other Serpents stood like statues, also watching.

Rhanglan sighed, turned his back on them all, and cast a lofting spell on himself.

Then he turned, ran down the passage, and bounded into the air, closing his eyes as he flashed between the two pillars.

When three breaths had passed, he brought himself swiftly to a halt—before he flew straight into the *next* waiting death, whatever it was—and came back down the passage. Lulkoun's eyes were upon him, and under their cold, steady weight Rhanglan prayed silently to the Supreme Serpent . . . and glided slowly between the pillars.

They stood as immobile as all stones should be, and from the rest of the Serpents a tentative, rather unsteady cheer arose. It ended in an instant as Lulkoun lifted his hand sharply—and said silkily into the silence, "Rhanglan's usefulness to us all is once again proved. Fangbrother Murskar, raise a shielding curved into the shape of a great arch—and keep it above each of us as we pass between the hammers."

He turned his head to regard the rest of the Serpents, and said simply, "You will make haste between the pillars, and go at least four paces beyond the place of their falling, so that everyone can get clear of them. You will not proceed farther without my command."

Murskar cast his shield spell, held it above each Serpent in turn, and all of them passed between the pillars without incident. When they were all past the trap, Lulkoun lined them all up along one wall of the passage with a silent wave of his arm and announced, "Fangbrother Murskar will now keep his shielding above the foremost man in line—who will be Faithful Brother Penstarn."

The guard named by the Lord Masterpriest turned as white as a cloud in a blue high-noon sky, and very slowly stepped forth out of the line of silent Serpents and went along them to the fore. As he passed a group of his fellow

Faithful Brothers, they heard him whisper, "He knows all of our names. Oh, Serpent, we are all doomed!"

"Weapons ready?" Lulkoun asked briskly. "Right, then—proceed."

They shuffled on, the Silent House dark and quiet all around them . . . and waiting ahead of them.

The passage opened out into another room that stretched away to the east until its far reaches passed beyond the reach their magical radiances. "Keep to our file," Lulkoun commanded sharply as the guards started to move apart to give themselves weapon-room. There was a hasty shuffling back into line. "Fangbrother Rhanglan," the Masterpriest added, "send light yonder."

The Fangbrother nodded, took a pace forward so as to have room for his arms to weave the spell—and the floor gave way under his boots, plunging him down a shaft so deep that his screams faded greatly before the silently swallowing Serpents heard, very faintly, the thump of Rhanglan's body landing on spears of stone, and the bones shattering.

A Faithful Brother whimpered, turned, and raced back the way they'd come. Lulkoun gestured to Murskar, who brought his shield down like a wall, and the guard fled right into it, striking his head against the unseen barrier.

In silence the Serpents watched the man slide down the invisible shield, stunned.

"In the words of Priest of the Serpent Sarthen," Lulkoun announced calmly, "when we follow the Scaly Way, we live—or die—together."

The Serpents stood like statues until he commanded, "Assist Faithful Brother Alansen to his feet, and return him to his place in line. I believe you know as well as I do that with the boy Raulin just crowned, barons and all returning to their own lands and holds to rebuild, this is our very best chance to reap what we can from Silvertree House without being noticed. Our chance will slip away if we spend days dawdling or allowing craven fear to dissuade us from our purpose—so proceed."

In grim silence the Serpents did his bidding. They lost another Faithful Brother two rooms later, to a rusty yet still massive scything blade that sprang out of the wall and lopped a head from armored shoulders on its way back into concealment. Two more were badly wounded in the passage beyond that, when similar blades stabbed down from above. Bleeding, they limped on, with increasingly sullen fellows beyond them.

Two chambers beyond that was a room where great stone stairs ascended from the center of the room—and beasts that looked like great cats with jutting tusks and horns on their heads prowled forward on stealthy paws to feed on followers of the Serpent.

Lulkoun himself wove a spell that turned two of the beasts into living torches, but they bounded into the ranks of the Serpents as they screamed and blazed, clawing and biting in their death-agonies—and only a hastily cast spell of hammerblows from Fangbrother Murskar thrust the burning beasts back from the men they were crushing and rending.

More of the tusked cats—and a few things that looked like tall, unwieldly walking columns of leafy tendrils, too—appeared through distant archways as the battle raged, and frightened curses were heard from the Serpents who slew them when Lord Masterpriest Lulkoun ordered an advance to be made through the archways from which the creatures had appeared.

The ways beyond met in a tangle of crisscrossing interesections, where monsters of several unfamiliar sorts—sheeplike things with spiked bone-club tails of fearsome bone-shattering force, and little scuttling things with heads like squids, who wore robes and wove spells that made the air itself cut like sharp swords—joined the leaf-things and the tusked cats to make fierce war on the intruding Serpents.

Far fewer Followers of the Scaly Way staggered on from those blood-drenched tunnels, proceeding towards a pulsing glow of sorcery in the distance, to battle through a handful of swooping flying foxlike beasts, and reach the source of the light.

It was a large chamber strewn with monstrous corpses both fresh and ancient, at the heart of which floated an upright, floating oval ring of pale fire that throbbed with almost painful intensity. Beasts were lurking among the heaped dead, waiting to pounce on what emerged through the ring out of an unknown otherwhere—and some of those arriving creatures were slain almost immediately, but others were formidable or swift enough to win past the hungry beasts.

One of these latter resembled a thin, long-tailed nightwyrm youngling—and it soared over the gate-guardians, tail wriggling, to come down upon the Serpents in a long, menacing glide, fanged jaws gaping.

Lord Masterpriest Lulkoun calmly wove a mighty spell as it swept down on him, and succeeded in causing one of its heads to burst into wet gobbets flung far and wide by a flailing neck—but the other head bit down on him and ended his cold commands forever, leaving only one kicking leg to tumble from its fangs as it turned, belly mere feet from the floor, and crashed through most of the shouting, turning-to-flee Serpents.

In the end Fangbrother Murskar abandoned all thought of hurling spells against the magical gate, or trying to examine it further, and rallied all the Serpents who could still walk—seven, besides himself—to try to get back out of the Silent House.

They almost made it.


The scene of the distant Throne Chamber on Flowfoam dissolved into a confused, swirling glow, and then into a cloud of dancing sparks . . . and then into nothing at all.

On the bed beside the sorceress who'd spun it, Hawkril Anharu—no longer an Overduke of Aglirta, and very happy about that—sighed contentedly, and rumbled in his deep voice, "So Raulin's turning out to be a fine Regent, and 'twas all for the best. Happy, my love?"

"Very," Embra Silvertree replied softly, turning onto her side to run one long-fingered hand the length of the corded muscles of his uppermost arm, "my Lord Baron Blackgult."

"Ho, there," Hawkril replied, embarrassed. "I never wanted the title, least of all through the death of the Golden—thy father. *You* are the rightful Lady Baron of both Sil—"

"Hush," Embra said, her hand drifting to a place that made him suddenly fall silent, even before she laid a fingertip over his lips. "I know. And I also know that I'm tall and beautiful and swift-witted—and hated and feared by half Asmarand besides. Yet there's only the one of me, and I haven't room in my head for spells and being the Dragon and a Guardian of Aglirta and *two* baronies, besides, so . . ."

Her caressing hand seized on a natural handle as she rolled back onto her shoulders on the bed, dragging Hawkril over atop her.

". . . I find myself distracted from all the grandeur and the duties by something *far* more important," she purred from beneath him, both of her hands busy now. "We've finally forged Aglirta into a land I'd like to raise children in. A son first, I think. . . ."

"Embra!" Hawkril gasped delightedly. "May we . . . should we? Uh—"

"Of course," his lady replied, moving hungrily under him. "Now you're not to spend the next few months groping for words like you are now, and pacing about restlessly. It's high time Silvertree House was cleaned out and made into a proper home, with room for all of our friends to be housed in style when they come to visit, and I see us having a *large* family, too—and I see *your* hands as the best to guide along this—this—"

And then she thrust her head up and bit at his mouth with a gasp, as Hawkril put his large and strong hands to very good use.


Dolmur Bowdragon raised his head suddenly, causing Maelra to look up from the spell she was weaving and ask quickly, "Uncle? Is something wrong?"

The tall man in robes lifted one hand in a "stay your

fears" gesture, stared at distant nothing for a long moment, and then smiled.

"No," he said, bringing his eyes down to hers. "The Dragon stirs, but it's for no bad reason this time. For once."

"Yes!" Embra Silvertree roared, as lustily as any armaragor bellowing a war cry. "Yessss—*Yes!*"

She raked at Hawkril's great shoulders, bucking and arching under him . . . and within her, what had once been Yuesembra leaped like an excited flame, shedding its cloak of mind-shadows at last, and flaring forth to meet—the astonished and brightly blazing golden fire of the Dragon.

Two sentiences rushed together, borne on Embra Silvertree's rapture, grappled in mingled apprehension and wonder, were pleased, and enthusiastically set about melding. . . .

And under an astonished and then frightened Hawkril Anharu, the lady he loved thrust up from the bed as if hurled, carrying him through its canopy as her skin burst forth into flames that snarled around their joined bodies as a golden glow kindled in Embra's sweat-soaked skin.

Blinding-bright it became, as Hawkril clung to her desperately and shouted out both his alarm and the soaring pleasure that had him in its thrall. Beneath him she sang, high and clearly and wordless, an endless ululation of glory.

The oval window at the top of their chamber burst above his back in singing shards whose tumblings Hawkril barely noticed, as he and his singing lady rose up into the moonlight blazing like an errant sun, wreathed in flames that did not burn.

He caught sight of their blazing reflection glimmering in the waters of the Silverflow, far below, as his lady's song became a voice that did not sound quite like Embra's, and said, "At last! Oh, my Raven, how I wish you'd lived to see this day! *Silvertree!*"

\* \* \*

The room shuddered, to the tune of what sounded like the peal of a great bell, and Maelra looked at her uncle in horror. "The *room* moved! What can the Dragon—?"

"The *tower* moved, little one," said her father, Ithim, from the doorway behind her. "A surge of power, sweeping across Darsar, like nothing I've ever felt before! Dolmur?"

"It's coming from upriver Aglirta," the patriarch of the Bowdragons replied, still smiling.

"From *Aglirta?*"

"Yes, brother, to us here in Arlund from a certain lady whose name I think you can guess."

"Graul! The Lady Dragon? What can it mean?"

"I believe the Dragon is conceiving an heir," Dolmur said calmly. "When the shaking stops, I'd say this calls for a toast. Something really fine from my cellar."

Maelra had always wanted to see what lay beyond that triple-spell-locked wine-cellar door, and asked eagerly, "Uncle? May I choose?"

And then the eldest Bowdragon did a remarkable thing. He stepped forward, hugged her, and said, "Bring up armfuls of whatever you like—and leave the door open so you can explore properly, later."

And then Dolmur Bowdragon threw back his head and laughed in sheer delight, as Maelra and Ithim stared at him in happy astonishment.


The whirling ball of flames above the table collapsed, spilling rat legs and a hound's tail in all directions—as the room rocked, something that sounded like the reverberating ring of a great bell came racing out of the east, washed over them, and was gone, roaring, into the distance . . . and the most powerful mages in Sirlptar cursed and staggered back from the ruined spell.

"What by the bebolten Three *happened?*" one of them roared.

"Is still happening," another corrected grimly.

"More power than I've ever felt before," gasped a third. "Oh, the Serpent and the Dragon battling probably unleashed more—but against each other, just the spillover reaching us. This was . . . this was . . ."

"Awesome," the youngest of them sobbed quietly, and burst into tears. "I . . . I'll never feel anything like that again. . . ."

"No," grunted an older and more sour voice, whose owner was removing still-bleeding rat legs from his face. "Not *quite* like that again, yes. A life of sorcery offers a wide variety of entertaining disasters—and in ninety winters, I haven't repeated one yet."

"But what *was* that?"

"The Dragon arousing," the old wizard said, scratching his chin with narrowed eyes, "and . . . ah, *mating*, I believe. Heh. With something else that's been around for a thousand-some years."

"Something else? *What?*"

"Huh. I've answered one question; that's *yours*, Mighty-Robes. Get on with it, will ye?"


The man kneeling alone before the altar opened his robes almost reverently, laying bare his chest for the lone serpent on the altar to bite.

It coiled, hissing, and drew itself up to strike, wavering higher and higher.

And the chamber shook, tiles falling with a clatter, a rolling shuddering that deepened until the walls were swaying and the room rocked. In the heart of that tumult, something that sounded like the reverberating ring of a great bell came racing out of the east, washed over the chamber with a fury that cracked the altar and toppled the hissing snake, and then was gone into the distance like racing thunder.

And the kneeling man rose, his body growing in size and height, scales racing into being along his lengthening, bulging arms. His mouth parted, growing fangs, and a forked tongue darted out from between them as the man let out a great hiss of fear and anger.

He was very far yet from being the Great Serpent, but it was a start.

Flaeros Delcamper paused with his ornate tallglass still a good hand-span from his lips. His skin was prickling.

"Lad?" Hulgor roared, from down the table. "Is it—poison?"

And then they all heard what he'd felt: a high, clear peal that grew and grew, racing out of the northeast at frightening speed. As servants scurried and heads all around the great table looked up wildly at the ceiling, it washed over them—something that sounded like the reverberating ring of a great bell, that shattered the tallglass Flaeros held in a spray of wine, and many other glasses in the room besides—and then was gone, to the accompaniment of some tentative screams from the well-bred ladies, racing on into the distance.

"*Well,* now," Hulgor growled, coming to his feet. "Well, now. Anyone hurt?"

His shaggy head swung back and forth, surveying the table—and then fixed on the figure seated at its end. "Orele? What by all the happy dancing Three *was* that?"

And the Lady Orele Delcamper smiled back at him, something that looked suspiciously like tears in her eyes, and said, "Something wonderful, Hulgor. When you're old enough, I'll explain it to you. It has to do with centuries of waiting fulfilled, and the Dragon rising, and babies."

"Babies?"

"Babies."

Hulgor sat back down with a grin growing slowly across his face. "Well, now," he said in satisfaction, to no one in particular. "Well, now."

Suldun Greatsarn hadn't been a gardener on Flowfoam for very long, but he prided himself on being a good one. He worked from dawn to dusk, bending his back with a spade and a claw-fork with a vigor that made younger men ache just to watch him, reminding the other gardeners that he'd inevitably be needed by the Regent to wear armor and hold a sword again soon enough—and so had less time then they did, to tame the growing things on Flowfoam that had been neglected in all the fighting just past.

Wherefore he was the only man still out in the grounds, long after nightfall, strolling in the moonlight. He did this on many nights, allowing himself this little time to enjoy the beauty that he wouldn't allow himself time to observe when the sun was up and there was work to be done.

Here, in this bed of flare-trumpets, and over *here,* where these kings'-helms were starting to bend under the weight of the blossoms that gave them their name. Aye, on the morrow he'd have to see to these, before—

And then there came a sudden trembling, from just to the north, across the river. From Castle Blackgult! Suldun trotted a little way along the beds, to where the valiant fallen were buried, so as to be able to peer across the water through the gap in the trees, and see—

The domed roof of the Dragon Turret burst up into the night, and flames roar up and out.

Suldun Greatsarn stood aghast. That was the bedchamber of Lord Hawkril and Lady Embra, and—and—

A ball of roiling flames as bright as the sun rose up out of the shattered turret, and Suldun cried out in pain and flung his arm across his eyes. Someone—a woman—was singing, a wordless song of soaring exultation, so beautiful and so happy that Suldun suddenly felt like weeping.

And then the song broke off into words that he couldn't quite catch, beyond fragments that sounded like "raven" and "here"—all except for the last one, which rolled out in a cry that echoed across the sky: "*Silvertree!*"

And around it rang a high, clear note, like the peal of a great bell, that flung Suldun to his knees and half deafened him as it raced away across Asmarand leaving him weeping in wonder.

And then there was a rumbling, right in front of him, and

a smaller glow, and he let fall his arm from his streaming eyes to behold . . .

A grave right in front of him cracked open, the earth shuddering as a glow shone out from beneath it.

The honored dead were rising!

Suldun Greatsarn was on his feet in an instant, and running like the wind through the gardens, not caring what he trampled.

He was—he was—being a warrior, even when Serpent and Dragon wrestled overhead in ruined Flowfoam Palace, and the fate of Aglirta hung in the balance, was safer than this, was—

He slipped in the soft earth of a bed, tumbled down a bank of rocks and mosses, and slammed into a tree, hard. Very hard.

Wherefore Suldun Greatsarn slept until morning, what he'd just seen fading from his memories . . . and so it came to pass that he never told anyone what he'd seen.

# Epilogue

The old man was staggering with weariness as he came up to the gaping archway in the pale gray mists of dawn, but he plunged into the waiting gloom of Silvertree House as if it was his own home, and his every step was along familiar ways.

He moved in uncanny silence for all his lurchings and stumblings, stopping in his purposeful stride only to peer down at a huddled, dark-robed figure lying in the passage.

"Will the Vale *never* run out of Serpents?" he asked the darkness disgustedly, straightening from his examination of Fangbrother Murskar's staring face, frozen forever in wild-eyed terror.

As usual, the darkness gave no answer.

The old man saw another dark, sprawled form in the distance, and sighed. "What've they been up to *now?*"

He found six more fresh bodies as he went on, and soon found himself staring into the agonized eyes of a silently screaming Serpent-priest who trembled upright in the grip of sorcery, many arrows frozen forever in the act of piercing his chest, and his own death-blood hanging in front of his mouth and nose in a crimson cloud.

The old man's face creased in disgust as he shook his head, muttering, "Even a Serpent shouldn't taste such a fate." Stepping around the stricken man, he strode on.

Pillars dark with fairly fresh blood promptly toppled across the passage. Their fall should have broken him, but somehow the old man was still standing when they righted themselves.

He turned and gave them a less-than-pleased look, hands on hips, and then went on.

When he stopped again, it was to glare down at a rusty blade that had thrust out of the walls through him. He stepped through it without apparent harm, shedding no blood, and after a moment it seemed to come to a decision and withdrew, grating back into hiding once more. This time, his glance back behind him revealed a bat flitting along the passage in his wake. It hastily veered to one side and was lost to view.

With something that just might have been the faint beginnings of a smile on his face, the old man went on, heading for the oldest rooms of the House: the riverfront chambers. Twice more traps failed to slay him, passing through him harmlessly, and he came at last to Old Gargoyle. There he stopped and gazed around.

Familiar rooms and passages, the same endless and somehow watchful gloom, and yet . . . yes, a new power was thrumming through the House.

The old man frowned, and took a step to the south, away from the river. The faint throbbing of power seemed just a trifle stronger.

By the time he'd passed through one of the archways in the south wall and left Old Gargoyle behind, the pulse he was following was definitely stronger.

He began to see gnawed bones, scattered here and there— beast bones. Fairly recent, not the crumbling relics of centuries past. There'd been much war in the House, hereabouts . . . where the throbbing of power was now a muted thunder.

The old man came at last to where he could see a faint, pulsing glow through an archway. He walked towards it, across several rooms littered with dead things, and emerged in a large room choked with heaped monster-carrion.

At its center was a floating ring of pale fire, an upright oval whose cool flames were throbbing with force enough to make the very air moan. Strange beasts were emerging out of the ring, slithering and padding and stalking—and other creatures, lurking amongst the dead, were pouncing on the new arrivals with fang and tentacle and claw.

The old man strode to where he could get a better view of

the carnage. A tentacle slapped through him almost immediately, curling back on itself almost in astonishment as it passed harmlessly through him. The old man ignored it and the lionlike thing that sprang at—and through—him a few paces later, as he walked carefully around the ring, peering at it. Tentatively he put out a hand towards it—and that arm pulsed and then seemed to *flow,* almost drifting away like smoke before he withdrew it.

The old man frowned. Something large and dark and bat-winged erupted from the gate and swooped right through him, clawing at something snake-like that rose from among the corpses to grapple with it—and then flew on into the wider darkness of the House.

The old man watched it go—until something caught the corner of his eye. He whirled in time to see the bat that had been following him, or possibly another bat (though he doubted this) flap through an archway.

"The Master of Bats sees all," he remarked in dry tones, and turned to look back at the magical gate.

Yawning jaws roared, right in his face, as a great rock-horn sprang. It plunged right through him, long-taloned feet slashing nothing, and landed on bones and half-eaten corpses beyond, skidding in carrion as it fought to turn around and launch itself at him again.

Snarling in anger and bewilderment, with bones spraying out behind it as its talons scraped the floor, it got itself around facing him again—as the old man turned calmly to watch, folding his arms across his chest—and sprang a second time, massive muscles rippling under its dirty gray hide.

Once more it plunged through him as if he was nothing but a shadow. Bewildered, the rock-horn roared again and raged around the old man, clawing and biting.

The old man stepped obligingly into its jaws several times, peering with interest at its fangs and the hue of its tongue and—its head snapped up, away from him, as those fiery eyes caught sight of something else.

The old man whirled around. A part of the smooth and apparently solid wall was opening like a door—it *was* a door, of course, a secret door. The face of the man who stepped out was melting like butter in the sun, shifting from that of a high-browed, scowling man into something far more feminine.

The Koglaur caught sight of the old man and the rock-horn—and ducked along the wall, leaving the no-longer secret door ajar behind it. With an eager growl, the rock-horn set off after it, leaping and scrambling over piles of the dead.

Still shifting into a tall, slender woman's body, the Faceless seemed to be peering at the wall, looking for something. Probably another door.

As the old man watched, the shape-shifter found whatever it was looking for, turned with a smile of triumph on its new—and beautiful, but entirely unfamiliar—face, and awaited the rock-horn's charge.

The hulking beast came at it in a rush, head lowered so that the horns for which it was named could gore, impaling the Koglaur and slamming her—it—into the wall it was lounging beside.

The shape-shifter kept still, and the rock-horn raced up to it, sprang—and came to a quivering halt, too dead to even shriek, as a row of four old and massive blades slammed down from the ceiling and cut it in half, the force of its rush slicing the rear part of its body into bloody sections. The severed head, jaws still gaping, skidded to the Koglaur's feet.

The shape-shifter looked down at its stare and fangs for a moment, and then looked across the room at the old man. They exchanged thin smiles as the Faceless did something to the wall beside it and another concealed door opened. It stepped through and closed the door in its wake.

Still smiling, the old man walked past where the dripping blades were rattling slowly up into the ceiling again, to another archway leading out of the room.

A withered, near-skeletal body lay a few paces along the passage beyond, crushed under the massive stone of a falling-block trap whose chain, thick with dust, ran up into the ceiling.

The body wore the crumbling remnants of boots and the

sort of robes favored by wizards who seek to impress. On the passage floor beside it, not far from one of its outflung hands—now shriveled into a bony claw—lay a long black staff.

As the old man strode nearer, a tiny, ruby-red radiance came into being at one end of the staff, and blinked at him.

The old man sank into a squat beside the staff, studying it for a moment, and then raised one of his hands in front of his face and stared at his fingers intently.

A long and silent time passed, during which the uplifted hand could be seen to tremble, and then sink towards the floor as if it had become too heavy for its aged owner to hold it up any longer.

The old man turned his hand over as it sank, so his fingers could—close on the staff.

His body quivered, then, still in uncanny silence . . . and his arm seemed to grow darker and more solid. He went to one knee, overbalancing, and as he waved his other hand to reclaim stability, his fingers passed down and through the flagstones of the floor for a fleeting moment.

Then the old man hefted the staff and held it up before him curiously, his hand now easily strong enough to support it, and more than that: he stood up with none of the weakness and stiffness of his earlier movements. More little lights appeared, here and there along the staff.

The gate in the room behind him flared into a sudden brightness of force that sent lurking monsters tumbling away from it. The old man turned to see what was happening . . . as a living counterpart of the withered body stepped out of the ring of fire, and glared around as if expecting trouble.

It was another tall, stag-headed sorcerer, also clad in dark robes. The stag-man had dusky brown skin, red-rimmed yellow eyes whose hue made him appear to be furious or wildly staring, and a pair of large black antlers sprouting from his skull.

The sorcerer stiffened at the sight of the old man, and wove a swift blasting spell.

It cracked across the chamber and passed through the old

man, who stood apparently unharmed—though his arm went pale again, and the staff clattered to the floor.

Leaving it where it had fallen, the old man strode confidently back into the gate-chamber, heading straight for the sorcerer.

The stag-man snarled out another spell. This spell-blast was larger and fiercer than the first, but when its flash and thunder had died, the old man was still advancing. More than that: he was smiling.

Astonishment and fear warred across the stag-sorcerer's face. "Who *are* you?"

"Sarasper Codelmer," the old man replied, circling swiftly to one side, "and this is my home."

"None dwell here but the dead and those doomed to die very soon!" the sorcerer snarled grandly, turning to face the old man and stepping forward. He raised ring-adorned hands to weave another spell.

"Indeed," Sarasper agreed—as a stone block the size of a small coach thundered down from the ceiling like the fist of one of the gods, smashing the sorcerer to a bloody smear.

He smiled mirthlessly, shook his head, and went back to retrieve the staff, his body crackling with vigor from all the sorcerous fire that had been poured into him. That had been the only trap in this room he'd known about.

When Sarasper was four rooms away from the gate, he perceived the distant throb of another, and went to find it.

He found not one, but two—and a dozen rooms beyond them, a third. There were heaps of bones around them all, and signs (long-dried trails of blood, dung, and talon-scratches on the walls) that beasts had ranged out into the House from these rings of fire, and survived for some time.

Sarasper shook his head, all traces of a smile gone.

He was turning grimly away from that last gate when it burst into bright fire behind him, a brilliance far more intense than that accompanying the arrival of the stag-sorcerer.

When he turned, staff raised as if he had the faintest idea of how to wield its magic, he saw—a nightwyrm!

Vast black wings spread, it was plunging towards him

with the fires of the gate still trailing from its wings.

Both of its heads promptly screamed its challenge at him—deafening in the enclosed chamber—and swooped down, biting and raking.

Its dark, sinuously cruel body blotted out the chamber as it came; it was as if a castle was racing at him.

There was nowhere for Sarasper to go, so he stood his ground, sad-eyed, as fangs and talons swept vainly through him. Then the great, blinding bulk swept on.

The nightwyrm shrieked in fury and alarm, moments before it crashed into the far wall with force enough to shake the room. Dust and small stones fell in clouds as the monster fought to turn, wings slamming into the walls.

Stone blocks dislodged by talons and wingtips spun down to the floor, shattering into shards, and Sarasper watched it realize it couldn't fly out of the chamber it had blundered into.

Then he sighed and strode out of the chamber, as the squalling nightwyrm beat and thrashed its great wings vainly, sending most of a wall toppling onto it.

Its screams and crashings echoed behind him for some time as he strode off down a passage, wondering when it would blunder back through the gate to freedom . . . or if it could.

He was heading towards one of the hidden libraries of the House, hoping its stone shelves still held their precious tomes of magic. If the Three were truly smiling on him—and on Aglirta—there'd be something helpful in at least one of them about sorcerous gates.

As he walked, Sarasper watched monsters slithering, scuttling, and stalking ahead of him. The bat circled his head once, before vanishing down a hall that ran off in another direction.

On an impulse, Sarasper turned aside from his chosen destination long enough to take an old, narrow stair up to a gallery he'd once spent many hours in.

It was still there, seemingly untouched. The bones of the last bustard he'd eaten here still lay in a neat pile on the windowsill where he'd left them.

He stopped at that high, arched window, where he'd tarried so often before, and gazed out of it, westwards down the Vale.

Gods, but Aglirta was fair. The ghost of Sarasper watched leaves dance and rustle in the bright light of morning, and shook his head again.

"A beautiful land," he murmured. "None dwell here but the dead and those doomed to die very soon, indeed. And if I don't find some way to close yon gates, all Aglirta just might become a Silent House of the dead. Soon."